"Fun . . . often amusing . . . always exciting."
—*Paranormal Romance Reviews*

"It would be hard to find a more exciting way to spend a few hours. Settle in for tons of fun and enjoyment."
—*Romantic Times*

"Four very enjoyable stories, with likeable, strong heroines. *Kick Ass* is not to be missed." —*Romance Reviews Today*

"There isn't a bad story to be found in *Kick Ass*."
—*All About Romance*

KICK @$$

Maggie Shayne

MaryJanice Davidson

Angela Knight

Jacey Ford

BERKLEY SENSATION, NEW YORK

THE BERKLEY PUBLISHING GROUP
Published by the Penguin Group
Penguin Group (USA) Inc.
375 Hudson Street, New York, New York 10014, USA
Penguin Group (Canada), 90 Eglinton Avenue East, Suite 700, Toronto, Ontario M4P 2Y3, Canada
(a division of Pearson Penguin Canada Inc.)
Penguin Books Ltd., 80 Strand, London WC2R 0RL, England
Penguin Group Ireland, 25 St. Stephen's Green, Dublin 2, Ireland (a division of Penguin Books Ltd.)
Penguin Group (Australia), 250 Camberwell Road, Camberwell, Victoria 3124, Australia
(a division of Pearson Australia Group Pty. Ltd.)
Penguin Books India Pvt. Ltd., 11 Community Centre, Panchsheel Park, New Delhi—110 017, India
Penguin Group (NZ), Cnr. Airborne and Rosedale Roads, Albany, Auckland 1310, New Zealand
(a division of Pearson New Zealand Ltd.)
Penguin Books (South Africa) (Pty.) Ltd., 24 Sturdee Avenue, Rosebank, Johannesburg 2196, South Africa

Penguin Books Ltd., Registered Offices: 80 Strand, London WC2R 0RL, England

KICK ASS

A Berkley Sensation Book / published by arrangement with the authors

PRINTING HISTORY
Berkley Sensation trade paperback edition / September 2005
Berkley Sensation mass-market edition / September 2006

ISBN: 0-425-21222-X

BERKLEY SENSATION®
Berkley Sensation Books are published by The Berkley Publishing Group,
a division of Penguin Group (USA) Inc.,
375 Hudson Street, New York, New York 10014.
BERKLEY SENSATION is a registered trademark of Penguin Group (USA) Inc.
The "B" design is a trademark belonging to Penguin Group (USA) Inc.

PRINTED IN THE UNITED STATES OF AMERICA

10 9 8 7 6 5 4 3 2 1

Contents

The Bride Wore a .44

MAGGIE SHAYNE

CH@%!*R

1

"No, no, absolutely not, Kira. Lilies could *kill* Aunt Thelma. You *know* she's allergic."

Kira sighed in response to her mother's ruling out another element of her dream wedding. Or at least, what she thought was her dream wedding. She was really only guessing, at best. But lilies had seemed right.

"Sit up straight, dear. Now why don't we go with something *reasonable* like roses. Red and white roses. Those stargazers as so tacky, anyway. Practically hot pink. We just don't *do* hot pink, love."

Mother tapped the desk to get the attention of the wedding planner, who was staring at Kira with sympathy in his chocolate brown eyes. "Pay attention, Marshall. We want red and white roses. Perfectly elegant. Write it down."

"If your daughter wants lilies, Mrs. Shanahan—"

"We've already established that lilies could kill someone, Marshall. We don't want a beloved aunt dropping dead at this event, now do we?" She looked from Kira to Marshall and back again, possibly because Marshall was looking so intently at Kira. So intently, Kira got the feeling he was trying to read her thoughts.

She stifled another sigh. It was his job to figure out what she wanted. He was her wedding planner. Hell, he couldn't know how little she really cared about any of this.

Mother glanced at her watch. "I have to run. Meeting with the caterer in ten minutes. Come along, Kira."

"You go ahead, Mom."

Her mother blinked in surprise. "You don't want any input into the final decisions regarding the menu, dear?"

"I'm not going to get any input whether I go or not. So I'm opting out." The words came out harsh and laced with sarcasm. Totally unlike her—so much so that it surprised her to hear that tone in her voice instead of her usual, docile, soft tones.

Her mother pressed a hand to her chest. "Kira?"

Kira softened her expression. Her mother had swooped in and picked up the pieces of Kira's life when it had been so torn apart she thought she'd never put it back together. She had screwed up. Everything. Badly. She didn't know how, exactly, but she had. Her mother never judged, never condemned, just swooped. And Kira had let her. Let her go just as far as she wanted with the coddling, the babying, the taking over and directing of her life. At first, she'd been physically unable to take charge for herself. Later, it was just easier to let her mother continue.

She couldn't hate her mom for doing it. She was the one who had allowed it. And she really didn't care about the details of the wedding, just as long as she got to marry the wonderful man her mother assured her she loved deeply. Peter was everything she had never known she had always wanted. And she had her mother to thank for remembering for her.

"Go on, Mom. I'm just a little overtired. And the wedding's only a week away."

Her mother nodded and pressed a palm to Kira's cheek. It was warm, soft, loving. "If you really want lilies—"

"Not badly enough to make Aunt Thelma sick." She didn't even know who Aunt Thelma was. "Roses will be great."

"All right, hon. I'll go on to the caterers and um—well, I'll see you for dinner. All right?"

Kira nodded and watched her mother go. The woman shot a few worried glances over her shoulder at her on the way out, but finally she was gone.

"So have you tried telling her that it's your wedding, not hers?" Marshall asked.

Kira turned, having all but forgotten he was in the room. No, that wasn't quite true. Marshall Waters had a presence that wasn't easy to forget. He looked for all the world as if he'd been scooped off the stage at a punk rock concert, stripped of his tight T-shirt and torn jeans, and dressed in a suit and tie. He'd kept the short and spiky dark brown hair, the rock star physique, and the intense brown eyes. He did not look like a wedding planner.

"Why bother at this point?" she asked, smiling. "She's already picked the dress, the bridesmaids' gowns, the cake, the invitations—"

"The groom?" he asked.

She shrugged and sank further back into the chair in front of his desk.

"Where is Peter today?" he asked, rolling a pen between his fingers. "I thought he'd be with you for the final run-through and that long awaited floral decision."

She drew a breath, sighed. "He had an important meeting."

"It's Saturday. He shouldn't be working on Saturdays," Marshall commented.

She got the feeling, and often, that Marshall didn't much like Peter. "Why not?" she asked. "You're working."

He shrugged. "Wouldn't be, if I had a gorgeous bride-to-be waiting at home."

She met his eyes even as the compliment hit her squarely in the chest and spread its warmth through her, then lowered hers quickly, because his were seeing a little too much.

"I should go."

"Stay," he said. "You're hungry. Your stomach's been rumbling since you sat down. And I have a sandwich order due here any minute."

"I have things to—"

"I know. You have an appointment with the caterer, which you already wriggled out of. Meaning you're free. Stay. As your wedding consultant, I recommend a half hour of stress-free relaxation and a meal."

Before she could answer, he picked up the phone, told someone to double his lunch order, and to bring it "up" when it arrived. Then he put the phone down and got to his feet, came around the desk, and took her elbow in his hand. "Come on."

"To where?" she asked.

But he didn't answer, just ushered her out of his office through a side door she hadn't noticed before, up a set of stairs that were not designed to impress, and finally out through the door at the very top—and onto the building's roof.

Buildings in Syracuse were not terribly tall. But this one was one of the tallest, and from it, the entire city's skyline spread out—not to mention the rolling hills beyond it, all the way to the deceptively blue sparkle of Onondaga Lake.

"Can you imagine it, a couple of centuries ago?" he asked her. "Iroquois country. Probably nothing as far as you could see besides smoke coming from an Indian village or two, and maybe the fort at St. Marie."

She smiled, trying to imagine it as he described it. The breeze blew bits of her hair free of its elegant French twist, and she managed to draw her gaze in again and focus on her immediate surroundings.

The roof was a garden. Decorative concrete urns, pots, and man-sized boxes lined it, all of them spilling over with greenery and flowers. A small patio table with an umbrella for shade stood near a four-foot-tall fountain complete with cement cherubs playing harps. He waved a hand at the chairs near that table. "Sit. Be comfy."

"This is nice," she said, doing what he suggested, taking

a seat. She tucked her navy skirt under her as she sat and unbuttoned the matching blazer. "You bring all your harried brides up here?"

"Only the ones I've been dying to talk to without their overbearing mothers present."

"She's not overbearing."

"No more than a buldozer." He paused. "I'm sorry. I shouldn't have—"

"It's okay." She held up a hand. "I know how it looks. But she's only acting this way because I sort of . . . I sort of need her to."

He lifted his brows. "I gotta admit, I've been wondering. You're not a skittish seventeen-year-old, Kira."

"Twenty-five," she told him. "But I wouldn't know about the skittish part."

He nodded slowly. "It's not that you're afraid to stand up to her," he said. "In fact, you seem to be forcibly restraining yourself from snapping her head off now and then."

Kira tipped her head to one side. "You're pretty insightful."

He shrugged and said nothing.

She leaned back in her chair and closed her eyes. The sun beamed down, the breeze blew, the traffic moved below, and she became acutely aware that she had utterly nothing to do, nowhere to be, no one to answer to for the next hour. For the first time in what felt like days, she breathed deeply, fully, slowly. "This feels good," she admitted.

"Enjoy it, then."

He didn't make a sound to intrude on her. Just let her sit there as the sun's heat and the sense of peace seemed to make her muscles unclench, one by one, bit by bit. Her body softened. At some point she heard footsteps and something being set on the table. She smelled fresh bread and tomato and turkey and maybe mustard.

When she got around to it, she opened her eyes, only to find Marshall leaning back in his chair across from her, his gaze fixed on her face. And she wondered if he'd been looking at her like that the entire time, and got the feeling he had.

"Food's here," he said. But he didn't look away.

She did, focusing instead on the sandwich in front of her. A pickle sat on the plate beside it. There were also a miniature bag of potato chips and a diet soft drink. "You eat up here every day?"

"Every day since I've been here. Unless it's raining," he said. "And sometimes even then."

"I don't blame you. It's nice."

He nodded, still watching her. When she looked back at him, he finally broke the intense gaze, and dug into his sandwich.

They ate for awhile, neither one speaking. Then finally, when he had finished, he said, "So why don't you tell me when you decided to let your mother run your life?"

She smiled and popped the last bit of her pickle into her mouth, then licked her fingers. "Right after I screwed it up so bad I almost lost it," she said. Then she shrugged. "I needed a break. And hell, she's doing a much better job than I ever did. At least, I assume she is."

He frowned. "Details?"

She wiped her mouth with her napkin, shrugged her shoulders. "Sure. Why not?" Then she leaned forward, reached out to clasp his hand in hers, and hesitated for a moment at the warm static that shot up her arm at the contact. But she quickly shook it off and drew his hand to the back of her head, pressed his palm there. "Feel that?"

"I sure do."

Something in his voice made her lift her eyes, and she realized they were leaning close, face-to-face over the table, in a posture that suggested they might be about to kiss. Her eyes locked with his very briefly, but she quickly closed them and drew away a little. "I meant the bumpy little ridge in my head."

"I know. Sorry, I was being a smart-ass. Yeah, I feel it." His fingers moved in her hair, either tracing the outline left by the surgery, or gently massaging her scalp. She wasn't sure which.

"There's a steel plate in there. Seems to be the result of

me running my life my way. It's been a long, slow recovery. Mom kind of took over. So far, I don't know, I'm just not compelled to take the responsibility back, you know?"

"You're scared."

She nodded. "Maybe I am."

He was still running his fingers over her head, and it was a little more than an exploration. The injury didn't even hurt much anymore. Hadn't, since the explosion that had nearly killed her. At least, not since she'd regained consciousness. Most people acted slightly repulsed if they happened to touch the place where her skull had been pieced back together. She'd stopped feeling hurt or angry over that a long time ago. It didn't do any good to get your skirt in a twist over what was basically a knee-jerk reaction.

He didn't pull his hand away, though. Instead, he slid it along the side of her head, then lower, until his palm rested on the curve of her neck. He stopped there, his fingers caressing, a very brief stroke against her skin that left her shivering, then took his hand away.

"You want me to feel anything else?"

"The rest of me is still pretty much intact," she said.

He shrugged. "So?"

Her lips pulled into a smile. The first genuine one she'd felt in recent memory. "You're kinda cute, Marshall."

"Hell, it's about time you noticed. So are you gonna tell me how that happened?"

"Nope." She picked up her soft drink and started for the stair door. "Maybe another time, though."

"I'll hold you to it."

"You do that." She had reached the door and she looked back over her shoulder. "Thanks for this, Marshall. I needed a break more than I knew."

"Anytime, Kira. Anytime at all."

CH@%!*R
2

She didn't sleep. Not all night. It was two thirty-five, and she wasn't even feeling a little bit bleary-eyed. Tomorrow she was going to be married.

And tonight, she was at the edge of panic. Something, something deep inside, was screaming to be heard. But it was garbled and incomprehensible. Something—more than likely—from the past.

She walked barefoot out of her bedroom and into the hall, down the broad curving staircase of her mother's opulent mansion, and through the house to the very back, and the little door that was almost hidden there. Beyond the porch, a path wound amid neatly trimmed rose of Sharon, every shrub higher than her head, creating a tunnel-like walkway that led to the garden, where she would be married tomorrow.

She walked along the path, smelling the scents of the fat blossoms, trying to imagine herself walking this same path tomorrow, dressed in the traditional bridal gown her mother had picked out, with its long train and multilayered veil, instead of the one she herself had liked: short, white, with spaghetti straps and crisscrossing ribbon at the bodice that made it look more like an antique undergarment than an actual dress. She'd called it "Goth-in-white." Her mother had called it an eyesore.

Whatever. It didn't matter. She didn't really know which one she would have liked better anyway. She didn't have a preference. She didn't care.

She barely *felt* anymore. She couldn't remember what it was like to feel, so she guessed she didn't miss it much. She wasn't excited about the wedding, but she wasn't nervous about it either. It was what her mother told her she'd been planning. What everyone seemed to expect. And since she had no personal preference anymore about much of anything, the easiest thing to do was comply.

Walking through the flowery tunnel, she emerged in the circular garden, with its fountain at the center. The sky above was clear and glittering with stars. No moon tonight, though, so it was incredibly dark.

A twig snapped behind her.

She spun without forethought, raising one arm in a defensive position, while jamming the other fist in a powerful thrust that connected with something, someone. He went down hard onto his back, and the next thing she knew, she was sitting on his chest, her knees on the ground on either side of him, her hands pinning his wrists to the ground.

He blinked up at her, something strange in his eyes as they held hers. "Kira?"

Something took over. Something alien, foreign. As if she were watching the scene play out, but not in control of it. She was leaning lower, pressing her mouth to his. He tugged his hands, as if he wanted her to let them go, but she slammed them soundly into the ground again and kissed him until she felt him start to shake, heard him moan, felt him hardening beneath her, and arching into her.

He tasted good. She wanted more.

What the hell was she doing?

She jerked her mouth from his, still feeling his tongue

inside her, and looked down at him, stunned to her marrow. Beneath her was her wedding planner!

"Marshall? Oh, God. Oh, God." She blinked, unable to hold his gaze as she scrambled off him, and then she just stood, covering her burning face with her hands. "I'm sorry," she muttered.

"I'm not."

He had gotten to his feet. His hands closed around her shoulders, and she forced herself to look up at him.

He was smiling. "It's okay."

"It's not. I hit you, and then I—"

"You didn't hurt me. And uh . . . the rest was my pleasure."

She lowered her head, but he squeezed her shoulders. "It's so unlike me."

"How do you know?"

She looked up sharply. "What's that supposed to mean?"

He didn't avert his eyes; instead, he used them to probe hers in the darkness. "I know you have some . . . some memory loss. From the . . . accident."

She sighed. "My mother told you. I'm surprised, she usually doesn't bring it up." She rubbed her arms, only then realizing she was wearing only a thin nightgown, and little else. "What are you doing here in the middle of the night?"

"Just a last-minute check. We want everything to go smoothly tomorrow, right?"

It was the first time she'd thought of her impending wedding day since she'd stepped into the garden. She thought she should have felt guilty. Oddly, she only felt embarrassed.

She lowered her head, closed her eyes. "I've gotta go inside."

"Tell me what happened to you, Kira."

She stopped walking, turned slowly to face him. "Not so much to tell. I was in the wrong place at the wrong time. There was an explosion."

He nodded slowly. "Where was the wrong place?"

"A village in Africa. Peter and I were both there, and so was my father. I was working for an aid organization. I'm still not clear why my father was there. Peter—had some kind of business connection there. Anyway, my father and I had gone to the market for supplies, when a bomb went off."

"I see."

She shrugged. "I don't. I don't remember anything, except waking up in a hospital a month later." She thinned her lips. "They told me my father was killed in the explosion."

He nodded slowly. "That must have been pretty awful."

She shrugged. "It should have been. I just—I don't remember him. It's horrible of me, isn't it?"

"It's physical. It's not like you can help it."

"Doesn't make me feel any better about it. At any rate, when I woke from the coma, I was as helpless as a toddler. Mom . . . she just took over. Brought me home, took care of me."

"It must have felt good, being taken care of like that."

She nodded. "I've kind of been letting her ever since."

"Why?"

She shrugged a little. "Because I don't care. I don't care about anything."

"Maybe you do. Maybe you just haven't remembered yet, what it is you care about."

Blinking slowly, she started for the house.

"What about Peter?" he asked as she moved away. "Do you care about him?"

She stopped walking, but didn't turn this time. "I must have once. I was engaged to him before the bombing." And that, a little voice inside her whispered, was why she was marrying him tomorrow. He and her mother were two things she knew for sure she must have cared about once. Two scraps of the identity she had lost. She couldn't let go—they were all she had.

Again she started walking toward the house. Again, he stopped her, with a hand on her shoulder, this time. She turned to face him there in the darkness. The breeze came between them, lifting her hair. He said, "Don't give up on yourself, Kira. You're in there, you're still in there. And I think you're close to finding you again."

She stared at him, wondering how he would know, and then she turned and hurried back to the house, grateful that he didn't follow her. She kept running, all the way through the hidden door in the back, and past the kitchen, to the back stairs and up the first flight, pausing on the landing.

To her right was the hallway. Her bedroom. The safe haven of her soft mattress and the warm fluffy comforter she could pull right up over her head. To her left, another flight of stairs. The third floor. The attic, and the trunks it held. She'd glimpsed them once, while exploring the place in search of anything that would trigger a memory. But her mother had caught her and sent her back downstairs, telling her the attic was strictly off-limits. "Just for now."

"But I must have had things of my own, things from . . . before," she'd whispered to her mother, when she'd first come home. Everything in the bedroom her mother had made ready for her was new. Brand-new. The clothes still had tags on them. Even to the underwear.

"Yes, and you're right. Your things are packed away in those trunks."

"Then shouldn't I—see them?"

Her mother had met her eyes, her own filled with worry. "When you start to remember the past, you can go through them. Until then—well, the doctors think your mind isn't ready yet. You don't want to do anything to force it. It could cause a setback that would make things even worse than they already are."

She shivered a little, somehow knowing her mother was right. It was better not to remember. It was easier.

But tonight . . . tonight, she needed to know. So she turned left instead of right, and she moved up the second flight of stairs to the door at the top. She opened it and walked into the darkness, one arm reaching out in front of her, searching for a light, and finally finding one. She flicked the switch, but only dim light appeared from a single, dust-coated bulb in the ceiling. The trunks stood in front of her, two of them, and she moved closer to them, feeling as if she were at the threshold of a doorway with something frightening on the other side.

Drawing a breath, she knelt, put her hands on one dusty lid and pushed, but the lid didn't give. The trunks were locked. Her mother had the keys. She ought to wait until morning, ask her mother then. She would open them.

"To hell with that," she muttered, and then almost wondered who had spoken. But she didn't wonder long. There was a hammer on the windowsill, coated in grime. A screwdriver beside it. She pushed cobwebs out of her face as she went to get the tools. Then she turned to face the two giant trunks that were the most recent additions to the collection of forgotten relics that filled the attic.

The trunks were not old ones, like some of the others filling the space. They were new, modern, in designer colors. Junk. She didn't feel any compunction about ruining them. She bent to the hasp of the first one, positioned the screwdriver, lifted the hammer, and wondered what secrets she was about to set free.

Her stomach was tied up in knots. Her heart beat rapid-fire, and she held her breath as she flipped open the lid.

Six months. It been six months since she'd come out of that coma. A month before that, she had been some other person, the Kira from before. A stranger. The person who was, maybe, locked away in these trunks like everything she'd ever owned.

The lid fell back. She knelt down and pawed aside the bubble wrap that was lovingly layered over her possessions. And then she sat very still, just staring.

Her hand trembled as she reached out and trailed her fingers over the glossy black metal. It was cold, hard, and unbelievably smooth. Kira closed her hand around the white grips and picked up the gun. The handle was pearl, she thought at first, but then decided it was white onyx. An oxymoron.

Kind of like the notion of the woman she believed herself to be walking around with a .44 Magnum.

And just how the hell do I know it's a .44 Magnum anyway?

CH@%!*R

3

In the morning, Kira's bedroom looked like an explosion at a punk and goth shop. She'd dragged the trunks down the stairs, using a folded blanket as a cushion to muffle the noise. Then she'd gone through them in the privacy of her bedroom, item by item.

There were clothes. Tons of them, but none that looked anything like the ones her mother had stocked in her closet. Nearly everything was black, from the sinfully short skirts to the tight leather pants and tank tops. What wasn't black was green. There were cargo pants with numerous pockets in six different styles. There were boots, black ones that looked for all the world like military issue. And there were straps that she at first took for some sort of S&M fetish gear, but finally figured out were holsters for her guns.

Yes. Guns. Plural. In addition to the pair of matching big black .44s, she'd found a nickel-plated snub-nosed .38 revolver, and a .22 with a twelve-round clip. Beyond those there were boxes of ammunition, a case containing a detachable scope, and two knives that looked so deadly they made her blood run cold, one big and one small.

Guns and clothes. That had been the sum total of the contents of the first trunk.

The second one had most of its space taken up by a black wetsuit, complete with flippers, goggles, and other items she couldn't identify, but which she guessed would attach to an oxygen tank. Tucked beneath those items she found a stun gun and a framed photograph.

The photo stunned her. It shocked her. And more than ever, it made her want to remember. Because it showed her, as she had been before.

Kira moved slowly to the mirror and stood there, looking from the photo, to her own reflection and back again. The girl in the glass wore a loose-fitting, white nightgown, and her skin was pale. The one in the photo was dressed in skintight black, and her skin was almost bronze from the sun. The one in the mirror had long, straight hair, a dull brown color. The one in the photo had short hair that curved around her face to her chin, and bangs the perfect length to somehow enhance the exotic tilt of her wide-set eyes. The brown had streaks of gold shot through it. The girl in the photo wore makeup, heavy on the eyeliner. Dark on the lips. And it looked good. *She* looked good. She looked confident, sure of herself, powerful, and strong.

And the man standing beside her, with his arm around her shoulders and his head tipped to rest against hers, wasn't the man she was going to marry in the morning.

He was her wedding planner. And the background that spread out behind them was one that was familiar to her— it was a small, impoverished village in Africa.

"Darling," her mother called, her voice a songbird's trill, as she tapped rapidly but softly on her bedroom door. "Are you up? Best get in the shower, dear, you have a hair appointment in an hour."

Kira opened the bedroom door and stepped out into the hall, quickly pulling the door closed behind her. She'd stuffed most of the evidence of her predawn raid into various drawers and closets and under the bed. She'd returned the empty trunks to their spots in the attic. But she didn't know how her mother was going to react, and she didn't want to upset her.

Abby greeted her with a warm hug. She was still in her filmy nightgown, but Kira had dressed—temporarily, at least. She wore a pair of slender, dressy pants, with knife-sharp creases, and a silk button-down top. The pants were brown, the top mustard yellow.

"Are you excited about your big day?"

Oh, she was excited all right. But not so much about the wedding. God, the wedding. What the hell was she supposed to do about that? "I am," she replied.

She returned her mother's hug, then held her hand as they walked down the stairs together.

"I hope you're not too nervous eat breakfast."

Kira smiled. "Actually, I'm famished." And eager, God she was eager to explore and question and try to find her past. Her identity. For the first time she wasn't afraid of it. Instead she was itching to delve into it.

If only she could remember.

"I'm so glad," her mother was saying as they moved down the stairs together. "I had Cook make your favorite. French toast with real maple syrup."

Kira smiled. "Was it always my favorite?" she asked.

"Since you were four. Maybe longer, but you were four when you informed your father and me." She closed her eyes briefly. "God, I wish he were still here with us, to see you married."

Kira nodded, wishing she could remember her father. The man deserved his daughter to mourn him, and yet she hadn't. Couldn't.

Her mother led her into the cozy breakfast nook, which was a sunny, glass-enclosed enclave off the dining room. The table was set, the sun streaming in through the window. Like magic, their cook, Anita, appeared with a silver coffeepot and a covered tray. She set the tray down, poured the coffee for them. It must have been nice, being raised in the lap of luxury, Kira thought. "Thanks, Anita," Kira said when her cup was full.

Anita nodded, saying nothing, but her eyes lingered on Kira's for a long moment before she hurried back to the kitchen.

Kira took a piece of French toast, set it on her plate. "Mom?"

"Yes?"

"Do you like Peter?"

Her mother blinked and frowned at her. "Well, of course I like him. Oh, well, I'll admit when you first introduced him, I had my doubts. But your father assured me you knew exactly what you were doing." She sighed, pressing a hand to her heart as she lifted her gaze to the photo of her and her late husband, Daniel, smiling, arm in arm. There were photos of him in every room of the house. She must have adored him.

"So Dad approved of him."

"He seemed to."

She nodded slowly, wondering how best to approach the new thought on her mind, and finally settling for the inane, "How do we know Marshall?"

Her mother lifted her brows. "He's your wedding planner, dear. Are you sure you're all right?"

"I'm fine. What I mean is, do we know him outside his job? Was he ever—a family friend or anything like that?"

"What a strange question." Her mother shrugged. "No, dear. We don't know him outside his job." Then she tipped her head. "Has he done something inappropriate, Kira?"

"Mother, really. Of course not."

Her mother studied her. But then the bustle of footsteps through the house drew their attention away, and they both turned to see Peter Nelson himself hurrying into the room. He wore a big smile—even white teeth in a tanned face— and beach blond hair.

"Peter!" Abby jumped to her feet and stood behind Kira's chair. "You're not supposed to see the bride before the wedding!"

"That's superstition," Peter said with a smile. "I promise, no disaster will result if I give my bride a gift before the ceremony."

"It's all right, Mom," Kira said, rising from her chair. "Hello, Peter." She watched him, searching his face. He was handsome. Polite. Good to her.

Hell, why was she having such misgivings about this marriage?

Maybe because you don't love him, have you thought of that?

She shrugged off that rationale. She didn't feel strong emotions for anyone or for anything. It was part of her condition. She'd loved him once. It would come back, probably when her memory did.

He clasped her elbows and kissed her cheek. "Morning, love. How are you feeling?"

"Wonderful. Join us for some French toast?"

"No time. So much to do. But I wanted to give you this." He brought a teddy bear from behind his back.

It was pink and wore a bridal gown and veil. Custommade for her, obviously. What were soon to be her initials were embroidered within a red, heart-shaped outline on the front of the dress, which was made of real satin, unless she was mistaken.

"It's incredible."

"Look around her neck. Under the dress," he added.

Frowning, she ran a finger under the dress's neckline and pulled out a strand of pearls. They were huge. "God, Peter, these must have cost a fortune."

"Nothing's too good for you. I hope you'll wear them today."

"I will. Thank you, Peter."

"You're welcome." Again, he leaned in, kissing her lips this time, lightly and gently. Then he turned and hurried away.

Kira sank into her chair, placing the pearl-laden teddy bear in an empty one nearby. "That was sweet of him," she said.

"It was amazing." Her mother dabbed at the corner of one eye with her napkin.

Kira sighed and dug into her French toast, eating quickly, because she was eager to get to her hair appointment. She finished up, said good-bye to her mother, and dashed up to her room to get the bag she'd packed. Then she headed for the salon.

Two hours later, the stylist, Nadine, said, "You're sure this is what you wanted? To look like you did in this photo?"

Kira nodded. "Yes, I'm sure, for the tenth time, I'm sure. Can I see? Did you do it?"

"*Oui*, it is done." Nadine spun her chair around so she faced the mirror. "Voilà!"

Kira stared at her reflection. Her eyes slammed closed against the tidal wave that suddenly hit her brain. Images, voices surged. There were people running around her, debris raining down, smoke, blood, screaming, and crying. There was a dead man beside her, a man she ought to know. And there was another man, leaning over her, his eyes stricken as he stared down at her. "Kira? Baby? Are you okay?"

She stared up at him for just an instant. Her lips moved to form words, but she didn't know what they were. And then she sank into darkness to the sound of his tormented whisper, "God, no."

"Oh, she hates it," Nadine moaned. "I was afraid of this. I can fix, don't worry—"

"No." Kira opened her eyes, but she couldn't get the image of those other eyes to leave her alone. They were Marshall's eyes. And they'd been way more intense than she had ever seen them. She focused again on her reflection in the mirror. And then she nodded. "I love it, Nadine. I love it. Don't change a thing."

CH@%!*R
4

Kira stood in her bedroom, gazing out the window to the back lawn and garden sprawling below. The flashes had kept coming. All morning. Frustrating bits, scraps of a mosaic, with more pieces missing than found. She saw bodies entwined. Hers and Marshall's. She saw their lips mating. She saw laughter and smiles and dark, intense looks filled with hidden meaning passing between them. And she felt a heat in her blood that she didn't remember feeling ever before. Or maybe it was a memory.

Now, on the back lawn, the chairs were set up. The string quartet was warming up, and people were arriving, mingling, talking. All of them dressed in black or white or both, as per her mother's instructions. Peter was there, already dressed in his tux, talking with men she didn't really know. His best man, his groomsmen. She'd met them, of course. Maybe she'd known them before. She hadn't cared enough to ask. She didn't care now.

Marshall was down there. He wore a tux as well as a headset and moved around the lawn. Her heart sped up as she watched him. Brisk, efficient, watchful. He had a way of moving that mesmerized her. It was powerful and yet graceful. Why hadn't she noticed before? Or had she?

Not like this she hadn't. Hell, she had shivers dancing up and down her nape and a shaky unsteady hitch in her breathing. And she didn't need a fully functioning memory to recognize animal attraction for what it was. She wanted Marshall Waters.

And she was pretty sure she'd had him. What would her mother think if she knew that her daughter was a slut? That she'd been cheating on her own fiancé with a wedding planner? God, what a giant mess this was. Why the hell had Marshall let her mother hire him? He wasn't the one without a memory.

There was a tap on her bedroom door. She turned, frowning. It wasn't her mother, she was down there milling around in the crowd, playing the perfect hostess. Hell, she wasn't playing it, she was it.

"It's Anita," a woman called.

Kira opened the door, not bothering to hide the two outfits hanging side by side from a pair of hooks in the wall. Not from Anita. Anita wouldn't rat her out.

"They'll be ready for you soon," Anita said, then she blinked, looking Kira up and down. "You're not dressed."

"Haven't quite decided what I'm going to wear," Kira said. She glanced toward the hooks on the wall.

Anita followed her gaze and sucked in her breath.

Kira studied the beautiful bridal gown. It was more *Cinderella* than *Midsummer Night's Dream,* but that was okay. It didn't matter. And if it did, she'd had her payback when her mother had seen her hair. Kira thought the woman was going to pass out.

Beside it, arranged on another set of hangers, were a pair of black leather pants, a ribbed black tank top, and a leather jacket. On the next hook there were holsters and guns.

"Did you know about all this, Anita?"

"All what, Kira? What's going on?" Anita narrowed her eyes and studied her.

"I don't know. I decided to go through those trunks last night. Anita, what was I doing with all these weapons?"

"Are you starting to get your memory back? Is that what this is?"

"Maybe. A little. Bits and pieces. But I don't know what it means." She turned and speared Anita with her eyes. "Has there been—have I been—involved with anyone? Besides Peter?"

Anita's shock turned to a look of stark disapproval. "You're getting cold feet, aren't you? You're thinking about calling off the wedding."

Lowering her head, she nodded. "Yeah. I am."

"You can't do that. Good God, you can't. Just . . . oh, hell. Wait here."

Anita turned and hurried from the room.

Hell, it didn't matter. She had to do what was right for her. She reached for the white dress. She would at least put it on. It would give her more time to decide what was the right thing to do. And if she decided to go through with this thing, she'd be ready.

She put the dress on. Even added the little glittering tiara and the layers of veils. Then she looked into the mirror. And then she rolled her eyes. "No way. It's just not happening."

"Marshall, we've got trouble."

Marshall tilted his head to one side when the voice came through his earphone, moved a few yards away from the crowd, and spoke into the mouthpiece. "What is it?"

"She's starting to remember. I think she's going to call off the wedding."

He thought every cell in his body smiled. God, it felt like it, and he was damned if he could keep the relief and joy from showing on his face.

"We've got to do something, Marshall. We can't make the arrest until the reception. Everything's set up there, not here. We have to stick with the plan. She calls off the wedding, it's going to ruin everything."

Marshall sucked in a calming breath and nodded. It wasn't as if the license she'd been issued was a real one, after all. The vows wouldn't be valid. But goddamn, it had been killing him to watch her moving forward with all this, and believing it was real.

Killing him.

Still, he had to stick with the plan. Peter would be taken into custody after the ceremony, when the rest of his cronies arrived. Some could only attend the reception. Marshall was to gather them up for a group photo, take them off a little way from the rest of the crowd, then give the signal for the troops to move in.

They wanted them all together.

Things had to move forward. Just as planned.

"Wait a minute," the voice on the radio said. "Wait, I think we're okay. She's coming out."

Marshall frowned. "She's going through with it?"

"Well, she's wearing the gown."

He looked back toward the house, and then he saw her. She stepped out the back door and waited there, shifting her feet. Swallowing the rush of disappointment, Marshall turned to face the crowd, signaled the string quartet.

They began to play, and the guests took their seats and grew quiet. As soon as they did, the quartet changed to the "Wedding March."

Marshall turned back toward the house.

Kira stood there, looking as if she were paralyzed. Hell. He was going to have to go back there. Talk her through it. Help her gather enough courage to walk down the aisle . . . to marry another man.

He took three steps toward her—and then all hell broke loose.

Kira didn't know what was happening. She'd run out of time for contemplation and had decided to go out there, as she was, send someone to fetch Peter for her, and then tell him as gently as she could that she didn't want to marry him. That she couldn't marry anyone, not until her memory was fully restored.

But the second she stepped out of the house, the band struck up, and the next thing she knew everyone was looking at her, and the "Wedding March" was playing. Hell! She just stood there, not sure what to do. If she walked down the aisle to her beaming groom, would she get caught up in the riptide and end up married? If she turned and ran back into the house, would everyone think she'd lost what little remained of her mind?

She stood there like a doe in headlights. And then she saw Marshall. He stepped into the aisle and started toward her. And she couldn't *wait* for him to get to her. She couldn't wait. She had to be near him, to touch him—to talk to him—now.

She gathered her skirts up and started toward him, but then gunshots rang out. Automatic weapons, her mind told her. And she launched herself at Marshall and knocked him flat on his back, landing on top of him. Her momentum kept them going as she wrapped around him and rolled to the side, out of the open, into the cover of the rose of Sharon hedges.

"Kira?" he asked.

"Stay down!" She pushed his chest, reaching to her side for a weapon and only belatedly realizing she had none. And why would she expect to find one there?

Marshall was easing her off him, setting her on the ground, beside him. She could see between the branches, everyone was on the ground. Men in black suits with blacker rifles fanned through the crowd. One of them gripped Peter by the shoulder.

"I gotta go, babe," Marshall said harshly. "Stay low. Stay under cover. You're not ready for this."

"Ready for what?"

He hesitated, then he yanked her hard against him and took her mouth in a kiss that was like a hurried mating. When he jerked his head back again, he said, "Just stay here."

She sat back on her heels, as Marshall crept out the opposite side of the bushes and, using them for cover, made his way back toward the wedding party.

Someone was doing the same on the other side.

The men were herding Peter away now. But then Marshall sprang from the cover with a gun pointed at them. And from the other side, Anita did the same.

Anita! Standing there in a crouch with her black uniform and white apron and a big silver gun in her hands. "Freeze!"

They *didn't* freeze. Shots rang out again. Anita went down, and the gunmen turned their attention to Marshall. But by that point, Kira was already charging down the aisle, screaming words she couldn't believe were coming from her lips.

"Drop the fucking guns! Now!"

Faces turned her way, as she drop-kicked the first guy, then sprang upright again to deliver an elbow to the throat of the second, and then she had his gun in her hands.

Someone hit her from behind—a big crack to the back of her head, not the least bit cushioned by the veils, no matter how many layers thick there were. Her tiara tilted over her eyes, her head swam, and she went down hard.

Blinking and sitting up, she saw the men running toward cars that had pulled onto the back lawn. Peter was shoved into the back of one. Marshall into another, a gun to his head. And then they took off, as she struggled to her feet.

The guy lying facedown on the ground beside her started to get up. She put the barrel of her rifle on his forehead. "Stay down for a sec."

He frowned at her, so she put her foot between his shoulder blades and slammed him down.

"It's all right everyone, you can get up." She nodded at the minister. "Hold him a minute?"

The minister nodded, came forward, and put his foot in the middle of the offender's back. Kira bent low. "Wiggle, and I'll pop you. Got it?"

"Yeah."

She kept one eye on the man as she hurried to where Anita lay still on the ground. Kneeling, Kira pressed a palm to her cheek. "You alive?"

"Yeah." It was a pained and breathless whisper. "You back?"

"I don't know what the fuck I am. Much less who. Hell, I'm not even sure what my mother's cook is doing with a 9-millimeter Ruger." She closed her eyes. "Or how I know a Ruger from a Glock. Hell."

"Go after him," Anita said, and Kira knew without asking that she was talking about Marshall. "They'll kill him. We can't wait."

"I'm going." She put an arm around Anita, helped her sit up, put the rifle in her arms. "You got him?"

"Yep," Anita said.

"Great." Kira looked around the lawn. Her mother had fainted, but a dozen relatives surrounded her. She would be fine. "I'll get my gear, Anita. Be two minutes."

"Make it one."

Her head was spinning, and she was damned if she knew what was going on. But she raced to her room, stripping off the veils and tiara as she went, kicking free of the shoes, unzipping the dress. She flung it aside and pulled on the other clothes, the ones she'd laid out, because they were the easiest ones to get to.

The leather pants, tank top. Then the straps and holsters. She didn't think first, she didn't need to. They went on automatically, shoulder strap, thigh strap, hip straps, slip into the boots with the hidden sheath, dagger in place. She checked the guns to be sure they were loaded and slammed them into their holsters. Put on the jacket and shoved spare ammo into her pockets. Then she was racing back down the stairs.

Her car was at the back door, a sacrilege parked across her mother's perfect lawn. Anita must have had someone bring it out for her. The cook was already shoving the thug into the passenger side. His hands were cuffed behind him. She slammed the door and looked up at Kira.

Kira eyed the bloody spot on her white apron. "You gonna be all right, Anita?"

"Cavalry is on the way. Medics, too. I'll be fine. And it's Kelly."

Kira lifted her brows and wondered what other revelations were awaiting her. But she didn't take time to ask, she just jumped behind the wheel and took off.

As she spun the tires and shifted the gears, she looked at the man beside her and told herself not to focus on the insane feeling that she didn't know who the hell she was, who this person was who seemed to have taken control of her body. It didn't matter, not now. All that mattered was finding Marshall in time. And Peter, too, she supposed.

"Now, you're going to tell me where they are, understand?"

He said something vile, so she cracked him upside the head with the gun. Then managed to shift gears without setting the weapon down. She headed out the driveway and left, the direction she'd seen the others take.

"Talk. Where are they?"

There was blood trickling from a small cut on his cheekbone. He thinned his lips. "If you think I won't kill you, you can think again," she said. "I've got nothing to lose."

He narrowed his eyes on her. "I was told you were harmless. That you'd been as good as lobotomized."

"Yeah? Well, don't believe everything you hear." She slanted him a look as they came to a crossroads. "Come on, Duke. Which way?"

She didn't know why she called him by name, she only knew his eyes widened when she said it.

"You do remember," he whispered.

"Which way, Duke?"

He swallowed hard. "Left."

She didn't move the car. "To where?"

His eyes shifted downward. "There's a house out in Kentport."

"Is there?"

He nodded.

She didn't move the car. Just revved the engine, letting the clutch up just enough to make the vehicle push itself forward, like a horse tugging at the bit. " 'Cause you know when we get to this house in Kentport, you're coming in with me. And if they're not there, I'll put this gun barrel in your ear and squeeze the trigger."

She saw him shiver and thought he actually believed her. Apparently, he'd known her in the past. Apparently, he had reason to think she could make good on the threat. Damn, what kind of a woman had she been?

What kind of a woman was she now?

"You know I'll do it, don't you, Duke?"

"Yeah."

"So you still want me to turn left?"

His Adam's apple swelled briefly. "Go straight. There's an apartment. Vacant. In the city."

She nodded, satisfied. "You get me to where they are, Duke, and you can walk. I never saw you. That's a promise."

He thinned his lips and nodded.

"You believe me?"

He met her eyes. "You never break your word. Everybody knows that. I'll get you there."

CH@%!*R
5

The apartment building was in a dead neighborhood. It sat below the base of a bridge across the river. Before they put the bridge up, this had been a ferry stop. Houses and shops cropped up around it. But once the bridge went in, the thriving community died. Shops closed. Owners moved and either sold their houses dirt cheap or rented them the same way. Things were let go. Repairs were seldom made. Some of the places ended up vacant, boarded up, and became way stations for the aging homeless, until they were pushed out by the street kids, who were pushed out in turn by the gangs. Now the decrepit buildings that hadn't fallen down, been torn down, or gone to arson, were crack houses, whorehouses, and gang hangouts.

Kira didn't know how she knew all this, but the knowledge was there, and had been there all along, lying silent and invisible with so many other things, like layers of sediment at the bottom of the sea. Only now, the formerly calm waters were rough and choppy, and the junk at the bottom was getting stirred up.

The bums holed up on the hill, underneath the bridge for

shelter. At night they came down and set fires in the barrels along the waterfront. Mostly the gangs left them alone, unless they were feeling particularly mean. There were other homeless they could roll, farther away. These were sort of their own.

She pulled the car to a stop behind the brick remnants of a one-time gas station, its upper half long gone, and killed the engine. "Which building?"

Duke nodded, because he couldn't point. "Farthest one down, right by the water. Red brick, see it?"

She nodded. And she believed him. So she reached behind his back and pressed the handcuff key into his palm. "Leave the cuffs and the key on the seat and get out of here."

He nodded.

She got out of the car and pulled the .44, leaving him to fumble with the key. It would take him a few minutes to maneuver it into the cuff's lock and get himself free with his hands behind him that way. She figured that gave her time—she doubted he'd try to screw her over, but even if he did, it would be ten minutes. Okay, maybe five.

She kept her back to the sides of buildings, inching along each one, then darting across the alley to the next. When she reached the redbrick building at the end of the row, she skirted it, in search of a less obvious entry than the front door.

Broken fire escape in the back. Twenty feet gaped between it and the ground. No good there. But she found a basement window busted out and crawled in there, standing still and facing the darkness to give her eyes time to adjust.

And her mind time to try to puzzle this out.

She'd been in Africa. So had her father, and Marshall, and so had Peter. She'd been engaged to Peter, but screwing Marshall. She didn't think she'd slept with Peter, or if she had, it must not have been too impressive, because she didn't have any memories of being twisted up naked with him. The memories of her and Marshall though—well, hell, they got her hot even thinking about them. And this was no time to be distracted, so she'd better stop.

Sighing, her eyes seeing things better now, she moved through the basement, avoiding the shapes of boxes and giant metal contraptions that might be normal basement things. Big, square, boxy.

So apparently, someone was involved with criminals. Armed men with automatic weapons who kidnaped people from weddings equaled criminals, right? They couldn't have been cops or feds or anything, she thought, because if they were, they wouldn't have brought their victims here. They'd have taken them to some official place "for questioning" or whatever.

So that meant the men in the suits were bad guys.

Apparently Anita was involved, though not on the criminals' side. Anita must be a good guy.

So why had the criminals taken Peter and Marshall? Were Peter and Marshall good guys, or bad guys?

More importantly, what about me?

Her black boot kicked something that scurried, and she didn't even wince. It was odd to expect to react and then feel nothing. She just kept moving and found a set of stairs leading upward. She took them, and when she reached the door at the top, she pushed it open slowly, peering around into a dimly lit hall. Sun filtered by a dirt-streaked window at the far end gave enough light to make her blink. Seeing no one, she stepped into the hall and started along it, pausing near each and every door to listen.

And hearing only silence.

She came to another set of stairs and crept up to the first landing, around it and up farther, but when her head reached above the floor of level two, she ducked quickly, pausing on the steps.

Someone was standing in front of one of the doors up there.

She dipped a hand into one of the numerous pockets of her jacket and came out with a little mirror. Then she placed it on the floor above her, facing the man, adjusted it until she could see him, left it there, and settled in for the wait.

Patience, she told herself, was as important as stealth or skill or smarts. And it only came with experience.

Must be I've been at this awhile, then . . . whatever this is.

It took time. And during that time, she found herself marking exits. The stairs that continued up. The window, at the far end of this hall, just like the one below. Probably within jumping distance of the ground. And the stairs back down again. That was about it, not counting any escape route inside the apartment itself. Number 207, she noted. And the guy standing outside the door was armed, and smoking, and flipping through a flesh magazine so old the pages were swollen.

Good. Take a good look, she thought.

She decided to hell with patience and crept up the stairs, making not so much as a sound. When she got to the top, she moved into the hall, in the opposite direction from where he was standing, and ducked into a door well. She had to press herself flat to do it, but hell, it was shadowy. He wouldn't see her.

Then she dug a coin from her pocket and tossed it toward the stairs. It flew perfectly, heading down a long way before hitting and pinging and bouncing the rest of the way down.

The guy's head came up fast. He dropped his magazine, lifted his gun, and started down the hall toward her. She pressed flatter, almost melding into the wood at her back.

He didn't see her. He moved down the stairs, rapidly.

Kira pushed off from the wall and ran up the hall, her feet landing like cat's paws, until she reached room 207. There was no time to hesitate or think it over. In a moment, the guard dog would be back. She twisted to the side, drew her knee to her chin and kicked, then burst into the room, gun pointed.

Marshall wasn't there. Instead it was Peter, standing in the room surrounded by the other men. She lifted the weapon, had the drop on all of them. "Don't even move. Not one of you."

Peter looked shocked, stunned as he searched her face. And then she said, "Come on, Peter, I'm taking you out of here."

His brows went up. "You're . . . rescuing me?"

"No time to explain, come on." She gripped his arm and tugged him with her as she backed toward the door. "Where are they holding Marshall?" she asked, glancing once, quickly behind her, and still not seeing the guard back in his place.

"Marshall . . . is one of them. He's in on this," Peter said.

She frowned at him, shaking her head slowly. "That . . . doesn't make sense." It made as much sense, she knew, as anything else did right now. But if Marshall were a bad guy, then didn't that mean she was, too?

She pressed her fingertips to her forehead, images burning in her mind. Marshall, touching her, kissing her, undressing her . . . .

"Are you all right, Kira?" Peter asked.

"Watch behind us," she snapped. "There's a guard."

"He's coming!" Peter shouted.

She spun around, but there was no one there. And now, Peter was pressing a cold gun barrel to the back of her neck. "My hero," he whispered. "It's kind of cute, actually, that you don't even know which side you're on. Tell me, Kira, just how far were you willing to go to get me? Hmm? All the way to the actual vows? To the wedding night? How many times would you have let me fuck you before you sprung your trap? Hmm?"

"I don't know what the hell you're talking about," she muttered, standing motionless and stiff.

He reached to her hand and took the .44, then slid its mate from the holster at her hip, and the bowie knife from its sheath on the other hip. "Don't you?"

He was running his hands down her body now, feeling for hidden weapons. He found none. Then he nodded, and two of his thugs came forward, one gripping each of her arms. "Bring her," Peter said.

They started forward, and Kira kicked one in the shins, and the next thing she knew they each grabbed a leg as well, and carried her that way, while she tried to wriggle free.

They carried her up a whole other flight of stairs, into a room on the third floor, where the first thing she saw was Marshall. His tux was gone, except for the pants. He was shirtless, his face bruised and bloody, his arms and legs bound to the straight-back chair in which he sat.

He lifted his head when they came in, and his eyes met hers. She felt the connection, felt the concern, but knew those eyes betrayed nothing to anyone else.

"Get the jacket off her," Peter commanded.

And the men did as he commanded, slinging her jacket to the floor.

"Shirt, too."

They peeled the tank over her head, but they had to let go of her arms to do so, and it gave her an opportunity. She elbowed one in the rib cage and punched the other in the jaw before they had her anchored again. She was wearing the white demi bra that had been on underneath her wedding gown. She hadn't had time to change, hadn't even thought about it.

"Here." Peter tossed them a rope. "Bind her hands at the wrists, then sling them over that beam right there. Keep her from breaking your jaw at least."

She twisted and resisted as they grabbed her wrists, but her attention was caught by Marshall, who shouted, "Jesus, leave her the hell alone. She doesn't know anything."

Peter smiled. "Maybe not. But you do."

She was still watching Marshall, though, saw him look down, and followed his gaze to her own hands. And then it was as if mists parted, letting knowledge seep through. She went still, let them bind her hands, but she pressed her palms together while keeping her wrists as far apart as she could. Even when they yanked the ropes, she resisted letting them push her wrists together.

Finally the rope's long end was tossed over a visible

beam in the ceiling, where most of the plaster had long since crumbled. They pulled it until her arms were up high, and kept pulling until she was standing on tiptoe. And then they anchored it there.

"Boots," Peter said.

They bent, each toward one leg, and she drew her knees up and kicked them so hard they both went down. Shaking his head in anger, Peter lifted a blade and walked calmly over to Marshall. He put the blade to Marshall's throat. Kira could see the sweat on Marshall's skin, the corded muscles in his neck, the pulse pounding there.

"Now, Kira, you give my men any more trouble, and you can just hang there and watch your wedding planner bleed out on the floor. Understand?"

She nodded rapidly.

He looked at the men who were dragging themselves to their feet. "Boots."

They got up and came to her, and she let them take off her black boots. They tipped them upside down in case anything was hidden inside, then tossed them into the corner with her coat.

Peter handed the knife to one man, who quickly took his former position at Marshall's throat. Then Peter himself came to her, put his hands on the front of the leather pants, undid the snap. Slowly, he lowered the zipper. His palms slid over her hips, pushing the pants down, and she knew he was doing it slowly on purpose.

"Go on, fight me," he told her. "I'd love to give my guy an excuse to slit loverboy's throat."

"Fuck you."

"Maybe."

He pushed the pants all the way off. And she was hanging there in her bra and panties. Every man in the room was eyeing her with a predatory hunger. And Marshall was no exception, although the anger in his eyes outshone everything else. Peter put his hands on her bra cups, squeezing, feeling for hidden weapons. When he found none, he smiled and pinched her nipples as hard as he could. Marshall lunged toward them, his chair coming up off the floor, but one of the other goons decked him, knocking him onto his side on the floor, chair and all.

She gritted her teeth, but didn't cry out.

Peter wasn't finished. He moved his hands to her panties and pushed one inside. She clamped her legs together, but he forced them apart, and shoved his fingers inside her. "You know damn well I don't have any weapons there," she growled.

"You can't blame me for being careful, Kira." He withdrew his hand again, walked over to Marshall, and wiped it on his chest. Then he righted the chair.

"So, Marshall, are you ready to tell exactly what evidence your friends in the Drug Enforcement Administration have on me, or shall I just tell the boys to make use of Kira in whatever way they like until you're ready to talk?"

CH@%!*R

6

The words *Drug Enforcement Administration* were still ricocheting through Kira's brain when Peter turned his attention to her again. "Let's start with something simple, while your partner thinks about his options," he said.

She tried not to let her confusion show on her face, but her gaze shot to Marshall's all the same. Her partner?

Peter clasped her chin in his hand and turned her head until her eyes locked with his. "How did you find your way here?"

"I followed you."

He lowered his head, shaking it slowly, then he turned from her and nodded at one of his men. The thug drove a fist into Marshall's stomach so hard Kira grunted in pain along with him. He doubled over as much as the ropes holding him would allow, head down, mouth open. She thought he was going to vomit, but he didn't.

"You wanna take another shot at that one, or are you going to let us kill him?"

Lifting her chin, she met his eyes. "You're not gonna kill him until he tells you want you want to know."

"Wrong, honey. We can get the same information from you."

She smiled slowly. "You think so? Well, you'd better have someone fill me in first, because I don't know shit."

"Bull. You got your memory back, or you wouldn't be here."

"I came here planning to rescue you from the bad guys, Peter. I didn't realize you were the biggest piece of shit in the sewer."

He backhanded her. Her head snapped sideways with the impact, and the pain shrieked through her entire head. But instead of making her cry or cower, it seemed to energize her. She touched the corner of her lip with the tip of her tongue and tasted blood.

Peter saw something in her eyes and turned away. "She didn't follow us here. You two get outside, search the area. Someone led her here, and ten to one it was Duke. You find him out there, kill him."

They rushed to obey.

Peter turned to the third goon. "You come with me. We're clearly going to need something a little more potent than our fists to make these two talk. Besides, my knuckles are getting sore." He turned to Kira. "I'll be back, sweetie. Maybe with a set of cables and a car battery, hmm?"

"I can hardly wait. Promise I get to go first?"

He glared at her before slamming out of the room with his thug on his heels. Kira released her breath all at once, then turned to study Marshall. He looked like hell. "Are you all right?" she asked.

He lifted his head, met her eyes, nodded once. "Good call, pretending you still don't remember anything. It probably kept me alive."

She held his eyes for a moment. "Marshall, I wasn't pretending. I *don't* remember anything."

He stared at her as if her words were not quite translating in his brain. "But your hair—your clothes—"

"I found a photo, and a few of my things in a trunk in

the attic. I thought if I put them on, did my hair the old way, maybe it would shake something loose. Help me remember."

"That doesn't make any sense. You charged those guys. You fought and you shot as if you knew how."

"Yeah. It surprised me as much as anyone, I guarantee you that. It wasn't like I thought about it first, I just did it. It was like . . . instinct."

"And the weapons? Were they in the same trunk?"

"Yeah." She looked around the room at her discarded clothing, and smiled slowly. "Yeah. And some of them are still in here with us."

He sent her a questioning look, and she nodded toward her boots, still lying in the corner where Peter had tossed them. Then he smiled, too. "The blade's still in the boot?"

She blinked, shocked that he could know that, but then shook it off and nodded.

She stretched out one leg as far as she could, but her toes came short of the boot.

"I can get over there, chair and all," Marshall said.

"Yeah, and make so much noise they'll hear you and come running. Just give me a second." She looked up, then carefully clasped the rope in her hands, pushed off with her toes, and began to swing. It was a pathetically small arc, at first, but she swung farther with each repetition until finally, she managed to grab the boot between her feet. She swung back toward Marshall and tossed the boot to him.

It landed right at his feet with a small thud.

She let her swinging subside and balanced on her toes once more.

Marshall stood the boot upright with his own feet, then began to move his chair. He had to go slowly, a little at a time to avoid making a lot of noise. But bit by bit, he managed to turn his chair around.

"Your left hand is four inches above the boot," Kira told him.

"Okay." He pushed with his feet, tipping the chair back onto two legs.

"Almost," she said. "Another inch."

He tipped further, hell, he was going to go over.

But he didn't. His fingertips found the edge of the boot, running along the inside. He finally located the hidden pocket and pulled out the blade. He found the button. The blade popped open, as he lowered his chair to the floor again.

"Now," she told him, "don't try to free your wrist. You'll never be able to do it." She eyed the knots, the ropes. "Looks like he looped your wrist, then wrapped the rope around the back of the chair, ran it to the other side, around the back, around the other wrist. If you can cut that rope . . ."

He twisted his wrist in an impossible angle, found the rope with the blade and began to saw. Kira held her breath. Finally, the rope gave way. He dropped the blade, then fumbled with the rope, tugging until his hands were free.

"Hurry, Marshall, they'll be back."

He nodded, grabbed up the blade, making quick work of his remaining bonds. Then he moved to her, reaching up above her. He had to stand very close to reach the rope that was looped over the beam. Very close. His body was touching hers, as he slid the blade over the rope, sawing. She felt the give when the rope was severed and finally lowered her feet to the floor. God it was a relief not to be on tiptoe.

She brought her hands down, rubbed her wrists, then looked up to see Marshall staring at her, and was reminded that she was damn near naked. He, she thought, hadn't forgotten it for a minute. "You're not a wedding consultant, are you?" she asked.

That drew his eyes up to hers. "No."

"Peter said DEA?"

"Yeah."

"He called me your partner. Just what kind of partners are we, Marshall?"

His eyes grew darker, she thought, before he averted them. "We'll have time for this later." Turning, he snatched the leather pants from the corner, the tank top, the jacket. "Get dressed," he said, handing them to her. "And make it quick."

She nodded. Her questions needed answers, but not at the risk of their lives. She pulled on the pants and tank, stuffed her feet into the boots and kept the knife in her hand. The jacket, she tucked under an arm, because it was faster than putting it on. Marshall took a step toward the door.

She touched his shoulder, stopping him. "There was a guard outside the other room when when I came in. I imagine he's outside this one by now. Let's try the window."

He nodded, and they crossed the room, stepping lightly, to stare out the dirt-streaked window. The broken fire escape was far to the left. Too far to jump for it. Before Marshall could say anything, Kira had spun around to the chair and was unwinding the ropes from it. She tossed him one end. "Quick, tie this to something solid."

He didn't hesitate, but quickly knelt and knotted the end of the rope around the base of the old-fashioned iron radiator beside the window. While he did that, she wrestled the window open.

"They're coming," he told her.

She looked up fast and heard the heavy footfalls in the hallway. "Hell, we're out of time."

Marshall held on to the rope. "Get on my back."

"You can't hold us both."

"I'll have to manage," he said, climbing out the window, feet braced on the wall, hands on the rope. "Hurry."

She slipped through the open window, clutching his shoulders and lowering herself until she could wrap her legs around his waist. "Go," she said.

He let the rope lengthen, dropping them drastically, then he pushed off with his feet and swung.

She heard shouting, knew the men were in the room, now, searching for them, even as they came short of their goal and began swinging back the other way. Heads appeared at the window. Then gunshots rang out. Marshall's feet hit the wall, and this time he pushed harder. They swung, arced over the fire escape.

He let go, and they fell.

She only had an instant to feel panic, before they hit the fire escape's landing with a terrible impact and a lot of noise. The entire structure groaned and wobbled, and for a moment she thought it would rip itself free of the building and send them crashing to the ground.

And then it did.

The fire escape fell like a giant timber, and as they were hurled toward the ground, Marshall gripped her arm and yelled, "Jump!"

They were airborne, then. The fire escape crashed, bits of rusted metal flying everywhere, and a split second later, Kira felt her own body hit the ground a few feet away from it.

Dazed, she lifted her head, giving it a slow shake.

"Come on, baby, they're coming." Marshall had her arm, tugging her to her feet, and then they were running.

She realized the men were no longer firing at them from the window, but were exiting the building, coming around after them.

"This way," she told Marshall. "The car's this way."

They changed directions, sprinting full speed, until they ducked into an alley, popped out the far side, and spotted the car. The keys had been in her jacket pocket. They were no longer there.

"Bastards took my keys."

"No problem," Marshall said, racing around to the back of the car, reaching underneath it, and coming out with a key in his palm. "You always keep a spare."

"You drive," she told him, scrambling into the passenger side.

He looked at her oddly, but didn't hesitate. He got behind the wheel, started the engine, and spun the tires as gunshots rang out behind them.

She ducked instinctively just before the rear window was blown to bits.

As they sped away, with armed criminals piling into cars to give chase, Marshall glanced sideways at her and said, "You really don't remember anything, do you?"

"No," she said. "I don't know why that's so hard for you to believe."

"Oh, I believe it now," he said, shifting gears, speeding ever faster.

"Why now?"

"Because," he told her. "You *never* let me drive."

CH@%!*R

7

"I think we lost them."

"Yeah, along with my stomach," Kira said. But though she knew the high speeds, split-second maneuvers, and two-wheel turns should have scared the hell out of her, she didn't really feel afraid. She felt alive. Her heart was pounding, blood flowing, skin tingling in ways they hadn't done since—since she could remember.

He put a hand on her shoulder. It was warm, firm. Familiar. "You okay?"

She nodded. "You'd almost think I was used to this kind of thing." Lifting her head slowly, she faced him, studied his profile. The strong nose, tanned skin, slight shadow of beard on his cheeks. Lips that were full and so sensual she got a little tingly as she stared at them. "I am, aren't I?"

He glanced her way, drew a breath, then let it out again without answering.

"Don't you think it's about time someone told me who the hell I am? God, Marshall, I have a right to know."

He nodded. "I know. I know you do. Believe me, there's nothing I want more than to tell you . . . everything. But—"

"But?"

He looked at her again. "I can't."

She lowered her head. "Can you tell me why not?"

"Because the doctors said you needed to remember on your own."

"That's stupid."

"No. No, it's not. Kira, things went down. Bad things. Things that could make the most heartless bastard in the world cry like a baby. You blocked it out for a reason."

"Yeah, and that reason was a head injury."

He licked his lips, said nothing, but she read his face, even though he kept it carefully focused on the road.

"Are you saying my memory loss doesn't have a physical cause?"

His deep sigh filled the car. "None they could find. The docs said you'd get things back a little at a time. And that would be the best way for you—remembering all of it at once could be . . . bad."

"Bad how?"

He shrugged.

She sighed, angry and impatient. "I have been getting things back. Little things."

"Yeah?" He faced her, and his eyes were alight with interest and something else. Something that looked like hope. "What have you remembered?"

She closed her eyes, and the images rolled through her mind again. She saw herself in his arms, saw him kissing her, laughing with her, making love to her.

"Kira?"

"Nothing I'm ready to talk about," she said.

"Okay. That's okay." He reached across the seat to put his hand over hers.

She opened her eyes and looked at it there, felt her throat tighten and her eyes burn, and didn't know why. God, she was so confused. "Where are we going?" she asked, to change the subject. "This isn't the way back to my house."

"We can't go back to your mother's place." He didn't call it her place, she noted, and wondered if she should read anything into that. "They'll be looking for us. We need a safe place where we can hole up, regroup, and phone our—my contact."

She nodded slowly. "How far?"

"Twenty minutes. Why?"

She shrugged. "You won't tell me who I am," she said softly. "So how about you use the time to tell me who you are, Marshall?"

He looked at her sharply.

She blinked and knew something without even trying. "That's not even your real name, is it?"

He shot her a startled look. "No. Do you remember what it is?"

She shook her head.

"Try," he said.

She closed her eyes, and again saw those images she'd seen before. Him, wrapping her in his arms, holding her, kissing her . . . her own voice whispering his name.

"Michael," she whispered.

And the image went on, spinning its web through her mind, playing out like a clip from a movie she hadn't yet seen. The kiss ended, and he backed away just a little, and she looked at him in his tux, and then down at herself. She saw white flowing all around her, pooling at her feet, and she heard a man's voice, not Michael's, but some other man, who stood there with them, saying, "Ladies and gentleman, it is my honor to present for the first time, Mr. and Mrs. Michael Waters."

Her eyes flew open. She stared at him, stunned.

"What? What's wrong?" he asked.

Kira could only blink. Then she moved her gaze lower, to his hands on the steering wheel, seeking out the left one. There was a gold band on his third finger. She clapped a hand to her mouth, then belatedly, thought to look to her own third finger. But she already knew there was no ring there.

"Kira, for God's sake, what's the matter?"

She swallowed hard. "You . . . you're my . . . husband."

He hit the brakes so hard she automatically braced her hands on the dashboard to keep from hitting the windshield, even though she was wearing a seat belt—had put it on thirty seconds into this mad drive.

She was vaguely aware of the car veering onto the shoulder, sending up a cloud of dust all around them. And then he was turning toward her, reaching for her, his face so incredibly filled with emotion she could barely believe it. He quickly released her seat belt and pulled her into his arms, his hands burying themselves in her hair as he held her so tightly she could barely breathe. His mouth moved over her neck, and then her jaw, and finally covered her lips. He kissed her with more passion than she would have guessed one man could possess. She went dizzy under the assault, and her body reacted without her mind's permission or concern. She kissed him back. She opened her lips to his questing tongue and twisted her arms around his waist and held on as if she would never let him go.

When he finally lifted his head, he stared into her eyes, his own glittering with unshed tears, and whispered, "You remember."

She lifted a hand, realized it was trembling as she touched his hair. "No," she said in a voice gone hoarse with some emotion she couldn't identify. "It was just a flash. Me in a bridal gown, you in a tux, a minister, a kiss."

Blinking in confusion he tipped his head to one side. "That's all?"

She nodded. "I'm sorry."

"Don't be, honey. It's not your fault." He smoothed her hair, reached across her to put her seat belt back on. Then got himself behind the wheel and set the car into motion once more. "Besides, it's progress."

"But I don't understand. If I'm married to you then— how was I engaged to Peter? Did we . . . are we divorced?"

His head turned sharply. "No way. You think I'd let a catch like you get away? No, Kira. It's . . . it's complicated."

"You were going to let me go through with the wedding. And my mother—"

"Your mother doesn't know about us. Hell, Kira, no one does. We were married in secret, in Africa, just before . . . damn it, I'm not supposed to be telling you any of this."

She closed her eyes, fought to make sense of things, but her head had begun pounding as if it would split, and she pressed her fingers to the bridge of her nose against the pain. "I have to know."

"You will. You'll know everything. It's coming back, Kira, be patient." He drove, and kept looking worriedly at her as he did. "You're in pain."

"It's just a headache."

"Information overload. The doctors said this would happen. Relax, hon. We're almost there. The place is stocked. I'll find you some pain reliever and a stiff drink as soon as we get there."

"And some weapons, I hope." She was leaning back against the headrest now, her eyes still closed. "I feel fucking naked without my Smith & Wesson."

She popped her eyes open, almost wondering who the hell had just spoken, but she knew it was her. Not the Kira she'd come to know over the past six months, the frightened, uncertain, confused one. But the Kira she had been before. The one she was coming to think of as the kick-ass bitch from hell.

The place was a small log cabin, situated on the shore of a looking glass lake. They pulled up as the sun was going down and painting the water in liquid gold. Pine trees backed the place, and the shapes of those same pines were cut out of the green shutters that flanked each window. A porch spanned the front of the place, a knotty wood porch swing dangling from its roof on black chains.

Kira got out of the car as soon as he'd brought it to a stop and stood there looking around, filling her lungs with the fresh tangy scent of the pine forest. "God, this is gorgeous."

He had been coming around the car toward her, but he stopped when she said that, and when she looked at him, she found him staring at her a little oddly. "Did I say something wrong?"

He shook his head. "You never liked it here. Said it was too far from civilization, too boring."

She shook her head slowly, her eyes skimming the lake now, noting the way the sentinel pines on the far shore were perfectly reflected in the water. "How could I ever be bored here?"

"I asked you that a thousand times."

Something floated into her memory with her next breath, gently painting the blank canvas with a stroke of vivid color. "My father used to take me to a place like this, when I was a little girl."

Marshall—Michael, she reminded herself—put a hand on her shoulder. "His hunting cabin in Seven Hills."

"You've been there?" She looked at him, surprised.

"No, but he told me about it."

She nodded slowly. "I didn't, though."

"No."

Kira narrowed her eyes and searched her mind, but found no answers. "So I loved it then, and I love it now. What happened to make me stop in between?"

His hand slid to the center of her back, and he rubbed small circles between her shoulder blades. "Don't push. It'll come to you."

She nodded, but she was impatient. She wanted her memory. She wanted all of it. Now. But she tried to at least give the impression that she wouldn't push too hard. "Is there a fireplace?"

"Yeah. You want a fire tonight?"

She nodded. "Will we be here long?"

"I don't know. I need to call in, update our . . . people."

"And check on Anita—Kelly, I mean," she said quickly, recalling the image of the housekeeper being skewered by a bullet. "I hope she's all right." She blinked then. "She wasn't really a housekeeper, was she?"

He lowered his head, digging a hand into his pocket.

"She worked with you . . . with us," Kira said.

Michael pulled out a key and handed it to her. "Why don't you go on in, take a look around while I get an armful of firewood?"

She knew he was trying to obey the dictates of her doctors, trying not to fill her in on things she would be better off remembering on her own. And she could tell it wasn't easy for him. So she stopped pushing and took the key, opened the door, and stepped into the house.

The entire place smelled of pine and cedar, and she inhaled deeply and let that scent tickle memories to life. She saw herself, pacing this very floor; back and forth over the wood, and the old-fashioned braided oval rug that covered most of it; back and forth in front of the huge fieldstone fireplace; pausing at the large picture window on the far side, to stare down toward the lake where Michael was relaxing on the dock with a beer in one hand and a fishing pole in the other. She heard herself mutter, "How can he be so content to just *sit there*?" Then as she watched, he turned back toward the house, almost as if he could feel her there, watching him, and he blew her a kiss. Her heart went soft, she smiled a goofy smile, grabbed her jacket, and headed out to join him, thinking she could even bear this godforsaken wilderness if he were with her.

For just a moment the emotion she had felt then came alive in her heart. For just an instant, she was filled to bursting with an overwhelming love so powerful it rocked her. She pressed a hand to her chest, as if to slow her suddenly rapid heartbeat, and turned slowly when she heard him come inside.

He met her eyes. "You okay?"

She nodded. "Yeah."

He didn't look as if he believed her. Crossing the room, he set the armload of wood into a metal rack made to hold it, which stood beside the fireplace. Then he straightened and brushed off his jacket before taking it off.

"We were . . . close," she said softly. Her heart was still

racing, her stomach in knots. "Our marriage, it was a good one."

He moved toward her, touched her shoulders. "The best."

She closed the space between them, sliding her arms around his waist and resting her head on his shoulder. "This must have been so hard on you."

"Nothing compared to what it's been for you, Kira." He returned her embrace, gently rubbing her back with one hand, stroking her hair with the other. "Just take it easy. Just let the memories come."

"I would if they weren't being so damn stubborn." She sighed and closed her eyes.

He held her a little tighter, then drew a deep breath. "I have to make that phone call. And I don't know about you, but I'm starved."

"Me, too." She loosened her grip, stepped away, but not without a twinge of regret. It felt right, being in his arms. "I'll go see what I can find in the kitchen while you make your call."

"All right."

Kira headed through the large room and into the kitchen off to one side. There had been a room off the other side, too, she realized as she stepped into the kitchen. And she thought it was a bedroom, with a bath attached, but she wasn't sure if that was a guess or a memory. An instant later, she knew it was a memory, because the images flooded her mind. Images of her and Michael, wrapped in each other's arms, a tangle of naked limbs on a bed whose four posts were knotty pine logs. She stood still in the middle of the kitchen, assaulted by a hunger that had nothing to do with food. It was a hunger for the man in the next room—a man who was a stranger to her.

CH@%!*R

8

He hadn't been kidding when he told her the place was stocked. The kitchen held a freezer, packed full of meats and vegetables, and the cupboards held enough canned goods to last a year. There was no bread, margarine, milk, eggs, or fresh veggies to go with anything, so she chose a couple of frozen pot pies and popped them into the microwave. In inspecting the drawers she located one that held paper, pens, tape, and batteries, and took out a notepad and a pen, then sat down at the little hardwood table and started making notes.

What did she know? She knew that she and Michael had worked together for the DEA. She guessed Kelly had been working with them as well. She knew that she and Michael had both been in Africa, that they'd been secretly married there. And she knew that Peter had been there, too.

And Dad.

She closed her eyes. Yes. Her father had been there, too. He'd died there. But why?

She wrote these things down, then tapped the pen on the

pad, making little dots of ink. "Peter's a bad guy," she muttered, and jotted it down. Apparently, she and Michael had been investigating him for some crime. She knew that much just from the things Peter had said when he'd been holding them captive.

But why was it that after the explosion, after the coma, Kira's own mother had introduced Peter to her as her fiancé? It made no sense.

And why were she and Michael keeping their marriage secret?

And where was her wedding ring?

She set the pen down, frowning as she got to her feet and returned to the big front room, where Michael was just folding a cell phone. He hadn't had one earlier. "Where did that come from?" she asked him.

He nodded toward an open door on the far side of the room, and she went toward it, reached inside to flick on a light switch, then caught her breath. The room was lined in weapons. Shotguns, rifles, handguns, and holsters hung from racks that covered three walls. A counter stood low on one wall, and it held several sets of walkie-talkies, a half dozen cell phones, spotlights, ammunition, and stacks of batteries.

"I guess this place *is* fully stocked," she muttered.

"And then some." He reached past her to flick the light off again, then closed the door, which vanished when shut, appearing to be just another part of the log cabin's wall.

"That's ingenious."

"Thanks. I thought of it myself." He was smiling, a teasing light in his eyes.

"How did your phone call go?"

His smile faded. "They haven't located Peter yet. We're to stay put until he's picked up."

"Is that really necessary?"

Michael nodded. "Peter doesn't like being fooled, Kira. You made him fall in love with you, when you were married to me. He's furious, and out for blood. Our blood."

Lowering her head, she nodded. "It was all part of a

case, wasn't it? You and I were investigating him for . . . something."

Michael nodded slowly, but said nothing. He wanted to, she could see that he wanted to, but he held it back.

"Won't my mother be worried?"

"It's been taken care of. And she's been temporarily re-located, just in case our boy gets the notion of using her to get to us."

"Oh."

"We'll be okay, Kira. No one knows about this place, not even within the agency. We're safe here."

"I never thought otherwise."

"But . . . you still have questions. I know it's frustrating, but—"

"Just one question. For now. And I think it's one that you can answer without making my head explode."

One corner of his mouth turned up in a half smile. "Okay, shoot."

"Where is my wedding ring?"

His half-smile faded. A look of longing replaced it as his eyes searched her face. He lifted a hand to his throat and tugged a silver chain from underneath his shirt. A gold band dangled from the end of it, spinning slowly and catching the light of the fire she hadn't even noticed he'd started in the hearth.

"I've had it stashed here for a while. Do you want it back?" he asked.

Michael was holding his breath awaiting her answer, she could see it, even though she had no idea what to say. If she said she wanted it back, would he take that to mean she wanted more? How could she come up with an answer that wouldn't mislead him or hurt him? She opened her mouth, thinking she had to say something. Anything.

He held up a hand. "No. I shouldn't be asking you shit like that, it's not fair. I'm sorry, Kira. You've got enough to deal with. Here." He took the chain from around his neck and draped it carefully around hers. "You can wear it under your blouse, or tuck it into a drawer. I'll never know the difference. No pressure, okay?"

She couldn't take her eyes off his face. The conflicting emotions in his eyes, which he kept so carefully from showing anywhere else. "Were you always this considerate of me?"

"When you let me be."

"Sounds like I didn't always."

He shrugged. "Not recently, no. You developed an aversion to letting anyone help you with anything. Said it was a sign of weakness."

"Guess getting my brain scrambled in Africa was an instant cure. I've been awfully dependent since I came out of the coma."

"Not on me," he said. And it sounded a little sad.

She lifted her brows. "I don't see anyone else around here."

The smile returned to his face. "I hadn't thought of that. Does that mean you're going to let me wait on you hand and foot while we're here?"

She shook her head. "No. But I'll let you show me how to use some of those weapons in that nifty little closet over there."

He tipped his head to one side. "You didn't have any trouble back at the uh . . . wedding."

"If you asked me how I did what I did back there, I couldn't tell you. And I'd rather not rely on my faulty memory or gut instinct if it comes down to life or death."

"Your gut instinct is flawless, Kira. Always has been. But yeah, I'll show you."

"Good." She smiled. "Pick out something simple. I'll go check on our pot pies."

He lowered his head, laughing softly.

"What?" she asked, frowning. "Did I say something funny?"

He met her eyes, his shining. "Pot pies. You always loved those things."

"I did?"

He reached out a hand to cup her nape, fingers brushing over her hair. "It's coming back to you, Kira. Little by little, it's all coming back."

"I hope so," she said, and her voice came out soft. "I want to remember you, Michael."

He started to lean closer to her, then stopped himself. Kira slid her hands over his shoulders and pulled him toward her, until his lips brushed hers. It was a light touch, but it lit a fire inside her. She linked her hands around his neck and pressed her mouth to his, felt him tremble, as he pulled her tighter to him.

The rapid-fire beat of her heart grew louder—and when the windows blew out of the cabin, she realized it wasn't her heart at all, but gunfire. In the next heartbeat, she was pressed to the floor with Michael's body covering hers. "Stay down." He growled the words into her ear. "Dammit, how did they find us?"

She couldn't speak, overwhelmed with the surge of adrenalin pumping through her body, itching to get up, to *do* something. "Duke. It had to be goddamn Duke. I left him alone in the car. He must have done something."

"Stuck a tracking device on it, more than likely," Michael said. "Come on, but stay low." He rolled off her.

On hands and knees, they made their way to the little hidden room. Michael opened its door, urged her inside ahead of him, then closed it again behind him. Only then did he get to his feet.

She heard him moving around as she crouched in the darkness. He never turned on a light, not even a flashlight, but she knew he was gathering weapons, ammunition. She jumped upright when she heard the cabin's front door crashing open, the sounds of heavy steps inside the house. Michael's hands closed on one of her arms, and he drew her body flush to his. "It's okay," he whispered, his lips touching her ear, moving with the words. "Just stay quiet. It's okay."

She nodded against the side of his face, then felt him moving, sliding a belt over her head, and around one shoulder, then another on the other side, so the two crossed at her chest. She felt a familiar, reassuring weight at her hips, moved her hands to her sides to caress the smooth grips of handguns and wondered at the flood of confidence that rushed through her.

Then Michael had her by the hand and led her toward the back of the room, where he knelt. And moments later, he was guiding her down a set of stairs in the floor. "Wait at the bottom," he told her.

Easier said than done, she thought, when she couldn't even see where the bottom was. Still, she made her way down into inky blackness, and there she waited. Only seconds ticked by, before he joined her there. She had drawn one of the weapons, held it ready at her side, even though she didn't remember pulling it. And her eyes were turned upward toward the ceiling, where she could see nothing but could hear the sounds of men stomping through the house, searching for them.

Michael slid an arm around her shoulders, started leading her forward, and she was surprised when they didn't run into a wall. "How are you doing?"

"Pissed," she muttered. "I didn't get my pot pie."

He squeezed her closer. "That's my girl."

She wanted to be. The thought danced through her mind without her permission. "Where does this lead?"

"Out," he said.

"Well, hell, I assumed that much."

"Comes out about a hundred yards from the house, pretty deep into the woods. The exit's camouflaged. There's no way they could have spotted it."

"Like there was no way they could find us at the cabin?" She felt him tense, and quickly added, "I'm not blaming you for it, Michael. Hell, it was my fault for leaving Duke alone in the car. I'm just saying . . . how do we know there's not a thug with an AK standing outside that entrance, ready to pop us when we come out?"

"Because," he said. "They want us alive."

"That's not exactly reassuring."

"I know. Just stay behind me, and if anything happens, I'll hold 'em off and you make a run for it."

The voice that answered wasn't hers—or at least, not the one she'd been thinking of as hers for the past six months. It said, "The hell I will."

CH@%!*R
9

She held her breath as Michael stood at the top of another set of stairs. She saw a sliver of gray twilight as he pushed the trapdoor upward and peered out, then sucked in a sharp breath when the door opened wider. Michael moved through it, and she started up behind him, only to have the trapdoor close all at once.

Frowning, she scooted up the steps, put her hands over her head, and shoved upward, only to meet resistance.

Hell, was Michael *standing on* the door?

"Well now, where the hell did you come from?" a man's voice said.

Kira froze. It wasn't Michael's voice.

"Like I'd tell you."

There was a terrible sound, a grunt of pain. Anger surged in Kira, and she shoved harder at the trapdoor.

"Don't!" Michael yelled. "I'll talk, just take it easy. I was out gathering firewood when I heard you guys shooting up the place. Decided it might be best to lay low till you left."

"And where's the little woman?"

"Relocated, for her protection. I couldn't tell you where if I wanted to, and that's the truth."

Kira closed her eyes. Damn him, he was determined to protect her.

"Bullshit," one of the men said. "You brought her here with you."

"No," he said. "I didn't. You really think I'd have stayed out here hiding if Kira were under fire at that cabin?"

The men were quiet for a moment, seeming to mull that over.

"He's right," one said at last. "He'd have charged into the cross fire to get her out. It wouldn't be the first time."

"Doesn't matter," Michael said. "She's no threat to you. She's got no memory, doesn't even know what this is all about."

"Search the woods, just in case," one of the men said. "I'll take this one back to the boss, figure out how he wants to proceed."

"I'm telling you, she's not here. You're wasting your time," Michael said.

"If she is, we'll find her."

"I wish she was lurking around here someplace. You can bet she'd have sense enough to lay low till you were long gone," he said. "She'd know she was my only chance. But as it is, I guess I'm screwed."

Kira closed her eyes, heard the message he had meant for her to hear. She had to stay quiet, stay safe, and rescue her husband from the grip of madmen.

For more than an hour she crouched in the darkness, underground. Eventually, she couldn't bear it any longer. She had no way of knowing if Peter's thugs still lurked outside, but she had to move. It was too easy to imagine what they might be doing to Michael.

She crept up the stairs and shoved at the trapdoor. It gave easily this time, and she peered out, saw nothing, then reminded herself that Michael hadn't seen anything either before stepping into the open and being spotted. So she crept out on her belly, pushing the trapdoor up only as much as she had to. When she was clear of it, she lay still on the ground, one gun in her hand, and she listened with every part of her. Carefully, she lifted her head, looked at her surroundings.

Darkness surrounded her. The only sounds were the occasional call of a nightbird, the songs of crickets, the whir of other insects buzzing past.

She pushed herself up, got to her feet, and glanced back at the trapdoor, then blinked because she couldn't see it. After a moment she realized it was completely camouflaged. It looked like a part of the forest floor, leaves, branches, grass actually growing from it. The thing was invisible.

She looked around, trying to get her bearings, and started in what she hoped was the direction of the cabin. Within a few yards, she saw soft yellow light, gleaming in the distance. She moved closer, instinctively moving without making a sound, creeping from one tree to the next. The light took form—it was coming from the cabin windows. And there were cars parked in front.

"They didn't take him away," she whispered. Then she wondered why they would bother. They had the perfect place here. Michael had told her himself, no one else knew about it. Not even the good guys.

Hell. She really was on her own. She worked the action on the handgun, then stopped, realizing what she had just done. No one had shown her how. She just knew. Just like she knew she wasn't going to miss what she targeted.

Just who the fuck do those assholes think they're dealing with?

The voice in her head made her smile, just a little. There was something familiar and comforting about it. About knowing it was *her* voice.

She crept closer to the house, moving around it, watching carefully for guards who might be posted outside and seeing none. Then she went still closer, skimming along the outer walls and peering in through the windows. Quick, careful glimpses, followed by slower, longer looks if she saw no one inside. By the time she'd circled the cabin fully she knew exactly what she faced.

Peter was nowhere in sight. She didn't think he was there. Michael was tied to a chair in the bedroom. One thug in there with him. The other three were lounging in the living room, eating.

My goddamn pot pies.

She returned to the bedroom, crouched below the window, and started to shake. The woman she'd spent the last six months believing herself to be was scared to death right now. She didn't want to do this. She wanted to run out of these woods, find a phone, call for help.

Kira closed her eyes, and immediately her mind was flooded with images. She saw herself, cornered by three men in a dark ally. She saw blood dripping from her nose, tasted it on her lips. Her weapons were lying on the ground, out of reach. She lifted her gaze to the men, knew with a grim certainty they meant to kill her, and sent them a smile. "Guess this is it, then."

"Maybe not quite," someone said from the far end of the alley.

The three men spun around, so surprised by the voice coming from behind them that they started firing without even aiming first. Kira dove for her guns, even as Michael strode into the ally, into the rain of bullets, his own guns blazing.

He dropped two of them, and she blasted the third, still lying on her belly on the ground, just as he drew down on Michael.

The echoes of the gunfire died and with them the ringing in her ears. She looked at Michael over the bodies lying between them. He smiled, and it lit his eyes. And she said, "You're late."

"I'm right on time," he told her. "Did you think I wasn't going to show?"

"Not for a minute." She moved into his arms, and he held her so tight she could feel him shaking just a little, and knew it was at having come so close to losing her.

Outside the little cabin, Kira blinked slowly until the memory cleared away. And then she realized that it was still there. She could still find it there. She *remembered!*

Not everything. Not yet, but . . . God, it was real. A real solid memory, and if she had time to sit and think she thought others would surely follow.

But there was no time for that. Not now.

"Well, well, what have we got here? Peeping Tom?"

The man had come up behind her, stood looming over her. "Peeping Kira," she said, then she jerked her head backward, slamming her skull into his groin so hard he dropped to his knees. She sprang up, spun around, delivering a kick to the side of the man's head in the process. His gun flew from his hand as he went over sideways, and even as he opened his mouth to cry out, she delivered a fist to his windpipe to keep him quiet.

He lay there, gasping, hands clutching his neck as he fought to breathe. She used her own weapon to put him down for the count, flicking the safety back on just before the butt smashed into his skull. Then she flicked it off again, picked up the man's weapon, tucked it into the back of her pants. All of this before she knelt beside the man to make sure he wasn't going to be coming around any time soon.

Her stomach convulsed when she realized he wasn't going to be coming around at all. He was dead. She'd killed a man without firing a shot. And she knew it wasn't the first time.

For a moment, she wondered if she really wanted to remember the woman she'd been. But then a sound from inside the cabin drew her attention, and she peered through the window. The man in the room with Michael was drawing the point of a blade slowly down Michael's cheek. The knife point left a scarlet trail in its wake. And it left a furious rage in Kira's belly.

She crept closer, ear to the wall, straining to hear.

"The boss will be here soon. Since you're refusing to talk, my bet is he's not gonna see much use in keeping you around."

"Sooner the better," Michael said.

The man stopped studying his knife blade and stood back. "If you're in that much of a hurry, I could do it right now."

"What, without your master giving you the okay? You haven't got the balls, pal."

"No?" The man brought the blade down hard, driving it straight into the back of Michael's hand, where it was bound to the chair's arm, and into the wood beyond. Michael shouted, and his face contorted in pain. Kira's ability to control her temper evaporated. She rose up onto her feet, leveled the gun on the bastard, and pulled the trigger, taking him dead center of his forehead. His head snapped back, and then he went down, dead before he hit the floor.

She met Michael's eyes for an instant. He was hurting, she could see it, but he mouthed the word "run."

The bedroom door slammed open, and men poured in. One of them yelled, "Get outside, it came from outside!"

Kira turned and raced into the cover of the forest, quickly skirting around to the front of the house, knowing they'd be focused on the rear, where she'd been. She moved quickly, as quietly as possible, back to the only place she could be certain they wouldn't find her. That trapdoor in the forest floor. She found it easily and realized that was because she remembered it.

She ducked into the darkness, lowering the door carefully over her and scooting to the bottom of the steps. Then she raced back along the tunnel, all the way back until it ended. The men would be outside by now. All of them, combing the woods for her. They wouldn't be worried about Michael being alone for a few moments. Not with a blade nailing his hand to the chair, his face cut up, his body bound so tight he couldn't even wiggle. One of them might be watching the front door, she supposed, but then, she didn't intend to go in through the front door.

She crept up the stairs, lifted the hidden panel in the floor, and quietly climbed upward, into the dark storage room.

CH@%!*R
10

Kira listened, her ear pressed to the closed door. Not a
sound came through. She reached into her boot in utter
darkness, unerringly closing her hand around the small,
folding knife and flicking the button that flipped the blade
out, then holding it in her teeth to keep her gun hands free.
She pushed the door open, very slowly, and crept into the
living room. No one was around. The front door stood part-
way open, the bedroom door was closed.

She moved fast, across the open living room, avoiding
the broken glass that littered the floor. There was no
cover, nothing to duck behind, and she would be visible
to anyone outside who happened to be looking in, so
speed was the only option. Limit the chance of being
glimpsed.

Outside, she could hear the men shouting to each other
as they searched the woods for her, though she couldn't
make out their words. She paused outside the bedroom
door, again listening, before slowly turning the knob and
opening the door.

She sighed in relief when she saw no one besides

Michael in the room, then tensed as she realized the blade was still in his hand.

He's been hurt a lot worse than that, she thought involuntarily, and then a rush of memories came, one after the other. Michael with a knife wound, a bullet hole, bruised and broken from a hellish beating. Hell, he'd even been hit by a car once.

She had to shake the memories away and focus on what she needed to do. When she did, she saw that he was staring at her, his face a mixture of relief, pain, and urgency. She closed the door behind her and holstered her gun. Taking the knife in her hand, she moved toward him, knelt, and quickly sliced through the ropes at his ankles, then the ones at his wrists. She paused then, her eyes on the blade through his hand, her hand hovering near it, shaking a little.

He gripped the hilt before she could, and gritting his teeth, jerked on the blade.

It didn't come out. His face was red, wet with moisture. His eyes shut tight, jaw clenched. "It's too deep into the chair. I can't get it with one hand. You've got to do it, babe. Pull straight up, hard as you can. Don't hesitate."

"Hell." She folded her own knife and pocketed it, then she closed her hands around the fat handle of the large hunting knife. She put one foot on the wooden chair, wedging it beside Michael's thigh. "On three," she told him. He nodded, braced himself. "One, two—" She yanked as hard as she could, her stomach convulsing as the blade came free so suddenly she almost fell over backward. She dropped the blade, her gaze shooting to Michael's hand as blood bubbled from the wound. He drew it to his waist and held it there with the good hand. Kira lunged to the nearby dresser, yanking open a drawer and taking the first piece of fabric she felt inside, which turned out to be a small T-shirt. She brought it to him, kneeling in front of him, beginning to tear it into strips with her teeth.

"Baby, we gotta get out of here. You can play nurse Nancy later." He took the shirt from her, twisting it quickly around his hand as he got to his feet. He stumbled a little, and she gripped his arm, started toward the window.

"They'll be watching that way."

Even as he said it, she heard the men returning through the front door. "Not now, they won't. Come on." She tugged him toward the window, yanking a blanket from the bed and throwing it over the sill so they wouldn't get cut on the shattered glass.

He shoved her through first, then followed, and then they were on the ground and running. She imagined the men were already in the bedroom before they got five yards from the window, but there was no time to look back, no way to judge whether the trees they'd put between them were dense enough to hide them. No way to know for sure whether the men were in pursuit.

Beside her, Michael ran, his gait uneven, breathing labored. He clutched the wounded hand to his side as he ran, and she knew he was hurting.

"This way," he said.

"That way's the lake."

"I know. They won't be looking there. Come on."

She trusted him, had no idea what he had in mind, but she trusted him. She always had. He would never let her down the way her father had.

Kira stopped running. What the hell was that supposed to mean? The way her father had?

Michael tugged her hand. "Come on, almost there."

"Yeah." She shook off the thought, the memory, filed it away to be mulled over later, when they were safe.

They emerged from the trees near the glistening lake's gently sloping shore. A boat rested there, far from the cabin, and she wondered if this was yet another of Michael's ingenious escape plans.

He grabbed the bow and shoved the boat into the water. "Get in," he told her.

"You get in. And don't waste time arguing, I'm not the one with a hole in my hand."

He got in. She shoved the boat farther into the water,

then she climbed into the boat with him, gripping the oars, dipping them into the water, and pushing them farther, both from the shore and from the house. Michael placed a cell phone call to someone, naming a meeting spot and a time. Rescue, Kira thought, was at hand.

"Easy," he said when he finished the call. "Don't row too fast. And try to stay low. Get us around that bend in the shoreline where we can't be seen from the cabin, and then we'll make for the far side."

She nodded, and followed his instructions, even while delivering a few of her own. "Rip that shirt up, and bandage your hand. Your face is a mess, too. You need stitches, Michael."

"Yeah, and probably a tetanus shot."

She shook her head. "You had one of those summer before last, when that lowlife Farentino jabbed you in the ass with that dirty meat hook."

She looked up slowly. He did, too. "You remember that?"

She nodded. "I remember . . . more and more. Little things, but entire incidents, instead of just snippets."

"What kinds of things?"

She shrugged.

"Tell me. I really want to know." He looked around them. "Besides, they haven't seen us. We got nothing but time now." He began tearing the shirt into strips and bandaging his wounded hand.

Drawing a breath, she nodded. "Okay."

The rowboat drifted on its own, slowly but steadily toward the far shore. She pulled the oars out of the water, let them rest in the bottom of the boat, upper ends held in the oarlocks. "Mostly, I remember things about us. Our wedding, that came back to me clearly. And then . . . well, just us. Together. Fighting, dodging bullets, laughing . . ." She averted her eyes before she went on. "Making love."

He was staring at her. She felt his eyes on her face, and chanced a look up. His eyes were warm, caring. "It's okay," he said. "Don't be embarrassed. If you knew how

hard it's been for me not to just tell you . . ." He reached
out, cupping her cheek in his palm. "That you remember
us, God, Kira, that means a lot."

She covered his hand with hers. "To me, too. I mean, for
you to keep quiet, for my sake, even though it meant
watching me make plans to marry another man—" She
frowned then. "But that engagement to Peter—it was never
real, was it? I was playing him, it was a cover."

He nodded. "The marriage wouldn't have been legit.
The license wasn't for real to begin with, and the plan was
for the troops to move in at the reception, when all Peter's
contacts would have been in one place. I never would have
let it go too far, Kira."

"But how could you know? I mean . . . I could have slept
with him, and you—"

His jaw went tight, and his hand fell from her face.
"No."

She blinked and shook her head quickly. "I'm not saying I did. I mean I'm pretty sure I didn't, I never, but—"

"I know you didn't." He pushed his good hand through
his hair, shaking his head. "Look, that was too much to
ask, even for your health's sake. I couldn't risk you letting
that guy touch you. Do you know how furious you would
have been later on, when you remembered that he was just
a suspect? That it was all a cover? No, Kira, I wasn't willing to risk that. I've had you . . . under surveillance this
whole time."

A heat sizzled through her veins. An anger that made no
sense to the new Kira, but fit perfectly with the old one.
"You had someone watching me?"

"Not someone. Me," he said. "Your phones are bugged,
your bedroom's miked, your car is wired, there are cam-
eras all over the freaking place. You've barely been out of
my sight since you left the hospital, Kira. And yeah, I knew
it would piss you off. But not as much as my letting you
sleep with a criminal would have."

She closed her eyes. "You . . . you were watching my
most private moments."

"Come on, Kira. I'm your husband. I was trying to protect you."

She heard his sigh and opened her eyes

"I know, I know," he said, "there's nothing you hate more than being dependent on a man for anything, but Jesus, I didn't see that I had any other choice."

He looked truly torn. She reached out a hand to cover his. "No, I don't see that you did either."

He blinked, maybe shocked by that.

"What made me so determined never to be dependent on anyone? Any man?"

He looked away, shrugged.

"Was I always that way?"

"No. Not always."

She gripped the oars, returning them to the water, giving a few strokes to get them moving faster again. "I keep getting . . . that it's something to do with my father. But the only glimpses of memory I've had of him feel as if we were—close. Really, really close."

He nodded. "You were. You and your dad were almost inseparable."

"There's something else," she said. "Something changed that, came between us, didn't it?"

Facing her squarely, Michael nodded.

"What was it, Michael?"

He hesitated, and she dropped the oars, gripped his shoulders. "Come on, the memories are returning. This is important, and it's not going to be too much for me to take. What came between my father and me?"

Without blinking or flinching away, he replied, "I did."

Kira frowned. "He . . . didn't approve of us?"

"He forbade you to marry me. Told me to stay away. He didn't want you working for the DEA in the first place, much less married to it." He shook his head. "It was only out of concern for you, Kira."

"But I married you anyway."

"In secret. We planned to tell your family after we returned from Africa."

She nodded slowly.

"Your father told you he'd disown you if you married me. You considered it a betrayal. After that, you just . . . you changed. He hurt you badly, Kira, and, I don't know, for a while there, it seemed like you expected me to do the same."

She nodded slowly. "I put up shields. Told myself not to love you too much, not to become too dependent, not to let myself need you."

"Is that a memory or a guess?" he asked.

She lowered her head, pressed her fingers to her forehead. "I'm not sure. Maybe a little of both." She drew a deep breath. "He . . . he was in Africa with us. He was killed. In the same explosion that nearly killed me."

"Yeah. Do you remember that?"

"I know it happened. But the event . . . it's still hazy. I can see parts. I remember pain, I remember trying to walk through this smoke and dust, calling for you, calling for Dad. . . ." She frowned, because no more would come. Then she narrowed her eyes. "Dad worked for the DEA, too, didn't he? That's why we were all in Africa together. We were gathering evidence. Peter had drug connections there."

Michael nodded. "Your father trained me. For a long time, he and I were almost as close as you and he were. Or . . . I thought so." He pointed past her. "We're almost to shore."

She picked up the oars and used them to push the boat to the shoreline, then she climbed out and dragged the craft's nose onto the beach. She reached for him, and he didn't wince when he moved. The cut on his hand had stopped bleeding, and he'd managed to wash the blood away as they'd crossed the lake, with strips of the T-shirt and lake water.

He stepped onto the shore.

She couldn't help but slide her arms around his waist, and his came around her as if the action were reflexive. Resting her head on his chest, she said, "God, this has been a nightmare for you. All of it."

His good hand in her hair, he whispered, "The night-mare would have been if I'd lost you. Have I, Kira?"

She lifted her head slowly and met his eyes, let them probe hers. "Even if I never remember another thing, I know that what we had was real, and it was good. And that I want it back."

His eyes roamed her face for another moment, and then he lowered his head and kissed her. His mouth covered hers, and then his tongue nudged her lips apart, and she opened to him, eager to explore the feelings he stirred in her. She held him harder, tangling her tongue with his, as her heart pounded and her breaths stuttered. And when she arched against him, she felt him, hard, and pushing back.

She opened her eyes, drawing her mouth away from his, and whispered, "I want to make love to you, Michael. Just as soon as your hand is patched up, I want us to—"

"Hand, hell." He scooped her into his arms, took her mouth even as he carried her further across the shore, and into a meadow of tall grasses and wildflowers. Dropping to his knees, he laid her down in the grass, stretched out be-side her, kissing her jaw, her neck. His wounded hand lay on the ground above her head, but the good one ran over her cheeks, and then her breasts, and then her belly. She wanted to touch him, too, and quickly unbuttoned his shirt and pushed it down from his shoulders. She ran her palms over his chest, and the fire inside her burned hotter.

Michael managed to lift up the top she wore, one-handed, then he pushed it higher, exposing her breasts to the night. As he fondled them he whispered, "God, I've missed you, Kira. The feel of you. The taste of you." He kissed a path down her neck, across her chest and breasts, and then he suckled her, and she clutched his head and whimpered in pleasure. His hand moved lower, between her legs, rubbing there, until she arched her hips off the ground. He responded instantly, easily unzipping the pants. She pushed them down as far as she could reach, then wriggled them the rest of the way off, and kicked them aside. She lay there, naked, and he rose up a little, so he could look at her. He stroked her thighs until she parted them, and then he put his hand between them, rubbing, spreading and exploring her.

She put her hand over his, and pushed him deeper, arching her hips, rubbing against his fingers, closing her eyes. She moved her own hand to the bulge of his pants, then, stroking him until he groaned. Then she unfastened the button, carefully lowered the zipper, and shoved the pants off him.

Impatient, he backed away, only for a moment. When he came back to her, he was as naked as she, and when he began to caress her and suckle her again, she clutched his hips and pulled him to her, wrapping her thighs around him, tugging him until he slid inside her. Then she closed her eyes and whispered his name. "Oh, God, Michael. Yes."

He drove into her then, beyond restraint, she thought. He drove the breath from her lungs and filled her so deeply she cried out, and moved to take him into her again and again. He kissed her as he plunged into her, pushing her closer and closer to heaven, and when she exploded around him, he clasped her hip in his hand, holding her to him to take even more. Her body shattered, shuddered, convulsed, and she moaned in pleasure, then held him hard as he spilled into her.

He held her tight in his arms while her body stopped shaking, and her muscles uncoiled, even as the sparks of pleasure played out. Eventually, he rolled onto his side, pulling her into his arms and holding her as if she were something precious.

His fingers framed her chin and jaw, and he tipped her head to his, kissed her. "You're the best thing that ever happened to me," he told her. "Thank you for coming back to me, baby. I couldn't have survived if you hadn't."

She drew a breath. "Things got tense between us, before all this."

He nodded. "I thought you blamed me for the rift with your father."

"No. It wasn't that. I was holding back, protecting myself from being hurt again, the way he hurt me. I remember so much more now. I'm sorry, Michael. I'm so sorry I hurt you."

"It doesn't matter."

"It does. But I want you to know that even though I remember that feeling, that fear, I don't feel it anymore. I left it behind. I know you'll never hurt me."

"I'd die first."

"I know. I really do."

He kissed her again, and she thought she tasted a tear on his lips, and she was overwhelmed with the intensity of her feelings for this man. Her husband.

But as much as she would have liked to lie there in his arms until sunrise, she knew they had to move on. He needed treatment. And they both needed to put more space between themselves and Peter's thugs. She sat up, reluctantly. "We should get dressed, get moving."

"I know. Our backup should be arriving to meet us about three miles from here."

She nodded, reached for her clothes and pulled them on. By the time she finished, he'd pulled on his pants and shirt, but was still struggling to fasten them one-handed.

"Let me get that," she said, smiling a little. She moved close to him, and he arched against her hand as she fastened the jeans. She stroked his chest, teasing him, as she buttoned up his shirt. When she finished, he covered her hands with his good one. "I never stopped loving you, Kira. I want to be sure you know that. Not for a minute."

Her throat went tight. "I—"

"Don't even twitch," Peter shouted from the darkness. "You're completely surrounded."

CH@%!*R

11

Michael's hands tightened on hers, and his eyes held hers for an instant before shifting past her to scan the darkness around them.

"Step away from him, Kira, or I'll drop you both where you stand."

She glanced downward, seeing her gun belts on the ground, concealed by the grass. "He's not well, Peter. He can barely stand on his own."

"Back away from him."

So they can kill him, she thought. *Peter would take me alive, avenge his wounded pride before he finished me off.*

She met Michael's eyes, then shifted hers downward, toward the guns in the grass nearby. She saw him follow her gaze.

"He'll drop like a rock if I let him go."

"He's gonna drop like a rock either way. Back off."

She met his eyes again, prayed he would do what she wanted him to do. Then she brought her hands to her sides, backing two steps away, deliberately staying between Michael and Peter. Michael slumped to the ground.

"Kill him," she heard Peter say.

Michael shouted, "Down, Kira!" And even as she dropped to her knees, he rose up onto his, tossing one gun to her with his wounded hand, while firing the other one in the direction of Peter's voice. The meadow exploded in gunfire.

Kira caught her weapon, turned and dropped to her belly in the grass, putting her back to Peter, firing at the muzzle flashes around them, one after the other. Gun smoke rose, because they were all so close and firing so rapidly. It stung her eyes, choked her.

And then the shooting stopped all at once.

She lay still a moment, trying to see through the smoke. It hovered there, in the heavy air, not rising or dissipating as fast she wished it would. "Michael?" she called softly, half expecting the sound of her voice to draw more gunfire.

When it didn't, she pushed herself upright. "Michael?"

No reply. She walked through the mists, trying to find her way and realized slowly that the sun was rising. Its rays pierced the mist, to fall upon bodies in the grass. Peter's body, those of his men. Bloody, still, lifeless. Dead, all of them.

"Michael?"

She searched for him, through the smoke and now the mist rising from the lake as well, and suddenly she was back in Africa. Blood was trickling down her face from the wound to her head, and she staggered as she walked through the rubble and smoke, searching for her father.

And then she found him. He lay beneath a pile of debris, and she fell to her knees, pushing it aside, gathering him to her. They'd been angry enemies for months by then, but suddenly, it didn't matter. "Dad. God, Dad, are you all right?"

His face was ashen, but his eyes blinked open, met hers. "Kira."

"I'll get help," she promised. "Lie still, I'll get help."

He clutched her hand in a grip surprisingly fierce. "No. Listen. Listen to me, daughter." She blinked, staring down at him. "I was wrong," he told her. "I was wrong, Kira. Michael's a good man. Maybe . . . the best I've ever known."

"What are you saying?" she asked, stroking his head.

"Your mother—she hasn't been happy in our marriage. Too many secrets. Too much I have to hide from her. But you . . . you're not your mother. You're strong. And you know."

"Mom loves you," she assured him.

"And suffers for it. I didn't want that for you. But . . . he loves you, Kira. You marry Michael. You tell him . . . tell him I'm sorry."

"You can tell him yourself." She bent closer, kissed his cheek. "I'm going to get help."

He nodded. "I love you, Kira. Be happy."

Then his eyes fell closed, and she knew he was gone. Even though she searched for a pulse, she knew he was gone, and when she saw the hole in his chest, she knew there was no chance to revive him. She held him in her arms, and she cried, until, swamped with dizziness and weakness, she let him go and fell to the ground beside him. Moments later, Michael was leaning over her, whispering her name, and she was staring up at him, trying to speak. And then there was only darkness.

The memory faded, and she was kneeling beside Michael, lifting his head, searching his body. Blood pulsed from a chest wound, and she pressed her hand to it to slow it down.

"Michael," she whispered. "Open your eyes. Listen to me. You are not dying, do you hear me? You are not leaving me, not now."

His eyes opened. He seemed short of breath, but focused, conscious, aware.

"I love you, Michael," she told him. "I don't just remember loving you, I feel it, maybe more so now than ever before. I love you so much it's overwhelming. It's all-consuming. Don't leave me."

He smiled weakly.

"Michael, I remember that final day. I remember what happened before I lost consciousness. I found Dad. He lay there, dying, but with his final breaths, he gave us his blessing. He said you were the best man he'd ever known. He loved you, you know."

Closing his eyes slowly, Michael whispered, "Thank you for that. It means . . . so much."

"It isn't gonna mean a damn thing if you don't hang on for me. God, Michael, I've been so empty. Walking around like a hollow shell. A body without a soul. And I know what was missing, now, Michael, because I've found it again. It was us. It was you."

She waited for his reply, but there wasn't one. He'd passed out. Or died.

She heard something then—the cell phone, ringing. She dug it from Michael's pocket and hit the button. "Where the hell are you guys?"

"Kira? Holy, shit, Kira, you almost sound like your old self."

She recognized Kelly's voice, not as her mother's housekeeper, but as a colleague. "I'm back," Kira told her. "The bad guys are dead, and Michael is down. We need a chopper."

"We're on the way," Kelly barked. Then, more softly, "Welcome home, Kira."

She was holding his hand, having put in the longest night of her life, when he woke in the hospital bed. He looked around the room, looked at her, smiled a little, and it even reached his eyes. "Hey, beautiful."

She was far from beautiful, she thought. Though her mother had brought her a change of clothes, she'd refused to leave her husband's bedside long enough to shower. Her mom brought her a basin of warm water, some soap, and deodorant, then stood guard at the door while she washed up beside the bed.

She looked down at the clothes her mother had chosen.

A dressy pantsuit, far from her usual attire. "Not exactly what I would have chosen," Kira said.

"I do love you in leather," he said. "Better out of it, though."

His voice was coarse, and she reached for the water pitcher, poured some into a glass, and then held the flexible straw to his lips.

He drank, then let his head rest on the pillows.

"How are you feeling?" she asked.

"Weak as a kitten. A little groggy. Not sure if I'm remembering what really happened, or if it's a bad case of wishful thinking."

She leaned over him, pressed her mouth to his. "You want me to climb into that bed and refresh your memory?"

He smiled against her lips. "Damn straight I do, so long as you don't mind doing all the work."

"I always liked being on top," she said.

Then she sat on the edge of his bed, better to cradle his head to her chest. "You're gonna be okay," she told him. "They got the bullet out of your chest. It missed your heart. You'll be fine."

"I've never been more glad to be alive, Kira."

"Neither have I." She sat up a little, but couldn't keep her hands off him, and so she stroked his shoulders, upper arms, occasionally his face as she spoke. "I had a long talk with Mom," she said. "Explained to her that I've been a deep-cover DEA agent for the past five years and that the whole thing with Peter was just a ploy to bust him for drug trafficking, and I was already married. To you."

"Must have broken her heart."

Kira smiled widely. "You know what she said?" She went on without waiting for an answer. "She said she kept wishing I wasn't engaged, because she would have managed to throw you and me together. She loved you from the minute she met you—in your guise as wedding planner."

"She said that?"

She drew an *X* across her chest with a forefinger. He nodded, smiling.

Then his smile died and he looked at her neck, frowning. "Where's . . . ?"

"My ring?" She held up her hand, showing him her wedding band, resting right where it belonged, on her finger. "I told you before, Michael. I love you. I want our life back. I want you back."

He closed his hand around hers. "You never lost me, babe." He glanced toward the door. "So you gonna lock that door and climb into this bed with me or what?"

She smiled, got to her feet, and went to the door, then she came slowly back to the bed, still smiling. "Now, you've been injured," she said. "I don't want to do anything that might hurt you. So I want you to lie *perfectly* still. Understand?"

"I'll do my best."

She kissed his jawline, his neck, and reached her hand underneath the covers to stroke him. "You just let me take care of you."

"Anytime," he said. "But there will be payback."

She squeezed him. "Oh, I'm counting on it."

The Incredible Misadventures
of Boo and the Boy Blunder

MARYJANICE DAVIDSON

For Jessica Growette,
who takes time away from her job
and family to help my books do well.

Acknowledgments

Thanks as always to Cindy Hwang, for asking, and to my husband, for doing.

Author's Note

There are vampire hunters, and there are albinos, but usually they aren't one and the same.

"Friends are *such* a mixed blessing."

—Berkeley Breathed

PROLOGUE

Although she hadn't been in his bar for five months and eighteen days, Jim knew her the minute she walked in. He would have known her anywhere, any place.

She looked exactly the same, though she had been coming to Doule's, on and off, for ten years.

Shoulder-length white hair. Not blond . . . *white*. Skin like milk. Eyes so pale a blue she looked blind . . . or like she had seen too much, and it had burned away all the trivialities in her.

Full mouth, long neck, and *real* long legs . . . he was six foot three and only had a couple of inches on her. High tits, firm and not too big. She was dressed in dark colors—she always dressed that way, as if to emphasize her striking coloring. Black jeans, a black T-shirt, black boots. Shit-kicker boots.

She sat down at the bar—though it was Friday night, a seat had instantly emptied for her—and nodded at him. He nodded back and had her drink—a Black Russian—in front of her a few seconds later.

She grunted her thanks and bent to her reading material.

She was reading the obituary section of the *Minneapolis Star Tribune*. He had never seen her read anything else, although they were in Boston.

It was just one more mystery about her. He didn't know her real name—everyone called her Ghost. But never to her face. He didn't know where she lived, but he suspected the Twin Cities; when she occasionally spoke, she didn't drop her r's and sounded, to his born-and-bred Weymouth ears, a little flat. He didn't know how old she was—her face was perfectly unlined; she could have been twenty-five or fifty-five.

He'd never seen her driver's license; it wasn't that kind of bar. If you were tough enough to get through the door, you could drink whatever the hell you wanted. And if you wanted to pay cash and leave without a receipt, that was fine, too.

He knew she was mesmerizing, stunning. And tough. Her job

(bounty hunter?)

took her to the area several times a year. Once

(FBI profiler?)

she'd come in without her jacket, wearing a black tank, and he'd noticed the muscle definition in her arms.

(traveling lumberjack?)

Sleek and pale and hard, like marble.

He knew she drank Black Russians and never had more than two an evening. He knew she occasionally carried a Beretta in a shoulder holster and her purse was full of spare clips. She always tipped 20 percent, and she never showed up two nights in a row.

He supposed he had a crush on her, a fragile one. It was a crush that wouldn't hold up under reality. She was probably in pharmaceutical sales and got the muscles working out in a health club like a gerbil on a wheel.

She was probably a perfectly ordinary person. The regulars let her through because she had a stony beauty, not because she was tough. And she probably read a Minnesota paper because she had a boyfriend there, or something boring like that.

He didn't especially care. He enjoyed seeing her the few times a year, and wondering. He'd never ask, she'd never tell, and things worked fine.

CH@%!*R
1

Boo Miller had just settled on her favorite stool in her favorite bar in her favorite city when she saw the tourist come in.

Tourist. When you hung out in places like Doule's, a tourist was defined simply as someone who did not belong. Doule's was a place for disgraced cops, con men (and women), thieves, parolees, and telemarketers. Not clean-cut boys slumming before going back to the Financial District first thing Monday.

That was okay. He wasn't just a tourist now; he was bait. It would make her job a helluva lot easier. And she had to give the boy toy snaps for even getting out of his car in this neighborhood, never mind coming inside.

"Excuse me," he was saying to Jim, the barkeep. Jim was typical of his clientele: Instead of a barbed wire tattoo around his biceps, he wore actual barbed wire. His nose had been broken at least twice, and he kept a twelve-gauge shotgun beneath the bar. Everyone knew it was there (well, everyone but the boy toy), and everyone knew Jim wouldn't hesitate to use it. Slugs would bring down a grown man just as easily as they'd take a ten-point buck. That's why *everyone* got along so well.

"What?" Jim asked, no inflection in the word at all.

"My cell's dead, and I've got a flat . . . do you mind if I use your phone?"

Boo shook her head without looking up.

"Pay phone's out back," Jim said.

"Oh." The bait seemed a little surprised, then resigned. "Well, okay. Sorry to bother you." Boy toy practically tiptoed through the filth on the floor (a stimulating combination of flat beer, piss, and mop water), and headed toward the back.

And the vampire got up to follow him.

Boo knew he'd do it. He couldn't help it, any more than a starving dog couldn't help stuffing itself and then puking. Bad neighborhood, clean-cut victim, a back ally behind a bar where the patrons wouldn't ask questions, or even look up—the boy toy might as well have written his blood type on his forehead.

After a minute, she went out after them.

CH@%!*R

2

It wasn't the worst night of Eddie Batley's life (his father's funeral still held the top spot), but it was close. First, his supervisor had busted him on all the surfing. The IT department had ratted him out, buncha spying brownshirts. *"Jawhol, Human Resources! Vee haff caught zee spy!"* He was amazed that they had nothing better to do . . . then remembered they really didn't. Making sure nobody had any fun at work was literally what they were paid for.

Then he'd had to work late, to make up for the time spent surfing. Then he'd left his cell phone in the car but hadn't plugged it in, so the battery conked out. Then he'd headed over to his ex-girlfriend's place to put in a cameo for her engagement party, had stupidly taken a shortcut, and blown a tire in quite possibly the worst neighborhood in the state.

His own fault . . . in Boston, it was prudent to stick to the path. Shortcuts were a bad idea, especially in a town where to create streets they'd simply paved the cow paths and called it good.

Now he was being mugged. Mugged! He felt like Comic Book Guy in *The Simpsons:* Worst. Episode. Ever!

Eddie wasn't especially big, and he wasn't especially strong—he led a sedentary life. But the mugger had muscles on muscles, because Eddie actually felt his feet leave the ground as the mugger pulled him close. Kissing close, as a matter of fact. As a further matter of fact, Eddie didn't swing that way. As a final matter of fact, the mugger wasn't going anywhere near his wallet. He was—uh—was he—

"Ow!" Eddie yelled. Worst *mugging* ever! The guy had *bitten* him on the *neck,* like some kind of—of—

Then the mugger dropped him, and just when Eddie was ready to ask him what the hell he thought he was doing, the mugger fell down dead with a big stick poking through his shirt.

That's when Eddie saw the mongo-babe who'd been in the bar earlier. She was standing right behind where the mugger had been. He'd never heard her come up behind them.

"What the *hell* is going on?" he yelled.

"Go home," mongo-babe said, poking the mugger with the toe of her boot.

CH@%!*R
3

"Wait wait wait. This is . . . a vampire, right?"

"Was," the babe said. She bent, pulled out the stick—stake, rather—and it slid out with sickening ease. "Past tense."

"And you're a vampire slayer."

" 'Bye," she said, whipping a wetnap pack out of her purse—ubiquitous in any woman's purse, with all the steamed lobster in town—tearing it, pulling out the nap, and wiping the blood off the end of the stake.

"Holy shit!" He was officially freaking out. Was he? Yep, he was. "I can't believe it! They're real! *You're* real."

The supercool vampire slayer grunted. Not much for conversation, but then, when you were heart-stoppingly gorgeous, he supposed you didn't have to be. He'd never seen a woman with such striking coloring before—her hair was silvery white, and so were her eyebrows. Her skin was almost as light as her hair. In the poor light of the alley, she almost seemed to glow. She looked like a beautiful ghost.

"Thanks for saving me from the fiendish clutch of the undead," he said, dazzled.

She grunted again, put the stake in her handbag, bent, and pulled a ring off the dead vampire's left thumb. Then she turned to leave.

"Wait!" He grabbed her elbow without thinking, then dropped it when she turned back and gave him her full attention. Her terrifying, knee-weakening attention. Her eyes were pale, and oddly mesmerizing. He hadn't been afraid of the vampire—everything had happened so fast, and being bitten was more annoying than scary—but he was afraid of her. *The vampire never heard her, never saw her,* he remembered. *Never knew what hit him.* "Uh, you're leaving?"

"Yeah."

"Well . . ." His voice cracked, and he cleared his throat and added manfully, "I'm coming with you."

Alarm flashed across her cold features. "No, no." She sounded . . . was it possible? Nervous?

"Listen, you saved my life. You *changed* my life!"

"It's only been," she said, "sixteen seconds."

"Right, but I can't believe it's all true! Vampires and vampire slayers, and—what else? Werewolves? Fairies? Trolls? Goblins?"

"Yes, yes, no, no, no, no. It's not that interesting," she said, which didn't convince him in the slightest. "It's just a job."

"No," he replied. "*I* have just a job. You—you're living a legend. You're like Buffy! Or Faith. Maybe Faith—you're kind of terrifying. But I've got to come with you now. Besides . . ." He groped for something that would appeal to her warrior's honor. "You saved my life, and that's a debt I have to repay."

"What bullshit," she said, and turned away.

"I'll follow you!" he yelled after her. From the other side of the street, dogs started to yowl. Well, his voice *did* get kind of high when he was excited. "It'll be hard for you to sneak up on vampires with me following your footsteps like—like a Watson to your Holmes."

She turned back and rolled her eyes. "This isn't a TV

show or a movie or even a book," she told him. "Real life is different. It's messy. It's hard to find a parking spot, and when you're on stakeout it's hard to find a place to take a shit."

"I know real life is different," he said, stung. And, frankly, a little disillusioned. Vampire slayers needed to take shits? "You don't have to tell me that. I'm not some dorky teenager." Hell, he'd been legal drinking age for five months and sixteen days!

"Yeah?" She was eyeing him in a way he wasn't entirely sure was complimentary. He looked down at himself, at his LUKE I AM YOUR FATHER T-shirt and the navy blue HE'S DEAD JIM computer bag. "I'm not sure you do."

"I can help," he said. "I want to help you. You saved my life, I've got to pay you back. Come on, I'll bet you could use an assistant."

"I don't even live around here," she said, looking more alarmed by the second.

"Great! I'm ready for a change of scenery." He was determined to tag along with the goddess of stakehood for as long as he could. This was the way out of his mediocre life. She was right, things *were* different in the real world. For one thing, they were massively boring. All the things he had long suspected as a kid—vampires, slayers, the fantastic and strange and wonderful—were true! He'd been a fool to ever believe otherwise. The question was, what else was out there?

The truth *is out there,* he thought, having a total Mulder moment. Oh, yeah!

"This isn't something you can wrap up with a few pop culture references."

"I bet you could use a guy like me," he insisted.

"A guy like you?"

"Yeah. I look like everybody else. Five minutes after I leave a room, nobody remembers I was there." The thing he had hated . . . could it be his secret power? Tonight, anything was possible. "But you . . . everybody remembers you, I bet."

She actually looked like she was mulling that one over. He pressed his advantage. "I can go into places for you and—be bait! Like I was tonight."

"You mean, be a dumbass on purpose?"

"Whatever it takes," he said doggedly. "Make your job a lot easier."

"Well . . ."

She was weakening!

"Great!"

"I haven't agreed yet."

"As good as." He had her! He had worn her down with the same über-geekiness that had scored him a date with his gaming partner for the prom. Maybe *that* was his power. The wear-down.

"You help me catch this one vampire," she told him. "This *one*. And then you go back to your life, and I go back to mine. No following me, no bugging me, no geeking out on me, no talking to me, no looking at me, no anything, ever. Agreed?"

"Don't worry. I'll help you catch the next one, and then you won't have to worry about trying to lose me."

"I'm not worried about trying to lose you," she told him. "I'd rather not kill you."

"Uh . . . what?"

"I only kill the dead," she said. "Come on, Boy Blunder."

CH@%!*R

4

How do I get myself into this shit? Boo asked herself as her new sidekick—sidekick!—gabbled happily beside her. *Because I'm a fuckin' softie and people smell it the way a vampire smells fear. That's how.*

"So, where's this new vampire we're going to kill? Is it close by? Do we have to get on a plane? Do you have a super-secret vampire killer plane? You know, like Wonder Woman's invisible jet?"

"Stop talking."

"What's your power? Do you have ghost powers? Or just, you know, strength and speed and stuff?"

"Stop talking now."

"I bet it's ghost powers. I never even heard you come up behind us. Can you walk through walls, too?"

She seized his shirt collar, twisted, and pulled him toward her until their faces were an inch apart. His brown eyes blinked at her from behind his wire rims. "Ghost powers? *Ghost* powers? What planet do you live on?"

"Hey, if you don't want to talk about your super-secret ghost powers, I understand."

She ground her teeth as an alternative to breaking his nose. "I don't. Have. Ghost. Powers."

"Okay, okay. Wh-what's your name?"

Shit. "Boo."

"Your name is Boo?"

"Listen carefully. I'm not telling you again. This isn't a comic book. I don't have any powers. The average person—that's you, dipshit—is so fucking unobservant, it makes it easy for me to off vampires. I look like I do because I'm a genetic *freak,* not because I have—Jesus!—ghost powers."

"Are you sure you're not super strong? Because my feet are practically off the ground, here. For the second time in ten minutes, I might add."

She let him go, disgusted with him and herself. "Come on, dickwad. Let's get this over with, so you can go back to your chat rooms."

"Sure." He pushed his glasses up and jerked his head, tossing a lock of brown hair out of his eyes. "But if it's okay with you, I don't want my sidekick handle to be dickwad. Or dipshit."

"Pick up the pace, fuckstick."

"Okay, well, I don't much care for that one, either." She could hear him hurrying after her. "How about Mack? I've always liked Mack."

"How about shut up?" Ah! Finally. She put her fingers between her teeth and whistled, a piercing note that cut through the night like a straight razor. "Taxi!"

"Ow! Is that your power? I bet that does a number on a dog's ears."

She sighed and jerked the door open. "Milk Street," she told the driver, then got in the front seat. Damned if she was sitting in the back with her own personal nightmare. "Get in, shitheap."

"Bad guys, here we come!" he yelled, and she fought the urge to groan and cover her eyes.

*   *   *

"By the way, my name's Eddie."

"I don't care."

"Eddie Batley," he continued, as if she'd said something else.

"Shut up and drink your kiddie cocktail, Eddie."

"It's a Shirley Temple," he snapped, and slurped it moodily. "You're the grumpiest vampire slayer I've ever met."

"Bad news."

"Actually, you're the *only*—what? Are we outnumbered by the denizens of the undead? Are their ghoulish minions cutting us off from aid?"

I only kill the dead. I only kill the dead. I only— "I don't see him."

"And that's bad because . . . ?"

"I have to keep sitting here with you."

"Aw," he said, still slurping. "That just means we can get to know each other better. Which did you like best, *Attack of the Clones* or *Phantom Menace*? Have you seen *Revenge of the Sith* yet?"

She motioned for the waitress to come over to their little table in the back. "Bring me three more of these."

"You got it, hon."

"And don't spare the booze," she muttered.

"So, Boo. That's kind of a weird name, you've gotta admit."

"I admit nothing."

"Is that a nickname, or is it short for something?"

"Shut up."

"At least it's not Casper or Ghost Girl or something like that. Boo's kind of cute."

"I'm going to let this vampire kill you," she informed him. "I'm not saving you this time. I'm never saving you again."

"You would betray your oath as a slayer?"

"What *oath,* nimrod? Guy asked me to take out the sucker at Doule's, same guy asked me to axe the sucker here, half in advance, the rest upon completion, thanks very much, have a nice fuckin' day."

"So you're like—like a paid assassin of the vampire?"

"Yeah."

"A vampire slayer!" he finished triumphantly.

"*No.* You make it sound like some romantic, amazing, incredible thing. It's just how I make a buck."

"A lonely calling, to be sure."

"Oh, for fuck's sake." Her Black Russians arrived and she gulped thirstily at the first one.

"So, what's that?"

"Shut up."

"Beer? Is it really dark beer?"

She groaned inwardly. "It's a Black Russian."

"Huh. So you drink Black Russians, you're wearing black boots and jeans, and a black shirt, and your purse is black—that's the biggest purse I've ever seen, by the way—and your hair is white and—huh."

"Yeah, it's all a bigass mystery, huh, Dorkson?"

"It's Watson, and you don't have to be so sensitive about it. I mean, you're really beautiful. The guys in here can't take their eyes off you."

"Super."

"If I had something like that—"

"Something like *what,* schmucko?"

"Well, you know. You're an albino, right? It sets you apart. If I was like you, I'd be—"

"You'd be what, Boy Blunder?"

"Happy."

"Eddie: Do I *look* happy?"

"Well, no. Frankly, I've been meaning to talk to you about that."

"Drink your cocktail, Babbly."

"It's Batley," he corrected her.

"You've heard the phrase I couldn't care less? I really, really, really couldn't."

A blessed beat of silence, broken by his, "So, if you could be Han Solo or Luke, which would you pick?"

"Batley, will you *shut up*?"

"I knew you'd get my name right eventually," he said smugly, and slurped down his maraschino cherry.

CH@%!*R
5

"This has been the greatest night of my life," her sidekick declared an hour later.

"Really? I was just thinking about how it was never going to end." Boo said this to her arms, since she had long ago put her head down and feigned sleep in a futile attempt to get him to stop talking.

"I can't believe they didn't even card me! I get carded for buying plant food."

"Nuh."

"So who is this guy? That you're going to slay? On a badass scale of one to ten, with one being my grandpa and a ten being Darth Vader—"

"Six."

"Huh. How about the one you already—"

"Four."

"He seemed pretty bad to me. Just walked up and grabbed me and chomped, without asking or even saying hi."

"That's a garden variety vampire. They're all like that."

"All of them? Aren't there any good ones like Angel, or season seven Spike?"

"No, numb fuck," she said kindly. "Vampires have to drink our blood to survive, they're pissed about being dead, and they never, ever say please. The one who got you was on my list because he *also* liked to cut up male strippers and leave the pieces scattered around the local playground."

"Gah!" he gahed. "That's disgusting!"

Boo shrugged. "Well. He's dead now, B.B."

"He was a *four*?"

"Yeah."

"Wh—what about the guy we're after now? The six?"

"Well. Um . . ."

"Oh my God! You're hesitating! You *never* hesitate. He's the Hitler of vampires, isn't he? He's sneaking up behind me right now, isn't he?" B.B. looked around wildly and accidentally knocked over his empty glass.

"Calm down before you hurt yourself. The vamp I'm supposed to kill—I haven't exactly got the job yet."

"You *don't*?"

"Killing the vampire earlier was kind of like . . . a tryout. The guy who hired me is meeting us here tonight to get proof that I did the first job, and he'll decide whether or not to send me after the other one."

"Huh. Cautious guy."

Exactly. She kind of liked her faceless employer for it. She was consumed with curiosity, and couldn't wait to meet him.

"That's why you took the ring?"

"No, it was shiny, and I wanted it, dumbass."

"I like B.B. better. I'm gonna pretend it stands for Brave—uh . . . what's another cool word that starts with B?"

"Boring," she suggested.

"Listen, *Boo,* I—"

"No."

"What, no?"

"You don't get to call me by my first name."

"What am I supposed to call you?"

"Why don't you go away and think about it?"

"Oh no you don't. I'm not missing all the fun."

"Yeah, we're having tons of fun tonight." She yawned. "Maybe the vampire will liven things up. He could hardly make things worse."

"Vampire? Where?" Another empty glass went flying. "Oh my God, is he behind me? He is, isn't he? I can feel his unholy cold breath on the back of my neck!"

"No, dumbass," she said kindly. "The wall's behind you. The vampire's standing just to the left of the stage. Denim shirt, khakis, necktie."

Eddie squinted. "Soulless bloodsuckers wear khakis?"

"Sure."

"Is it the one we're supposed to kill?"

"No." And that was odd. She could go weeks without seeing a vampire, except through work. It was an interesting coincidence that she had killed one earlier, was setting up to kill another, and here was a third.

Big surprise, the vampire was ferociously good-looking. Boo was used to that; in all her sixteen years of killing the dead, she had yet to stake one that was even plain. It wasn't such a mystery when you thought about it. All vampires were by definition murder victims. And everybody liked their food to be pleasantly presented. It was why they served pheasants under glass, and sushi with fake grass.

This one was no different—tall and broad shouldered, about six foot three. Dark blond hair pulled back in a ponytail that stopped between his shoulder blades. And even across the darkened club she could see how blue his eyes were. Long, straight nose and the *de rigueur* full mouth, which, she had no doubt, hid a mouthful of fangs when he was hungry.

The Boy Blunder was gripping the table while he stared. "What's he doing?"

"Probably looking for a drink."

"You mean a victim."

"Sure. Most vampires have to drink every night. He's scoping for singles. Someone who looks lonely or upset—

stood up, or abandoned. They're like hyenas, B.B. They don't go for groups. They cull from the herd."

"Oh my God! He's going up on stage! He's—he's going after the stage manager!"

"No . . ." She stared with dawning horror. "He's . . . he's . . ."

B.B. glanced at the sign over the bar. "The Tickler. I thought this was some sort of weird sex bar, but it's—"

"A comedy club," she finished, and rested her forehead on her arms again.

". . . and what's the deal with coffins? Have you ever tried to sleep in one? They're the worst! Hard—no support for your lower back, and pointy at the end, so your feet can't even breathe. It doesn't matter how many Dr. Scholl's you put on; your feet just smother in those things.

"I mean, it's bad enough you die and find out nobody remembered to put your funeral into their Palm, but then you've got to give up your Select Comfort Bed for *this*?"

Gregory Schorr barely heard the laughter—not that he ever got the big belly roars of a Robin Williams or Jim Carrey—because he couldn't take his eyes off Ghost. Unbelievable! The most feared vampire killer of the last hundred years was sitting twenty feet away. Listening to his routine! She had a look on her perfect, white face that he couldn't read . . . she could have been bored or anxious.

"And let me tell you something else about being dead," he continued, on automatic, the better to stare at the Ghost. "You still have to put quarters in the meter. Hell, for that matter you still have to find a parking place! Try finding that little detail in Anne Rice's latest." She was stunning, utterly breathtaking. Slim, with that unearthly pale skin— she was paler than he was!—and riveting light-colored eyes. Her hair looked like white silk, and he longed to touch it, to run it through his fingers, see it spread out on his pillow.

He had been dying to meet her—almost literally—for

the last decade, but the gossip and rumors simply did not do her justice. She was breathtaking. She had killed more vampires than he had ever seen but, having little love for his kind, that just made her more appealing.

He finished his routine, accepted the modest applause—he was learning not to hypnotize the audience into laughing, and paying for it with less overt clapping—and practically ran over to her table.

"Look out!" her companion, a dark-haired, bespectacled youngster, warned. "Here he comes!"

"Thanks for the heads-up," she told him. To Gregory, she said, "That was—uh—well."

"You're hired," he said.

CH@%!*R

6

"You can't hire me," Boo told the vampire, who, amazingly, had pulled up a chair and was sitting two feet away.

"Excuse me, but I just did."

"I don't work for dead guys."

"What do you think you've been doing?"

Her eyes widened and almost bulged, and Eddie happened to know there was a gun in the small of her back and three stakes in her purse, so he jumped in. "So, you're a comedian?"

The vampire looked away from her, at him, and Eddie squashed the instant urge to leap from his chair and exit the building. Boo had explained that the way to spot a vampire was to look for the ones who couldn't join a crowd. The ones on the fringe, looking on. Pale, and quick—unbelievably quick. With mesmerizing charisma—the ones you wanted to follow all the way home. Or to a car. Or a hotel room. Or an alley. A stranger you were instantly drawn to, and trusted. And feared.

Eddie was afraid of the vampire, but wanted to stay and

listen as much as he wanted to leave. And that scared him worse than anything that had happened all night.

"Yeah, amateur," the vampire said. Eddie wasn't sure if he was referring to himself, or Eddie. "What'd you think?"

"It was . . . interesting." To put it mildly. A vampire riffing on vampires. Huh. He'd been afraid Boo would swallow her own tongue. She hadn't been that appalled when he'd tagged along for the night. "So this is what you do?"

"Sure. In my old life I was a cop, but I swore if I ever got a second chance, I'd try stand-up. Just for fun, a parttime thing. So after I came back from the dead—"

"You didn't come back from the dead," Boo interrupted. She looked rattled. Frankly, he didn't think she could *get* rattled. "You *are* dead."

"Semantics," the vampire said easily, and smiled at them both.

"You have a great smile," Eddie said, dazzled. Not that he swung that way (not that there was anything wrong with that) but the vampire seemed genuinely nice. Charming and, like, urbane. It was kind of—

"We're out of here," Boo announced, standing. "Let's book, B.B."

The vampire put a hand on her arm. "Don't you want to—"

"I *want* you to let go of me before something felonious happens to you."

He let go. Eddie nearly shriveled with relief. "Look, let's all sit down and have a drink."

Boo gave him a look that nearly scorched his eyebrows. "I don't drink with the dead."

"No," the vampire said cheerfully, "you just get hired by them. You pretty much do their bidding. You don't think I'm the first one to ever think of it, do you?"

She sat so hard, the chair rocked. "What."

The vampire clicked his fingers at the waitress. "Another round, please."

"Sure, Greg," the bodaciously cute woman with purple

curls replied, giving him a smile and switching her butt as she walked away.

"What."

"Is that supposed to be a question? I'd heard your social skills were fairly poor, but I like to judge for myself before—ow."

"Ow?" Eddie asked. He'd heard an odd sound—zing!—but couldn't place it. Then he saw the vampire look under the table, put his hand down—on his leg, maybe?—and bring it back up, dripping blood. "Oh my God! You *shot* him?"

"I shot him."

"That wasn't nice," the vampire said reproachfully. "That's my favorite shin. Not to mention, all my other slacks are at the dry cleaners."

"I don't get some answers quick, I'll be a lot less nice and your dry cleaner will be a lot more busy."

Eddie's mind reeled. "Ack! Dude, tell her what she wants to know! And put the gun away," he hissed at Boo. "We're not in the *Star Wars* cantina."

"Oh, God, if only." She saw the vampire flinch and smiled. It wasn't an especially warm smile. "Oops. My bad."

"What do you want to know?" he asked reasonably, reaching for a napkin and wiping the blood off his hand. Eddie noticed it was very dark blood, and that the vampire didn't bother to use any napkins to blot his leg. Could they heal that quickly? And why wasn't he screaming and jumping up and down? Did they not feel pain?

"Why did you hire me?"

"To kill vampires. Two unbelievably awful ones, in fact."

"But—*you're* a vampire," Eddie couldn't help pointing out. "You can't—I mean, you guys are supposed to stick together."

"Why?" the vampire replied. "You guys don't. Besides, I used to be a cop. There's some stuff you just can't look away from. Ghost can do the job, so I hired her."

"Don't shoot him again!" Eddie screamed in a whisper.

"I don't like that name," Boo told the undead, soon-to-be-all-the-way dead guy.

For the first time all evening, the vampire looked mortified. "Right. Sorry about that. What shall I call you?"

"Shut up."

"All right, but doesn't have a very nice ring to—"

"What did you mean when you said you weren't the first one to think of it?" she interrupted.

"Well, what does it sound like? Vampires are territorial. Sometimes we don't get along too well. Luckily, there's a famous vampire killer who happens to be for hire, and she doesn't check ID. She just takes the cash and does the job. What could be simpler?"

Boo went paler, a feat Eddie didn't think was possible. It was obvious this had never occurred to her before. It wouldn't have occurred to him, either. Vampires hiring vampire slayers to kill vampires? Yech. Chilly bastards.

"It's the way of the world," the vampire was saying, sounding concerned. "I thought you knew."

"Of course she knew," Eddie interrupted, too heartily. "You think there's something you bloodsuckers are up to that we don't have the 4-1-1 on? Ha! And again, I say ha."

"Well, good, I'd hate to think I took the intrepid vampire killers by surprise." The waitress came back, put down drinks—the vampire was drinking something dark red in a wineglass, surprise—and gave them all a nice flash of cleavage as she took her tip. "So! I take it you've killed that asshole, Weatherly?"

There was a "clunk!' as Boo dropped the dead (?) vampire's ring on their little table.

"Nice," the vampire said, picking it up and looking at it. "Just outstanding. How'd he go?"

"He went easy."

"Yeah," Eddie said, sounding, to his own ears, tough and cool, if slightly squeaky. "Piece of cake."

"Really?" The vampire's gaze lingered on Eddie's neck,

and he couldn't help fingering the bite mark, which still stung. "That's good. Only one to go."

"I can't work for you," Boo said, looking like a grasshopper was crawling around inside her mouth.

"You'll let Martigan walk around free?"

"Martigan would be . . ." Eddie prompted.

"A real piece of work," the vampire said, sounding disgusted. And what would disgust a guy who routinely drank blood, Eddie had no idea. But he suspected he was about to find out. "As far as I can figure, he's been around since the thirties. Likes to eat children. He'll stay in one place, a bunch of kids will disappear, but before the mob can get pitchforks and torches—or even an Identi-Kit—together, he disappears. Then he'll pop up somewhere new, and in a few days, there's more third graders missing."

"That's horrible," Eddie said, feeling faint. As a mostly grown man it had been one thing to face off against a vampire. But a child? "That's—"

"But he fucked up. He's in my territory now. And we're gonna get him." The vampire smiled, looking wolfish and cheerful at the same time.

"We?" Boo said, and Eddie could have sworn her expression had eased a little. Aw. She and the vampire had something in common . . . their hatred of scumball vampires. It was all right out of . . . well, he wasn't sure what.

"He's too dangerous, too old. I can't in good conscience let you go after him by yourselves. Especially with a child who has no idea what he's doing."

"Hey!" Eddie said hotly. "I'm not a child, I'm twenty-one!"

The vampire rolled his eyes, and the corner of Boo's mouth twitched.

"I'm an intrepid vampire killer, deadly apprentice to the most feared and—and blond vampire killer of them all!"

"Oh, stop it," the vampire told him. "You've never even met one before tonight, I'll bet my watch on it. You're probably tagging along because you think it'll be interesting and fun. And the lady here is too nice to tell you to fuck off."

"Heh," Boo said.

"But *I'm* not," the vampire said. He leaned forward, and Eddie suddenly noticed how huge the man's pupils were, blotting out the blue of his eyes, blotting out the room, the world. "Fuck off."

CH@%!*R
7

"I'm not working with you," Boo said, watching Eddie get up and walk away like a robot. "Although, uh, thanks."

"Really, what were you thinking?" Gregory scolded her. "I can't think of a better way for an ordinary fellow to get hurt than to spend the night hanging out with you."

"I would have looked out for him. Off my case, dead guy," she snapped.

"We'll let that pass for the minute. And would you rather go after Martigan by yourself and possibly fail, or let me come along and increase your chances of success?"

"Mmmm . . ."

"Not that you would be 'letting' me do anything," he added silkily.

"You're really pushing your luck, dead guy."

"Maybe you could stake me after," he added helpfully, and she almost laughed.

In fact, this was the most intriguing vampire she had ever met. Not that she'd ever spent much time getting to know the dead. But Gregory Schorr was an interesting mix of hard and compassionate.

Kind of the way she thought of herself, truth be told.

"That's an interesting proposition," she admitted. "And you *did* get rid of the Boy Blunder for me."

He'd been sipping his wine, and choked. "That's what you call him?"

"One of the things." She finished her last Black Russian, then shook her head. "No, I can't. I should be killing you right this second."

"Please," he said, offended. "You've already ruined my pants. That reminds me, I've got a locker in the back of the club—I'll have to change."

"Never mind about your pants. I should stake you, then go after Martigan. He won't be the only awful vampire I've ever killed."

"No, but he'll be the oldest."

She was silent. He was right. How did he know that?

"We have a newsletter," he told her, anticipating the question.

"You *what*?"

"All right, we don't. But there are files on you in the library in Minneapolis. There's not much, but you *have* left witnesses, unwittingly or not. I've sort of been a fan."

"That's gross."

"Fine, play hard to get."

"I'm *not*—"

"Anyway, you do what I do. You get rid of the scum, the creatures you absolutely can't abide walking around on the same planet you are. Listen, when I was a cop, I had the highest clearing rate in the city. I wasn't about to let being a vampire change that. Put yourself in my shoes: You've got fifteen years of BPD experience, and suddenly you're a lot harder to kill. What would you do?"

"What all of you do," she replied in a hard voice. "Make victims. Every night."

He made an impatient sound. "Yes, I drink blood, I take victims just about every night. You're telling me you're a defender of rapists, of murderers? Because that's who I drink from."

She sat in silence. She was a lot of things, but she wasn't a hypocrite. She wasn't about to ride his ass because he ate bad guys. If you thought about it, he was doing a public service.

She shook that off. Sitting here in the gloom with him, *not* killing him, *did* make her a hypocrite. All vampires were bad. Gregory was a vampire. Gregory was bad. Simplistic but then, the basics always were.

"It's just a job," he reminded her gently. "Don't you want to stack the deck as far as you can in your favor? There's plenty of time to worry about other things after we—after you take care of Martigan."

In the end, that was the straw she grasped: the job. She had been telling herself for years that killing vampires was just how she made a buck. If Gregory could help her do her job, she was a fool to stand in his way.

And there would be time to worry about other things. Later.

CH@%!*R

8

Gregory worked hard to contain his elation. If the darling Ghost had the tiniest hint how thrilled he was to be spending the night with her, she'd likely shoot him again. Worse, she'd leave.

"I suppose we'd better get B.B.," she observed as they left the club and went into the autumn Boston evening. "Not that I don't appreciate you getting rid of him. But I'd feel better if I saw him safely home. Otherwise he'll just—"

"Wander around, fucking off," Gregory confirmed. "Not to tell you your business—"

"So don't."

"But what were you thinking, letting him tag along?"

"He caught me in a weak moment," she admitted. "Not to mention, I was sort of impressed. Most people in that situation would have pissed themselves with fear, then cried themselves to sleep. He wanted to tag along and help me."

"Can't blame him for that one," Gregory murmured.

She gave him a sideways look, one without the slightest

drop of flirtation. "Don't start the whole vampire seduction bullshit, unless you like the taste of wood."

"Wanting to seduce you has nothing to do with my being a vampire," he told her.

"Right." She managed to cram an amazing amount of disgust and disbelief into one word.

"Is this the part where you pretend that you have no idea you're fantastically beautiful?" he asked politely.

Her lips went so tight they almost disappeared. "No, it's the part where I kill you and then sit down to a chicken dinner."

"After we get Eddie," he reminded her, cheering up, as always, at the prospect of distracting death. Not to mention possibly buying death a drink.

They found Eddie stumbling around along the water-front, more vacant-eyed than usual. The vampire, Boo noticed, didn't look remotely ashamed at the state he'd left Eddie in.

"You're coming with us, looks like," he said, snapping his fingers before Eddie's eyes.

"Whoa!" Eddie shook himself like a Labrador fresh out of a lake. "I am? Great. Okay! Great. That was weird. Man, you totally Jedi'd all over my butt."

"Yeah, sorry ab—"

"That was awesome! You used your dark powers of the night on me."

"I'm going to use my dark powers of my foot up your ass if we don't get going," Boo said, possibly more irritated than she'd ever been in her life. "Let's go, Boy Blunder."

"I really hate that name," Eddie confided, falling into step beside her. "So what's the plan?"

"What *is* the plan?" Gregory asked, behind her. He could see at once she didn't care for that at all, as she immediately slowed so he could walk abreast. It was a little disconcerting, but he couldn't blame her for being practical.

"You're asking me?" she replied. "You're the incredibly ancient wise old creature of the night."

"I'm only sixty-eight," he said, irritated. He had no idea how old the lady was, but chances were he had a decade or two on her at least.

"Well, you don't look a second over twenty-eight," Eddie comforted him. "In fact, you're a great-looking guy. Not great looking for your age; great looking in general. I mean, I'm strictly hetero, but I have to say, if I ever made an exception to the rule, I'd definitely do it for you."

"That's adorable," Boo said. "I think you two make a great couple. I foresee a spring wedding."

"It's possible I haven't entirely shaken off your little Jedi trick," Eddie admitted.

"I'm *sure* that's not it," Boo said, actually grinning a little. Gregory was torn between exasperation at the Boy Blunder and happiness that she was smiling.

"You were telling us the plan."

"Was I? Well, my plan was to meet you, get the green light to axe Martigan, then go find Martigan and axe him. But it's turning into one of those nights," she finished in a mutter.

CH@%!*R
9

"You know, you don't have to stick around," Boo said. Bad enough she had one sidekick she didn't know what to do with, but now a vampire was tagging along. A damned vampire!

It serves me right, she thought, sighing internally. *I earned every bit of it. It's mine. I shouldn't have put Blunder out there for bait, and this is my punishment: The guy I thought I was supposed to kill is sticking to me like gum on a shoe.*

"You can't take Martigan by yourself," he reminded her.

"Says you. Besides, what do you care?"

"Hey, I'm still a cop."

"No you aren't!" she almost shouted. "You're dead, you've been dead for years, and dead guys make lousy policemen."

"In my heart, I'm still a cop." And he said it so sincerely, she couldn't think of a retort.

"So you hired her to kill this vampire," Eddie piped up, "this Martigan guy?"

"Sure."

"How'd you even know how to find her? How'd you even know about Martigan?"

She opened her mouth to say something like "Shut up, Boy Asunder," but she was curious about those points herself, and wanted to hear Gregory's answer.

Gregory had his hands stuffed in his pocket, past the wrists, and kicked at a rock while they walked together. "I run my own security company."

"Like private cops."

"Yes."

"Cool."

"We can always use another Web geek," Gregory said, and Boo could practically hear Eddie getting the thrill of his life.

"Really? You'll give me a job? Because the one I have *sucks*. No offense. If that term offends you. And I hope it doesn't."

"You can't work for him," she said, exasperated.

"*You* do."

"That's just for tonight," she snapped. "And I'm an independent contractor, not an employee."

"Well, you can't spend your whole life slaying vampires," Eddie said. "Can you?"

She found that honestly puzzling. "What else would I do?"

"Lots of things. With your God-given powers of light, and his fiendish powers of the night—"

"Eddie, you're so completely full of shit."

"Not completely," Gregory said.

"Yes, completely. The very idea is beyond ridiculous."

"We'd make a great team," the vampire said, actually sounding wounded.

"Yeah, we would," Boy Hinder enthused.

God, God. "I'm sure you've both heard this before, but I don't work for vampires, I kill them."

"How many have you killed?"

"That's none of our business," Gregory said quickly.

Ha! That made him a little twitchy. She decided to answer. "I stopped counting when I got to twenty-five."

"Why?"

"Because it was depressing," she admitted.

"Just for the record, I don't have a problem with you killing vampires per se," the vampire announced.

"How utterly super of you."

"But, I feel like I have to clarify, vampires are like everybody else: Some of them are assholes, and some of them are saints, but most of them are somewhere in the middle."

"All the ones *I've* met have been assholes."

"But you've met me," he said, visibly hurt.

"Gregory, most of the vampires I've killed have started it by trying to kill *me*. How can you defend them?"

He opened his mouth, then closed it without a word.

"All righty then. Now, if you've got some information on where we can find Martigan, let's have it so we can *please* get off this grungy waterfront, find the fucker, *kill* the fucker, and I can go home and never see you again."

"Which one of us?" Eddie whined.

God, God. "Just *give*, Gregory. Please. I'm begging. I really am."

He grinned. "All right. In the interest of saving Eddie from federal assault, your wish is my command. According to my latest update, the fucker will be at the Park Street Station tomorrow night at eight. Fund-raiser for the Y."

"That's nice and specific," Eddie commented.

"And it matches with what I was able to find out, so it's probably accurate." *Score another one for Gregory. Damn it.*

"How'd you know this?" Eddie asked with exhausting excitement. "The ultra-secret society of vampires? Or vampire killers? You received an update? A secret update?"

"No, we read the neighborhood newsletter, dumb shit," Boo said kindly. "You have to know how things work, and why things work, and what's going on around you, all the time. Not only will the place be crawling with kids, it'll be crawling with kids in the foster program."

"No parents to notice they're gone," Gregory explained.

"Duh," Eddie snarked. "*That* much I could figure out on my own."

"And the state system . . . well, they do their best, but they're understaffed and underfunded. I'm sorry to say it would take days for anyone to notice a missing orphan."

Sorry to say? Why does he even care? "It'll be a smorgasbord for Martigan," she added. "He won't be able to resist."

"If it's not till tomorrow, why did we—you—go out tonight?"

"Sometimes it takes a few nights to case the dead guy—or gal—in general. Remember: Know what's going on around you, all the time."

Incredibly, Eddie had whipped out a pen and was taking notes on his palm. ". . . all . . . the . . . time . . ."

"Besides, killing two vampires in one night is too much to ask of anyone," Gregory said.

"Hmf," she replied.

"Two vampires or two dozen, we'll be there," Eddie said, sounding tough and flinty, tucking the pen behind his ear. Then, "Uh, right? We'll be there?"

Annoyingly, the vampire and the vampire hunter traded a look. "Sure," Gregory said with a total lack of conviction.

CH@%!*R

10

"You live here?"

Gregory stifled a laugh; it was obvious Eddie was being disabused of one cherished notion after another. They had pulled up outside a perfectly ordinary looking apartment building in Quincy, a perfectly ordinary southern suburb of Boston.

"Yeah."

"It's nice." He himself had a house on the beach on the Cape but then, he'd had a few decades to save up for it. And the security business was, as always, very good. "It's nice and . . . unassuming."

Boo snorted, but she didn't shoot him again, so he was marginally encouraged. He'd changed into a hole-free pair of slacks, but that was it until he went home.

Frankly, he was amazed she had brought them to her *home,* of all things. But then, quite a bit about the evening had amazed him.

He wondered if she was lonely. It was a thought that had never occurred to him in the same context as the dreaded Ghost.

But it was something to think about.

"So this is your fortress of solitude, huh?" Eddie asked as they stepped into the elevator.

"Yes. I retreat here to bind the wounds inflicted upon me by man's inhumanity to man. I use justice as my poultice."

Gregory coughed hard, so he wouldn't laugh hard. He caught Boo's eye but had to look away. Judging from the bite on Eddie's neck, his evening was going badly enough.

And . . . for a second . . . he could have sworn she winked at him.

Impossible. He was just getting sentimental in his old age.

Even in the flickering fluorescent elevator lighting, she was stunning, and though he'd looked away to avoid cracking up, he found himself looking at her again. To his surprise, Boo was eyeing him back. This was nerve-racking, while at the same time stimulating.

Eddie, the game little fellow, hadn't given up. "So you moved here after the grisly death of your parents?" he asked, following her to apartment 9C.

"My parents are still alive," she replied.

"Really? That's—wait!" Eddie threw up his hands and Gregory walked right into them. "She has to invite you in."

"No I don't, dumbass," she said kindly, unlocking the door and walking in.

"It's just an old wives' tale," Gregory said, patting the boy on the shoulder. He felt a little sorry for Eddie; the kid was getting more crushed by the minute. "You know, you could be a *little* nicer," he told her.

"I *could*." She was already shrugging out of her jacket, revealing a black tank top, smoothly muscled arms, and gorgeous breasts, real old-fashioned breasts like the ones Ava and Marilyn had.

Boo tossed her black jacket onto the end table. Which was also black. As were the sofa, coffee table, chairs, and lamps.

"Whoa," Eddie said, staring around the room.

"My home away from etcetera," Boo said. "I'd offer you guys a drink, but one of you is a parasite and the other one isn't welcome."

"Ha ha," he said to Eddie, "you're a parasite."

"Your apartment is *all black*."

"I'm glad you've pointed that out. It's been on my mind for some time." She twirled a ghost-white strand of hair on an equally white finger. "Do you think it has some sort of deep psychological meaning?"

Eddie seemed to realize he was stating the obvious (not to mention skating on thin ice), so he switched tactics. "You said earlier—you said your parents are alive?"

"Sure. They're still running the café, last time I checked."

"Oh. Well, that's . . . that's good."

Gregory looked around inside the slightly cluttered, conventional-except-for-the-color-scheme apartment. There were black stuffed animals—a dragon and a bear—on the couch, a black blanket crumpled in the lap of the recliner, a chess set in the corner—both sides black. "How in the world did you get into the business you're in?" *And how in the world do you know which piece is yours?*

She took a Beck's Dark out of the fridge, used the edge of the counter to snap the cap off, and took a drink. Her long throat worked thirstily as she sucked it down, and he had to look away. "I took an aptitude test in high school and it came back 'vampire killer.' "

"You had a mysterious destiny," Eddie guessed, "and fate called upon you."

"I had a mysterious Poli Sci test," she replied, "and a vampire called upon me. Luckily, my shotgun worked fine."

"You killed a vampire with a shotgun?"

"No, shit for brains," she replied kindly. "I made him mad with a shotgun. I killed him with my pasta scoop."

"Well, I've got to hear the rest of this one," Gregory said, and pulled out a black chair and made himself comfortable.

CH@%!*R

11

"Do you know what happens to an albino in the wild? It gets eaten. It stands out with its freakish coloring and predators just can't resist. They move in and snap it up."

"I think I see where you're going with this."

"Listen, Luke Dorkwalker, I'm not in a sharing mood very often, so shut up and listen, willya?"

"Sorry."

"Just . . . hush up for five seconds, okay? I saved your life, and in return you're gonna be quiet."

"That doesn't seem—"

"*Eddie.*"

"Sorry."

"I had a perfectly ordinary life. In fact, if I go back there, my perfectly ordinary life is waiting for me. I worked in the café to earn money for college; I'm welcome back home anytime.

"And speaking of college, that's where it all started. It wasn't that I survived a vampire attack and it changed my life. It's that they kept attacking me. The first time, living through it was dumb luck. The second time, I was more pissed than scared."

"You were probably more pissed than scared the first time, too," Eddie suggested.

"Shush. There aren't that very many vampires, Eddie. There's lots more of us than there are of them. You've got a better chance of being killed in a plane crash than being attacked by a vampire."

"I never fly."

She rubbed her pale eyebrows. "But I've been attacked a bunch of times. It's like I said. I stand out, and they can't resist. The third time, I found out there had been a reward for the vampire that had attacked me. It paid my rent for eight months, and bought my schoolbooks for the year. So I thought, why not survive vampire attacks for a living?"

"That's it?"

"That's it."

"So . . . it really is just a job."

"Yep."

"How'd you get so good at it?" Gregory couldn't help asking.

"You mean besides years of practice? Look, I understand you guys, okay? I have to stay out of the sun, too . . . I go outside at noon for five minutes, and I've got a nasty sunburn. I prefer it at night, just like you. My senses have sharpened over the years because of it . . . like you. I've got shitty day vision but can see well at night. Like you. That's all there is. That's the big secret."

"Why are you telling me this?" For him, Eddie had disappeared; he was focused only on her. For him, everyone might have disappeared.

"I—I don't know." She looked frightened for a moment, an expression so fleeting he wondered if it had been wishful thinking on his part. "I really don't."

Eddie's mouth was moving, but he wasn't saying anything. Oh. Yes he was. They just weren't listening. ". . . nice of you to let us crash here."

"It's not nice," she replied shortly. "I can't get rid of you for the time being, and I can't let *him* walk around."

"You mean to pen me up like a dog?" Gregory asked pleasantly.

"I don't know what I mean," she muttered, and stomped out of the room.

CH@%!*R
12

"Checkmate."
　"Shit."

"Checkmate."
　"Shit."

"Checkmate."
　"Shit!" She leaped to her feet and kicked over the coffee table. "Son of a *bitch*!"
　"Hey, keep it down," Eddie said. "I'm watching the *Buffy* marathon."
　"Shit! Shit! Shit!"
　"Up for another one?" he asked, careful not to smile. From the way she was kicking things around the living room, he guessed not.
　"I don't know what you're getting so mad about," Eddie commented, staring at the screen. "He's got, what? Forty-five years of experience playing?"

"Forty-nine," he corrected.

"I hate vampires," she muttered, stalking into the kitchen.

"Hmm, the mighty vampire killer is a sore loser. Who would have guessed?"

"Shut up, fangs-for-brains." He could hear her slamming cupboard doors open and closed.

"Can I have another Zima?" Eddie asked.

"You didn't have a first Zima. Do they even make Zima anymore?" He heard her sigh. "Gregory, do you want a beer?"

"I don't drink . . . beer."

Eddie chortled.

"God, God."

"Don't do that, it hurts my head," he called.

"*That's* too bad."

"What?" Eddie asked. "Saying God? You mean there's finally one thing about the myths that are true?"

"Apparently so."

"But how come? I mean, you seem like a really nice guy."

"Seem like," she called from the other room.

"You're a comedian when you're not helping bad vampires get staked, for G—for crying out loud. Why shouldn't you be able to, I dunno, say the Lord's Prayer or whatever?"

Gregory shuddered all over. "I imagine it's an intrinsic part of being a vampire, like needing to drink blood. Can we not talk about it?"

"Does it mean you're *intrinsically* evil?" Boo asked, coming back to the living room. She set down her beer and righted the coffee table. Gregory got down on his hands and knees to help her pick up the scattered pieces.

"You don't go to church," he pointed out, picking up the queen. "Does that mean you're bad?"

She stared at him, a rook in her fist. "How did you know that?"

"I didn't," he admitted. "I guessed. I would imagine you're out late on Saturday nights, so you sleep in on Sundays. At least, I always went there on Sunday mornings."

She blinked. "Tons of good people don't go to church. It's just—their choice, is all."

"Exactly."

"So it's a choice issue? Are you arguing that needing to drink blood is—is no different than eating meat?"

"Meat is murder," Eddie said automatically, clicking past Nickelodeon.

"Yes."

"Because that's—that's not the same thing."

"No?" He smiled at her.

"No."

"Yes," Eddie said.

"Who's talking to you?"

"Shhhh. I love this part."

"God, God." She went back into the kitchen.

Gregory sat down beside Eddie just in time to see the vampire on the screen disappear in a cloud of dust. He snorted. Typical TV fairy tales. Really, they were part of the problem. It wouldn't be so hard to convince Ghost he was a man worthy of her feminine attentions if she hadn't been exposed to . . .

Well. That wasn't fair. She'd been attacked, several times by her reckoning. And ridding the world of scum was her job. It was enough to make anyone jaded. He remembered when he was on the BPD and despaired of meeting a woman who wasn't a prostitute, thief, husband-killer, or political fixer. Heck, back then there hadn't been any women cops, even.

He imagined she had much the same problem.

CH@%!*R
13

"This should be fine," he said cheerfully.

She stared at him. "The bathtub."

"Sure."

Eddie peeked over her shoulder. "Oh, man, the tub?"

"He has to," she replied. "There aren't any windows in here. It's either here or under my bed." She gave Gregory a look. "Under my bed isn't an option."

He tried not to think about her bed. "Really, it'll be fine." He inspected it again. "Is that Comet?"

"I cleaned house the day before yesterday," she admitted.

"It *does* look sparkling and fresh," Eddie said.

"Just let me borrow a pillow and a blanket and I won't trouble you anymore."

"If only," she mumbled.

"I'm not even going to ask if you need a coffin or the soil of your native land," Eddie said.

"Good," Gregory said in unison with her.

"This night is just getting weirder and weirder."

"Tell me about it," she said, leaving to get a pillow.

*   *   *

"I think he's asleep," Eddie said, ear jammed to the bathroom door.

"I doubt it. He won't sleep until the sun comes up." Boo checked her watch. "About three hours from now."

"So what's he doing in there?"

"Reading the *Pioneer Press,* last time I checked."

"How do you even have the—never mind, what if he gets hungry and tries to . . . you know."

"Then I'll kill him," she said flatly.

"Just like that?"

"Just like that." She was making up the sofa bed for him, unfolding crisp, clean black sheets, and Eddie thought—not for the first time—that she was an interesting mix of thoughtful domestic and hardened killer. Just like Grandma!

"Come on, we've been hanging around him all night. We watched the Buffy marathon together! He made the best sangria I've ever had. He tried out his new stand-up material on us."

She shivered. "Don't remind me."

"So how can you treat him like he's one of the bad guys?"

"Because—he is."

"Come on, that's like saying the French are cowards, or Polish people are dumb."

"It's not the same thing," she said, sounding offended. She was tucking in the sheets in savage, economical motions, and he edged away from her a little. "At all."

"Boo, it's exactly the same thing. Admit it, he hasn't done one bad thing to either one of us."

"He mojo'd you."

"For my own good. I mean, I wish he wouldn't have—although it was kind of cool—but he had good reasons. And he hired you to kill Martigan."

"Territorial," she suggested.

"Or a really good guy who's using every resource he

can—including you—to get a child killer off the streets.
You just can't give him a chance because you think he's
scum, like the ones you killed."

She didn't say anything.

"This is why you're a lone wolf," he guessed. "Roaming
the world completing your sacred mission—"

"Eddie. *Please* don't."

"—because you've thought you were all alone. And you
have been alone. Except there's someone out there for
you . . . maybe . . . if you give him a chance. You just have
to overlook him being the undead."

She shook her head.

"Look, I'm not saying you should, y'know, get married
or anything. Just give him a chance."

"He hasn't been staked yet, has he? He's in my bathtub
right this second, isn't he?" she griped. "That's as much as
a chance as I've ever given any dead guy."

"*Un*dead."

"Same thing."

"You know that's not true." Actually, he didn't know—
she was pretty firmly prejudiced in that idea. But she
wasn't unreasonable. Just abrupt. And bitchy. And quietly
furious all the time. He hated to think of the state of her
stomach lining.

And lonely. Very, very lonely.

"He's sort of perfect for you."

She snorted and fluffed a pillow. "Maybe you should
date him."

"His Jedi trick totally wore off already. I think of him
solely as a tall, great-looking blond guy with the shoulder-
length locks of a god and eyes the color of the Caribbean."
Eddie frowned. That had sounded less gay in his head.
"*Anyway.* Here's a guy who's interesting, smart—whipped
your ass in chess pretty good, didn't he?—challenging,
cool, funny, and he would overlook your staking tenden-
cies. Heck, he'd probably help you, if you wanted."

"I don't need—"

"Yeah, yeah, lone wolf, work alone, die alone, I get it.

All's I'm saying is, you could do worse than Gregory. In this whole apartment, there aren't any pictures. It doesn't look like you have anything. No boyfriends, nothing of you, not even your parents. How do you live?"

She fluffed the pillow again. Actually, she punched it. He guessed she was imagining it was his head. "I have my work."

"Lame," he announced.

"I have plenty of things besides that!" she almost shouted. She "fluffed" the pillow by kicking it. "I live a rich and satisfying life, Eddie Batley!"

"Lame," he coughed into his fist. He supposed death was right around the corner, but unlike *some* people in the room, he really did feel he had lived a rich and satisfying life, and could go to his grave (after being beaten to death by an angry albino vampire slayer) a satisfied man. "So massively lame."

"Goddammit," she snarled, and stepped up on the sofa bed, walked across it, stepped down, grabbed two fistfuls of his shirt, and mashed her lips to his.

"Eh?" he managed.

"Kiss me," she demanded, then mashed on him again.

"Let go, or I'll get my pepper spray," he mumbled around her lips. Her breasts were pressed against his chest, her pretty mouth was against his, her long legs against his thighs.

It was mildly terrifying.

He got an elbow up in an attempt to fend her off. "Boo, I'm really super flattered, here. But I'm also kind of scared of you, which doesn't entirely do it for me."

"Shut up, Boy Blunder."

"See, calling me names isn't erotic." He managed to wrest his mouth free. "Not those kinds of names, anyway. Look, I'm out of my mind, okay? I mean, a woman as great-looking as you is never, ever going to throw herself at me ever again."

Despite the circumstances, she grinned a little. "That's probably true."

He resisted the urge to smell her hair. "But you're only molesting me because you'd rather be in the tub with *him*. And you're afraid to face it."

The grin vanished. She glared into his eyes. "I'm not afraid of anything."

He squashed the impulse to grab her boobs. "Prove it."

CH@%!*R
14

The bathroom door crashed open, and Gregory jumped. He'd long mastered the art of ignoring the input of his enhanced hearing, so as not to eavesdrop on people (unless he needed to, naturally). So he'd peripherally heard the two of them chatting and moving around, but beyond that hadn't paid much attention.

Ghost was framed in the doorway. She stepped into the tiny bathroom and slammed the door. He dropped the newspaper (and his jaw). This was it! She was going to kill him. Try, anyway. He wondered how best to fend her off without really hurting her. Maybe crack her hard enough in the jaw so she went down in one? Get an arm around her throat until she passed out from lack of oxygen? That might bruise her, assuming he wasn't coughing up splinters by then, but maybe she—

"I'm taking a poll," she said in a voice that shook. "If I stripped and tried to seduce you, you'd have sex with me, right?"

He blinked. Was it a trick question? Had to be. "Of course."

"Right! And it wouldn't be because I'm some pathetic loser, right?"

He was trying to process current events. "You're not pathetic. You're not a loser, either. And I'm not just saying that because you appear to be not killing me."

"Exactly!" she said triumphantly.

"Er—what's this about?"

"I'll tell you what it's about," she said, stabbing a finger in his direction. "We're going to *date*. Starting right now!"

"We are?" he gasped.

"Damned right!" She moved the rest of the way into the small room and climbed into the tub, falling on top of him when her grip slipped. If he'd had any breath, it would have whooshed out of his lungs. "If I kiss you, you're going to kiss me back, right?"

"Of course." Then he cupped the back of her skull in his hand and pressed his mouth to hers.

"M'not a loser," she muttered, and her mouth bloomed beneath his like a perfect white flower.

He sucked on her tongue, his hands busy at her shirt, and her hands were occupied, too, and they groped and wrestled in the supremely uncomfortable bathtub. He didn't especially care—he would have taken her in a rose garden, a swamp, a dead forest, a basement.

He got her shirt off, shredded her jeans, and pushed her bra up around her neck, as she clawed for his belt buckle. "Do *not* bite me," she said, chewing on his earlobe.

He gritted his teeth as her pale breasts filled his hands, her scent—daisies and Tide—filled his head. "That's . . . not going to be easy."

"Gregory. I couldn't handle that."

"All right."

"I mean it." Her hands were on him, stroking him with a feathery touch, and he groaned.

"All right, hon." *Oh boy. Don't bite, don't bite.*

"I'll make it worth your while," she whispered, her grip firming, her touch like rough silk.

"Yes," he said. "You will." He slipped a finger through

her downy crease and found her damp, felt her squirm against him, and ground his teeth harder. *Don't bite, don't bite, don't you dare bite.*

She wiggled, her knees coming down on either side of him, and he put his arms around her and pressed on her lower back. Sliding into her was like gliding into a fantasy with sight and scent and sound. She moaned and rested her forehead on his shoulder, her white hair brushing his mouth.

"You're every dream I've ever had," he told her, and kissed her throat.

"My name is Boo," she said, and shivered against him.

He nuzzled her nipples and badly wanted to take one into his mouth, but was afraid he'd bite her . . . holding back was getting *very* difficult. But her squirming and gasping was delectable, and he felt his eyes roll back as he pulsed within her.

"Oh boy," he managed as she sprawled on top of him.

"I think I've bruised my elbows," she admitted, trying to sit up.

"You probably bruise like a peach."

She grinned down at him. "I've never heard it put quite like that before. And you're right."

"Want to show me?"

"Sure. But mostly," she admitted, "I want to get the hell out of this bathtub."

CH@%!*R
15

"Okay!" Eddie enthused when Boo came into the living room around two the next day. Gregory was still conked out in her bed—she'd rigged up some black blankets across the window before they'd gotten busy again—and super geek enthusiasm was a little tough to take first thing in the afternoon. "So, what? When's Gregory getting up? When do you want to leave? I assume you want to get there first, so Martigan can walk into your clever trap. Do you think I can take a piss? Will the G-man care? Will he notice?"

"Don't call him that, ugh." Then, "You haven't gone to the bathroom yet?"

"I can't do it if someone's watching," he whined.

"Well, he's not in there. I—I changed my mind and let him sleep under my bed." They'd crept across the hall so quietly the night before, Eddie had never woken up. Thank God.

"Oh." Eddie galloped past her, and she heard the door slam. She sighed and went into the kitchen for a glass of juice. One problem solved.

Several remained. What had she done? It hadn't been

just to prove something to the Boy Blunder; she knew herself well enough to realize there was more to it than that. And she'd wanted Gregory—no doubt about that. Despite proof of his—his condition. Two hours ago, feeling morbid, she nevertheless couldn't resist taking his pulse as he . . . rested? Slumbered?

Eight per minute. Respiration: four.

She had heard the rumors over the years—that vampires weren't dead, it was a virus and you either caught it or you didn't. If you did catch it, your pulse and breathing slowed down permanently, you couldn't go out, your senses and reflexes improved, you couldn't tolerate solids. She had always dismissed it as vampire fantasy: "We're not the awful night creatures you think we are, we're sick."

Yeah.

Sure.

Whether it was true or not—and she was no scientist—Gregory was no—how would Eddie put it? "Ravenous member of the undead hell-horde."

She gulped more juice, remembering his hands on her, his cock *in* her, his mouth . . . his mouth. He had wanted to bite her. Badly. And hadn't, because she had asked him not to. That had touched her . . . had been enough to let her relax enough to reach orgasm, a very rare thing.

He'd been more careful the second time, and so had she, and they had ended up caressing each other and sliding together for a lovely long time. He'd chewed through her black puma pillow and mock-threatened to eat Eddie before they were done, and she found herself laughing in bed for the first time in . . . ever.

It was all rather strange and wonderful.

"Okay!" Eddie said again, coming back out. "Want to get a bite?"

"Sure, dumbass," she replied cheerfully. "I'll buy."

The bedroom door opened, and Gregory was stretching as he strolled through it. He opened his mouth, and she grabbed his shirt and arched up on tiptoe to hiss into his ear. "Don't say anything to Eddie."

Fortunately, the object of her concern was entranced by *A Very Brady Christmas*.

Gregory blinked at her. "What? Why not?"

"Because, okay?"

His blue eyes narrowed. "I'm your dirty little secret, is that it?"

"Yes, that's exactly it, now don't say anything."

"You were supposed to deny that."

"Well, I can't. Please, okay?"

"Mmm."

"We'll have to work that one out."

He still looked disgruntled, but sounded mildly encouraged. "All right."

"Okay, great." She forced the word out. "Thanks."

"I'm just a man, you know," he told her gently. "There's nothing special about me."

"Ha," she said, snuck a glance over her shoulder, then gave him a quick kiss.

CH@%!*R
16

"Okay, are we ready? We're ready." Eddie jogged in place. "My reflexes are razor sharp. Let's go kill a vampire! A bad one, I mean."

"Sounds like a plan," Gregory said, and punched him in the back of the neck. Eddie dropped like a rock into a pond.

"Oh, excellent," Boo said. "Grab his ankles."

"It's just that it's dangerous," Gregory said half-apologetically, picking Eddie up and placing him on the couch. After a moment, he tucked the remote into the snoring man's hand.

"Hey, you don't have to tell me. I was ready to tie him up."

"Oooh."

She gave him a look. "The last thing we need is him stumbling around in an alley babbling Buffy-isms while we're trying to flank Martigan."

"Agreed." He gazed at her. She was dressed in a black sweater, another pair of black leggings, and her hair was caught back with a black headband. She was checking her tote bag, and chewing gum. "Frankly, I'm not happy about you being there tonight."

She glanced up from her rummaging. "Is this the part where you're all annoying and overprotective?"

"Yes," he admitted.

"To quote the Boy Blunder: lame."

"Since he's unconscious . . ." He opened his arms.

She evaded his embrace, smiling regretfully. "First we kill the bad guy. Then we can have sex."

"Slave driver," he grumbled, following her out the door.

"So have you heard about the vampire queen?"

Boo was watching the crowd and tipped her head toward him. "I've heard . . . some things," she said carefully.

"Rumors, I suppose."

"It's as silly as vampirism being something you can catch, like the flu."

"It *is* something you can catch."

"Let's argue about it later. Besides, you're wrong. And I don't know whether what I've heard about Elizabeth The One is true or fantasy."

"There is something to that. I doubt she can endure sunlight and wear . . . religious icons."

"If it sounds like she's becoming a problem, I'll go out to the Cities to kill her. I've been watching the local papers . . . there hasn't been a sudden increase of missing people. The crime rates are essentially unchanged."

"I doubt it will be as cut-and-dried as that. She overthrew what's-his-name . . . Nostro. Killed him and took the throne."

"What are you saying?" She was afraid to look away from the milling adults and children, afraid to look him in the eyes.

"I'm saying if she becomes a problem, I'll go out there with you."

"Well." *I work alone. Don't bother. Butt out. That's so sweet of you. I loved having you in my bed. I don't want you in danger.* "Thank you."

"There, now. Was that so hard?" he teased.

"Oh, shush." She stiffened. The man on the fringe of the crowd, talking to a cocoa-colored girl—she looked about eight, and he looked about twenty. He was crouched in front of her, listening intently, hands relaxed and loose, head cocked attentively. Dark hair. Dark eyes. High cheekbones, pale skin, scar on the chin.

Gotcha.

"Oh, you prick," Gregory was muttering; he'd spotted the killer, too. "Get the fuck away from her."

"Easy."

"If he puts a finger on her, I'm cutting off his head."

"We'll do that anyway."

"Okay," he said, comforted.

Martigan pointed, and the child nodded warily. He said something—Boo couldn't pick it up over the murmuring of the crowd—and the girl laughed and nodded again, more relaxed.

"Prick. Prick. Prick."

"Don't tell me what he's saying to her, I don't even want to know."

Martigan gestured, and the girl followed his hands. He caught her chin, gently forcing her to look back at him, and spoke again.

Gregory twitched. "Easy," Boo said.

The child nodded yet again, much more slowly this time, and even from a distance Boo could see her eyes had gone glassy. It occurred to her that Gregory had never tried to pull any vampire mind tricks on her.

Probably he doesn't dare.

And maybe he wouldn't do that to take advantage. Just for someone's own good, like Eddie.

And maybe you should keep your mind on business, dumbass.

"Okay," she said, and they followed Martigan and the child through the crowd and into Public Gardens.

"We're too far away."

"We're fine."

"He could hurt her before we get to her."

"You can get to her in time."

His lips thinned. "I appreciate your confidence, but . . ."

"Gregory, I do this for a living, okay? Trust me. Cripes, you're a nervous wreck."

"It's just . . . she's so little."

"It'll be fine." There were fewer and fewer people in the park, just the occasional couple leaning against a tree, talking softly. Martigan had a hand on the child's shoulder and was leading her onto a deserted path.

"Ready?"

"So ready."

Gregory went left, and Boo hurried forward, dropping her hand into her bag. "Excuse me?" she called, her voice high and sweet. "We're looking for our little girl? Jenny? Is that you?"

Martigan turned, his hand tightening on the child's shoulder. He was relaxed, smiling. "Sorry, this isn't her." He got a good look at Boo as she got closer and the smile faded. "You look—kind of familiar. You—"

"I'm too old for you," she said sweetly. "Why don't you let go of the kid before something unbelievably awful happens to you?"

He showed his teeth, and the girl yelped as his hand clamped down, but her dreamy expression didn't change. "You're Ghost."

"Remind me to get a wig."

"Come a step closer, and I'll unzip her like a bass."

"Oh, John." She smiled. "You'll do that anyway." Then the stake burst from his chest, and Gregory was there, yanking the girl away, stepping back as Martigan thudded to the ground. Boo watched the killer's eyes go as glassy as the girl's, cloud over, die.

"It's the little things in life that make it all worthwhile," she said, and took the child's hand.

CH@%!*R
17

"We make a good team."

"Screw that." She noticed he had tightened up—she could feel it in the arm against her shoulders—and clarified. "We make a *great* team."

"We do, don't we? That piece of shit never knew what hit him."

"All part of the plan." She was getting out her keys; an hour had passed, and they had seen the child safely back to her group. Mercifully, the little girl remembered nothing.

"Scumbag," Gregory said. "It was too quick for him."

"It's over for him, and that's the important thing." She swung open the door, and they beheld an enraged, disheveled Eddie, who had clearly been on the way out. Gregory's arm slid off her shoulders, but Eddie was too puffed with outrageous indignation to notice.

"You guys suck! *You* sucker-punched me and *you* let him! Bad!" He shook his finger at them. "Very very bad!"

"We just didn't want you to get hurt," Gregory tried to explain.

"Yeah, dumb shit, we would have felt all awful inside if

something had happened to you. Besides, you would have cramped our style."

"Oooh, I like that," Gregory said, kissing her ear. " 'Our' style."

"Hey, hey. You're supposed to be my deep dark secret, remember?"

"Sorry, I forgot." He was actually nibbling on her ear now, and she was laughing and trying to shut the door and fending him off at the same time.

"Sure you did. Big undead jerk."

"What the *hell*?" Eddie gasped. "What did I miss?" He looked around wildly. "How long have I been out? What month is it?"

"You were out long enough," she said, and put her arms around Gregory, and kissed him.

"Not such a secret anymore?" he asked, kissing her back.

"Eh, it's just the Boy Blunder. If he blabs, I can always kill him."

Eddie's reaction was best left to the imagination.

Warfem

ANGELA KNIGHT

Acknowledgments

Several good friends helped me with this story by diligently checking it for logic holes. Any I failed to plug are my sole responsibility.

My thanks to Martha Punches, Morgan Hawke, and Katherine Lazo, as well as my wonderful critique partner, Diane Whiteside.

And as always, thanks to my agent, Roberta Brown, and my wonderfully patient editor, Cindy Hwang.

CH@%!*R

1

The thugs followed Alina Kasi out of the bar. Three of them. Two were obviously muscle—a big, beefy blond and a wiry rodent of a man who looked like the kind who'd carry a blade. Then there was the one she figured for the brains of the trio, a thoroughly unremarkable brunet with a pleasant smile and cold, cold eyes.

Alina, planning her trap, was careful to give no indication she'd seen them. Instead she strolled down the ped-walk, tilting her head back like a woman enjoying the cool evening air. Zipcars ghosted overhead, sighing softly in the darkness. Across the river, Jarnalda's two moons rode high over the arches and spires of the city skyline. It was all pretty enough for a tourist trid, if not for the three men skulking along behind her like a trio of wolves.

Just out for a stroll, boys, she thought. *Come try your luck.*

Rajin would be outraged, of course. The Femmat aristocrat would expect Alina to tuck herself safely away in that miserable hotel Kasi House had booked for her. After all, Alina was only scheduled for a one-day layover on this planet, waiting for the jumpship that would take her on to Calista. She shouldn't be out looking for trouble.

All true. A responsible courier working for a responsible employer would never take this kind of chance with a file. But Alina wasn't working for a responsible employer, and she was just frustrated and pissed enough not to care. Besides, these three were no real danger to her.

They were, at best, entertainment.

The trio had been shadowing her since she'd arrived that morning, except they'd changed height, weight, and even species with every encounter. Alina figured they were using some kind of imagizer to project disguises over their true forms. Must be using high-end equipment, too. The illusions would have been good enough to fool her if her sensors hadn't told her the same three men had been tailing her all day.

All of which added up to data thieves. She wondered how they thought they could get the file out of her computer implant. The comp wouldn't give it up if even if they killed her, so they must believe they could force her to upload it to whatever storage unit they had.

Idiots.

She did hope they didn't have a data stripper, though. In theory, one of those devices could bypass her comp's security and gut its files. Of course, to use the stripper, the thieves would first have to hack open her skull, since her comp wound through her brain in a mirror of her neural pathways.

That wouldn't exactly be easy, because Alina was a Samurai Class Warfem, genetically engineered for combat. Her bones and muscles were so heavily reinforced, she was stronger than all three of the men who stalked her. And given her battle computer and the sensors implanted throughout her body, she could also out-think and out-fight them.

As she would shortly demonstrate.

So what are they carrying? Alina thought to her comp.

The leader and the blond have stun batons, while the

small dark one has a nano-knife, the computer replied in its soundless mental voice.

That all? Every other time data thieves had jumped her, they'd been armed like men going after a Soji Dragon. Alina had still protected her files, but she'd had to work at it.

There are stiff penalties against carrying beam weapons on this planet.

Which means nothing to data thieves. Any interesting talents? Cybernetics?

Standard human. No apparent implants beyond data jacks.

She frowned, wondering if they might be setting a trap of their own. What kind of fool would send three standard humans to take a Warfem?

Fools or not, though, they were getting ready to try for her. Alina could almost smell it in their sweat. *Go to full alert.*

Instantly, the implant began readying her body for the coming battle, preparing the chemical dump she'd need if she decided to go into the berserker state called *riaat*. She didn't think it would be necessary, but one never knew.

As the comp did its work, Alina took a moment to decide on her next move.

It was 2500 hours, almost midnight on this planet. Alien constellations spilled overhead, the star population thinner out here on the galactic rim than back home on Vardon. Stores and shops rose to either side of the pedwalk, utilitarian boxes built of ferocrete, square and unimaginative compared with the soaring, curved shapes back home.

Trid signs, some of them amazingly lewd, gave the scene what color it had. Women, strutting eternally in midair, wearing some designer's idea of the latest fashion; men posing in jump shoes and very little else; an alien doing . . . whatever that was. All of them cooing come-ons or chanting their respective stores' hours.

But the only sound that interested Alina was the scrape of her pursuers' boots on the dirty pedwalk behind her.

There were no other footsteps. Despite the illusionary company of the signs, she was alone with them.

Which was exactly the way she wanted it. She needed room and privacy to break a few bones and get a few answers. Who were they, and who were they working for?

And in the process, they'd hopefully put up a good enough fight to let Alina blow off some steam. After years in the emotional cage Rajin had built for her, she needed it.

They were almost close enough. One . . . Two . . . Three . . .

"Kaaassssi!" Lifting her voice in the ringing battlecry of her House, Alina spun and charged.

She caught them completely by surprise. Somebody shouted as she slammed her fist into the big blond's jaw. He rolled with it at the last moment, so the punch didn't quite land as hard as it should have. Still, backed by her genetically engineered strength, it put him down.

In the same smooth motion, she grabbed the right wrist of the rodent-faced one as he went for his knife. Spinning him around, she seized his left shoulder and cranked his right arm up and back until the joint gave. He howled in agony, and she shoved him aside.

Cold pain sliced into her ribs, ripping her breath away. Instinctively, she whirled and rammed her fist into the cold-eyed leader's nose, winning a howl. His stun baton lost contact with her ribs, and she could breathe again.

Her computer snapped a mental warning, and she ducked the blond's roundhouse as he came at her again. Pivoting on one foot, she slammed a knee into his balls, then gave him an uppercut that clicked his teeth together. He hit the ground. He wouldn't be getting up anytime soon.

Her comp confirmed it. *Opponent unconscious.*

"Fuck this." The rodent man reeled off. Apparently the dislocated arm had discouraged him. She turned her full attention to the leader.

He bared his teeth at her, his nose streaming blood. "If you're smart, you'll give the file up now."

"Got a better idea, thief." She bounced on her toes, her blood singing with the raw enjoyment of a good, clean fight. Finally, something she could hit. "You tell me who sent you, and I won't break every bone you have."

The leader only smiled.

Alert! the computer howled. *Tevan combat cyborg, closing fast from the rooftop!*

"Told you," the thief mocked, evidently reading the instant alarm on her face.

Blazing hell, it *was* a trap. Alina snapped into a spinning kick that slammed into the side of his head. His jaw broke with a wet crack clearly audible to her enhanced hearing.

Then she whirled and ran. No way was she going to try to fight a Tevan cyborg. One of those bastards could take on a Warlord and win. He'd beat her into paste.

Worse, if the Tevan had a data stripper and got his hands on the file, Rajin would take out her anger on Galar.

Should have thought of that before you went after these fools, she thought, furious with herself.

The Tevan hit the ground behind her with a meaty thud. "Warlord's slut, get back here!" His rumbling roar made her blood chill. Big boots boomed on the pavement. She put her head down and ran faster.

What have we got?

Tevan cyborg, 2.3 meters tall, two hundred and ninety kilograms. Skeletal structure reinforced with titanium laminate. Nano-cybernetic muscle implants give him strength superior to a Warlord in riaat. *And he's gaining on you. Eight meters . . . 7.9 . . . Seven meters . . .* Those pounding footsteps grew louder.

Give me riaat. *I need to outrun him.* She certainly couldn't outfight him.

Fire flooded her consciousness, as the computer released a wave of neurochemicals from reservoir implants throughout her body. In seconds, the chemicals did their work, quadrupling her strength and decreasing her ability to feel pain. Euphoria replaced her fear with a hot, feral joy she knew was an illusionary product of *riaat.*

Time to make things a little tougher on the Tevan. She lengthened her stride, bounding now, feeling as light as if somebody had suddenly cut gravity in half.

The Tevan is still closing. Four meters . . . 3.8 . . .

A low building stood off to her left, no more than three stories, its gray face gleaming ghostly in the light from the two moons. Alina veered toward it and leaped. Her feet hit the roof, knees bending to absorb the impact.

Something heavy slammed into the side of the building behind her with a crunch. Before she could jump clear, a massive seven-fingered hand clamped around her left ankle and spilled her to the roof. She rolled, trying to kick free. The reptilian bastard hung on the edge staring at her, his four yellow eyes glittering with battle madness. Before she could kick him in the head, he plucked her off the roof and slung her across the pedwalk.

Alina twisted in midair, tucking in her chin and saving herself from a headfirst collision with the building. The impact still knocked the breath out of her.

Stunned, she hit the walk with a teeth-rattling jolt. This time she did see stars.

Up! the computer demanded, its metal voice as strident as an enforcer's siren. *The Tevan is closing!*

Alina lifted her spinning head. Blood poured hot and wet from her nose, and her scraped face stung. She glimpsed the Tevan's armored boot drawing back, aimed right for her head. She flung herself clear as it flashed by.

Panting, bleeding, Alina reeled to her feet.

The Tevan stalked her, two meters plus of muscle, orange scales, flame-red armor, and cybernetic implants. He had a short, bearlike muzzle, with a crown of spines that protected his four small yellow eyes. His hands and feet were broad, with seven thin, agile digits on each. Peeling back his orange lips, he revealed a mouthful of razor teeth. "Surrender the file, and I won't kill you," he rumbled in Standard, his voice a chilling basso growl as inhuman as the rest of him.

"Blow that," Alina snarled, knowing if she lost this fight

she was dead. And worse, so was Galar. "You want it, you're going to have to bleed for it."

"Warbitch, I'm not the one who's going to bleed." He lunged.

She ducked the huge fist flying at her face. Pain faded as her computer pumped endorphins into her bloodstream. Her concentration narrowed on the task of staying alive.

Alina shot a punch into his ribs hard enough to shatter ferocrete, but he just plowed another punch toward her gut. She twisted aside and pumped a kick into his thigh.

The Tevan growled and sprang. Alina leaped back to circle just out of reach, looking for an opening. With *riaat* jacking her strength to superhuman levels, she could stay out of his way, but that wasn't good enough. Her reserves would run out long before he tired.

Despite his vastly superior strength and reinforced bones, she had to put him down long enough to make good her escape.

Then it happened. Alina ducked one vicious fist—right into the path of the other. A sun went nova in her skull. The world spun as she slammed into a wall for the second time. Then the ground came up and hit her in the face. Her comp shrieking warnings, Alina tried to scramble to her feet.

She didn't make it. Her knees gave out, and her cheek collided painfully with the pedwalk.

The Tevan's massive boots rang on the rough surface as he stalked her. "Now, Warbitch, you're—"

A male bellow cut him off in mid-sentence. Something massive flew out of the darkness to barrel into his back. This time the Tevan was the one to hit the wall.

Dazed, Alina watched the flurry of movement—fists, feet, arms, big bodies surging and striking at one another. *Who the . . . ?*

Command beads glittered in her savior's long hair. *A Warlord.*

A Warlord had come to her rescue.

CH@%!*R

2

Yes! They had him now! The thought banished Alina's pain, sent strength pouring through her. No matter how battered she felt, she damn well wouldn't just lie there while a Warlord fought for her. Reeling to her feet, she yelled her battle cry and charged.

The Tevan rolled one yellow eye toward her, but he didn't dare take his attention off the Warlord who was powering punches into his head and body. The air was full of meaty thuds and grunts, the smell of sweat, and the Tevan's lizard reek.

The Warlord has cracked the Tevan's armor, her computer said as she looked for an opening. *Right side, between the eighth and ninth rib.* A set of red crosshairs popped into her vision, pinpointing the weakness.

Alina rammed her fist dead in the center of those crosshairs. Something in her own side shrieked in agony with the force of the blow, but the cracks widened. The Tevan roared and twisted to strike out at her. She ducked his wild punch as the Warlord hit him squarely over his cracked armor. The acrid scent of alien blood rose.

With a bellow of frustrated rage, the Tevan broke and ran, lumbering like a galloping bull. Alina and the Warlord raced after him, tearing down the darkened pedwalk in the exaggerated strides of full *riaat*. A zipbike flashed low over their heads, probably a passerby wanting a closer look at the chase. The Warlord reached out a powerful arm for the Tevan's armored shoulder.

But the alien leaped straight up, grabbed the back of the zipbike, and heaved himself astride behind the driver. Before Alina and the Warlord could do more than curse, the bike arched skyward, its gravlevs glowing blue against the night.

She broke stride, panting as she stared after the Tevan in rage. "Well, that absolutely grinds." Shaking her head, Alina turned toward her Warlord savior. "Thanks for—" She broke off.

He was easily two meters tall, with the lean, powerful build of a Comanche class Warlord, built for agility and speed as much as strength. His hair was a rich dark sable, and a small, neat beard framed his sensual mouth. The intricate tattoo of Arvid House spilled down the left side of his handsome face in brilliant iridescent blue and scarlet.

Her attention narrowed into the small circle at the base of the tatt, right over the hollow of his strong cheekbone. The circle had not been filled in. Like her, he was still unmarried. After all these years.

The lust that was one of the side effects of *riaat* rolled through her in a hot and burning wave, blended with pure longing. It had been so damn long since she'd seen him, touched him. "Baird," she choked, her voice shaking. Sweet Goddess, she wanted him.

Too bad she could never have him.

Baird stood frozen, staring at her, taking in the blood smearing the side of her face, the loneliness and hunger in her eyes. His own blood burned with *riaat* lust and pain, and he took a step forward, tempted to push her to the pedwalk and take her right there.

Instead he stopped and clenched his fists, fighting himself. He didn't mind the desire—he understood that. The aftermath of *riaat* always engulfed his body in an erotic storm.

What bothered him was the pain. It felt as if someone had scooped a huge, aching hole out of the center of his chest, and the only thing that would fill it was her. Despite the investigation, despite duty and honor, despite the long, bitter years that had passed, he wanted her still.

He couldn't afford that. He had a job to do.

Comp, kill the riaat lust, Baird ordered. Instantly, the desire began to drain away, leaving his body feeling cold. Yet the pain remained, searing him like a beamer burn.

"Damn you, Alina," he gritted. She had no right to such power over him.

She opened her mouth as if to retort, but her face suddenly paled. Her eyes widened and rolled back in her head.

Baird jumped forward to catch her before she hit the ground. She felt lighter than he remembered as he lowered her to the pedwalk. *What are her injuries?*

Concussion, fractured cheekbone, two cracked ribs, and extensive bruising and lacerations, his internal computer replied. *Given the extent of her injuries, a medtech is advisable.*

And yet she'd waded back into the fight with the Tevan to back him up, then helped him chase the bastard down the alley. Some of that lunatic endurance had been *riaat,* but the rest had been pure, stubborn Alina.

Call a unit, he ordered. Aloud, he said, "Alina? Alina, talk to me."

She lifted her blond head, combat beaded braids clinking. "Baird. Goddess, Baird, been so long. Missed you . . ."

He had to control the impulse to tighten his grip on her. His comp was draining off the chemicals of *riaat,* but he was still more than strong enough to hurt her without meaning to. "I missed you, too, brat." He had to stop to clear his throat. He'd always hated seeing her hurt.

Her eyes rolled. "Galar. Where's Galar?"

"What?" He remembered his files. Galar was Rajin's ten-year-old son. Why was she asking about him? But before he could question her, her head dropped against his shoulder.

Maybe Rajin had her working as the boy's bodyguard when she wasn't using her for . . . other tasks.

The rising wail of a medunit's siren drew his eyes skyward. The big vehicle came in fast and low, riding on its intricate arrangement of gravlev fields. As it set down, Baird walked to meet it, cradling Alina gently in his arms.

A woman in the blue uniform of a medtech towed a gleaming transparent tube from the back of the unit. "Put her in here," she said as the tube's lid slid back.

Baird placed Alina in the tube and stepped back, watching anxiously as the curving lid sealed and a pink gas pumped to fill it.

A trid of Alina's body appeared over the tube, her injuries outlined in red. The tech studied them and murmured a few soft commands before turning toward him. Her skin was a metallic silver that contrasted vividly with the pale blue of her hair. She was as human as Baird was, which meant her coloring was either a product of genetic tinkering or cosmetics—it was tough to say which. Faint lines around her eyes suggested she was well into her eighties. "How about you? You've got some bruises, too," she said, stepping over to aim a handheld scanner at him. "What the hell happened, anyway? Did you do that to her?"

Outraged, he glared at the tech. "What, beat her like that? Don't be ridiculous. We're both Vardonese warriors."

The woman's gaze lifted, belatedly taking in his braids and command beads. "Oh, yeah, I've heard of you." Cynicism gleamed in her eyes. "You guys take some kind of vow. Vardon is one of those matriarchal planets, right? You've got that female aristocracy, the Femays or something."

"The *Femmats*."

Two hundred years before, a group of idealistic scientists had colonized Vardon, intent on creating a utopia. Since most violence was committed by young men, they decided to tinker with their own genetic code to eliminate male aggression. But they'd also realized they needed protection from all the aggressive colonies around them, so they created a defense force of super warriors—the Warlords and their female equivalent, Warfems.

Raised in Warlord Creches to learn loyalty and obedience, the Warriors were indentured to the companies that created them, then sent into military service. They all took a vow to protect those weaker than themselves, male or female, adult or child.

Now guilt pricked Baird's outrage. Alina had been his partner, his lover and his best friend for five years. For him, that had been a very strong bond, even if Alina had turned her back on it in the end.

Yet his actions today had put her in that regenerator.

Still, if what they suspected was true, her bond with him wasn't the only one Alina had violated. That was why Baird had volunteered for this mission. He had to find out if she was guilty, prove her innocence if she wasn't, and stop her if she was.

It was a matter of honor.

"So if you didn't do it to her, who did?" the tech asked.

"A Tevan cyborg."

Pale blue eyebrows flew upward. "A Tevan? Who did you two piss off, anyway?"

"I have no idea. The Tevan was beating her, so I stepped in." Which was the truth—more or less.

The tech snorted. "Good thing you did. The lizard probably would have killed her."

"It certainly looked that way." And when he got his hands on the bastard, Baird was going to kick his ass.

Alina woke as the regenator's pink mist drained away. Disoriented, she watched the transparent lid slide back, blinking hazily at the stars overhead.

"Alina? Are you all right?" The deep voice cut through her mental fog, snapping her instantly to attention.

"Baird?" Her heart leaped. He stood beside the tube, looking grim as a medtech trained a scanner on her. Alina started to roll off the tube stretcher. The world reeled around her, almost dumping her on her face.

Baird caught her. "Take it slow, Alina. You always get the spins after a session in regen."

She gave him a look as she steadied herself against his strong chest. "I'm touched you remember." She was surprised he'd even care, particularly after that last row they'd had over Rajin's ultimatum.

Twenty years ago.

A long time. No wonder he's changed.

Baird had been barely twenty the last time she'd seen him. He was taller now, harder, more muscular than the boy she'd fought beside for five years.

That was only to be expected, she supposed. They'd been half-starved little animals then, fighting the Xeran invaders with all the savagery of wolf-cats. Now the Xer were gone, and the great Femmat Houses of Vardon were richer and more powerful than ever. Which wasn't exactly a blessing, at least in Alina's case.

Baird frowned down at her, visibly worried. "How are you feeling?"

She straightened away from him, though she wanted nothing more than to rest against his strength.

Unfortunately, it was a luxury Alina couldn't afford. In all the ways that mattered, nothing had changed where she and Baird were concerned. "I'm fine." And she was, she realized, probing her face with cautious fingers.

"You weren't half an hour ago," the medtech told her. "Concussion, fractured cheekbone, cracked ribs. Stay out of fights with Tevans, okay?"

"I'll take that under advisement." Alina inhaled, pleased to note the lack of pain. Everything felt solid and sturdy again. The regenator had done its job with its usual efficiency.

"Good." Nodding, the tech turned to shepherd her machine back into the emergency unit.

As it lifted off, Alina couldn't resist another look at Baird. Examining the beads braided into his hair, she spotted a ruby that signified a captaincy in the Vardon Stellar Command, along with twenty years' worth of service and combat decorations. They made a glittering display against his sable mane.

He was wearing the uniform, too, a blue unisuit piped with command red, a captain's scarlet insignia decorating his high collar. The dark colors drew attention to his face, with its strong, angular bone structure that was, if anything, more handsome than she remembered.

Yet there was something in those golden eyes that was much older than she knew him to be. Warlords didn't live as long as Femmat aristocrats, but forty was still quite young.

So why did those eyes look so weary, so hard and disillusioned? What had happened to him on the way to all those combat decorations?

Still, Alina felt a twinge of envy for his military splendor. All she wore were the beads she'd won in the invasion. Rajin Kasi had refused to let her serve after that. *"Kasi House spent a great deal of money on your genetic engineering, your cybernetics, and your education,"* the Femmat aristocrat had told her. *"We mean to get a return on our investment."*

As a gesture of gratitude, most Houses had emancipated the genetically engineered warriors who'd fought to free Vardon from the Xer. The reasoning went that no matter what each company had spent creating their Warlords and Warfem, the fighters had more than paid it back during that five-year guerrilla war.

Rajin, as Kasi House president, hadn't agreed. At least not when it came to Alina. But when she'd forbidden further contact with Baird, Alina had seriously considered suing for her freedom. Unfortunately she knew what price Rajin would exact.

She hadn't even dared tell Baird why she hadn't, which had resulted in that last bitter fight. He hadn't spoken to her since.

Until tonight.

"The Tevan hurt you," Baird said, jolting her out of her painful preoccupation. His golden eyes were fixed so hungrily on her face, she'd have thought he was still in the aftermath of *riaat* if her computer hadn't told her otherwise. Lifting a big hand, he brushed his knuckles across her healed cheekbone in a tender gesture at odds with his curled lip. "He's lucky he got away. I'd have killed him for that."

Alina inhaled sharply at his warm, callused touch. She tried to cover her reaction with a smile. "You always were protective."

"I've missed you." His deep voice sounded a little hoarse.

"You're not . . . still angry?"

Those beautiful eyes flickered, and she knew he lied. "No. You were only doing your duty to your House."

Which wasn't what he'd said at the time. He'd called her a coward then, too gutless to stand up to Rajin's blatant abuse. And she hadn't been able to explain.

For ten years, Alina had wondered if he was right about her cowardice. Then Galar was born, and she'd known her sacrifice was worth it.

Too bad she still couldn't explain to Baird. She'd love to damn the consequences and spill the whole story, but she wouldn't be the only one to face Rajin's rage. She couldn't take the chance.

Instead she changed the subject, gently tugging one of the braids that swung by his temple. "Judging by the beads, you've done well for yourself."

His smile flashed white. "Judging by the murder attempt, you're still pissing people off. What was that all about, anyway?"

She stiffened with the automatic wariness of twenty years as a courier for Rajin Kasi. Then she forced a shrug and a grin. "As you said, I must have pissed someone off."

"Need a bodyguard?"

Goddess, yes. Data thieves might dare an attempt on her, but they'd steer well clear of a Warlord. And if they didn't, they'd regret it. But . . . Reluctantly, she shook her head. "Rajin would throw a rod. You know how she is about us."

He lifted a dark brow. "Is Rajin here?"

"Waiting for me on Calista."

"Calista is twenty-four light years away. She doesn't have to know." Baird frowned. "Besides, hasn't Kasi House emancipated you by now? Even if you weren't a Xeran Invasion veteran, most Houses demand no more than ten years' service."

"Rajin says soon." She'd been saying "soon" for the past ten years. Alina knew "soon" would never arrive unless she found a way to force it.

"You could take Kasi to court, sue for emancipation."

Not a day went by that she didn't dream of doing just that. "It's complicated."

Perceptive golden eyes studied her face. "Why don't we go someplace a little more secure, and you can explain it to me?"

She wavered, tempted despite the risk. Goddess, she'd love to tell him the whole story, face his rage, and get it over with. Maybe he'd listen and forgive.

Maybe he'd even help her get Galar away from Rajin. She'd sacrifice anything for the boy's safety. Hell, she had already sacrificed her heart, her happiness and her honor. Nothing else was left.

Except the boy's life.

No, she couldn't risk that. But she could be with Baird, if only for tonight. Feed her hunger for him. Make love to him again. Store up memories. Surely she deserved that much? "Yes," Alina said, her voice hoarse with need. "I'd like to . . . catch up."

She wanted to do a great deal more than catch up. And judging from the bulge in those snug uniform trousers, so did Baird.

CH@%!*R
3

Baird's smile flashed white against his darkly tanned face. He took Alina's hand. "My hotel?"

His hotel. His bed. "Sounds good." He probably rated better accommodations than she did. Kasi House always booked cheap lodgings for her, which usually meant a spacer's hostel in the worst section of whatever port city she landed in. The theory was that she could look out for herself. Which she could, but she'd frankly gotten very tired of sleeping in vermin-infested sackracks.

As Alina watched, Baird turned his gaze skyward, his handsome profile outlined against the stars, and sent out a call for a zipcab through his communications implant. Automatically, she looked up, too.

"Alina," he said suddenly.

She half-turned, and he stepped against her, all dark male strength, his hands big and warm as they came to rest on her waist. Then his mouth lowered to hers, and she forgot all her worry and bitterness. Hot, wet, flavored with some delicious alien spice, his lips moved over hers. They were much more skillful than they'd been when he was a pretty young warrior just coming to his power. This was the kiss of a man who knew exactly what he was doing and the best way to go about doing it. She found herself sinking against him with a low moan of need.

God, she wanted him. On her, in her, however she could get him. Now. She wasn't even all that sure she could wait for a bed.

A burst of musical notes played, jerking them from each other's arms as the zipcab descended. It came to a hovering halt, announcing its rates in a purring female voice. Shaped roughly like a curving wedge, it wore a brilliant paint-job advertising some local bar. Its forward passenger door slid open in invitation.

Baird looked down at Alina, a warm gleam of anticipation in his eyes. "Shall we?"

"Goddess, yes."

They scooted inside to sink into deep blue upholstery. Alina sat back with a sigh, her tired body enjoying the luxury. The seats adjusted as they settled in, cupping around backs and butts. In the event of a crash, they'd also surround the cab's occupants with soft, protective cocoons.

The cab had no driver, though it did have a triangular yoke that thrust from its dash—part of its manual emergency controls in case the navigation computer went down. Baird murmured the address of his hotel, and the cab took off, soaring straight up to merge with the traffic overhead.

Alina barely had time to glimpse the lights of the city receding below before he pulled her out of her seat and into his lap. His mouth claimed hers, demanding and hot. She moaned and kissed him back.

For long, sweet moments, she simply forgot herself in the kiss, in the heat of his mouth, so familiar and yet so different. She wrapped one arm around his shoulder and the other in his long hair as he cuddled her in his lap. It was a pose they'd assumed a thousand times all those years before, but it felt very different now. He was hard and strong and broad in a way he hadn't been then, making her feel almost delicate. She found the differences deliciously arousing.

And so were his big, clever hands.

He found his way beneath the hem of her tunic to the skin that lay beneath, stroking gently across her waist and belly, then up to the curves of her breasts. "You're bigger than you used to be," he said softly, cupping her in long, warm fingers.

Alina smiled against his mouth. "So are you."

"You have that effect on me." He rolled his hips against her backside. The bulge of his erection was thick and long, making her shudder in longing greed.

She drew back to bite tenderly at his lower lip. "Taller. I meant you've grown taller."

He looked into her eyes. There was regret in his. "I was a boy then."

"Well, you're definitely not anymore." Alina wrapped her fingers in the thick black silk of his hair. Lowering her head, she took his mouth in a slow, sliding kiss.

He groaned, the sound vibrating deep and rough, and kissed her back.

Fear and bitterness spun away.

Despite Baird's suspicions, despite everything he knew about her, the taste of Alina was magic. In her arms, he felt a boy again, trembling with need and hunger for his first lover. Finally he had to draw back, gasping, to look into her face. The regenator's mist had cleaned the blood away, and the bruises and swelling were gone. He could see her now.

Alina looked even lovelier than she had twenty years ago. She'd lost the haunted look of partial starvation, flesh filling in the stark hollows under her high cheekbones. Her body felt solid with healthy muscle, and her breasts filled his hands with their soft weight.

But her pretty mouth had the same sweet curve, and those eyes were just as big and violet as they'd always been. Even the beads in her blond hair were the same. That probably galled her; she should have a collection of promotion and campaign honors as impressive as his. That bitch Rajin had refused to let her serve.

She'd evidently had other plans for Alina.

Hate stirred in his heart, chill and bitter. If his lover had violated her oath, it was because of the Femmat.

Yet Alina could have walked away at any time. The girl he'd known would have, rather than be involved in Rajin's crimes. Why hadn't she? What hold did the Femmat have on her?

"Baird?" Alina lifted her head, frowning. "Is something wrong?"

He forced a smile and raked his thumb over a tight nipple. "Nothing, sweet. Nothing at all."

They were still caressing each other when the cab chimed, announcing their arrival at their destination. With a groan of frustrated reluctance, Alina drew back from Baird's deliciously tempting mouth.

Resting his forehead against hers, he said huskily, "Patience, love. I want to take you in a bed, not a zipcab." He drew back and rested his palm on the cab's payment screen, authorizing it to charge his credit account. The fare paid, the cab popped its door and let them out on the pedwalk.

Straightening the hem of her tunic with a jerk, Alina looked up at the hotel towering over their heads. She'd been right—this was no sackrack, though not an aristocrat's lodgings either. It was the sort of inexpensive, decent place that catered to travelers of Baird's rank and class. She should be able to get a good night's sleep here, uninterrupted by sexual groans penetrating inadequate soundproofing.

Though she strongly suspected she'd be too busy making pleasure noises of her own to notice anyone else's. She really didn't anticipate getting all that much sleep, not judging from the hot male hunger in Baird's eyes.

Though there'd been a moment when she'd seen something else, something that looked a lot like rage. Something fresher than two-decade-old anger over their breakup.

But when he reached for her hand, she gave it, threading her fingers gratefully between his long, strong ones. Even that chaste contact made her body hum.

They walked into the building together, past the trids advertising exotic liquors, restaurants, clothing, and sex entertainers. The lobby itself was bright and well lit, decorated in bright colors, with a soaring, transparent ceiling. A massive central mobile constructed of flowing shapes dominated the vast space, chiming softly.

Alina and Baird didn't linger to sightsee, instead heading straight for the glass-enclosed antigrav lift. It opened at their approach, and they stepped inside. The double doors closed with a musical trill, sealing them in the tube as it slid smoothly upward. Through the glass, she noticed a pair of grav-dancers soaring around one another in the center of the lobby, their bodies nude except for swirls of glittering paint. No sooner did they come together than one or the other swooped away, so that they dove and soared like birds. Watching them, Alina felt her heart ache.

"They're a pretty good metaphor for us, aren't they?" Baird asked softly, watching her face.

"You always were far too good at reading my mind." She turned away from the dancers and forced a smile. "I don't want to think about that now."

His face hardened. "No, I don't suppose you do." The doors opened. "And neither do I."

Before she could move, he bent and swept her up into his arms, startling a laugh out of her as he carried her out into the hall. Alina wasn't used to feeling delicate, yet cradled in those powerful arms, she did—and she loved it.

Baird strode down the corridor with her, surefooted and powerful. Alina stared up into his tight profile, wondering at the hint of danger she felt from him, the edge of anger.

Yes, this was more than the old grudge. But what?

His room responded to his biological signature at their

approach, and its door slid open in welcome. He carried her inside without breaking step.

The room was a simple enough affair. Its only furniture was a small table in the corner flanked by a couple of chairs, and a huge oval bed covered in dark blue slick-sheets that matched the carpet.

Baird tossed her lightly on the bed. Alina landed with an unwarrior-like gasp and giggle.

"Strip," he growled.

She'd have told another man exactly what he could do with his commands, but this was Baird. Smiling wickedly, she rolled onto hands and knees and stared at him through the curtain of her blond braids. "Do I look like one of your recruits, Captain?"

"You look like a Warfem who's about to get fucked." He grabbed the seal of his unisuit and dragged it down in one ruthless motion. As she watched, breath caught, he stripped the suit off to stand boldly naked. His cock bobbed free, flushed and thick.

Alina swallowed, her hungry gaze fixed on his broad, sculpted chest. It was furred in a dark ruff of chest hair that narrowed to a trail leading straight to that impressive cock. His legs were long, the thighs and calves thick and round with brawn. As she stared at him, dry-mouthed with desire, he strode to the wall. A panel slid open at his approach, and he reached inside to pull out a length of flexible forcecable.

She raised a brow, interested but not shocked. Warlords tended to be fairly inventive when it came to sex. "We never did bondage before."

Baird shrugged, braids swinging beside one high cheek-bone. "It seems to suit my mood. You're still not naked." His eyes were glowing red, a Warlord's indicator of stark lust. He was on the verge of losing control.

Heart pounding, Alina reached for the hem of her tunic and pulled it over her head. He went still, watching as she flicked open the closure of her breastband. The band fell away, freeing her breasts. His eyes widened and flared bright red.

Deliberately taunting, she rolled onto her back and slid her boots and trousers off, taking her time, letting him get a good look. Smoothly, easily, she lifted on leg and pointed the toe at the ceiling. He licked his lips and dropped his gaze between her thighs, and she hid a smile. "Is this naked enough for you, Captain?"

"Perhaps a little too naked," he said, his voice hoarse. "I think you need to accessorize."

Baird moved so fast even Alina was taken by surprise. One minute he was across the room, staring hot-eyed at her nudity. The next, he was on the bed and spinning her around so she was on her knees with her back to him. He pulled one of her wrists behind her back and wrapped it in the forcecable, then bound the other wrist, too.

Alina inhaled at the wild arousal that exploded low in her belly. She twisted around to grin at him. "You taking me captive, Baird?"

For just a moment, she thought she glimpsed bitterness in his golden eyes. "It seems to be the only way I can keep you."

CH@%!*R

4

Before she could question that flash of dark anger, Baird caught her breasts in his warm, long-fingered hands, and she gasped. Skillfully, he rolled her tight nipples between thumbs and forefingers until pleasure furled through her like a red silk ribbon. "Believe me," she wheezed, "I have no desire to go anywhere."

"Are you sure?" He raked his teeth gently over the straining cords of her throat.

She shivered. "Ooohhhh, yes." His fingers tightened, pulled, pinched. Each tiny motion created glittering sensations that raced through her body in a river of fire headed straight between her thighs. "Especially when you do that."

"Then I'll do it some more. You have the most luscious nipples." He twisted the little tips until she squirmed her butt against the hard ridge of his cock.

"Glad you"—she had to stop to pant—"glad you approve."

"Oh, I definitely approve." Baird reached down between her thighs, finding the very spot that craved his touch. His fingers slipped easily in the slick cream that had risen as he'd played with her. "And I'm not the only one."

"That's putting it mildly." Alina let her head fall back against his shoulder as he strummed nipple and clit.

"Bed," he ordered the mattress, "I need a little hump. About fifty centimeters high and forty across." Obediently, the bed extruded a soft mound of mattress. Baird draped her belly-down across it, then moved in behind her.

Alina licked her lips in anticipation. With her wrists bound at the small of her back, she felt deliciously vulnerable and intensely aroused. She'd never played sexual games before—which probably wasn't surprising, given that her encounters had been rare and hurried, usually driven by *riaat* hunger more than true attraction. The only man she'd ever really wanted had been Baird.

And now, for tonight at least, she had him.

The bed shifted under her knees, and she tensed, swallowing. Shooting a quick look over her shoulder, she saw him kneel at the foot of the bed and lower his head to her backside. His fingers parted her labia for his tongue.

Alina groaned as he gave her sex a long, slow lick that ran right between the seam of her lips up to her clit. "Oh, sweet Goddess!" She stopped to pant. "You do realize I don't really need any more foreplay?"

"Perhaps not." He took one of her lips between his teeth and gave it a gentle, teasing tug. "But I've waited for this a very long time, and I'm going to make it last." He released her, then went for her clit, his tongue dancing over the hard little nub.

Pleasure jolted through her body like bolts of current. "In that case"— she had to stop to moan—"be my guest."

A long forefinger slid into her sex, slowly, as he angled his head and licked. Each flick of his tongue felt like a hot little flame, and Alina writhed, maddened. She could feel her climax heating, stoked by that working finger and his clever mouth.

Her sweet young lover had grown into a big, skilled, outrageously sexy stranger.

The orgasm built like a storm about to break, hot and fast and . . .

He stopped. "Not yet."

"*What?*" Outraged, she tried to grind down on the finger so temptingly deep inside her.

Baird snatched it away from her and slapped a hand down on her hip, stilling her. "Not yet."

"You can't . . ."

"I can." His tone was hard and inflexible, one she'd never heard from him before. "This time I set the course. Not you. And fucking well not Rajin Kasi." The tip of a callused finger circled her clit. Sparks of heat and arousal danced at the contact.

"Yes, master." She'd intended the words as mocking, but they emerged too faint, straining under the weight of desire.

"That's better." The humor was back in his voice again, though it had that dark, bitter edge she kept glimpsing in him.

"You carrying a grudge, Baird?"

"Who, me?" His laughter was a sexual rumble that made tiny muscles ripple inside her. "What gives you that idea?"

And Baird drove his cock into her sex in one hard, long thrust that made her back arch. "Just wondering," she wheezed.

"You okay?" The question was abrupt, almost as if he didn't want to ask.

"Fine," she managed. He began to pull out, and the sliding pleasure made her moan. "Better than fine."

"Good." There was that dark satisfaction again. He was definitely working off a grudge. And he was entitled to one. Imagining his reaction if he knew her secret, she winced.

Then Baird was pushing inside, and she forgot everything else but how good it felt to be full of him again.

He thrust slowly, taking his time. Sometimes he added artistic little touches, working his way to the balls and then grinding his hips, raking both her clit and the walls of her sheath with merciless pleasure.

Alina hunched back at him, dying to come. But every time she was about to go over, he pulled away.

"You've got a mean streak," she managed, the third time he stalled her orgasm.

"Now that you mention it"—he drove in yet another hard thrust that tormented her sweetly—"I do. Maybe you should keep that in mind."

"Noted." He did that wicked little thing with his hips again. Unable to stand it any longer, she writhed, whimpering. "God, Baird, please . . ."

"Please, what?"

Her temper snapped. "*Let me come,* blaze you!"

He drew out, eased in. "You could always have your computer send you over."

"I don't want the flipping comp! *I want you!*"

Male satisfaction rang in his voice. "That's all I wanted to know." He started pumping, long and strong and hard, grinding just enough.

The climax he'd been holding off exploded through her body in a silent rain of sparks. She yowled, almost blinded by its savagery. It was so much fiercer than anything she'd ever felt, a feral erotic storm that made her convulse like a woman in a seizure.

Distantly, Alina heard Baird's triumphant roar as he began to shoot his seed deep inside her.

Limp and thoroughly sated, she scarcely noticed when Baird untied her wrists and told the bed to flatten out again. She roused only when he picked her up, flipped the covers back, and slipped between them with her. "That was . . . I can't think of a word to do it justice."

He curled muscled arms around her and pulled her back into the sweaty warmth of his big body. "I can safely say it was my pleasure."

Sweaty or not, he felt good. "Goddess, I wish I could stay with you."

Baird stiffened. It was slight, but she knew him well enough to notice. "Do you have to leave now?"

Alina sighed. "Not now. I'm supposed to ship out to Calista in the morning. Rajin's waiting for me there."

"As it happens, I'm headed for Calista, too." When she glanced up in surprise, he shrugged. "I'm joining my new ship there. We didn't have anything headed that way, so I'm taking a civilian transport. *The Antares Empress*."

"That's the same ship I'm booked for." Alina hesitated. Had he been a stranger, she'd have found that detail a little too coincidental. But this was Baird, and he would no more work for an enemy of Vardon than he could breathe hard vacuum. "We could spend more time together."

He lifted a dark brow. "Won't that torque Rajin?"

Alina grinned, feeling suddenly reckless. "I'll argue I need a bodyguard. After the business with the Tevan, she won't kick too hard."

Baird studied her face, his golden gaze perceptive. "Why do I get the impression you're not terribly happy with the old . . . Femmat?"

"I haven't been happy with Kasi's esteemed president in twenty years."

"Then sue. You know damn well you'd win."

Alina looked away. "I can't afford an attorney."

Baird frowned, visibly puzzled. "Aren't you a member of the Guild?"

"Of course." She'd joined the Vardonese Guild of Warriors decades ago.

"Then they'd provide you with an attorney, given the circumstances. That's what they're for—to intercede between warriors and the Femmatocracy."

He was right, of course, but there was a great deal he didn't know. "As I said before, it's complicated." She gave him a hot grin. "And I'd much rather make love than explain."

Baird looked at her for a long moment, his gaze wary. Then he smiled, though it looked a little tight. "You've got a very good point."

*   *   *

The night passed in a delicious blur of passion that ended in sated, exhausted sleep.

Baird woke the next morning as he'd woken so many times twenty years before—with Alina cuddled against his side, warm and trusting.

He lifted his head and looked down into her sleeping face. One of her blond braids lay across a high cheekbone, adorned in the campaign beads she'd won risking her life beside him. In the bright morning sunlight, he suddenly noticed faint shadows under her eyes, as if worry and guilt were constant companions.

And well they should be, if his suspicions were true.

Seeing her lids lift, he forced a smile. "Good morning, sweet. Hungry?"

Alina yawned hugely and gave him a grin that made his heart catch. "After all that *riaat*—and all that sex? I could eat a Soji Dragon. Raw."

His smile was more genuine this time. "I trust the hotel restaurant can produce something a little more tender than that."

"God, I hope so. Does this place have a real water shower?"

"I think so."

She rolled out of bed, long and lithe and breathtakingly naked. Her breasts were high and full, and she had a tight waist, a sweetly curving backside that felt perfect in his hands, and long, muscular legs. "Good. The sackracks Kasi likes to stick me in have nothing but sonics. I know they get you clean, but I never really feel like it."

His eyes followed her delectable backside as she made for the bathroom. He rose and strode after her. "Then by all means; let's get wet."

By the time they emerged from the shower, they were both prune-skinned and pleasantly sore from yet another dizzying sexual encounter. "Why don't you go down and order for us," he told her as they dressed, him in his captain's uniform, her in the violet tunic and black pants that made the most of her dramatic coloring. "I need to make a few calls."

She gave him another of those flashing, wicked grins. "Make it quick, or I'll eat your breakfast, too."

He forced a grin. "I'll risk it. Get me something with plenty of meat."

"Okay." She frowned, scratching her eyebrow. "We're going to need to catch a cab and swing by my hostel before we head to the shuttleport. We have to be aboard *The Antares Empress* by 1400 hours."

"I know. We've got plenty of time."

Alina nodded and sauntered out. Baird's gaze lingered on her swaying hips until the door closed behind her. He locked his sensors on her as she walked down the hall, scanning her progress through the walls.

It was only after he knew she was gone that he walked to the wall panel that hid his secure com unit. He could have used his internal communication system, of course, but there was a chance Alina would somehow manage to intercept it.

And considering the call he was about to make, that would be very bad.

CH@%!*R
5

The panel sensed him and slid open. Baird pulled out the oblong bag that held his gear, opened the seal, and spilled the hand-sized unit into his palm. Popping open the small screen, he sat down on the bed and murmured the voice command. There was a long, annoying wait while the unit set up communications with his contact.

Then the Tevan's familiar face appeared on the screen. They'd been partners for five years, ever since Baird left ship service for the intelligence branch of the Vardonese military.

"I'm in," Baird told him. "We don't have to keep trying to convince her she needs my protection."

Four yellow eyes rolled. "Gods and goddesses, that's the best news I've had all day. You broke my ribs, you bastard."

"You deserved it. I told you not to hurt her, Ualtar. She had to go into regen."

"So did I." His partner's amber gaze searched his. "And may I remind you, if she's involved, a few bruises are the least she deserves."

Baird frowned. "I still can't believe she knows what's going on."

"You don't sound as convinced as you were last night."

He raked a hand through his long hair. "She seemed . . . unusually evasive."

"You mean guilty." Ualtar shook his spiked head. "I told you, Baird. She's in this up to her horns—if she had any."

"Ualtar, there's no way she's working for them. Not Alina."

"It's been twenty years, brother. You don't know what she's capable of." The Tevan leaned closer to the pickup, his expression grim. "And I don't want you finding out the hard way."

"I can handle her."

"Not if you keep thinking with your dick. You have to maintain your objectivity on this, or you're going to end up dead. These people do not play around."

"Believe me, Ualtar, I know exactly what they're capable of."

"Yeah, but they're not the real problem, are they? She is."

Baird killed the com link and clicked the unit closed. Brooding, he tossed the little device aside and leaned an elbow on his thigh.

He'd become an adept and skillful liar after joining Vardonese Intelligence, but lying to Alina had been surprisingly difficult. He ached to confront her with their suspicions and beg her to prove herself innocent, but he couldn't. There was too much at risk. If she was involved in treason and discovered he was on her trail, the enemy would slip through their fingers like smoke.

Still, he couldn't believe the laughing lover he'd known during the occupation could have become a traitor. She'd been too forthright, too loyal, too courageous.

Restlessly, he rose from the bed and began to pace in long strides. As much as he hated to admit it to himself, two decades had changed Alina. She'd become closed and wary. Too often last night, he'd seen fear in her eyes. But fear of what? Him? The thought made something clench tight in his chest.

Because she had reason to fear him. If she was a traitor, he'd destroy her. Considering the rage that boiled through him at the very idea, he didn't think he was even capable of showing her mercy.

He hated traitors. Over the past five years, he'd watched them work to destroy their own people for personal advancement. He'd do anything to stop them. Anything at all. Lie, kill, whore, or steal, it didn't matter. Nothing mattered except stopping them.

He'd loved Alina with everything in his soul, and she'd turned her back on him. But had she also turned her back on everything they'd once believed in? Everything he still believed in? Sweet Goddess, he hoped not.

Because when he'd lain with Alina in his arms last night, looking down into those brilliant eyes, he'd realized he loved her still. Despite everything she'd done to him, despite the decades of separation. None of it mattered. He loved her.

If she was a traitor, her destruction would be his own.

The Antares Empress catered to professional spacers and soldiers from a dozen different worlds. Its accommodations were not lush by any means, but they were relatively comfortable.

The ship itself was shaped roughly like a star, with a globular central body that housed passenger and command functions. Several long, spine-like pylons thrust out from the core, housing the generators that created the jumpspace bubble around the ship, permitting it to travel at supralight velocities.

Baird and Alina got settled into their respective quarters, then arranged to meet in the ship's workout deck. Building and maintaining muscle was almost a religion for Vardonese warriors. The trip time was an opportunity to get in a little training.

Among other things.

They could have ended up with worse facilities, Baird

decided when he walked onto the exercise deck. It was completely open, wrapped around with a heavily shielded viewport that gave a stunning view of jumpspace. Stars streamed past, bleeding a kaleidoscope of hot colors—the radiation of this alien dimension, where the laws of physics no longer quite applied. If it hadn't been for the bubble of normal space that protected the ship, the bizarre forces around them would have torn the *Empress* apart.

The deck itself was equipped with benches and assorted equipment designed to work specific muscle groups. Baird preferred the simplicity of gravity bars. He picked up one of the featherweight rods from the rack that held them and chose a spot where he could keep an eye on the lift.

He was doing arm curls with the gravity bar when Alina walked in. The sight of her was incendiary, clad in that narrow breastband and hipsnugs that displayed every lush curve of her long body. Baird almost dropped the bar as his cock hardened with a rush of approval.

Evidently his body didn't share his doubts.

Alina grinned and returned his hungry gaze, violet eyes mischievous. Since he wore nothing more than a pair of snugs, there was a lot of him on display. He barely suppressed the urge to flex.

She strolled over to one of the racks that held the bars, chose one of medium length, and lifted it down. Steadying it with both hands, she murmured, "One hundred kilos." The wiry muscles in her arms leaped into relief as the bar immediately increased its weight to the setting she dictated.

Lazily, she began to rotate the rod like a quarterstaff as she strolled toward him, arms flexing as she worked to control the weight. "There's something about a man concentrating on working up a sweat that makes me want to . . . distract him." Looking at the rod he held, she lifted a blond brow. "But considering how much weight you've got on that bar, I'll refrain. Hate for you to put a hole in the deck."

Baird breathed deeply and did another slow, deliberate curl. His arms felt as if they were on fire, but his ego wouldn't even let him grunt. "I'll try not to drop it."

"You never used to lift that much." She grinned. "But then—you've grown."

"Like I said, so have you." His gaze lingered on the full mounds of her breasts, barely contained in that band. "I remember when you were a skinny little fifteen-year-old, all legs and bravado." The thought of her innocence then stabbed him in the heart. He had to look away.

Alina laughed and moved away until she had room to swing the rod without hitting him. Falling into a combat stance, she took a deep breath and leaped into the air, whirling her weapon in a mock attack on imaginary opponents. Unable to resist, he found himself watching her again, admiring the flex and play of her slender muscles.

"I was so damn green, I pissed chartreuse," she told him. "Which I did frequently, since I was terrified all the time." She stopped, one knee lifted high, the bar held in perfect balance. It was a breathtaking display of strength and athleticism even by Warlord standards.

Baird lowered his own bar to watch. "I thought you were very brave." And honest, and loyal. Had he been wrong?

"Had you fooled." She whipped around, slicing the bar in a hissing arc. "But the lieutenant saw through both of us."

He smiled slightly, remembering. "Lieutenant Grev and Sergeant Avo. I wouldn't be alive today if the sergeant hadn't saved my ass. Five or six times." Baird had been a half-grown kid fresh out of House Arvid Creche, pressed into duty only because the invading Xer would have shot him on sight simply for being a Warlord. Grev and Avo had taught him and Alina tactics, discipline, and the art of staying alive.

Pumping a kick at one imaginary opponent, Alina thrust the bar in a move Avo had taught them both. "God, those two loved one another. First time I'd seen married warriors."

Baird nodded. There had been six warriors in their guerilla unit to start out with, but two of them fell to the Xer early on. Over the next four years, Alina, the Warfem Grev, and her Warlord husband, Avo, had become the closest thing Bard had ever known to family.

The two adults had loved each other with such utter commitment, they'd inspired Baird and Alina to start playing at passion. In time, what had begun as imitation love grew into the real thing.

"There's a reason you don't see bonded warriors that much, though," he said, brooding. "His wife's death at the Xer's hands gutted Avo. He got reckless and sloppy. And it got him killed." Good thing Baird and Alina had been nineteen by then, seasoned by four years in combat, or they'd never have survived without him.

"Love always carries a cost." The long muscles in her arms were beginning to tremble slightly, but she didn't seem to notice. Her gaze had turned inward, brooding. Then she smiled, sudden and blinding. "But it's worth it."

No. No, it wasn't. There'd been a time after Alina had left Baird that he, too, had courted death. But he'd been in the stellar service by then, and too many other lives depended on him. He'd steadied down, done his job, earned his medals.

But he'd never fallen in love again.

"You remember the Ortaris?" Alina asked suddenly.

Brows lifting, he looked up at her. "Yeah." They'd encountered the little family right after Sergeant Avo was killed. Baird himself had been badly hurt in the failed attempt to rescue the sergeant. Since there had been no regenator available, he'd had to heal the hard way. For the month it had taken him to recover, Mr. and Mrs. Ortari had hidden Baird and Alina in their basement. "The Xer would have killed us if it hadn't been for them."

Alina nodded. "Big risk, particularly considering the three kids."

"Yeah, that's right," Baird said, remembering. "There was the little baby, the ten-year-old son, and that teenage daughter."

"The one with the crush on you."

He grinned. "Suyo." The girl's attention had been almost as flattering as Alina's incandescent jealousy.

Apparently catching sight of his smug expression, Alina

turned and stuck out her tongue at him, a gesture she'd learned from Suyo herself. Baird roared with laughter, then had to throw up an arm to ward her off as she waved the gravity bar at him. "I should have known you'd remember her, rodent," Alina growled, thoroughly irritated.

"Rodent" had been her favorite insult before Avo taught her how to swear. Baird laughed even harder.

With a huff, she turned away and pretended to ignore him while he tried to get control of himself.

When his gasping laughter died, they settled into a companionable silence. Suddenly Alina asked, "Did you ever wonder what it would be like to have a mother?"

Baird frowned. Technically, neither had any mother beyond the genetic engineers who'd constructed their DNA. Both had been raised in their respective House Creches among several hundred other genetically engineered children. Their caretakers had been civilians and a few warrior instructors.

"I suppose," he admitted. "But I've always been a little skeptical about the whole mother concept. It seems a bit like one of those stories they tell little children, like the ones about fairies and talking wolves. It can't possibly be as good as they say."

Alina gave him a wicked little smile. "Actually, I've met a talking wolf or two."

Baird shot her an impatient look. "Cyborgs. You know what I mean."

"Yeah." She took up the combat pose again. "You were unconscious most of the time, but I got to watch Mrs. Ortari with her children. It was like Avo and Grev with us, except more so. Very warm and . . . nice." She swung the staff in a circle. "I envied those kids. She let me hold the baby sometimes."

"Oh?" Interested, he looked at her. Somehow he had the feeling this detail was more important than it sounded. "What was that like?"

"Frightening. And yet it was . . . there was this tiny person with these big eyes and miniature hands, and she looked at me the way nobody has ever looked at me before. Like I was . . . everything. At first it was uncomfortable, because I was so afraid I'd hurt her. But then"—she shrugged—"I liked it. I missed her when we left."

Baird frowned, realizing this had obviously been a major experience for her. "You never mentioned it."

"No. Thought about it a lot, though." Alina turned her attention to the bar. "Off," she told it, and went to put it away. "There's a zee-gee tank next door. Want to . . . practice?"

Something about the way she said the last word told him she had something more than martial arts in mind. "Sure. Why not?"

Already hardening in anticipation, he followed her across the corridor to the soaring, three-story, zero-gravity tank. Like most jumpships, *The Antares Empress* maintained simulated gravity, but the fields had been known to fail, especially during combat. Thus, anybody who ever served in space made it a point to practice zee-gee hand-to-hand techniques.

Besides, it was a hell of a lot of fun.

In zee-gee, Baird's size and weight advantage became mass he had to maneuver, which meant he and Alina could compete as physical equals. More or less.

Not that either of them had much competition in mind.

CH@%!*R

6

As they entered the tank, Baird checked it out with the wariness of long habit. You could get seriously hurt in a poorly designed tank.

Luckily, this one was first-rate, with well-padded curving walls one could hit at speed without breaking anything. More important, the jutting handholds were of the breakaway type, rounded and flexible, so a fighter didn't have to worry about impaling himself or his opponent during a throw.

"Gravity off," Alina told the ship's computer.

For a moment, Baird had the sickening sensation they were plunging downward, as if the chamber had become a elevator in free-fall. But that was just an illusion created as the artificial gravity vanished, and in a moment, his battle computer compensated.

From the corner of his eye, he saw Alina flex her legs and launch herself at the opposite wall. She hit the thick padding, bounced, and shot straight back toward him like a deliciously curved cannon shell. Baird kicked off and twisted, grabbing for her as she shot by. He managed to snag her upper arm and got towed along for his trouble, but as they tumbled toward the wall, he started wrapping himself around her. He needed to get those long arms and legs under control.

Then he'd have her.

Yet Alina had no intention of allowing herself to be had, at least not yet. She twisted as they hit the wall, grabbed a handhold, and heaved him clear before he had time to get a good grip. While he flailed, she kicked lazily away.

By the time Baird got himself stopped, she was grinning at him from the other end of the tank. "Point for me," she said, gently mocking.

Baird bared his teeth at her as his competitive instincts awakened in a hot rush. "That's the last one you get."

"I don't think so." Alina sprang.

This time he was ready when she barreled into him. Allowing her momentum to carry them toward the wall, he snagged her right wrist and slung a leg over her hip. Zeegee or not, he was still stronger than she was, and his arms and legs were longer. If he could get a good grip on her, he could do whatever he wanted.

And he wanted to do plenty, especially with that round little backside rubbing against his groin.

For whatever time they had together, he wanted all of her.

Unfortunately for his frustration level, Alina had learned her way around a tank sometime in the past twenty years, and she was flexible as an eelcat. She rammed an elbow into his sternum, squirmed loose when he gasped, and kicked away. He shot after her, his cock as hard as ferocrete behind the tough fabric of his snugs.

Alina hit the wall an instant before he did and caromed off like a billiard ball. He bounced after her, kicking hard enough to give himself the speed to catch her.

The trouble was, all that mass and momentum was hard to stop. As he overtook her, she twisted, grabbed him by the hand he reached with, and heaved. The physics of equal and opposite reactions sent him shooting in one direction while she shot in the other.

Laughing.

"That," he told her, "was a mistake."

She grinned. "Probably, but it was fun."

Baird peeled his lips back from his teeth. "We'll see."

There was something wickedly intoxicating about pushing her luck with Baird.

Probably because Alina could see the exact moment when it ran out. He looked at her across the width of the tank, his eyes flaring bright red with frustration and erotic hunger. His black hipsnugs barely contained his cock, which looked on the verge of escaping his waistband any minute. Hard muscle flexed all along his body as he gathered himself.

He wasn't playing anymore.

Her heart pounded hard, and her nipples were tight beneath the fabric of her breastband. She was already wet between the thighs.

Most men got sloppier when they were ticked off. Not Baird. Thanks to his training, he grew colder, more controlled. More dangerous. She deliberately gave him a goading grin and watched him explode.

He shot across the tank like a mortar shell. Alina launched herself off at an angle, determined to stay out of his grip as long as she could. She knew if he got his hands on her this time, she wouldn't be getting away until he was finished with her. And they'd both enjoy it more if she made him work for it.

Behind her, Baird's feet hit the tank wall with a meaty bang. She could almost feel him barreling after her, but she didn't look back as she bounced off one wall and shot toward another. A big hand swiped at her ankle and missed. She didn't stop to gloat, too intent on ricocheting off every flat surface she could find.

Chancing a quick look, she saw him at the other side of the tank, clinging to a handhold and watching her with predatory intensity. Her eyes widened as he launched, hard and fast. She tried to twist away, but she had too much momentum.

He hit her with a growl of male triumph, snapping one arm around her torso and knocking them both into a dizzy tumble. Blinded by her own whipping hair and flying beads, Alina tried to plant an elbow in his gut and kick free. He refused to let go. Instead he wrapped one long leg around her right hip and the other around her left calf. She drew a fist back for a quick punch, but he engulfed her wrist in one hand. Cursing, she tried for a left cross, but before the blow could land, he'd captured that hand, too.

Alina looked at him as they tumbled in midair. Her sense of humor pricked her instinctive competitive streak like a balloon, and she smiled. "Oops."

He grinned darkly at her from a tangle of free-floating hair and glittering beads. "Oops indeed. You seem to be caught."

"Maybe." She gave him a testing wiggle, but he tightened the grip of both legs, silently making it clear she wasn't going anywhere. If this had been a true fight, she'd have had to do some real damage if she wanted to break his hold.

Instead, Alina rolled her hips against the thick ridge of his erection. It felt so hard, she licked her lips in anticipation. "Well, now," she purred. "Apparently you've got me after all. What are you going to do now, Warlord?"

"What I'd do to any captured enemy." Baird's teeth flashed as he circled both her wrists with one big hand. "Search you for weapons." With his free hand, he pulled up the hem of her breastband. Freed, her breasts bounced, nipples tight and tingling. He grinned at them. "You do seem to be well-armed."

He swooped down to engulf one of the hard peaks with his mouth, gave it a slow, thorough suckling as he caressed the full mound with his free hand.

She inhaled sharply at the lazy rise of pleasure. "You've got a weapon or two of your own."

Baird looked up, gave her a slow, heart-stopping smile,

and rolled his hips slowly against her belly. "And I know how to use them."

"That's putting it mildly." With a moan, Alina savored the teasing promise of that big shaft, imagining how it would feel thrusting deep inside her. She rocked against him sinuously. "Here's a thought. Why don't you let me show you what I can do with that particular blade?"

He lifted a brow, intrigued. "You've talked me into it."

When Baird released her wrists, she went for the waist-band of his snugs and started pulling them off. It wasn't an easy maneuver in zero gravity. They found themselves tumbling slowly while she peeled and he tried to squirm free.

Baird started to laugh in a rich, almost tactile rumble that soon had Alina joining in. The laughter, and the clumsiness it engendered, only made them tumble faster.

Finally he snagged a handhold and steadied them long enough for them to strip, clinging together like giddy children.

"Damn, that felt good," Alina said, wrapping her arms around his waist as their clothing floated away. "It's been too damn long since I laughed like that."

The humor faded from his eyes as he studied her face. "I gather Rajin hasn't mellowed out of her bitch streak."

"No, not exactly." Alina looked into those golden eyes and thought about telling him everything. But secrets, after all, develop their own inertia, and she found she didn't know where to begin.

Instead she reached between his muscled thighs, cupped his full balls in one hand, and watched his gaze go vague as passion rose. He'd softened a little as they'd played, but at her touch he hardened again. She stroked up from his sac, exploring his warm silken length. He groaned, the sound full-throated and hot with pleasure.

Anchoring herself with a hand on his butt, she bent to take him in her mouth. His taste was instantly familiar, even after all these years—the clean male scent of his body, the tang of his arousal. Her eyes drifted closed.

Gods, she'd missed him. She'd been so lonely.

As she suckled him slowly, a big hand came to rest on her head, threading through her blond hair. "Let me taste you," he asked hoarsely.

Agile and eager, she drew back and twisted around in the air until she hung head-down relative to him. Strong, warm hands caught her hips and pulled her close. She spread her legs, giving him access to her sex even as she caught his shaft in her fingers and bent close to suckle. He tasted salty with pre-come as she took as much of his thickness as she could.

Baird spread her lips with two fingers. Alina felt the warmth of his breath an instant before his hot tongue claimed her in a long, delicious lick. She moaned around his cock and sucked harder. His tongue danced over her clit in answer, and an index finger slid deep in her core. He groaned approval.

So they licked and nibbled at one another, spinning slowly, bouncing gently off walls, but too lost in each other to care. The pleasure rose and fell in shimmering waves, each crest building on the next.

Until Baird tore his head away, only to pull her around in the air until they were face to face again. "I've got to have you," he gasped. "Now."

"Yes!" She spread her thighs for him, and he slid between them.

His thrust made them both moan. Desperately, she wrapped her arms and legs around him as he began to pump. The sensation of gliding thickness was hot and slick and wonderful, and it made every nerve in her body vibrate with arousal and delight.

"God, that's good!" Baird clamped a hand over her hip and one thigh, bracing her so he could ride faster, surging hard and deep. She writhed against him, loving the way he felt, relishing the steep build of climax.

It burst free with a soundless pop of glittering heat, ripping a startled cry from her throat as she arched, coming.

Aware even as she lost herself of Baird's strong hands, his big body, his crooning words of praise and pleasure.

Alina looked so beautiful as she came, her face taking on a hot, lost glow as she threw her head back and cried out. The sight alone would have been enough to bring him.

Given how slick and tight she felt on top of it, he didn't have a prayer of holding off.

Baird climaxed with a wordless shout, clinging to her as they spun lazily in the air. Out of control, and not caring.

Long moments passed with his mind empty of anything but her lush curves.

"Forget her." The words burst from his mouth without any conscious thought on his part.

She opened those lovely violet eyes and blinked lazily, startled. "Who?"

"Rajin." This was insane, and he knew it. Yet he couldn't seem to keep the words from spilling out of his mouth. "Don't meet her on Calista. Come with me." His hands tightened, pulling her closer. "Bond with me. Marry me."

CH@%!*R
7

For just a heartbeat, joy blazed in her gaze. Then it guttered and went out. "Baird, I can't do that. I'm a courier. I've got to deliver a file she's expecting."

"You don't have to do a damn thing. She's kept you a virtual slave for twenty years. You owe her nothing."

Alina sighed. "Baird, Kasi House is a military contractor. If they're using me to carry this file, it's probably important."

"So why the hell are they sending it to Calista? That's not a Vardonese colony, and there are no Vardonese contractors there."

"It's not a courier's job to know what he's carrying. I just go where they tell me to go and protect my files until I get there. You *know* that. Why are you asking me these questions?"

Baird pushed away from her, the better to fight for control. He could almost hear Ualtar cursing him for his impulsiveness. He was on the verge of blowing the whole thing, yet he'd made the offer anyway. Goddess, he wanted to save her so badly.

But what if she didn't deserve saving?

He needed to shut his idiot mouth—and distract her until he could figure out what the hell was going on and what he was going to do about it. "I'm pushing because I'm tired of missing you, Alina. Because I don't understand why you won't sue for emancipation, when you know perfectly well Kasi can't legally keep you. You've served your time. What hold has Rajin got on you?"

Baird turned back just in time to see the telltale guilty flicker in her eyes. "Nothing. Not a bloody thing. I'm just making a living and doing my job. The same as you. Kasi pays well enough."

"Not well enough to afford a lawyer, evidently."

"There are other benefits than money." Her jaw jutting stubbornly, she looked around for her clothes. He watched her kick after her floating breastband, collect it, and jerk it on over her head. "Look, this has been a delightful trip into nostalgia, but we're not kids anymore, Baird." Her breasts bounced as she went after her hipsnugs, but for once he was in no mood to appreciate the view. "The fact is, it's been twenty years. We don't really know each other now. You have no idea what my life is like, and no business pushing me into running off with you." She tried to wiggle back into the snugs, but between her anger and the lack of gravity, it was tough to do. Frustrated, she snapped, "Computer, gravity up."

Anger simmering, Baird sank toward the floor as his weight slowly increased. He watched her jerk on the snugs, roll to her feet, and stalk toward the door.

Just before she stepped outside, she turned to look back at him. For an instant, pain, longing, and fear filled her face before she wiped away all expression. "I don't think it's a good idea to see each other again, Baird."

"Dammit, Alina, let me help you!"

"I can't." She turned and walked out.

Alina spent the next two days in her cabin, brooding. About Baird, of course, wishing for the hundredth time she could explain without risking an implosion of everything she loved. She hated leaving it like this, but she couldn't risk it. At least when she'd lost him before, there hadn't been this anger and bitterness.

Then there was Galar. She missed him with an aching intensity, as she always did whenever Rajin sent her out on one of these interminable missions. She almost hoped the Femmat would bring him along, except Rajin only did that when she intended a little extortion.

It would be best if the boy stayed back on Vardon. Especially since Baird had a point—why had Rajin sent her to Calista with the file when Kasi House had no contractors there?

Alina frowned as a cold, creeping fear slid through her veins. Rajin loved pushing the bounds of common decency, true—but treason?

And if she had turned traitor, what the hell was Alina going to do about it?

Under normal circumstances, the answer was obvious— stop her cold. But there was Galar. Alina couldn't turn a blind eye to treason, but she couldn't allow Rajin to use the terminal command either.

Yet the fact that the Femmat would even implant such a command was a strong indication she'd gone beyond her former petty sins. Alina had been afraid of something like this ever since she'd learned what Rajin had done to Galar.

Softly, Alina cursed Rajin and herself with equal bitterness. She should have killed the bitch then, even if it meant being executed as a rogue. The trap had closed so slowly she hadn't seen it coming until it was too late.

Alina had unintentionally created the trap herself when she'd impulsively decided to have Baird's child after they'd learned the war was ending. It hadn't been difficult; her computer gave her perfect control over her own reproduction. She'd wanted a baby like Mrs. Ortari's, and she'd expected Kasi House to liberate her. She'd planned to ask Baird to bond with her.

They'd have been a family, raising Galar together.

But when she returned to Kasi House for what should have been the last time, the medtechs discovered she was pregnant. The House was losing all its warrior veterans to emancipation, so when Rajin spotted a way to keep one, she jumped at it. She'd refused to emancipate Alina and ordered the fetus removed and placed in cryostorage. Rajin told Alina she could have the baby back only if she agreed to serve Kasi House for another ten years. By then, the next crop of warriors would be mature and able to serve.

Rajin also forbade her from seeing Baird again, and warned her not to reveal their son's existence. Alina had considered flouting those orders, but soon realized she'd stepped into legal quicksand.

For one thing, half Galar's DNA had been created by Arvid House engineers. Even if she and Baird bonded and successfully sued Kasi House for custody of their son, Arvid House could also put in a claim. After all, a Warrior was an expensive piece of property. She and Baird might win a suit against one House, but two? The fetus could end up in legal limbo for years. In the end, she decided that the only way to keep her son was to play Rajin's game. It was infuriating and terrifying, but she'd felt she had no choice.

Rajin was good at taking away choices.

So Alina had served Kasi as a special courier for ten uneventful years, carrying files containing warship designs between the company, its contractors, and the Vardonese military. As they'd agreed, at the end of nine years, doctors reimplanted the fetus. Galar had been none the worse for his time in cryostorage, and Alina had carried him to term. Kasi House even implanted the computers, sensor, and Warlord neurochemical reservoirs the boy would one day use to go to *riaat*.

Then Rajin had sprung her next ugly surprise. Though Alina might have completed her service, the boy was the product of Kasi House engineering through his mother, and as such, was legally company property. He was to go to the Warlord Creche—unless Alina agreed to continue her service. If she agreed, Rajin would permit Alina to raise him. When Alina was off on missions, Rajin would see to his care.

She'd had no choice but to agree.

For the next nine years, Alina had no cause to regret the deal she'd made. Galar was a bright, intelligent boy, the image of his father, mischievous and handsome. They existed in a happy bubble of contentment. And they were able to spend a great deal of time together, since other warrior couriers had come into service and her missions were relatively infrequent.

Until the day last year when Rajin called her into her office and gave her a pouch of firegems she wanted delivered to a buyer on Calista. Kasi House didn't deal in gems, and they both knew it. *"Consider it a personal favor,"* Rajin said, with a sly smile.

Rajin was stealing from the company.

Alina had delivered the stones, found out who the buyers were and which Kasi House department the gems had disappeared from.

At last. Here was the evidence she needed to free her son. But before she could present it to the Kasi House Council of Femmats, Rajin called her into her office and told her she'd ordered a termination virus into Galar's computer implant. It had programmed his computer to fill his *riatt* reservoirs with a neurotoxin. All she had to do was broadcast the code, and the boy's comp would flood his bloodstream with the poison. He'd die in agony, his body so damaged no regenator would be able to repair it.

Reading the death in Alina's eyes, Rajin said, *"Keep your mouth shut, give me one more year of service, and I'll erase the code and free you both. But if you touch me, he dies now."*

One year.

It was a devil's bargain, and Alina had known it. She would have killed Rajin on the spot, except she feared she wouldn't be able to do it before the Femmat transmitted the code.

It was tempting to try some surprise means of assassination, but she knew she'd be executed for murdering a Femmat, regardless of her reasons. Her son would be left an orphan, the child of a rogue.

So Alina had agreed, secretly planning to hack into the boy's implant and disable the code. Unfortunately, she'd quickly discovered that any attempt to destroy it would result in its activation. And she didn't dare go to the authorities for help, because Rajin would activate the code and kill her son. She'd had no choice but to abide by the agreement and hope Rajin kept her vow.

Rajin had taken full advantage of her blackmail. There had been other deliveries after that—not many, but a few. Mostly gems, some objets d'art. All were items that had mysteriously gone missing from Kasi's treasury.

But was Baird right? Had Rajin gone beyond petty theft to treason—and made Alina an accessory to the crime?

It was time to go to Baird and tell him all the painful truths Rajin had forbidden her to tell. If anybody could help, he could.

But what if something went wrong? What if he tried to move against Rajin and got Galar killed?

By the time the *The Antares Empress* arrived at Calista, she'd decided it was time to take a chance. Back when they'd fought together, Baird had always found a way to turn defeat into victory. If anybody could help her get out of this mess, it was him. Besides, she was tired of shouldering the burden alone.

When she called his quarters, he'd already left, so Alina hurried to meet the next shuttle, hoping for a chance to talk to him before he caught transport elsewhere. But arriving at the shuttle deck, she found the line to board reached all the way down the corridor.

There was nothing for it but to wait and pray she got to him in time.

*   *   *

Alina descended the shuttle's ramp behind a lushly curved woman with a mass of bright green curls spilling down her back. Her boots clicked as she stepped onto the tarmac.

Warily, Alina scanned the port. All around, other shuttles stood—long, sleek shapes with aerodynamic lines designed for travel into planetary atmospheres. The beacons encircling one of them suddenly began flashing. With a blaring hoot of warning, the huge craft lifted off, floating slowly upward balanced on a delicate antigravity field. It drifted gently higher, lazy as a soap bubble, until its thruster fields abruptly cut in and shot it toward the horizon with a rumbling sonic boom. The field generators in its stubby wings glowed a shimmering blue as it zipped off over the obelisks and broad flat discs that made up the city's architecture.

Baird was somewhere out there. And she needed to find him quickly, if she was to have any hope of escaping the trap she was in.

Scan for him, Alina told her comp.

Pinpointed, it replied after a pause. She looked around to see a set of red crosshairs appear in her field of vision. Hefting her bag over her shoulder, Alina strode in that direction, ignoring the rest of the travelers headed for the sprawling terminal building.

At last she reached the edge of the buffer zone of vegetation that lay around the landing field. The local equivalent of trees were blue with alien chlorophyll, their leaves feathery, more like giant ferns than anything else. The "grass" that covered the ground beneath them was just as blue and equally feathery, leaves spreading out rather than up.

She'd just stepped out under the trees when her comp began howling. *Warning! Xer lifesign! Baird is under attack.*

What? Sweet gods. What the hell were Xer doing here?

Their home world was fifty light years away. She slung her bag across her back by its strap and began to run through the trees. *How many of them?*

Six. The comp flashed her a mental image of what her sensors were picking up—seven figures, six of them attacking a lone man.

Where the hell did they come from?

Unknown. It appears to be an ambush.

Give me riaat. She clenched her teeth as the burning chemical storm began, swirling through her body like a wave of lava. In a moment, strength poured in after it, and she was bounding.

What kind of capabilities do they have?

Insufficient data at this distance.

Well, tell me when you figure it out! Alina put her head down and concentrated on running, darting around trees and leaping any shorter vegetation in her path.

She burst into a clearing and almost ran right into them. The six Xer wore civilian clothing: long tunics split for leg room, and one-piece pant-boot combinations, all in dark colors. Silver skull rings jutted from their shaved heads, implanted in patterns. Like the Vardonese, their ancestors had been human colonists, but a couple of hundred years of genetic engineering had left its mark in great strength and vicious intelligence.

Just the sight of them sent rage searing through Alina. Twenty years ago, their kind had invaded Vardon and laid the planet waste. They'd raped and murdered and stolen every bit of Femmat technology they could get their hands on. It had taken Vardon's warrior class five long years to drive them off, and countless good Warlords and Warfems had died in the process.

Alina didn't even break step before slamming into the first of them with a howl. The impact tumbled them both halfway across the clearing. When they rolled to a stop, Alina was straddling him, powering her fist again and again into his face. He was out before he could get in a punch.

Then she was on her feet again, leaping for the remaining five, who had Baird down on the ground and were struggling to hold him there. She grabbed one and spun him around into a punch.

As he fell, Alina danced back, more than ready to fight. To her relief, she saw Baird throw off one of those holding him pinned and hit another in the face. The Warlord surged to his feet, bleeding, his lower lip swollen, his eyes burning red with *riaat*.

"Change of heart, Alina?" he snarled, dancing backward, slamming punches into the three remaining Xer warriors who were attempting to close in on him again. "Or don't you have the stomach for treason?"

CH@%!*R
8

"I'm not a traitor!" she spat, and grunted as the Xer she was fighting rammed his baton into her side. The blaze of pain sent her to one knee, fighting to breathe.

"Lights out for you, bitch," the Xer snarled, stabbing his baton toward her unprotected neck. If it touched her spinal cord, she'd be out for hours. She threw up an arm in an instinctive block.

"Shit." Baird barreled into her opponent, taking him down hard. Alina gasped in relief and reeled to her feet. Despite the pain, she aimed a kick at the Xer's balls, as he struggled with Baird on the ground. She hit her target; he convulsed with a bellow. Baird threw him off and rolled upright as the remaining Xer closed in. For a moment, he and Alina exchanged a single, searing glance. "You can't believe I'm working for these monsters!" she spat.

She watched doubt war with their battle-tested bond. The bond won. "If I had, I'd have let him hit you." Baird and Alina moved into the fighting pose that had become habit twenty years ago—back-to-back.

Where the hell did these guys come from? Alina commed to him through her computer.

Don't know. One minute I was cutting through the park to meet somebody, then . . .

She caught movement coming through the trees and glanced in that direction. Rajin Kasi stepped into the clearing. The Femmat had forgone her usual aristocrat's robes for a civilian tunic and leggings. Her shimmering violet hair was piled on top of her head, held there with an intricate arrangements of combs.

But Alina's attention was focused on Galar. The boy's young face was cold with a terrible rage. Alina could almost feel the fear he was struggling to hide.

Rajin rested a hand on his shoulder in a gesture that might have been mistaken for motherly. Alina knew it for the threat it was and felt her heart catch in her chest.

The Femmat's chill silver eyes met hers across the clearing. *Stop at once.* The command rang through her comp's communication's unit on the private frequency Baird couldn't hear. As a Femmat, Rajin had a communication's implant, but no battle computer or cybernetics, and no more than human strength.

Sick fury rolled over Alina. *"You are working for the Xer! You traitorous bitch!"*

"Take him down."

Her gut turned to ice. *"Who?"*

"You know who." Rajin's commed voice was implacable. *"The Warlord. Your lover. Take him down now, or watch the boy die now. Choose, Warfem."* Something vicious rose in that metallic gaze, and Alina knew she'd do it.

But the idea of betraying Baird wrapped her in sick horror. He trusted her, had asked her to marry him.

Then an image flashed through her mind: Galar writhing in agony, his face blackening, his eyes begging her silently to save him.

"Now!" Rajin screamed. Her slender hand tightened on the boy's shoulder.

Galar's golden eyes blazed. *"Don't do it,"* he said through his own comp. *"Don't let her . . ."*

Rajin's lip curled. *"I will not tell you again. Now, or watch your precious boy shriek out his life."*

Galar half-turned toward Rajin, tensing. He was going to attack her, and she'd kill him.

With a howl of anguish, Alina pivoted with all the power of *riaat* and slammed her fist into the side of Baird's head. He stumbled and went down.

For just an instant, the golden gaze so like their son's met hers. *"Damn you, Alina,"* Baird said on their old battle frequency. *"Damn you to hell. I believed in you!"*

Before he could roll away, one of the Xer leaped forward and jammed his shock stick into the base of his skull, where spinal cord met brain. He went limp, instantly unconscious.

Sick, Alina looked away as another of the Xer stepped forward and snapped some kind of collar on him. Goddess only knew what it did.

She wanted to throw up. Then her gaze fell on Rajin. A cold, deadly rage replaced her guilt.

Galar saw his chance, and knew he'd better take it. The situation had reached critical mass, as he'd always known it would. Rajin had finally pushed his mother too far. People were going to start dying.

Galar was going to make flogging sure it wasn't him or his mother. Or the Warlord. He'd grown up hearing stories about Baird, his mother's heroic partner—and his father. He badly wanted to get to know the man who'd sired him.

Fortunately, a Xer sprawled unconscious barely a meter from his sneakbooted feet. The agent's stun baton lay forgotten by his head. Better yet, nobody was watching; the agents were too busy collecting the Warlord and dealing with their injured, while his mother and Rajin were focused on the hate swirling between them.

In one smooth motion, Galar stepped forward, scooped up the baton, collapsed it by pushing on either end, and slid it into a pocket. The baton was one of several weapons his mother had trained him to use. All he needed now was a chance.

His stomach knotted at the risk he was taking, but he ignored his fear. Kid or not, he was a warrior.

Pretending to need reassurance, he moved to his mother's side and leaned against her hip. Normally she'd rest a hand on his shoulder, but now she stood coiled, almost vibrating with rage. Yet her face was perfectly cool and expressionless. Oh, yeah. She was getting ready to kill somebody. She'd put up with a lot out of Rajin over the years because of him, but this had pushed her into a meltdown.

If she went rogue . . . Galar swallowed. He'd seen a rogue warrior shot down once when he was six. As he'd watched the man writhe and die, Rajin had leaned down and whispered, *"See what could happen to your mother . . ."*

He had to do something.

Silently, Galar told his comp to eavesdrop on the conversation. The adults had no idea he'd figured out their private frequency and codes. It was a good thing Rajin had never thought to keep him from using his computer to its full potential. But then, she wasn't a programmer, so there wasn't much she could do about it anyway. One of her flunkies had designed the virus that installed the terminal code and programmed his computer to manufacture the neurotoxin.

Besides, she persisted in thinking of him as a normal ten-year-old, and he was careful to maintain the illusion. She hadn't known enough warrior children to realize how computer implants stimulated brain growth and intelligence. And Galar was good at playing dumb.

"What's in the file, Rajin?" his mother asked in that cool mental voice of hers. Above the clearing, a white zip-truck swooped low and prepared to land.

"That's none of your concern."

"Given that you've made me an accessory to treason, I think it is."

Rajin folded her hands, her elegant face serene. *"It's nothing of great import. Not compared to the money they're paying me."*

"Been gambling on Wekita, again, I assume." As Rajin's eyes widened, she smiled coldly. *"Yes, I know about that. I've investigated you thoroughly."*

The Femmat shrugged with an elegant lift of one shoulder. *"The Wekita are not a forgiving people when it comes to so much money. They go to great lengths to ensure debts are paid."*

"Yet you keep gambling there."

"The risk is part of the attraction. And there was a very pretty little dragon flying in the Soji races. Quite fast. Just not as fast as I'd hoped."

"So you betray Vardon to pay for your vices."

"I do what I must. And so will you, unless you want me to transmit a certain word to the boy."

Gelar went sick and cold. If Rajin used the command, there was nothing he could do to save himself.

His mother reached out and put her arm protectively around his shoulders. *"I strongly suggest you think twice about that,"* she said. *"I may not be able to open your file, but I can delete it. And I doubt the Xer would be particularly understanding."*

The blood drained from Rajin's face. *"You wouldn't dare."*

"I once attacked a Xer tachyon cannon emplacement with no backup except Baird. There's very little I wouldn't dare."

"The Xer will kill us all!"

"So be it. This isn't petty theft anymore, Rajin. Vardonese Warriors will die if you hand over military secrets to the Xer."

"What of it? We'll just make more of them." Her lip lifted in a sneer. *"But can you make another Galar?"*

He felt her hand tighten on his shoulders. Daring a glance up at her face, he watched cold determination flare in her eyes. *"I'll make you a bargain, Rajin. I'll give the Xer the file if you erase the code and free us."*

Rajin stared at her a long moment. "Very well, then, damn you. You have your bargain."

His mother's grip eased, and Galar slumped in relief.

The truck landed, and the Xer got busy loading their men into the vehicle. He hoped none of them noticed the agent's missing stun baton.

A tall, muscular Xer approached, implants shining in the sunlight. He eyed Alina dubiously, then turned to Rajin. Beyond them, a long, black zipcar landed beside the truck. "If you will accompany us, Femmat Kasi, we will make the transfer."

Rajin nodded in an abbreviated Femmat bow. "It will be my pleasure, sir."

Galar followed the adults as they got into the car. As he prepared to slip inside, his mother's hand fell on his shoulder.

Coded transmission from your mother, his comp said.

"Nice work on stealing that baton," she said, her comp transmitting in the private code they'd created. *"I assume you remember how to use it."*

His palms were sweating. *"Jam it into the base of the skull. Knocks them right out."*

"Right. That's going to be a tricky spot to get to, since you're shorter than the Xer. But luckily, Rajin tells everyone you're her son, so they won't expect you to be as strong as you are. Pretend you need to go to the bathroom, then stun your guard and run. The Xer have a jamming field set up to prevent our calling out, but as soon as you're beyond it, contact the Calista authorities. Tell them the Xer have kidnapped a Vardonese agent and plan to kill him. The Calistans will set Baird free and clean up the mess."

What mess? *"What about the terminal code?"*

Something cold and dark flickered in his mother's violet eyes. *"You let me worry about that."*

Pain rolled in a searing wave from the base of Baird's spine, burning its way all the way into his skull. Despite his fight for control, it jerked all his muscles tight, arching him into a bow of agony in the chair. Somehow he kept the scream between his teeth.

One thought kept hammering in his brain, adding to his agony. *Alina betrayed me. I was wrong. She's working for the Xer after all.*

His beautiful Alina was a traitor. And if he escaped, he was bound by duty to kill her.

After a white-hot eternity that was probably a minute and a half, the pain faded, leaving him to slump, sweating and nauseated. But worse even than the pain was the black despair.

Alina.

"I can keep this up all night," the Xer torturer said, her voice light, almost pleasant. "And so can you. That's the wonderful thing about the collar. It doesn't break bones, it doesn't burn the skin off your body, it doesn't ram spikes into your eyeballs. It only feels like it."

Panting, Baird glared at his enemy as sweat rolled stinging into his eyes. The control collar they'd put on him felt as if it was slowly choking him, but unfortunately, it wasn't.

He wouldn't get off that easily.

They sat in what looked like a perfectly ordinary office of the kind found in private homes. Baird knew the Xer didn't have a military compound on Calista; it appeared they'd had to make do with renting a house. The carpet under his feet was thick and lush, and the walls were a soothing blue. The Xer was seated comfortably behind a faux wood control desk, while Baird sprawled in a blue, thickly upholstered armchair in front of it.

He wasn't even bound, though he might as well have been. The collar interrupted his brain's signals to his body, leaving him completely paralyzed, though his muscles responded well enough to whatever stimulation the torturer chose to inflict.

"Come on, Baird, don't do this to yourself," she said, her smile flirtatious. She could have passed for pretty with her platinum blond hair and perfect face, if it wasn't for the viciousness in her sky-blue eyes. "What do you boys know about the *Femmat*? We know you've been following her courier."

He licked his lips. "Look, Alina and I are old friends. We just got together for a little sex."

The torturer's perfect pink mouth drew into a bow. "Don't insult my intelligence. We know who you work for. We . . ."

"I want my daddy!" A child's voice rang clearly through the closed door. Apparently there was no soundproofing in here at all.

"Look, kid, your daddy's not here," the guard in the hallway said, sounding frustrated. "You go on back to the Femmat now."

"You're lying! I know you've got him in there!"

"Kid . . . Shit!"

Thud.

"Dadddyyyyy!" the boy yelled at the top of his lungs.

"Retar, you idiot!" With a huff of frustration, the torturer rose and stalked to the door. Baird rolled his eyes, trying to see what she was doing, but she passed out of his field of view. The door sighed open. "Retar, could you get that child under . . . AH!" Feet scuffled. Baird heard the distinctive buzz of a stun baton, then the thud of a body hitting the floor.

Somebody grunted with effort, followed by rustles and a series of thumps that sounded like a body being dragged across the floor. "Damn, lady, what have you been eating—ferocrete?" Baird's eyebrows rose. That sounded like the kid.

Another series of thumps, and the door closed.

Frustrated, paralyzed, Baird growled, "All right, somebody want to tell me what the hell is going on?"

To his astonishment, a ten-year-old boy walked into his field of view and sat down at the torturer's desk. The kid gave him a bright, white grin. "Hi, Dad."

CH@%!*R

9

Baird blinked in utter astonishment. He recognized the boy from a trid in his files. It was Rajin Kasi's son, Galar.

But though Baird had been paralyzed, his computer and sensors still worked. And both were telling him the boy was not the purely human child he should have been. "You're a warrior."

"Yep." The boy didn't look up, too busy peering intently at the desk's touch screen, evidently trying to puzzle out the controls.

"If you're trying to deactivate the collar, hit the red square." He'd gotten another agent out of a Xeran collar once before. "Why aren't you in a creche?"

"Because I'm a hostage." The boy touched the desk.

The collar opened and fell into Baird's lap. Cautiously, he stretched, making sure everything was working, but his attention was focused on Galar. "The Xer are holding you?"

"No, Rajin is. She's been using me to blackmail my mother."

Baird blinked, belatedly seeing the resemblance. "Alina."

The kid nodded, his blond hair the exact same shade as hers. His mouth was drawn into a familiar line Baird knew from a hundred combat missions. "And you're my father."

About to roll out of the chair to have a go at the computer desk, Baird gaped at the boy. He'd assumed Galar had been joking when he'd called him Daddy, but it sounded as if he actually believed it. "What leads you to that conclusion?"

Galar shrugged. "Mother says so." He frowned down at the desk console, frustrated. "I know all about you. She told me all kinds of stories about when you were her partner during the war."

The pain was stark and breathtaking. Alina had dared tell her son such a lie before betraying Baird and handing him over to the Xer. *I never knew her,* he thought in sick rage. *I never knew her at all.* He fought the anger down long enough to address his comp. *Does he actually think I'm his father?*

Sensors indicate he believes what he says.

Despite the fury sizzling through him, Baird rose and stalked to the desk. He had a job to do, which meant he needed to disable the Xerian's communication jammers so he could call the Vardonese embassy.

The child moved aside for him without being told. Baird glanced him and felt a stab of pity. None of this was his fault. "I don't know what they've told you, Galar, but your mother and I haven't been together for twenty years. I couldn't be your father."

Level, golden eyes met his. For a moment, it was like looking into a mirror, but he knew that was an illusion. "My mother loved you, Baird. That's why she had me."

He wanted to rage and swear, but forced himself to speak calmly instead. "She misled you. If you were my son, you'd be nineteen."

"My mother doesn't lie!" Temper flared in those too-familiar eyes. "Look, she thought Kasi House would emancipate her, but Rajin refused. Mom was still pregnant with me when the old bitch ordered my fetus surgically removed and put in cryostorage. She said Mother could have me back if she continued to work for Kasi. So she did. Eleven years ago, they thawed me out and let her have me. Rajin's been using me to manipulate Mom ever since."

Baird frowned, considering the idea. It sounded plausible. Goddess knew it sounded like the kind of thing Kasi would do.

Could this boy be his? Had Alina given birth to him as an expression of love for Baird? The thought was so staggering, so painful, he shoved it away. The little traitor had lied to her son, just as she'd lied to Baird. "Look, I don't have time to argue about this . . ."

"No, we don't," Galar said. Fear and impatience whitened his face, though to his credit, his voice remained controlled. "We've got to get to Mother before she tries to kill Rajin. Because if she's not fast enough, I'm dead, and even if she succeeds, the Xer will kill her."

"What are you talking about?"

As Galar explained the trap he was in, Baird used the desk unit to hack into the Xer's communications and security systems. By the time the child finished describing the death he faced if Rajin used her codes, a great deal was painfully clear. "So that's why Alina went along with Rajin's treason," Baird said. "It doesn't make it forgivable, but . . ."

"My mother is not a traitor!" The mouth so like Alina's drew into a mutinous line. "She didn't know Rajin was working for the Xer, and now that she does, she's going to kill her. And as many of the Xer as she can take with them!"

Baird frowned. "She'd put you in danger like that?"

"No, she told me to leave and call the authorities so they could rescue you, but I took the chance of turning you loose instead. You owe us, Warlord. And if you don't help us, we're both dead."

Lifting a brow, Baird studied the boy. Galar had taken a hell of a chance to free him—not only in tackling three full-grown Xer, but in braving Baird's own disbelief and anger by telling him his story.

And those golden eyes—it was like looking into a mirror. *Computer, give me a DNA scan of this child. Is he my son?*

The mental silence that followed was long and nerve-wracking.

Yes.

"Sweet Goddess," Baird whispered, stunned.

Sometime in the past twenty years, the Xer had figured out how to build neuroweb computers, probably with tech they'd stolen from the Vardonese during the invasion. According to Alina's sensors, the leader of the Xer agents had one, though her computer pronounced it inferior to Kasi House tech. Too, given Major Jenci Csaba's age, it must have been implanted in adulthood rather than infancy, so it wasn't as well integrated into his brain.

Inferior comp or not, Alina's instincts told her she'd better keep an eye on Csaba. The number of sensor scans he'd sent her way over dinner certainly indicated he was suspicious. That was no doubt why he hadn't requested she transfer the file to him. He was afraid of a virus.

As well he should be—she had one all loaded up and ready to send him. He'd be dead before he hit the ground when his comp stopped his heart. Of course, the Xer could restart it again with a regenator, but Alina figured dropping him would still cause some very satisfactory chaos. With luck, she could use the confusion to escape and free Baird.

Though if Galar had succeeded in getting away, the boy might even now be summoning the Calista authorities. The fact that the Xer hadn't raised the alarm over his escape was a very encouraging sign.

Alina leaned back in her seat, playing with her fork as their server brought in dessert—something showy and flaming. Her attention was focused across the elegant table, where Rajin flirted with the Xer major. Csaba probably wanted to enlist the Femmat as a long-term asset. And Rajin, the traitorous bitch, seemed interested.

Alina rolled her fork between her fingers and calculated the angle and force she'd need to bury it in Rajin's eye-socket. It was a tricky shot, but doable.

But if she missed, was Galar far enough away to be beyond Rajin's code transmission? The boy had been gone half an hour. It was a good thing Rajin and Csaba were so wrapped up in their little waltz of treachery. Alina needed to move before either of them missed him.

And Goddess only knew what the Xer were doing to Baird in the meantime. The thought made her stomach twist, so she pushed it away.

She'd get to him in time. She had to.

Suddenly Rajin looked over at her as she and the Xer rose. "Alina, come. It's time to give Major Csaba what he's paid for."

Finally. Alina smiled easily, put her fork down, and stood. She considered telling her computer to prepare for *riaat,* but Csaba might notice. She'd have to do this at normal strength, but if she hit Rajin hard enough, fast enough, the woman should be unable to get the command out.

Hopefully. It was the only game in town, in any case.

She rounded the table, mentally cursing herself for not killing Rajin earlier. She'd delayed too long, hoping for a better chance, for a way to both save Galar and keep him.

Csaba and Rajin were moving ahead of her into the next room. She lengthened her stride to catch up. Her breathing slowed, calmed. Her mind went cold and still.

In one smooth, powerful motion, she scythed her leg up and across, aiming for the side of Rajin's head with her boot.

Csaba whirled in an blur of inhuman speed, throwing up a forearm to block the kick that would have shattered the Femmat's skull. Alina didn't hesitate, throwing herself at him, punching, kicking, trying to drive past his guard to get at Rajin. Her heart slammed in panic. *No! Galar!*

From behind the protection of the Xer's shoulder, Rajin stared at her with infuriated terror. "He's dead, bitch!" the Femmat screamed. "You just killed your son!"

Alina cried out in anguish as her comp picked up the stream of code pouring from Rajin's communication's implant.

If Galar wasn't out of range, he was dead.

Go to riatt! she ordered the computer, as she kept trying to beat her way through the Xer's guard. *Keep a lock on Rajin, I want to be able to find her when I'm finished with this bastard.*

The Xer's fist shot toward her head, and she jerked aside, backhanding him so hard he slammed into the wall behind him. But before she could close in to finish him, a dozen agents charged into the room. She spun to meet them, her teeth bared in despair and rage. She might be done, but she was going to take as many of them with her as she could.

Then a familiar war cry stopped her in her tracks. A big male body charged in behind the Xer, beads flashing in his braids.

"Baird!"

"Yeah, it's me." Baird plowed into the agents like a tachyon shell, sending some of them reeling, as the others whirled to fight.

With a cry of joy, she ran to help.

"*You do realize,*" he said on their old battle frequency, "*I'm going to kick your ass when I get done with these idiots.*"

Alina plowed her fist into a Xeran's gut. "*I guess I've got it coming.*"

She only hoped she wouldn't have to tell him their son was dead.

Heart in her throat, Rajin slunk out of the room, praying neither of the warriors saw her go. She knew she had to catch a flight to whatever ship was in orbit, or she was dead. Alina wouldn't stop until she had revenge for her brat's death.

Sweet Goddess, but this situation had melted down with staggering speed. She'd be lucky if she . . .

A door hissed open behind her.

With a strangled shriek, Rajin whirled to see Galar step out of what looked like a closet. Something silver gleamed from around his throat. Shocked, Rajin gasped, "Why aren't you . . . ? And why are you wearing a Xer control collar?"

"To block your fuckin' signal, bitch," the brat said, and flicked his wrist, snapping the stun baton out to its full length.

Before she had time to jump back, he shoved it right into her belly. Rajin bent double with a howl of agony. She never felt him jam it against the base of her skull.

The boy watched her tumble to the ground at his feet, out cold. He bounced the baton in his palm and grinned. "Damn, that felt good."

They were fighting back-to-back again as the Xer circled, looking for an opening. Baird growled, *"These odds really grind."*

"We've faced worse." Alina was sweating, and her mouth tasted of blood from her cut lip.

He snorted. *"Not in the past two decades."*

Suddenly her computer began to howl. *Tevan lifesign approaching!*

What?

Alina jerked her head around just in time to see the huge reptile step through the door, a tachyon rifle lifted and aimed in his seven-fingered hands. A number of other figures followed behind him, all armored and armed. Alina's heart sank. *"Oh, we're screwed."*

"Not exactly." Aloud, Baird added, "What the hell took you so long, you big lizard?"

"Traffic was a bitch," the Tevan growled, as his armored

backup leveled their weapons at the Xer agents. "Hey, ass-holes—you gonna give us an excuse?"

Cursing, the Xer straightened and backed away, throwing their batons aside.

"Mother!" A small figure raced around them.

"Galar!" Alina caught him as he leaped for her. "Sweet Goddess, you're all right!"

"I knocked Rajin out!" he told her happily. "The Warlords took her away. Baird reprogrammed his control collar and put it on me so her signal couldn't get through, and then he told me to hide in the closet, but when I heard Rajin in the hall . . ."

"What—wait, slow down!" She put the boy on his feet, barely noticing as the Vardonese agents started forcecuffing their prisoners and hustling them off. "What are you talking about? Explain."

"Actually," Baird drawled from beside her, "he's not the only one with some explaining to do."

Alina paced at Baird's side, every muscle tense with a blend of fear and hope. They'd stepped outside the Xer's headquarters while he questioned her. Now they walked together under the alien trees, as zipcars sighed overhead and a warm wind blew in their faces.

He told her he worked for military intelligence, which in retrospect made a great deal of sense. It was obvious their encounter yesterday had not been chance.

It turned out an official at Kasi House had learned about Rajin's theft of those gems. Yet because she was the company's president, it was virtually impossible for the lower-ranking Femmat to confront her. Then Rajin began showing an unhealthy interest in a Vardonese warship the company was building, and the official reported her to military counterintelligence.

Baird was one of the agents assigned to the case. When he learned Alina was involved, he volunteered to make contact with her.

He explained all that with a cool dispassion that somehow hinted at boiling rage. Alina had tried to blunt his anger by holding nothing back, from the night she'd decided to get pregnant through Rajin's blackmailing her into carrying the gems. When she finally worked her way to the present, he said nothing for five steaming minutes.

When he finally spoke, it wasn't what she'd expected. "Obviously, I have a conflict of interest here. One of the other agents will have to question you further. You'll be required to undergo a deep scan of your comp's memories to verify your story. Assuming you've told me the truth, I doubt you'll be charged, though the ultimate decision will, of course, be up to the Femmat chief prosecutor."

Assuming you've told me the truth. She winced. "Baird, I'm sorry."

He shrugged, his broad shoulders stiff. "You did what you believed necessary to protect your son."

"Our son."

Baird's golden gaze flicked to hers. The rage she'd sensed blazed up in his eyes. "I do have one more question. Were you *ever* going to tell me?"

Her mouth went dry. "As soon as we were free, we were going to come to you. I wanted to be with you. That's why I got pregnant. I saw a baby as the physical embodiment of our bond. Then he was born, and I realized how much more he was. He was so precious, so fragile, and he depended so completely on me."

A fine muscle worked in Baird's jaw. "And you didn't trust me to protect him. That's what really galls me—not that you didn't tell me your plans, not even that you smuggled for that bitch. I *always* trusted you."

"Baird . . ."

He stopped and spun to face her, big hands fisted at his side. She forced herself to meet his angry gaze. "Deep down, I trusted you even when my superiors, logic, and simple common sense told me you had to be knowingly involved in treason. Part of me knew Alina Kasi would never stoop to treason. Period. Hell, when you coldcocked me and I woke up in a torture collar, the minute your son showed up with another explanation, I leaped at it. But you wouldn't trust me to do the one thing I was born to do— the one thing I took an oath to do: protect the innocent."

It was then she saw the pain. Deep beneath the incandescent anger was a stark hurt that she hadn't believed possible in him.

"And you did find a way to protect him," Alina said softly. "Nobody but Baird Arvid would have thought to reprogram the same torture collar the Xer had used on him to save Galar. I kept trying to come up with ways to block Rajin's signal to the comp. It never even occurred to me to block the comp's signal to the reservoirs."

He said nothing, simply staring down at her from his great height, his eyes burning.

She gathered her courage. "You're right. I didn't trust you, and I should have." Reaching out, she took one of his hard, strong hands. "I'm trusting you now. I love you, Baird. I've loved you from the time I was fifteen years old. Forgive me. Bond with me. Give our son a father."

He blinked as if she'd said the one thing he hadn't expected. "Alina, I've never been a father. I've never even had a father. How do you know I won't get it wrong?"

Alina smiled, despite the hot prickle behind her eyelids. "I trust you."

His smile was so white and wide, it was blinding. Then she was in his arms, so strong and sure around her. "Thank you for our son, Alina," he said, the instant before his mouth covered hers, hot and joyous. They clung together in the kiss as the pain drained away.

CH@%!*R

10

Alina leaned her shoulder against the bulkhead, watching her son and Ualtar play some alien board game the Tevan had produced to kill time on their trip back to Vardon.

His little face lighting with triumph, Galar moved his stone piece and clicked it against the reptile's. "Hah! Got your *behrooz*!"

The big alien sat back with a grunt of disgust. "Kid, you're a menace. You sure you've never played this game?"

"I learn fast. Gimme."

Ualtar shook his horned head and reached into a pocket of his unisuit to pull out a credit chip. As he handed it over to her crowing offspring, he said, "You've raised a hustler, Alina."

Baird stepped up behind her and slid his arms around her waist. "It's like I keep telling you, partner—if they've got a battlecomp, don't play strategy games with 'em."

"That wasn't just computer. He's definitely your kid."

Baird grinned. "Thank you."

"It wasn't a compliment." To Galar he added, "Set the board up again, brat. I want my credits back."

Baird cleared his throat. "If you two are going to be busy for a while, we're going to go in the back and . . . check the prisoners."

The boy looked up at his new friend, his expression mischievous. "They want to get gooey again, don't they?"

Ualtar reached over and ruffled his hair. "Get used to it."

With a laugh, Baird tugged Alina back out of the wardroom and into the hall. "Man knows me too well."

She threaded an arm around his waist. "I can't believe you had me convinced that scaly teddy bear was a killer data thief."

Baird shrugged. "Ualtar's a good actor. We've been running scams like that for years." He slanted her a look. "Though that particular fight got a little rougher than I intended. I'm sorry about that, by the way."

"Considering you thought I was selling the plans for the next Vardonese warship to the Xer, I wouldn't have blamed you for shooting me on the spot."

"Well, we did need you to lead us to your contact." They started down the corridor of the little ship together. "And as I said, I couldn't believe you knew what was happening."

"I didn't, but I certainly should have. I did know Rajin had been stealing from Kasi House."

"It's quite a jump from there to treason."

"Maybe, but the Kasi board of executives will probably bring me up on charges anyway. I knew what I was doing when I transported those gems for Rajin."

Baird laid a comforting hand on her shoulder. "Given the threat to Galar, I doubt they'll charge you. Particularly when you've got excellent grounds for a lawsuit. According to the evidence we've collected, our source at Kasi House wasn't the only one who knew Rajin was dirty. The others cooperated because she paid them off in advancements and incentives. I wouldn't be surprised if some of them even knew about what she'd done to Galar. Somebody definitely helped her poison his implants. When we find out who they are, they'll be charged as an accessory to attempted murder."

"I only wish I could get to them first." Alina gave him a wicked grin. "Hey, there's an idea. How about looking the other way while I slip off to the brig and beat the bitch out of Rajin?"

Baird grinned back. "No. First, I need her in a large enough piece to stand trial, and two, you're about to be much too busy to worry about her." A corridor door slid open, and he waltzed her into his quarters, a room scarcely big enough for both of them and his bed.

"Does this mean we're about to get gooey?" She wrapped her arms around his neck.

"Oh, yeah." He leaned down to take her mouth with his.

His lips were just as warm and clever as she remembered, and she sighed in pleasure. "You know, you're very good with that mouth," she told him when he let her come up for air.

"Want to find out what else I'm good at?" He slid his hands under the hem of her tunic.

Alina smiled as his long fingers caressed and explored their way up her ribs. "I've already got a . . ." He reached a nipple, and she caught her breath. "Ah! . . . Pretty good idea."

Baird withdrew his hands and started to turn away. "Well, if you're not interested . . ."

"Wait one minute! Where do you think you're going?" She bent, caught him behind the thighs, and hefted him off his feet. He made an awkward armful even with her enhanced strength, so before she could lose her grip, she turned and tossed him lightly onto the bed.

Flat on his back, Baird smirked at her. "Now, is that any way to treat a Warlord?"

"Yep." She pulled her tunic off over her head and popped open her breastband. Her breasts bounced free and bare.

"Okay, you've got me there." He sat up to watch with lecherous interest as she bent and started wiggling her way out of her tight pants. "Why don't you bring those pretty little nipples over here, and I'll show you all my favorite tricks."

She propped her fists on her hips. "Take off your pants, and I'll show you mine."

Laughing, Baird started stripping off his uniform. Alina took advantage of his distraction to pounce just as he got his boots off, knocking him back so she could straddle his broad, brawny chest. "Got you."

"Possibly." He caught her thighs in his big, warm hands, high up, right at the groin. His thumbs stroked her labia. She gasped at the sweet rise of pleasure. His golden eyes glinted up at her. "Then again, maybe I've got you."

Alina settled back on his muscled belly, gazing down into his handsome, angular face. The joy that swelled in her heart was almost giddy. Finally, she was free to touch him, love him as she chose. "Or maybe we've got each other." She sobered and touched his tattooed cheek. "I'm sorry."

He lifted a dark brow. "Sorry you've got me?"

"Sorry I hurt you."

He gave her a tight smile. "I got you back. I sicced the three-hundred-kilo Tevan on you."

"Mmm." Alina bent low over him and licked one of his nipples, her gaze on his. "And yet, I feel the need to atone."

Baird drew in a breath as she gently nibbled. "Well, if you insist."

She smiled, spreading her hands over the warm, muscled ridges of his chest. Licking, suckling, she stroked her way gently downward, exploring the tight line of his abdominals. They flexed as he gasped. Tenderly, she raked her nails through the thick ruff of hair on his chest. She inhaled, drinking in his scent.

One of his hands slipped between their bodies to cup her breast. He squeezed gently, then rolled her nipple between his fingers, sending sweet pleasure radiating through the peak.

But this was for him, so Alina drew away and moved

lower down his body. His cock curved over his belly, thick and silken, more of that thick hair covering his balls. She cupped him with one hand, and the big shaft leaped in anticipation. "Hi, there," she purred, bending over the silken head.

"Hi, yourself." His voice sounded hoarse with need. A bead of pre-come gathered on the tip of his cock, silent testimony to his hunger.

She flicked it off with her tongue, enjoying his moan, then circled the thick rod with her fingers. Angling him upward, she took him into her mouth, slowly, taking her time. His skin felt slightly nubby against her tongue as she swirled it back and forth. Tightening her lips, she began to suck in deep, slow pulls.

"Goddess, Alina!" Baird gasped. One hand came up catch the back of her head, fingers tunneling through her hair.

Smiling around his width, she slid him deeper, slowly, a centimeter at a time, spinning out the pleasure as long as she could. At the same time, she cupped him, stroking his heavy balls through the velvet skin of his sac.

He twisted under her. There was something so delicious in his arousal that she felt her own cream gathering. Baird wasn't a passive lover; she knew it wouldn't be long before his control snapped.

He lasted longer than she expected under her slow, delightful torment. But when he finally broke, there was no doubt about it.

"Enough!" Baird sat up, grabbed her around the hips, and rolled her under him. She spread her thighs eagerly as he settled between them, wrapping them around his backside as he lifted himself just enough to aim his cock for her slick core.

He entered in a single hard, deep thrust that took him all the way to the balls. "Goddess!" When he threw his head back, the cords stood high and stark on his powerful throat.

"Oh, more!" Alina writhed in mingled pleasure and joy as he began to shaft her in long, hard strokes. Each deep entry raked her clit with sweet friction, while every withdrawal pulled her inner flesh.

Her climax began to gather like a hot offshore storm, building every time his hips slapped hers. In the instant before they blew into pleasure, Baird's golden gaze met hers. "I love you."

"Yes! Goddess, Baird, I love you!"

The fire poured over them, blinding and hot, slinging them into sweet, dizzying heights. When the pleasure faded, he collapsed panting beside her, then promptly pulled her into his arms.

She lay across his hard chest, listening to his heart pound a fierce rhythm her own echoed. Her mouth drew into a sleepy curl. "It took me twenty years, but I'm back where I belong."

Baird's strong arms tightened, drawing her even closer. "We both are."

Painkillers

JACEY FORD

CH@%!*R

1

Lauren Devlin knew the pain was coming and tried not to tense up. She was familiar enough with this particular brand of torture to know that would only make it worse. She shivered as expert hands pinned her legs down so she couldn't move.

God, this was gonna hurt.

A ripping sound rent the air and Lauren flinched, knowing the pain was only a split-second away. Then it was upon her. Her legs spasmed, trying to clench together protectively, but the firm hands on Lauren's thighs held them apart. She gritted her teeth and tried to blink back the tears in her eyes, but couldn't stop them from falling.

Even worse, she knew this was just the beginning. Her torturer wouldn't let up until the job was finished.

"I swear, I am never going to do another swimsuit shoot," she grumbled, pressing her palms into her eyes to stem the tears.

The spa employee who was doing Lauren's bikini wax just nodded blandly and continued slathering hot wax on Lauren's tender parts with a Popsicle stick. Lauren figured anyone who voluntarily took on this job must have worked in a Nazi concentration camp in a former life, because they seemed to enjoy inflicting pain on others. She'd never met a waxer who didn't, at some point in the process, assure her that "This won't hurt a bit." Yeah, right.

Before the woman could tear another strip of Lauren's hair out by the roots, she held up a hand and said, "Wait a sec." Then she reached over and grabbed a tiny bottle of Isla Suspiro rum from the nightstand in her hotel room. She twisted off the metal cap, took a deep breath, and chugged half the bottle in one gulp.

"Okay, go ahead," she said to the resort employee, who put one firm hand on Lauren's knee before grabbing the edge of the strip of cloth she'd smoothed over the hot wax and ripping it off.

There were days when being a supermodel was anything but glamorous, Lauren thought as she peeled off a packet of aspirin that was attached with a rubbery adhesive to the bottle of rum. She was down here on Isla Suspiro—*Island of Sighs*—shooting an ad for the rum named for the island. Some marketing whiz at the company had decided to package their beverage with aspirin as a promotional gimmick. "A rum so good you'll be tempted to drink the whole bottle. But try to restrain yourself," the adline read. Apparently, the aspirin was for those who could not resist that temptation.

So much for encouraging moderation.

Lauren took another swig of rum as more hot wax was applied to her crotch. The sweet liquor burned going down, but at least it was an effective painkiller. The next strip that was ripped off didn't hurt quite as much as the last one had.

The photo shoot for Isla Suspiro Rum's print ads started today, hence this morning's torture. Lauren had already checked out the location for today's shoot—a beautiful stretch of white-sand beach here on the tourist side of the island, with swaying palm trees and water such a clear blue that it almost hurt to look at. Sadly, the tourist areas on this

island had to be protected by machine gun– wielding security guards, and travelers were advised not to leave these
secure locales without proper protection. Most U.S.
tourists who visited the island remained cloistered within
the concrete walls of their all-inclusive resorts, but even
they were sometimes accosted by drug runners on Jet Skis
who peddled their pharmaceuticals to anyone who swam
far enough from the beach.

Lauren, however, had no intention of remaining on Paradise Resort's property during her stay on Isla Suspiro. Not
because she had a hankering for mind-altering drugs, or
even because she believed that her status as an interna-
tional celebrity afforded her any more protection from
crime than a regular tourist.

No, it was because Lauren had come to Isla Suspiro on a
mission.

Because aside from being a supermodel, Lauren Devlin
was also a spy.

"Did you know your American friends have sent an agent
here to Isla Suspiro?" Emilio Santos asked quietly in his
second-story office at the Isla Suspiro Rum Company. He
kept his back to his brother, his hands clasped behind him as
he pretended to watch the activity on the production floor
below. Instead, he studied his older brother's reflection in
one of the windows overlooking the first floor.

Tomas Santos—a ruggedly handsome man who had
clawed his way to power two years before, after an election
fraught with allegations of fraud, blackmail, and bribery—
frowned at his brother's back. "Are you certain?" he asked.

Emilio kept his gaze focused on the floor below, where
employees in dark brown Isla Suspiro Rum Company uniforms scurried around like so many cockroaches. Emilio
knew his presence at the factory made the workers nervous, but he didn't care. Not in his company would the
mañana attitude that was so pervasive elsewhere be tolerated. When he demanded that something be done, he ex-

pected it to be done. *Now*. Not tomorrow—not *mañana*. Not in his factory.

"Yes, I'm sure," Emilio answered his brother's question before turning to walk back to the large mahogany desk that dominated his office. Tomas was seated across from the desk in a dove gray leather chair, his large tanned hands resting in his lap.

Where Emilio was small and wiry, both his older brother, Tomas, and his younger brother, Rafael, had the same broad shoulders and tall frame as their father had before his death. Unfortunately, Rafael also shared his oldest brother's hunger for power, a trait that had gotten him exiled two years ago to the primitive jungle that blanketed the wet southern coast of the island. Emilio made certain that Tomas never underestimated their younger brother's ambition. According to Emilio's frequent reports on Rafael's activities, banishing the youngest Santos son to the jungle had not stifled his desire to rule. Instead, it had merely provided Rafael with the isolation he needed to begin recruiting and training his own army—an army he would use to overthrow Tomas once Rafael had become powerful enough to attempt a coup.

Emilio suspected that Tomas wasn't as troubled as he should be by the threat Rafael presented, because he believed that the U.S. government looked favorably upon Tomas Santos remaining in power. Under his rule, the island was relatively safe for American tourists to visit. Crimes against U.S. citizens were taken seriously, and the perpetrators of these crimes were always promptly found and harshly punished. And if sometimes the wrong man was jailed for another's crimes? Well, once America felt that justice had been served, their eyes turned quickly to other matters.

In order to keep their relationship on stable terms, the United States had intervened several times in the past two years—quietly and without much fanfare—on Tomas's behalf. A suspicious bank account would mysteriously be frozen, a dissenter's camp would suddenly disappear.

Emilio knew the only reason Rafael had survived this long was because he had his own powerful allies that helped him keep one step ahead of both Tomas and the CIA. Plus, Emilio guessed that no one but him suspected how strong Rafael's army had become.

And Emilio, who was as intelligent and power-hungry as his brothers, had no intention of sharing that information with his older brother. At least, not until the time was right.

He sat down behind his desk and slowly sipped a cup of the rich coffee the island was famous for. "Why would the CIA send an agent here without arranging for him to meet with you?" Emilio asked, as if truly perplexed by the question.

Tomas's eyes narrowed, and his hands tightened convulsively in his lap. "I don't know. Perhaps the agent is simply here on vacation," he suggested, obviously resisting the idea that the CIA might turn against him.

"Or perhaps he's meeting with Rafael instead? Perhaps the Americans are unhappy with the job you're doing and wish to remove you from power," Emilio countered.

Tomas's gaze flicked to the busy production floor below. "Surely they don't expect that I can right a lifetime of wrongs in two years? Building better lives for the people of Isla Suspiro will take time. I can't increase spending to build much-needed roads and improve our port and airports until our people can support the higher taxes. It will take years—probably decades—before things begin to improve. There's no quick fix to our problems. Not unless the Americans are willing to send us more money than they already have."

"And if they do, you will be perceived as a puppet for the United States," Emilio said. His brother was in an impossible situation, and they both knew it. Tomas—fool that he was—was committed to doing what was best for the people of Isla Suspiro over the long term. That meant he would not resort to selling illegal drugs for a quick inflow of cash, which would have assured his popularity with the people and cemented his position as leader of the island. Instead, he was trying to get the fledgling rum and coffee industries off the ground, as well as building new schools to help educate the people and prepare them for better jobs. Only, these things took time, time Tomas wasn't certain he had—not with both his youngest brother and the CIA watching for the slightest sign of weakness.

"It's possible this agent is only here to observe conditions on the island," Tomas said.

"And it's also possible he's here to kill you," Emilio responded, his voice eerily devoid of emotion.

Tomas sighed heavily and rubbed the back of his neck with the air of a man well acquainted with adversity. "Yes, that's possible," he admitted.

"You know the Americans are impatient. If I can prove that their agent is meeting with Rafael, will you finally take my advice and do something to defend yourself against him?"

"He's our brother," Tomas protested softly, looking up at Emilio with his sad, dark eyes.

"He's your adversary," Emilio corrected. "One who would like to remove you from your duly elected position with violence, uncaring about the wishes of the people of this island."

Silence hung heavily in the air between the two brothers. This war had begun long ago, with Tomas's insistence that the only way to lead Isla Suspiro out of poverty was to work within the system for change, while Rafael argued with equal ferocity that the system itself was the problem and must be overthrown. Emilio just stood back and let his brothers argue. He didn't have the charisma to inspire people to follow his leadership. He knew that his only hope to obtain the power he wanted was to win it by default. And so he had stealthily laid his plans, waiting for the right moment to close his trap around both of his brothers.

Now. Now was the time.

Soon, the presidency would be his.

Finally, Tomas nodded and stood to leave. "All right.

Prove to me that this CIA agent is working with Rafael, and I will attack. I cannot allow our brother to gain any more power, not if he's already managed to win support from the United States."

From across his desk, Emilio nodded his approval, although he knew his brother neither wished for nor cared about his endorsement of his decisions. In politics, Tomas Santos would do what he felt was right, and to hell with what his younger brother thought about the matter.

Fortunately for Emilio, however, his brother did not show the same concern about the rum business. If he had, Emilio could not have let him live as long as he had.

No, Tomas left the running of Isla Suspiro Rum entirely to Emilio—a wise decision that was validated as their profits continued to climb. Of course, that also meant that Tomas had no idea *why* their income had increased so sharply in such a short amount of time, but Emilio figured that it was none of his brother's business. As long as the money kept coming in as expected to fund his own pursuits, Tomas left Emilio alone.

Emilio waited until the sound of his brother's footsteps faded before making certain the hallway was deserted. Then he closed and locked his office door and hurried back to his desk. From a secret compartment under the top drawer, he removed a key and unlocked a larger hidden compartment in the bottom drawer to his left. He pulled a cell phone out of the drawer and checked the scrambler before he hit redial. The call was answered on the first ring.

"The CIA has sent someone to interfere in your business. It would be in your best interest to stop him," Emilio said without preamble.

"Do they know about our plans for Sunday?" the man on the other end of the line asked, his voice clipped and abrupt.

"Not unless one of your men leaked the information. I just spoke to Tomas and it's clear that he does not know. At least, not yet," Emilio added ominously.

"It's possible, then, that this agent is here to tell him

about our plans," Rafael Santos said, then paused, as if considering what to do next.

Emilio impatiently tapped his fingers on his desk, willing his brother to come to the conclusion that Emilio himself had when he had first learned of the CIA's presence on the island.

"I must stop him from reaching Tomas," Rafael said finally.

Emilio had to resist the urge to clap, as if his younger brother were a trained seal at a circus that had performed its trick well. "Yes. But you must make it appear as if he came to you willingly. That will confirm Thomas's suspicions that the Americans have turned against him."

"Yes. Yes, you're right," Rafael agreed. "I will have my men take care of it immediately. Where can I find this American spy?"

"Paradise Resort. I was not able to get the man's name from my source, but he did tell me it was someone who arrived on the island this morning and is staying at the resort. The rest, I'm afraid, I must leave up to you." Emilio didn't like leaving so much in the hands of his brother, but he couldn't call the resort to try to get more information without risking Tomas finding out. His older brother had spies everywhere.

This game of playing brother against brother was becoming tedious, but as Emilio hung up the phone and replaced it in the secret compartment in his desk, he allowed himself a small smile. In a short time, the game would be over and he could just imagine Tomas's and Rafael's surprise when they realized who had wrested their power away from them.

Yes, it wouldn't be long before Emilio had it all—the money, the power, and the admiration of the people of Isla Suspiro. Too bad his satisfaction at seeing his brothers defeated wouldn't last long. Once Emilio had what he wanted, they would both have to die.

CH@%!*R

2

"Haven, you are one lucky bastard," Jake Haven muttered to himself as he opened Lauren Devlin's hotel room door and caught a glimpse of the turquoise waters of the Caribbean Sea lapping away at the beach outside. He stepped inside the room, put his bag down on the marble tiled floor, and whistled. In the movies, spies always stayed at posh resorts and got laid by gorgeous women. In real life, however, CIA agents were government employees who did not have unlimited expense accounts and were more likely to be holed up doing surveillance in their rented Ford Tauruses than snuggled in at the Ritz. And as for the women . . . well, let's just say there was fantasy and there was reality and, although Jake talked a big game with the support staff, he spent more time alone than he cared to admit.

The thing was, Jake liked to keep the fantasy alive. He wanted others to believe that his was a glamorous, high-danger, high-excitement life. Hell, he *himself* wanted to believe that. So, yeah, when he finally did get assigned an op that looked as though it had come right out of the script of a James Bond movie, he felt pretty fucking lucky. What red-blooded American male wouldn't?

He looked around the room, from the disheveled sheets on the bed to the empty rum bottles lying on their sides on the nightstand and the silky women's panties draped over a rattan chair near the French doors leading out to the beach. Jake eyed those panties and sent up a silent "thank you" to his partner, Race. It was only because of Race's girlfriend, Aimee, that Jake had been assigned this job. Or rather, because Race's girlfriend Aimee had a supermodel for a sister.

Jake had been photographed standing on Aimee's porch chatting with her sister just often enough for the tabloids to hint that Jake and Lauren were more than just casual strangers. Two days ago, when Jake's boss suggested they exploit those rumors to provide Jake with a cover story for this op, Jake had nearly whooped with joy. He'd been trying to get up the nerve to ask Lauren out for months, but something always held him back.

Unfortuantely, Jake knew exactly what that something was—fear. He was as confident as the next guy, but he wasn't about to toss his ego down in front of a supermodel and watch her stomp all over it with her five-inch heels.

He'd been astounded to learn that Lauren worked undercover with the Agency, but he supposed he shouldn't have been so surprised. As a supermodel, she traveled extensively and got to meet heavy-hitters from all over the world. And because of her looks, she no doubt got treated like arm candy a lot, which meant no one worried about saying something in her presence that she might actually understand.

"Never underestimate the treachery of a woman," Jake muttered as he crossed the room to a desk in the corner. He didn't know where Lauren was—probably off sunbathing somewhere in an incredibly small bikini. Just the thought of seeing her nearly naked made Jake hard, but he tried to remind himself that he had about as much chance getting laid by Lauren Devlin this weekend as did the bellboy who'd offered to take his bag when he'd arrived.

Women like Lauren didn't pay much attention to guys like him. Not in the real world, where government salaries were part of the public record.

Still, that wasn't going to stop Jake from enjoying his fantasy to the fullest.

When his boss had told him his mission was to provide backup to an informant on the CIA's payroll, Jake hadn't thought much of it. He'd done this many times before: providing support to a highly placed official in a hostile government or relaying information for an agent who had gone deep undercover. He'd never had a model as an informant before, but Jake sure as hell wasn't complaining.

And it wasn't like Lauren was a *real* agent. According to her handler, Martha McLaughlin—a smug, egotistical woman Jake had come to dislike over the years—Lauren had been recruited by the Agency to do nothing more than provide low-risk intel. Who attended so-and-so's party? How many armed bodyguards does Prince such-and-such travel with? What time and from which airport is this suspected drug dealer arriving? That sort of thing. She'd probably never so much as picked a lock during her "career" with the CIA.

On this op, Lauren had been sent in to see if she could discover who was funding Rafael Santos's army. Unfortunately, the CIA had just uncovered evidence that the rebel army was gearing up for an attack, so Jake had been sent in to take over the case. He had to find some way to trace the source of Santos's funds and stop the flow of money to the rebel forces. If he could stem the tide of money, a coup attempt could be averted, and thousands of lives could be saved.

And that was what his job was really about. Not glamour or excitement or fun, but saving lives. Most of the time, it was downright boring. But at least his partner on this op would be easy on the eyes.

Jake sat down at the desk and pulled open a drawer to

find some paper and a pen, then chuckled to himself when he realized that Lauren had taped a manila folder to the bottom of the drawer.

"Great hiding place." He snorted, tugging the file loose. He flipped it open to find satellite photos of the island along with a map and pictures of the key players in Isla Suspiro's political arena. Jake had been given a duplicate file, but he'd studied the information and then destroyed it before coming to the island.

Jake pulled a piece of resort stationery out of the drawer and quickly penned a note to Lauren just in case she returned to the room before he found her. He'd left a message on her cell phone after getting off the plane from Miami giving her his ETA at the resort, but she hadn't called him back. He wrote down his cell number again and told her to meet him in the lobby at one o'clock if she got his message. Then he started whistling again he crossed toward the French doors that opened up onto the white sand beach. The first place he was going to look for her was down near a cluster of palm trees where the Isla Suspiro Rum photo shoot was supposed to be taking place.

Oh, yeah. Babes in bikinis, here I come, Jake thought as he pulled open the door and stepped out into the sunshine to find his new partner.

Lauren winced as the hairdresser's comb jerked to a stop at the knot in her hair.

"I'm sorry, Miss Devlin," the woman apologized as she gingerly picked at the tangle.

This was the fourth time in less than two hours that Lauren's hair had had to be blow-dried, and the spray-on detangler was no match for saltwater. What she really needed was to go back to her room and condition her hair, but the psychotic photographer kept insisting that he was only one click away from getting the perfect shot. In the meantime, Lauren's hair was being systematically destroyed by the combination of sea air, sand, and blow-drying. Not to mention that, even with the water a balmy 85 degrees, her nipples were killing her from rubbing against her cold, wet swimsuit. But the client was paying for a surf shot, so a surf shot they would get.

Lauren sighed as she exited the hair and makeup tent. The caterers had brought a cooler full of bottled water and sodas in addition to the sandwiches and salads that were always ordered on photo shoots but that no one ate. Lauren didn't know any models who would actually eat in public—some because they had serious eating disorders, like bingeing on doughnuts and fried chicken and then throwing it all up, and others because they were uncomfortable with the scrutiny they were under when they ate. Lauren didn't eat because she'd had her fill of cereal, fresh fruit, and rum that morning after the sadist from the spa had come to rip her hair out by its roots. She didn't typically drink alcohol for breakfast, but sometimes a girl had to do what a girl had to do.

And right now, she had to get back into the water, spread her legs, and act as if she were making love with the surf, chafed nipples, crispy hair, and all.

Right-e-o.

"Lauren, there's a good girl. Hurry up now, will you? I'm going to lose my light," the photographer said as soon as he caught sight of her emerging from the tent.

Lauren rolled her eyes heavenward. Brad Klein was from Cleveland, but he insisted on using a fake English accent and acting as though every photo shoot he did was of the utmost importance. Like what they were doing really made a difference. Not that Lauren had anything against advertising or models or even sadistic photographers. They just weren't exactly saving the world here.

She sighed as she stepped into the surf and felt the bathtub-warm water lapping around her ankles. She couldn't wait for this shoot to be over so she could get back to her real mission. As soon as her backup arrived, she wanted to head out into the jungle to gather more intel on the rebel troop's movements and see if her hunch was correct that a coup attempt was imminent.

She didn't know who the Agency was sending in for backup. She'd been told the agent would contact her when he arrived on the island, but cell service here was spotty, and it wasn't like she could pack a cell phone in the tiny bikini she was wearing. Last time she'd tried to check her messages, she couldn't get a signal. Hopefully, this photo shoot would be over soon and she could go back to her room and get in touch with her contact.

"Okay then, back into the water, love," the photographer said.

Lauren grimaced and started to lower herself into the sea, but stopped when a familiar voice said, "Lauren, baby. Why'd you run out on me like that back in Atlanta? I've missed you."

Huh? Run out on who? And what was with that *baby* crap? She looked up, shielding her eyes from the sun's rays as Jake Haven sauntered toward her with the usual wiseass grin plastered on his face.

Ever since they'd met, she and Jake had had what could be termed an "interesting" relationship. He tried to charm her with his tales of danger and adventure as a CIA operative, and she discounted about 85 percent of everything he said. After all, she'd been trained at The Farm just like he had, and she knew bullshit when it was plated up and shoved under her nose, even though Jake tried to convince her it was filet mignon.

She was certain Jake hadn't known she was CIA before now. If he had, he never would have tried to convince her that his outlandish tales of adventure overseas were true.

But there was only one reason he could be looking for her on this beach—he'd been sent here as her backup. Which meant they were ready to roll. Which also meant this photo shoot was now a wrap. But how could she end it? She squinted, trying to recall if the *Secret Agent's Handbook* her handler had given her after her training was complete had any advice for such a situation. She didn't think it had, so she supposed she was on her own for this one.

"My gosh, I'm feeling dizzy," Lauren said, dramatically fluttering the eyelashes her makeup artist had just finished lengthening to twice their original size. Then, as artfully as possible, she sank into the sea, being careful to fall forward onto her knees so as not to get her hair wet again. She couldn't take another bout with the blow-dryer.

Although Brad had been the one standing closest to her, Jake was the first to reach her. Through half-closed eyes, Lauren saw the tips of his brown boots digging into the sand as he squatted down on the beach. Then she nearly forgot herself and opened her eyes with surprise when, in one smooth move, he scooped her up out of the water with one arm under her knees and the other beneath her shoulders.

"Someone get her some water," he ordered in the most serious tone Lauren had ever heard him use.

She kept her eyes screwed shut as Jake carried her toward the hair and makeup tent. His grip on her was surprisingly firm, as was the chest her right cheek kept banging against as he walked.

"Lauren? Are you all right?" he asked once they were under the shade of the tent.

"She probably just needs some food. These silly models are always fainting from hunger," she head Brad say from behind Jake.

Asshole, she thought. She wondered how he'd like to lie out there under the sun for two straight hours with nothing covering his head. Not to mention having people whisper behind his back that he was getting fat if he happened to gain half a pound.

But, hey, if it would get her out of this photo shoot, she didn't mind if Brad thought she was some delicate flower. *Give them what they expect.* That was her motto.

Her eyes fluttered open, and she found herself staring up into Jake's dark green eyes. She'd never really noticed his eyes before, but they were quite nice, fringed with golden brown lashes a shade darker than his hair.

"Are you okay?" he asked softly, shifting his weight back onto his heels and holding her even closer to his chest.

Lauren pulled her bottom lip into her mouth to moisten it. She was so close she could hear Jake's heart beating slowly and rhythmically and could smell the faint traces of laundry detergent still clinging to his black T-shirt. It was interesting how you could know someone for months and then suddenly be smacked in the head with this awareness that he might be something different—something *more*—than you thought.

"I'm fine," Lauren whispered, their gazes still locked together. Then she closed her eyes, shook her head. "No, I mean, I feel so weak," she corrected, louder this time, so Brad could overhear what she was saying.

The photographer came over with a bottle of water and held it out to her. "Here, drink this," he said.

Lauren gave a disappointed little sigh and forced her hand to tremble as she brought it to her throat. "Oh, not that water, please. It has an aftertaste."

Brad scowled at the bottle in his hand and then at her. Lauren heard him mutter something about "freaking spoiled models" as he went back to the cooler and rummaged around in the half-melted ice to find her another brand. "How's this one?" he asked, holding up a different bottle.

"Maybe . . . could you find the kind with the electrolytes?" she asked shakily and felt Jake's chest rumble beneath her right ear as he coughed.

Brad finally found the brand of water Lauren had requested. She waited for Jake to put her down, but he seemed perfectly content to continue holding her. Since that made her look even more weak and helpless, Lauren didn't protest. Not that she really wanted to. His hold on her was startlingly comfortable.

She twisted the cap off of the bottle and took a tiny sip as if she couldn't force herself to drink any more than that. Then she nestled her head back against Jake's chest as if even that small effort had exhausted her. "I don't think I can go back out there," she said in a breathy tone.

"She's had enough for the day," Jake announced decisively, turning toward the resort as if he intended to carry her across the beach and back to her room.

"But what about my light?" Brad protested.

"It'll have to wait until tomorrow," Jake said.

Lauren let her hand drop to her side, leaving it dangling in the air as if she were too overcome to move.

"Who are you, anyway?" Brad grumbled.

"I'm Jake Haven. Lauren and I are, uh, friends," Jake said, pausing just long enough for Brad to get the idea that they were more than friends. "And I'm not going to let her go back out there and get sunstroke. Can't you see that she's dehydrated?"

Lauren smacked her lips as if to prove Jake's point that she was parched. She *was* thirsty, but didn't want to swallow the entire bottle of water until Brad was out of sight. Better to let him think she was at death's door. Not that he had much say in the matter. That was one thing about being a supermodel—when you were in such high demand, you got to call the shots. At her level, diva-ish behavior was not only tolerated, it was expected. Show up late. Throw a temper tantrum if the room was too hot or too cold. Bitch about how awful the three-thousand-dollar-a-night hotel room was. Complain about the food, the photographer, the wardrobe, the hair and makeup people. You could pretty much make everyone around you miserable, and you still got callbacks because you had the look clients wanted.

Some of the girls let it go to their heads, but Lauren had learned early in life that all this attention wasn't about *her*, it was about how she looked. Yeah, in the beginning, she'd thought she was pretty hot stuff. She'd led a charmed life in high school—always trying out for, and making, the cheerleading squad, always getting the extra help she needed in her classes, always getting the guy she liked to ask her out.

Things started to change the first time she had sex with

a guy. She'd waited until her eighteenth birthday. In the harsh light of maturity, she now saw that she'd been on a power trip. It hadn't been about waiting for the right guy to come along. It had been about proving that she was the one in control. So she picked the time, she picked the place, she picked the guy, and in the arrogance of her youth, she was convinced that she'd be the best he'd ever had.

Only, she hadn't been. She'd had no clue what to do once the clothes were off and there was nothing between them but naked skin. And afterward, she'd realized that her partner hadn't been disappointed because she was all that bad in bed, he'd been disappointed because he believed that a woman who looked as good as Lauren did should come packaged with some sort of Super Vagina that would guarantee a guy the most incredible sex he'd ever had. With her, they expected multiple orgasms. Nonstop sex every five minutes for the entire night. Swinging from trapezes and God only knew what else.

It had occurred to Lauren then that, underneath the pretty exterior she'd been blessed with, she was really just an ordinary person who was no better than anyone else.

It was a lesson she would never forget.

Which was why she didn't take the attention she received too seriously. She knew how meaningless it really was. But that didn't mean she was above using her power when it suited her.

"All right. But don't be late tomorrow morning. Remember, we're meeting in the lobby at 10:30 to drive out to the rum company to do a shoot out there," Brad said, as if he were the one in charge.

Lauren simply nodded in the photographer's direction as Jake started across the hot sand. Then she remembered something. "Wait, I need my bag," she said, waving toward the tent where she'd left her beach bag, which contained her *Secret Agent's Handbook*, room key, wallet, sandals, and a see-through cover-up to wear over her bikini bottoms. Jake detoured, effortlessly slinging her bag over his shoulder before heading back to the hotel.

Once they were out of earshot of the crew, Lauren allowed herself a small smile and said, "You can put me down now. I'm perfectly capable of walking."

"What? And ruin that Oscar-worthy performance?" Jake said with a chuckle.

"Yeah, I was good, wasn't I?"

"You were," Jake acknowledged. "I can see why you'd be effective at gathering intelligence."

Lauren grimaced as Jake stepped into the cool lobby of the hotel. "People think models are weak and stupid. I just give them what they expect."

As they turned down the hallway leading to her room, Jake seemed as though he were about to say something, but he stopped abruptly when two men stepped out from behind an enormous potted plant. Jake hurriedly stepped backward, but stopped again when two more men came up behind him.

Just in case anyone was wondering, four-to-two odds in the real world—especially when neither of the two were armed and one of the two had his hands full of the other one—weren't good. Yeah, in the movies, James Bond would whistle, and his high-tech car would come roaring out of nowhere to save him, or he'd push a button on his watch, and his attackers would all fall to the ground in agony. But if Jake were to push a button on his watch, all that would happen is his stopwatch would start. And Lauren wasn't even wearing a watch—just a skimpy metallic-looking bikini and a whole lot of sand.

"Shit," Jake said as one of the guys stuck something that felt suspiciously like the barrel of a gun in his kidneys.

"Welcome to Isla Suspiro, Mr. Haven," the man holding the gun said pleasantly.

"Please come with us," the thug ahead of him and to his right said.

"And if you make any noise, we'll kill you both right here," another man added.

Jake looked down at Lauren, then back up at the men. "Okay," he said. "Just let me get rid of the girl."

"I don't think so," the guy on his right said, eyeing Lauren appreciatively.

This was not good at all. A barely clothed Lauren Devlin was making Jake's palms itch. He could only imagine what these goons had in mind.

"She stays here. She's got nothing to do with whatever it is you boys want from me," he said firmly, unconsciously tightening his hold on her.

Unfortunately, they didn't buy his argument. Instead, the thug with the gun moved the barrel up so that it was resting just below Jake's elbow, right against Lauren's side. A point-blank shot there would puncture her lung and go straight through her heart and keep on going. She'd die right here in his arms, with no chance that he could get help in time to save her.

"All right. Let's go, then," he said, slowly turning around to follow their lead. He braved a quick glance at Lauren, who had remained silent during the entire exchange and who was now looking up at him with more than a hint of fear in her heart-stoppingly gorgeous blue eyes. "Sorry," he mouthed, wishing the apology didn't sound so lame.

Her eyes narrowed ferociously for a split second, and then the wide-eyed fear was back so quickly that Jake thought that maybe he'd just imagined it. That is, until she curled one hand around his neck, leaned so close he felt a lock of her dark brown hair tickling his chin, and whispered, "This is perfect. They're going to take us right into the rebel camp."

Jake sighed and started walking. He had a feeling this weekend wasn't going to turn out at all like he'd planned.

CH@%!*R

3

By the time they reached camp, Lauren had managed to make the rebels wish they'd left her back at the resort. She'd pretended to be frightened about everything from the wild parrots that screeched overhead to an imagined spider that she insisted had dropped into their jeep when they'd stopped for her to relieve herself. She forced them to give her her beach bag back by refusing to go into the jungle without shoes on and then complained so much about the possibility of getting sunburned that one of the men had finally given her his shirt just to shut her up.

Whatever happened next, she wanted them to be convinced she wouldn't try to escape. It amazed her how easily most people bought her act. Did they not consider it possible that all that whining was just for show?

Apparently not, Lauren thought as she snuck a look over at Jake, who had his eyes closed and appeared to be asleep. The warm heat of the tropical sun peeking out between heavy jungle foliage was certainly conducive to napping, but Lauren didn't know how he could sleep when they were in danger. He should be formulating an escape plan, not napping. What kind of a spy was he? Lauren stifled a yawn and forced herself to sit up straight. She had to pay attention, to memorize the route the rebels were taking so she could lead them out once they escaped.

Their journey took several hours, the jeep winding its way up a narrow muddy mountainside. They passed the occasional vehicle, each one full of men dressed in camouflage gear with machine guns at their sides who nodded without smiling to the thugs who had kidnapped Lauren and Jake. The men didn't talk much, communicating more in a series of grunts and nods than anything else.

Typical, Lauren thought. She was certain if she asked what they were thinking, they'd all say, "Nothing" . . . and mean it.

In her mind, she pictured the satellite photos she'd been provided with before coming on this mission—photos that clearly showed this path through these mountains. She had been sent here because recent photos showed a marked increase in traffic along this road. The CIA didn't have clear pictures of the rebel camp itself, the jungle was too good at hiding Rafael Santos's headquarters. But they were able to estimate where Santos had set up camp just by tracking traffic patterns on the roads leading into the jungle.

On her first day here, Lauren had hired a local helicopter pilot to take her up and give her an overview of the island's layout. On her second day, she went up again on a group tour of the local waterfalls as an excuse to get access to this specific region. She figured that if anyone became suspicious of her activities, she could say she was just helping to scout locations for the photo shoot. But even as recently as a few days ago, there had been little traffic on this road. Unlike today, she hadn't seen even one vehicle as they'd flown to Nuevo Rios, a popular tourist destination with stunning waterfalls and clear lakes where bathers could escape the jungle heat.

It was obvious that things had changed in the last few days, since the rebels weren't even trying to stay out of sight. Lauren just hoped she and Jake could figure out when the rebels planned to attack so they could communicate the details to Tomas Santos. Should be easy. All they had to do was to stay alive long enough to make their escape.

Lauren took a sip of the bottled water she'd brought along and then glanced over at Jake to see if he was awake and would like a drink. He still had his eyes closed, so she put the cap back on the bottle and tucked it back into her bag, just as they skidded around a corner and the driver slammed the vehicle to a stop.

Lauren blinked at the scene in front of her. From around the corner, she hadn't heard anything—not the buzz of voices or the sound of truck engines or anything. When the driver turned off the jeep's engine, she realized that part of what was muffling the sound of the rebel camp was the constant roar of a not-so-distant waterfall. She looked around and couldn't see anything but the dense jungle surrounding them, but the waterfall had to be near.

"Get out," the man in the passenger seat ordered, turning around to wave a machine gun under Jake's nose.

Jake started as if he'd been jerked awake. He rolled his shoulders back and stretched his arms before standing up and jumping out of the jeep. The man sitting between Jake and Lauren got up next, his heavy boots hitting the packed dirt with a thud. He held his hand out to indicate that he wanted his shirt back, so Lauren obliged, being careful not to flash the men as she slipped the T-shirt over her head. Then she gingerly stepped over to the side of the vehicle and looked down at the ground as if afraid she'd bruise her tender feet if she had to jump all that way by herself. Jake noticed her hesitation and stepped forward to help her, but the man in the passenger seat stopped him with a pointed thrust of his gun in the direction of Jake's gut. Lauren clambered awkwardly out of the vehicle, taking care not to land on anything that might puncture the soles of her thin sandals.

She took a deep breath. Okay, here was the part where she

was gang-raped while the thugs held Jake's arms and forced him to watch. Funny, she hadn't really been scared up till now. She wasn't sure why—maybe because she'd felt that their affiliation with the CIA would keep them from being harmed. After all, the rebels had to know that the CIA would retaliate if they killed one of their agents.

But did they even know she and Jake were CIA? What if they had come for Jake for an entirely different reason?

And if there were no witnesses to their kidnapping, how would the Agency even know who to retaliate against?

Lauren swallowed. Hard. Then she forced herself to turn around, surprised to find a tall, handsome man striding toward them. Like the men around him, he wore a dark green T-shirt tucked into a pair of jungle camouflage pants that were, in turn, tucked into a pair of heavy black boots. His skin was the color of an expensive lambskin coat. His hair and eyes were dark brown, his features strong, his face smooth and unlined.

She knew from the file she'd studied earlier that this was none other than the rebel leader himself, Rafael Santos.

"Well, what do we have here?" Santos asked, looking at Lauren with amusement.

"You've obviously been in this jungle way too long. I'm a woman," Lauren said, raising her eyebrows and forcing herself to project an air of bravado she didn't feel.

Santos laughed and eyed her appreciatively. "I've not been out here *that* long. What is she doing here?" This last was addressed to the man in the passenger seat, who was apparently the highest-ranking goon in the bunch.

The rebel shrugged. "She was with Haven. I didn't think you wanted witnesses."

"Ah. Well, this is certainly a welcome surprise. You men take Haven over to the west compound. You know what to do with him." Santos didn't even spare Jake a glance as he reached out to take Lauren's arm. "My name is Rafael Santos, and I'd be delighted if you'd dine with me this evening. I apologize for the crude state of my camp, but I can at least offer you a warm bath and some clothes."

Lauren slid a look at Jake as she walked past, hoping her eyes conveyed the message she knew she couldn't voice: *Don't worry, Jake. I'll save you.*

Rafael Santos was in high spirits as he entered his tent two hours later and found his brother Emilio pacing the floor, waiting for him. He believed that God had sent the beautiful American girl to him as a sign that he was destined to succeed in his mission to lead the people of Isla Suspiro to freedom and wealth. Wasn't that what America symbolized? And to have this woman dropped in his lap such a short time before he was to reclaim his birthright? Yes, surely she had been sent from heaven to show him that his mission was blessed.

"Glad to see that one of us is in a good mood," Emilio grumbled, flopping his thin frame down onto a heavy wooden chair.

Briefly, Rafael considered telling his brother about the woman, but he changed his mind as he quickly pondered what Emilio's reaction might be. Emilio trusted no one. Most likely, he'd tell Rafael to have his fun with the girl and then kill her, but Rafael had no intention of so carelessly tossing away God's gift.

No. Better to keep this secret to himself for now.

"Our plans are proceeding according to schedule," he said instead, reaching out to take a tumbler from off the top of a bookshelf. He poured two fingers of rum into the glass and added several ice cubes from a small portable freezer before handing the glass to his brother. He made a similar drink for himself and pulled out a chair to sit down when he noticed several Isla Suspiro Rum boxes stacked near the door of his tent.

"Some of the new shipment?" he asked, nodding toward the boxes.

Emilio grunted. "Yes. And the last of the funds you'll need before Sunday."

"Ah. Excellent," Rafael said. This was indeed a good day.

"Did you capture the American agent?"

"Of course," Rafael answered, taking a sip of rum and letting the smooth liquid roll around on his tongue for a moment before swallowing. Isla Suspiro rum was some of the finest on the market. Too bad the rum itself didn't provide enough profits to make anyone rich. If it had, this split between Rafael and his oldest brother might have been unnecessary. But, who knew? It still might have come to this. He and Tomas might have the same goals, but they would never agree on how to achieve them.

Tomas was already losing favor with the people, after only two years in power. If he were allowed to remain as president, someone—someone other than Rafael, who had the people's best interests at heart—might overthrow the government and bring more pain to the nation. As Emilio constantly reminded him, Rafael was the only one who could ensure that did not happen.

"I will hold the American until our mission on Sunday is complete," Rafael said.

"And then what?" Emilio asked. "You can't just let him go. The CIA will not look favorably upon someone who has kidnapped one of their agents."

Rafael frowned and set his tumbler down on the table with a loud *thunk*. "Would you have me release him now? I can't take the risk that he'll interfere with my plans once he's free."

Emilio Santos closed his eyes and gritted his teeth as he counted to ten. His brother was such a fool. "No," he said after he'd calmed his temper. "You must kill him and have your men bring his body to me. I will make it appear as if Tomas had him assassinated. This will help turn the Americans to your favor when the time is right."

Rafael's eyes narrowed. "I can't do that. What if the CIA discovers that I was the one responsible for their agent's death?"

Emilio clutched his glass with both hands and prayed for patience. *Two days*, he promised himself. In two days, Tomas and Rafael would be dead and he would be in power, and this would all have been worth it. "Pick some-one expendable to do the job and have him deliver the body to me. I will take care of seeing that the murder cannot be linked to you. Or are you willing to risk the welfare of Isla Suspiro's people by allowing this spy to stop you?"

Rafael seemed to ponder the question for a long time before raising his gaze from his drink. He looked troubled, sudden lines appearing around his eyes that had not been there a moment before. "I suppose," he said, raising his glass to his lips once more, "in war, one must be prepared to carry out reprehensible tasks to ensure the greater good." He took a sip of his drink and paused for a moment, then brought his gaze back to Emilio's. "I will send my man, Hector, to you with the body of the American. It will be done."

CH@%!*R
4

Lauren gasped with surprise when the flap of the tent she'd been shown to was suddenly jerked aside. A large man with a head like a steel toaster stepped inside and tersely said, "Come."

She'd had over two hours to fret, pace, and primp and was glad to get out of there. At one point, she'd tried going outside, but was stopped by one of the two heavily armed guards stationed at her tent. The tent was near the middle of the camp, with men walking all around, so she couldn't attempt an escape out the back until it quieted down. Or until the sun set and her disappearance wouldn't be quite so noticeable. In the meantime, she'd been left alone to worry.

How badly had Jake been hurt? What did the rebels want from him? Would they release him once they had the information they wanted, or did they plan to kill him?

She'd paced the tent, searching for something to use as a weapon, but hadn't found anything. One of the rebels had brought her a pair of loose white cotton pants and a matching tank top. She was glad to have something to put on over her skimpy bathing suit, but there was no way she could escape unnoticed wearing white.

Which may have been exactly why this outfit had been chosen for her.

She had asked for a sturdier pair of shoes than the strappy sandals she'd tucked into her beach bag that morning, but her request had been ignored. Instead, the rebel who had delivered the clothes brought her a bucket of warm water, a washcloth, some soap, and a hairbrush. Her request for a mirror had been met with the same stony silence and dark look that she'd gotten when she'd asked for better shoes.

So much for befriending the enemy.

It had taken her ten minutes to get cleaned up. The rest of the time she'd spent pacing the dirt floor of the tent, trying to eavesdrop on the men outside and sitting on the lone cot studying her *Secret Agent's Handbook* for ideas of how to free Jake. The *Handbook* was, written in special ink. To the casual observer, it looked like nothing more than a popular novel. But when viewed through the secret lens hidden in an ordinary-looking bookmark, it became a textbook filled with tips about everything from fending off an alligator attack and communicating with another agent in a prison camp to surviving a trip down a waterfall and seducing the leader of a band of guerillas. Lauren paid particular attention to that last one, since she figured she might need to use those skills later in the evening.

By the time Santos's thug came for her, she was ready to start digging her way out of the camp with her bare hands—and to hell with the manicure she'd gotten yesterday. She wanted to be doing something, not just sitting here waiting. This was her first real op since graduating from the Agency's accelerated training program the month before, and she wanted to put the skills she'd learned, both during training and by nearly memorizing every word of her *Secret Agent's Handbook,* to use. For the first time in her life, she had the chance to make a real difference in the world. Now if only an opportunity would present itself so she could make her escape and get started.

In the meantime, she had no choice but to follow Santos's man across the camp, ignoring the way her progress was watched by the rebels. It was difficult not to feel somewhat like a piece of rare beef being dragged on a string through a pit of hungry lions. She scooted closer to the man who had come for her, as if he might protect her if one of the lions suddenly swiped out a paw to grab her. The training she'd gone through had made her fairly confident in her own abilities to protect herself, but there was no way she could single-handedly take on a platoon of determined men.

When the rebel stopped in front of another, larger tent and rapped on a wooden support post, Lauren couldn't hold back a shiver. Then she straightened her shoulders and told herself to start acting like a real agent. If Santos had planned to throw her to his men, he would have done it already.

There was a muffled "Come in" from inside the tent and Toaster Head stepped aside to let her pass. Lauren raised her chin and breezed past the man, determined to behave as if this sort of thing happened to her every day.

"Good evening, my dear. You look lovely," Rafael Santos said as she walked into the tent, a warm glint in his molten chocolate eyes. He had changed out of his camouflage gear and into a pair of tan linen slacks and a cream-colored shirt that highlighted the golden tone of his tanned skin. He stood near a large mahogany table that dwarfed the room, his right hand resting on the back of a chair, and a glass half-full of some amber liquid in his left.

Lauren quickly scanned the room, hoping to spot a gun or some other weapon that might aid in her escape. There was a low bookcase along one wall. On top of the bookcase was a small assortment of liquor bottles and glasses.

Hmm, the bottles were a definite possibility in the weapon category.

Next to the bookcase were several cardboard boxes with

the words *Isla Suspiro Rum Company* printed on them in black. The only other things in the room were a small refrigerator, a portable wardrobe rack where several uniforms were hung, and a cot that wasn't much larger than the one in her tent—nothing Lauren could use to get herself out of this predicament. So she would just have to play along, it seemed.

"Thank you," she said with a half smile, acknowledging Rafael's compliment as she took a step toward the table where he stood watching her.

"Would you like a drink?" he offered, inclining his head toward the bottles on top of the bookcase.

"A small one, thank you."

Ice cubes clinked against crystal as Rafael poured a drink and brought it to her. He smiled down at her and took her hand, leading her to the head of the table, where he pulled out a chair carved from a wood so dark it was almost black. He indicated that she should sit, so she did, her pants softly swishing as she crossed her legs.

"So tell me," Rafael began, studying her intently as if trying to gauge her reaction to his next question. "What were you doing with our friend, Mr. Haven?"

Lauren took a sip of her rum and shrugged, quickly trying to think up a plausible lie. She had no way of knowing how much Santos knew of what went on in the outside world. She and Jake had been photographed together numerous times, so she couldn't pretend that they didn't know each other.

If Rafael had done his research in the past two hours, he would know she was lying. So she went for a modified version of the truth instead.

"Jake and I had a few dates back in Atlanta, but we were never anything serious." True. Yes, those so-called dates always included her sister, Aimee, or Jake's partner, Race, but Santos couldn't know that. The tabloids had been quick to link Lauren romantically with her mystery man.

"I had no idea he planned to follow me down here," she continued. Also true. She hadn't known the Agency was sending backup until yesterday. She took another sip of rum and smiled right up into Santos's eyes and said, "He means nothing to me." Not true, Lauren was surprised to find herself thinking. Before that surprise could show on her face, she blinked it away and concentrated on the man standing across from her.

"Your country is very beautiful," she said, changing the subject and hoping flattery would loosen the rebel leader's tongue.

"Yes it is," Rafael agreed. He took a seat next to her and reached out to touch her hair. "And so are you," he added softly.

Yeah, yeah, yeah, Lauren wanted to say. Like she'd never heard *that* before. Instead, she batted her eyelashes, thanked him again, and asked, "How long have lived here? In the jungle, I mean."

"A few years," he answered evasively.

"It must get lonely. Hard to meet new people up here," she joked.

He chuckled. "I manage to stay busy. But I will admit it's not often that a woman such as yourself shows up in my camp. Today must be my lucky day."

I wouldn't exactly say that. Lauren smiled. "Yes, and mine too."

Rafael leaned forward, looking as if he were about to kiss her, when a knock sounded from outside. He swore under his breath, but soon recovered his manners. "This must be dinner. I hope you're hungry."

"Starving," Lauren said. She didn't have to lie about that. She *was* starving.

Her stomach grumbled hungrily as two men entered the tent wheeling a cart between them. Whatever they had brought, it smelled heavenly. She slowly sipped her drink, mindful that Rafael was watching her and would think it odd if she left her drink untasted, as a feast was laid out before them on the table.

As they ate and chatted pleasantly, Lauren tried to come up with a plan to stash some food for Jake. She'd bet he wasn't being treated as well as she was, and he was certain to be hungry by the time she managed to get them both free. Unfortunately, the outfit she'd been given didn't have any pockets, and, even if it had, she'd have been sure to arouse Rafael's suspicions if she stuffed them full of roasted pork and stewed peppers.

When they were finished eating, Rafael went to the door and murmured quietly to someone who must have been standing just outside, because a man entered the tent immediately and cleaned up their dishes.

Lauren watched the plates disappear and tried not to frown. She hadn't gotten anything out of the rebel leader that the Agency hadn't already known. He'd talked about growing up on the island and about his family's ancestral home on the beach near the resort where she was staying. Then he'd told her how much he admired the spirit of the people of Isla Suspiro and wanted only what was best for them. He'd mentioned his brothers with a wistful sort of smile, but hadn't elaborated when Lauren tried to get him to tell her more. She could hardly come right out and ask about his source of funding, though it sure would have made her job easier if she could. Perhaps she could get him to talk about his social connections, however. That might give them the lead they needed.

"You must know a lot of people, having lived on the island your entire life," she said, leaning back in the straight-backed chair and doing her best to look relaxed.

"I have my allies," Rafael said enigmatically. Then he came up behind her and put his hands on her shoulders and squeezed. "Your hair is so lovely," he murmured.

Yes. Her hair. A fascinating topic. And yet, Lauren was not intrigued. What would he comment upon next? Her eyes? *The color of a calm alpine lake,* one admirer had called them. What kind of complete narcissist would one have to be to find this sort of fawning attention flattering?

"Thank you. I use Clinique hair care products," she responded coquettishly, unable to stop herself.

Rafael chuckled.

Lauren rolled her eyes heavenward, grateful that he was standing behind her and couldn't see the expression on her face. She was about to ask him more about his family home when he bent down and pressed a soft kiss on the side of her neck. Lauren shivered, but not from desire. How was she going to get out of this? She closed her eyes and tried to think. Her *Handbook* had only given tips for how to seduce a rebel leader, not how to get *him* to stop seducing her.

She wondered what Jake would do in this situation, then had to swallow a laugh. If Jake were being seduced by an attractive rebel leader—a female one; she got the impression that he was decidedly heterosexual—he probably wouldn't think twice about having sex with her. Whatever he had to do to complete his mission. She doubted he'd think of it as much of a sacrifice, either.

Well, Lauren hoped she didn't have to take this charade that far.

She stood up and turned around, letting Rafael's arms envelop her. He smiled down at her, then slowly lowered his mouth to hers for a kiss. He tasted of the island's rum, his lips firm and warm on hers. Lauren slid her arms around his neck, tangling her fingers in his hair.

He pressed her body to his and whispered her name.

"Oh Rafael," she murmured.

And then, with no further warning, her eyelids fluttered open and she gave a bloodcurdling scream.

"I'm getting too old for this," Jake groaned, wishing he had some of that Isla Suspiro rum Lauren had left on the nightstand back at the resort to kill the pain in his bruised ribs. He'd been taken to what Rafael Santos had referred to as the west compound, where the rebels had done their best to politely coax his secrets out of him with their fists. Through it all, Jake had maintained that he was just a tourist, silently wondering the entire time who the hell had sold him out. He'd broken out in a cold sweat when it occurred to him that whoever had ratted him out may have told Santos that Lauren was CIA, too. While getting the shit kicked out of him, he'd tried to listen for any sounds that would indicate she'd been found out, but fortunately, all he'd heard aside from his own grunts of pain were the sounds of birds screeching in the jungle overhead, men's voices shouting in the distance, and the occasional rumble of a vehicle's engine.

Once he'd been sufficiently worked over, he was tossed into a ten-foot-deep hole that had been dug into the soft earth. That would have been easy enough to escape from, but then one of the goons had climbed down into the pit on a rickety ladder and handcuffed his right arm to a tree root that was nearly as thick as Jake's wrist. Then the bastards had taken his boots, obviously figuring that he'd be unable to make it in the jungle barefooted.

He wasn't stupid enough to believe that Santos and his goons bought his story about being a tourist. He knew that they knew he was CIA. But he figured if they had wanted to kill him, they'd have done it (or tried to—he liked to think he had a few tricks up his sleeve—or down his shorts, as the case may be) once they'd finished working him over. Instead, they'd dumped him here for safekeeping.

So, for now at least, they obviously wanted him alive.

"Glad we're all in agreement about that," Jake muttered as he tore open a seam on the left leg of his tan cargo shorts and pulled out a slim metal multipurpose tool. Regular pat-downs missed catching it 99 percent of the time, and, because it was sewn into a false seam just above a zipper, even when caught by a metal detector, it was often dismissed.

Jake pulled out a small shovel and sank it into the soft dirt about two feet off the ground. Crouching down made his already sore ribs ache even more, but he ignored the twinge of pain as he dug out another scoop of dirt. He could have removed the handcuffs first, but didn't want to chance one of Santos's goons checking on him and seeing him loose until he had created an escape route for himself. If they'd been smart, they'd have cuffed his hands together behind his back, using the tree root as an anchor. Instead, they'd clapped one of the cuffs to the root and the other to his right wrist, leaving his left hand free. If they'd done the former, Jake would have been forced to take the riskier route of freeing himself first.

"Thank God for amateurs," he said as he reached up to dig out one last foothold. But he supposed he ought to give them their due—enthusiastic amateurs could inflict more pain on a guy than a professional. The professionals usually preferred a quick bullet to the brain. Easy. Painless. Fast. Unless, of course, they wanted something from you first. Then the amateurs had nothing on the pros. And he had the scars to prove it.

Jake shuddered and ruthlessly shoved back memories he'd rather forget. James Bond never pined for the dead he'd left behind, and neither would he. *Focus on the mission*, he told himself, stepping back to assess his handiwork and erasing all thoughts of the past from his mind.

He couldn't just pop up out of this hole like a prairie dog. That was a good way to get his head blown off. First, he had to know if someone was out there watching him.

Jake flipped the shovel back in place and pulled out another tool that looked like a dentist's mirror. Cautiously, he raised the mirror above his head and twisted it around to see if the entrance to the hole was being guarded, half-expecting to find some well-armed thug smirking back at him in the glass. Fortunately, it looked as though they'd either underestimated him or overestimated themselves, because no one appeared to be lurking around topside. Jake figured his unguarded state wouldn't last forever, so he hurriedly picked the lock of his handcuffs with another of his tool's handy accessories and used the footholds he'd dug into the earth to scramble up out of the hole.

He didn't waste any time slipping into the jungle. While he would have preferred to be wearing his boots, his bare feet actually made it easier to avoid stepping on twigs or anything that might alert the enemy to his presence since he could actually feel what was in front of him before stepping on it. He made his way toward the center of the camp, where several large green tents had been pitched. He had to find out what Rafael Santos was up to or thousands of Isla Suspiro's residents would suffer during the coup attempt. Jake knew all too well that it was the regular people—the ones who wanted only to raise their children and live their lives in peace—who bore the brunt of political unrest. Most struggled just to survive and were not prepared to rise up against the armies that invaded their towns and villages, burning their homes, murdering their children, and raping their wives, sisters, and daughters.

Jake would not allow this to happen on the island—not if there was any way he could prevent it. Tomas Santos's rise to power had been sanctioned—and, yes, partially funded—by the CIA. The oldest Santos brother had a vision for his people of stability, prosperity, and hope for a better way of life. And Jake intended to see that Tomas's dreams came to fruition. No matter the cost to himself.

Which was why he was intent on finding out more information about the rebel troop's movements. He had to trust that Lauren could take care of herself, although the temptation to rescue her and make a hurried escape was so great that Jake found himself torn between doing what he knew was right and getting her the hell out of here right now.

No, he *would* complete this mission. Jake roughly shoved all thoughts of Lauren from his mind and crept toward a tent that was lit from within and hummed with activity. He slunk to a spot in the shadows and pressed his ear to the canvas, longing for the listening devices that were safely tucked into his luggage back at the resort.

". . . have our troops positioned here and here to cut off a counterattack," he heard someone say and wished like hell he had X-ray vision so he could see where "here and here" were.

"The vans will help," another man said.

A low murmur met the second man's statement, and Jake swore under his breath because he couldn't make out the words. What vans? When were they planning to attack?

Then he stiffened and froze when he heard the unmistakable sound of several pairs of boots thumping the ground just around the corner from where he stood.

Shit. Now what?

If the men came around the corner, they'd see him for sure. Jake hurriedly looked around the darkened camp for cover and saw the outline of a jeep about twenty feet away. He'd have to make a run for it. He turned and sprinted out of his hiding place, but was still five feet away from the jeep when the first line of troops came marching into sight. He dove for cover like a batter diving for home plate and hit the dirt at the same moment a woman's scream rent the air.

CH@%!*R
5

Jake lay motionless under the jeep as sweat beaded on his forehead and dripped into his eyes. He blinked away the salty sting and reminded himself to breathe. It was Lauren who had screamed, and, despite his determination to stay focused on his mission, the urge to leap from his hiding place and go to her rescue was so strong that he clenched his hands into fists, his legs twitching with the desire to run to her aid.

Several months ago, he had callously told his partner, Race Gardner, to leave the woman he loved at the mercy of a wealthy gunrunner for the sake of their operation. They needed information, and Aimee Devlin—Lauren's sister—was in a position to obtain it. At the time, Jake couldn't understand why Race had struggled with the decision. As uncaring as it may have seemed, they both knew that stopping the gunrunner from trafficking in weapons of mass destruction was far more important than saving the life of one woman—even if she was a woman Race had feelings for.

Now, Jake had some small idea of how his partner had

felt. No wonder Race had wanted to rip Jake's head off during that op.

Jake slowly raised his hand and wiped the sweat off his brow. He couldn't do it; couldn't leave Lauren to suffer whatever torture Santos was putting her through. She hadn't gone through field agent training, wouldn't know what to expect or how to escape on her own. He'd have to get her out of here and return tomorrow, maybe have a helo drop him a few miles from the camp and hike back. Yes, that would be best, Jake convinced himself.

He heard raised voices and scooted up an inch so that he could see around the jeep's left front tire. He gritted his teeth when he saw Lauren, wearing a white outfit that made her stand out in the darkness, being led away from a tent in the center of the camp by two armed guards. Rafael Santos stood outside the entrance to the tent and watched her go before turning back to his men and waving, as if telling them to disperse.

The rebels who had almost stumbled upon Jake immediately moved back into formation—four men deep by three wide—and began marching straight toward the jeep Jake was hiding under.

Of course, Jake thought with a heavy sigh. Where else would they be headed?

He hurriedly rolled to the other side of the vehicle and slipped out from under it. Fortunately, there were several crates stacked near the jeep, and Jake moved behind them and then crept back into the jungle without being spotted. He crouched down and followed the line of vegetation encroaching upon the camp until he was directly across from the tent Lauren had been led to. The two armed guards had remained outside, one standing at the entrance while the other slowly made the rounds of the perimeter.

Which meant there were only about two minutes during which any spot was left unguarded.

It wasn't much, but it would have to be enough.

Jake waited until the second guard moved out of sight before sliding the multipurpose tool from one of the zippered pockets of his shorts. Then he stepped out of the jungle and ran toward the tent, a knife in his outstretched hand. He plunged the blade into the thick canvas about six inches above the ground and pushed downward. Praying he'd made a large enough hole for him to slip through, he dropped to the ground and tried to wiggle in, but the tear was too small to accommodate his shoulders.

He swore and, counting the seconds off in his head, he plunged the knife in again to enlarge the hole. He started to sweat again as the sound of approaching footsteps reached his ears. He didn't have time to make it back to the jungle before the guard rounded the corner.

This hole better be big enough.

Jake scrunched his shoulders to minimize their width and dove headfirst through the tear in the tent. He pushed hard against the canvas and felt it give as the footsteps outside grew louder. He tucked his legs inside the tent and spun around on the ground, grabbing the two edges of ripped green fabric and holding them together just as the guard's booted feet came into view.

Jake held his breath, willing the man to continue his patrol without noticing the tear.

One second. Two. Three. And, finally, the footsteps passed the spot where Jake was crouching.

He whipped around, expecting to find Lauren watching him with gratitude and, yeah, okay, more than a hint of admiration shining out of those gorgeous blue eyes of hers. After all, he was here to save her from hours—maybe even days or weeks—of torture.

Instead, all he found was . . . an empty tent.

He knew that Santos's goons had brought her here, so that meant only one thing. Somehow, Lauren Devlin had managed to escape without his help.

Lauren really didn't enjoy traipsing around the jungle wearing nothing but a bikini, but she didn't have much choice. She'd shed the white outfit and stuffed it—along with a piece of broken glass she'd managed to steal from Rafael's tent after she'd pretended to see a large and no doubt deadly spider dangling from his ceiling—into her beach bag. After she'd screamed, she'd leapt back out of Rafael's embrace, intentionally knocking their glasses off the table with one flailing arm. Her theatrics had brought Santos's men running, which immediately cooled his ardor and also allowed her to slip away with a shard of glass tucked into her bikini bottoms.

She'd used the glass as a makeshift knife to cut a hole in her tent and escape, but she knew that if she didn't take off the outfit Santos's man had brought for her, she'd stand out like a chubby girl at a cheerleading competition. Until she could find something else to wear, she'd have to brave getting scratched by all manner of jungle vegetation as she searched for where Jake was being held prisoner.

She hurried as fast as she could while taking care not to expose herself or trip on any downed trees, roots, or any of the dozens of coconuts that had fallen to the ground. She hoped she wasn't too late. As Santos's men had ushered her away from his tent, she'd heard Rafael giving the order to someone to "take care of the American spy" and knew she didn't have much time to save Jake.

As she made her way out of the center of the camp, the jungle became eerily quiet, with no sound but the constant pounding of the waterfall in the distance. The moon peeked in and out of the treetops, painting the world below with a ghoulishly gray tint. Lauren clutched her chest as a bird suddenly screeched overhead, like a portent of doom in some horror flick.

She peered out from behind the tree she was using to shield herself and swallowed a gasp when she saw the moon reflecting off the barrel of a gun. One of the thugs who had kidnapped them stood in front of a hole in the ground, pointing his gun at the darkness below. Lauren was pretty sure she knew what—or, rather, *who*—was in that pit.

Jake would have no chance of surviving. The goon was

going to shoot him at near point-blank range and there was nowhere for Jake to hide.

She had to save him.

But how? There was nothing in her *Secret Agent's Handbook* about fending off a gunman with nothing in your arsenal but a pair of flimsy sandals, a shard of glass, and a book.

The rebel was bigger than her by six inches and at least a hundred pounds. The only thing she had on her side was surprise.

Frantically, Lauren looked around for a weapon—something that would enable her to strike without getting into close range, where the goon could easily overtake her. She'd never be able to get close enough to overtake him with the dull piece of glass in her bag. But what else could she use? She needed a stick or a rock or . . . Hmm. She spied a fallen coconut on the ground near her feet. It was about the size of a cantaloupe and had a sharp, pointy ridge on the bottom.

She eased down and picked it up, careful not to make any noise that would alert the rebel to her presence. The coconut was heavy, its outer shell hard and rough beneath her fingers. She lowered her beach bag to the ground at her feet and narrowed her eyes, calculating the distance between herself and the rebel.

Yes, this just might work.

Thank God for her three-hours-a-day/seven-days-a-week sessions with personal-trainer-to-the-stars Aaron Richardson, who was known to leave his clients sobbing if their workouts weren't strenuous enough for his liking. At twenty-nine, Lauren knew she would be lucky to have one more year in modeling, and that was only if she continued her grueling workout schedule. Gravity and age were making it harder for her to keep those extra ounces off. And so she let Aaron torture her into staying in shape—a decision for which she was grateful as she brought her right arm back in preparation for hurling the coconut at the rebel's head.

"Hey," the goon said just then, sounding surprised as he stared down into the pit.

Lauren didn't wait to discover what had startled the man. Instead, she brought her arm forward with all her might, releasing her missile when her arm was fully extended in front of her.

As if sensing that something was amiss, the man turned, but not in time to do anything more than suck in a breath as the coconut hit him full in the face. He took an instinctive step backward, lost his footing, and fell into the hole behind him, his arms flapping at his sides as if that might stop his descent.

Damn. That hadn't gone exactly as she'd planned.

Lauren hurriedly looked around the camp to make sure she was alone before stepping out of the shadows. She dashed over to the edge of the pit and gazed down into the inky darkness.

"Jake? Are you all right?" she whispered loudly. Having two hundred fifty pounds of dead weight land on you unexpectedly had to hurt.

The only answer from down below was a groan.

Great. Now what? If she jumped into the hole with the two men, she'd be just as vulnerable as Jake—and would be no help if any of Santos's men came running to see what had happened to their *compadre*. No, she'd be better off hiding in the jungle until Jake came to.

She took a step back, toward the jungle, and then opened her mouth to scream when she bumped up against a warm, firm someone. She inhaled a deep breath, which was trapped in her throat when a man clamped his hand over her mouth and began to drag her away from the camp.

She was about to slam her heel down on his instep when Jake whispered in her ear, "Lauren, it's me." Then he dropped his hand and released her, and Lauren was shocked at how much she wanted to turn and throw her arms around him in relief. Instead, she nodded once and they headed for the cover of the jungle. She stopped for a moment to search for the bag she'd dropped earlier and found it near the base of a misshapen tree. She picked it up and turned to find Jake watching her. He made a motion for her to follow him and they both remained silent as they walked deeper into the jungle and left the camp behind.

When they'd traveled what Lauren guessed had to be a quarter of a mile through dense forest, they reached a clearing and Jake finally stopped and turned to her.

"You okay?" he asked gruffly, then cleared his throat. His gaze was focused on a spot about a foot above her head, and Lauren twisted around to see what he was looking at, but couldn't see anything of interest in the light reflecting off the trees from the moon overhead.

She shrugged. "Yeah. How about you? Your feet must be sore."

Jake waved a hand dismissively. "I'm fine. As we drove up this afternoon, I noticed a rebel encampment about another half mile from here. When we get there, I'll see what I can do about procuring some shoes."

"I thought you slept all the way up here," Lauren said with a frown.

Jake looked at her then, his green eyes meeting hers for just a second before sliding away.

"Oh," Lauren said. Right. Of course he hadn't been sleeping.

"Can you keep going? I'd like to get out of this jungle before morning if we can."

Lauren gritted her teeth. "You know, that whole 'fainting flower' thing is just something I do to get people to underestimate me. I'm a lot tougher than I look."

One corner of Jake's mouth tilted up in a half-smile. "And next you're going to tell me that you can kick my ass any day, right?"

Lauren crossed her arms over her chest and rocked back on her heels, looking up at him. She was five-nine, but he still had a good three inches on her. And after he'd toted her around the resort earlier that day without so much as breaking a sweat, she knew he was a lot stronger than she'd ever suspected. She wasn't sure why, but she'd never really looked that closely at him before. Most likely, it was because he put on an act whenever he was around her—as if he wanted her to see him as this larger-than-life man of mystery who simply wasn't real.

It was almost as if he thought the real Jake Haven wasn't good enough for her.

Lauren blinked and slowly dropped her arms to her sides. Oh my God. That was it. Jake Haven, a man who routinely put his life on the line for his country, felt he didn't measure up to *her*. How screwed up was this world if any guy thought he wasn't good enough for someone who made her living by staring into a camera?

"Uh," Lauren began, nervously shuffling her feet in the dirt. "No. I don't think I can kick your ass. But I *can* keep going. I assume you plan to go back to the rebel camp now that we know where it is? I wasn't able to get anything from Santos," she added as she started walking, hoping Jake would follow. She didn't know why, but he was watching her intently, and she suddenly felt uncomfortable about her state of undress. Moving away from him seemed like the smart thing to do.

She shivered when Jake laid a hand on her bare shoulder. His fingers were cool on her heated skin, his touch strong, yet gentle at the same time.

"You're going the wrong way," he said softly.

Lauren turned around, felt goose bumps rise on her skin when she found Jake standing only inches from her. She hadn't even heard him move.

"Am I?" she whispered.

He nodded, but didn't step back. Instead, his hand tightened on her shoulder. Lauren held her breath, knowing that he was going to kiss her and suddenly wanting him to, very much. The air between them crackled like dry firewood under a match's caress. Lauren leaned into him and wet her bottom lip with her tongue.

He lowered his mouth to hers, and it was like no other kiss Lauren had ever experienced, not because of its intensity, but because it was . . . sweet. Sincere.

When he pulled back, Jake was smiling a self-mocking sort of smile. "I've wanted to do that since the day we met," he said.

Lauren gave him her own self-mocking smile. "Why? Because of how I look in a swimsuit?"

Jake didn't even look down at her body, clad in a string bikini, which she was certain didn't look nearly as attractive on her now as it had this morning when she'd first put it on. "Of course," he answered, then took a step back, leaving Lauren with the impression that there was much more to this man than she had ever suspected.

CH@%!*R
6

"What are those vans doing here?" Lauren whispered as she and Jake sat at the edge of a clearing, hidden by a large plant with prehistoric-sized leaves. Parked in the clearing were several tan delivery trucks with the Isla Suspiro Rum Company name and logo painted on their sides, as well as half a dozen olive-drab jeeps, one of which Jake intended to steal. Or, rather, as he put it—procure.

"I overheard one of Santos's men talking about an ambush and another said, 'The vans will help.' I didn't know what he was referring to at the time, but I imagine they're planning to use those vehicles"— Jake jerked his chin in the direction of the tan trucks—"to get close to Tomas Santos's compound without arousing suspicion."

"We need to warn him," Lauren said.

"We will. As soon as we get out of this damn jungle," Jake agreed, swatting at a fly that had seemingly been following him for the last thirty minutes.

"I don't suppose they left the keys in the ignition." Lauren gazed hopefully toward the jeeps.

Jake shrugged and shot her a grin. "Doesn't matter. I know how to hot-wire a car."

"I must have been absent the day they taught that," Lauren said dryly. Her training had definitely not included hot-wiring cars. Mostly, she'd learned how to fill out Agency forms, how to tell if a phone line was secure, and how to communicate with her handler if she thought she might be under surveillance. When she got back to the States, she was going to request more training. It was clear that the training her handler, Martha McLaughlin, had assured her would be adequate for her job was not enough.

"When we get back to Atlanta, I'll teach you," Jake offered. Then, as one of the guards patrolling the clearing came into view, they hunkered down beneath the plant. The guard ambled around the vehicles, one hand resting on his machine gun. The minutes ticked by as he stopped to lean against one of the delivery trucks and enjoy a cigarette. When he was finished, he flicked his cigarette butt onto the ground and crushed it under the heel of his boot. Then he walked to the edge of the jungle—fortunately, several feet from where Jake and Lauren were hiding—unzipped his fly, and took a leak. Lauren shuddered thinking about having to remain still while someone peed on you. Being a spy in the real world was not nearly as glamorous as she'd imagined.

Finally, the guard moved away. She and Jake stood, and Lauren winced as her thigh muscles cramped in protest of having to crouch for so long. Her personal torturer, er, trainer would accuse her of being a wimp if he saw her cringing like this, though, so she shook it off without complaint.

Jake reached into his pocket and handed her a slim metal object. She turned it over in her hand as he said, "Use the knife to puncture a tire on each of the vehicles except the one I'm stealing. I'll get to work hot-wiring us a jeep."

Lauren nodded and ran to do as she'd been told. After she'd finished, she jogged back to the jeep Jake was working on, tossed her beach bag onto the floor, and curled up in the space in front of the passenger seat so she wouldn't be as easy to see if the guard came back.

"Ready?" Jake asked, his hands buried beneath the dashboard.

"Yep," Lauren said.

"Okay. Here we go. Keep down," Jake warned.

Then the engine sputtered to life. Lauren held on to the seat as the jeep bucked forward. They were going to have to drive straight through the clearing in order to get to the path on the other side, which presumably led to the main road. They'd counted four guards while they'd sat in the jungle, formulating their plan.

Lauren could only pray that all four were bad shots.

She heard men shouting and engines revving as the rebels realized what was happening, but she remained right where she was. Jake didn't need to worry about her poking her head up and getting it blown off in addition to trying to avoid being shot himself. Besides, there wasn't anything she could do to help, so she might just as well stay out of the way.

The jeep hit a pothole, and Lauren was certain the impact jarred several of her teeth loose. She didn't have a lot of time to think about it, though, because the guards began shooting at them.

"Shit. Hold on," Jake shouted just before he jerked the steering wheel sharply to the left. Lauren *was* holding on, but the force of the turn still threw her across the floor, where her cheek became intimately acquainted with the side of the dashboard.

Ouch. That was going to leave a mark.

She pushed herself back into a sitting position as Jake cranked on the steering wheel again. This time she was thrown against the door. The back of her head hit the metal with a resounding *thwack,* but she was thankful at least that this bruise would be covered by her hair. It was going to be tough enough to explain away all the scratches on her legs and torso in addition to the bruises she was quickly acquiring.

Someone rammed them from behind—obviously a flat tire wasn't enough to stop the rebels from driving short distances—and Lauren began to feel like a crash test dummy when her head slammed into the dashboard again.

Jake gunned the engine and laid on the horn, shouting, "Get out of the way!"

A spray of gunfire shattered the windshield, spraying glass all over the front seat, and Lauren winced when she heard a thud and then bounced off the floor when the jeep ran over something. But at least the gunfire had stopped.

Then they were roaring through the jungle, the moonlight suddenly disappearing as if someone had flipped a switch. Lauren wiped the glass off the seat, but stayed down on the floor until the sound of the vehicles pursuing them faded away.

Slowly, she pushed herself up, peering above the back of the seat to make sure the rebels were gone before turning to sit down.

"We did it," she said.

Beside her, Jake snorted. "You sound surprised."

She laughed when she realized that he was right. "Sorry. If it's any consolation, it's not you that I doubted. This is my first real op. I've never had to deal with anything like this before," she admitted.

Jake shot her an unfathomable look, and then asked, "How long have you been with the Agency?"

Lauren twisted in her seat again, so she could make sure they weren't being followed. It didn't seem smart to relax their guard. After all, she hadn't had time to puncture all the tires, and it wouldn't take long for the rebels to replace a flat and come after them. "I was recruited about five years ago for minor surveillance work. Basically, I just attended a lot of parties and fed information back to my handler. I've been asking for over three years to get upgraded to field agent. They finally gave me the promotion a few months ago." Lauren shrugged as if the upgrade to field agent meant little to her, when, in fact, she was more proud of that accomplishment than of anything she'd ever done in her life. But for some reason, she didn't want to let Jake know that. Maybe because she was afraid he'd make fun of her. Becoming an agent and being taken seriously had probably come easy for him, but she'd had to fight for it. Martha McLaughlin had refused her request time and time again, always hinting that she wasn't field agent material. Lauren figured it was her tenacity that had finally convinced her superior to put her in for the promotion. Martha must have realized that Lauren was not going to give up.

"So you went through the full training course at The Farm? I didn't realize that. I'd been told that you were just an informant. How were you able to explain such a long absence from your modeling job?" Jake asked, glancing into the rearview mirror and narrowing his eyes as if that might help him see into the utter darkness behind them.

"I went through a special accelerated program so the Agency could get me into the field right away. I was only at The Farm for three weeks." Lauren had thought it strange that she was the only agent going through this accelerated training at the time, but Martha had explained that it was a pilot program the Agency was testing. They wanted to see if they could get agents who already had some fieldwork behind them up and running faster than new recruits who had no experience. Since Lauren was the first to graduate from this special training program, she felt an even greater pressure to succeed on this op. Lauren hated to think that her handler's faith in her had been misplaced.

"There's no—" Jake began, but was cut off when a bullet hit the dead center of their rearview mirror.

Lauren threw herself back onto the floor before Jake could instruct her to get down. She knew the drill. "Is there anything I can do?" she shouted.

"Just sit tight," Jake yelled back. "We're almost to the main road. We might be able to outrun them once we get there."

Lauren nodded and remained crouched on the floor. If this were the movies, there would be several cans of gasoline in the back of the jeep that she could empty out behind them and then set on fire to blow up their pursuers. Unfortunately, even if there had been extra fuel in the back, she didn't have a match to light it.

Guess I'm going to have to take up smoking, she thought.

"There's the main road. Hold on," Jake warned.

If they'd been on pavement, the jeep's tires would have left a trail of rubber on the concrete as they shot out of the jungle and turned a hard 90 degrees to the left. Since the road was hacked out of the dirt, though, the tires spun wildly, seeking traction in the soft earth. The rear of the vehicle fishtailed, and Lauren peeked up over the passenger-side door as Jake fought to keep control of the vehicle. There was a steep drop-off on the other side of this narrow mountain road, and if they were going over, she at least wanted to know beforehand that she was going to die.

A wave of dizziness washed over her as she looked down onto the treetops a hundred feet below. Okay, maybe she'd been wrong. Maybe she didn't want to know.

Beside her, Jake swore and pressed hard on the accelerator. The engine protested his abuse as the right rear tire of the jeep spun in the empty air. Fortunately, the other three tires sank into the dirt and pulled the vehicle back onto the road. Jake didn't let up on the accelerator as the jeep pitched forward.

Lauren wrapped her arms around her beach bag as they skidded around a bend in the rutted road. "Do you think we can outrun them?" she asked. From her seat on the floor, she couldn't tell how close the rebels were.

Jake's face hardened, and Lauren saw him turn his head to glance behind them and then look forward again. "Well," he said, "I think we could have, but they must have radioed for help. Now they're coming at us from both directions."

"Damn," Lauren said, sounding a lot calmer than she felt.

"Yep," Jake agreed.

"Only one thing to do," Lauren said with a nod. She reached out to brace herself to avoid getting slammed into the dashboard again.

"Yep," Jake agreed again.

"Back into the jungle we go." Lauren held tight as Jake jerked the steering wheel to the left again. They were immediately swallowed up by the jungle. Jake had to slow down so he wouldn't ram into any trees, and Lauren heard the faint noise of men shouting behind them. They had maybe a five-minute lead on the rebels.

She closed her eyes and pictured the satellite photos of the island in her mind, trying to pinpoint their location. The helicopter tours she had taken had helped. Although it was dark, she was able to imagine the terrain they were traveling through; the thick leafy trees with hanging vines draping off of them like elegant scarves, the occasional coconut tree that hadn't yet been overshadowed by a larger, more aggressive tree, the flowers that somehow managed to bloom in the smallest patch of sunlight.

The sound of their engine was dwarfed by the constant roar of rushing water, louder here than it had been even back in Rafael Santos's camp, and suddenly, Lauren knew exactly where they were. They were approaching the waterfall at Nuevo Rios.

Even better, she had an idea about how to get the rebels off their trail.

She pulled the multipurpose tool that Jake had handed her earlier from out of her beach bag and, without hesitating, flipped open the knife and cut her arm. She smeared the white clothes in her bag with blood and then reached up to untuck the T-shirt clinging to Jake's taut abdomen.

Startled by her touch, he took his eyes off the jungle for a second. "What the hell—" he began.

"I have a plan," Lauren interrupted. "Just keep driving straight, toward the river."

Jake grunted, which Lauren took as agreement. She hastily jabbed several ragged holes in Jake's T-shirt and then pulled off one of her sandals and eyed it ruefully. She hated to sacrifice it—it was a Sesto Meucci that had set her back two hundred and fifty dollars for the pair. But it had to be done.

The roar of the waterfall got louder as they approached the river. When Lauren had flown over the area a few days before, the sight of millions of gallons of water a minute dropping 125 feet into the lake below was awe-inspiring. The sound of it was no less impressive tonight, although she guessed that they were still some distance from the actual falls because, while the constant hum of rushing water was loud, it wasn't as deafening as it would be up close.

Jake abruptly slammed on the brakes and Lauren lost hold of the knife. She felt around on the floor for it, her fingers tightening around the cool metal as she raised herself up onto the seat. The jungle had ended without warning, the river brutally stealing its path from the heavy vegetation that grew right up to the water's edge.

"I hope you're not going to suggest that we go over the falls," Jake said, sliding a sideways glance in her direction.

Lauren grinned. "No, but that's what I want the rebels to think we did."

"You think they'll buy it?" Jake asked. He turned to face her, his right arm draped over the back of the seat as if they were having a casual conversation and not running for their lives.

Lauren took comfort in his calmness. He behaved exactly the way she expected a field agent to behave. He was cool under pressure, his mind focused on the mission as he logically assessed each problem that arose. She took a deep breath and tried to emulate his attitude. "Yes," she answered. "I'm sure they've seen all the movies where people routinely go over the falls to save themselves."

"But you don't think we should do that?" Jake asked, lifting his hand to scratch under his chin, where a hint of coarse beard was just beginning to show.

"Not if we want to live to die another day," Lauren said, stealing a line from her favorite Bond movie. "There's no way we'd survive. I suggest we send the jeep down the falls with our clothes in it. The rebels will find the jeep and our mangled clothes will wash up farther downstream. They'll most likely assume we were thrown from the jeep and drowned, and we'll have bought ourselves some time."

"And how do you suggest we get out of this jungle without the jeep? It'll take us days to walk out of here."

"We won't have to walk," Lauren said smugly as she stepped out of the jeep and tossed her sandal and the white outfit onto the passenger-side floor. "Take off your shirt," she ordered, half-expecting him to argue.

He didn't. Instead, he stepped out of the jeep and stripped off his shirt, his skin glowing golden in the moon-light overhead. At first, all she could see was hard muscle covered with all that smooth skin. But then, as he bent to twist his shirt around the steering wheel, Lauren noticed the purplish bruises covering his back.

She flinched. So, while she had been pacing around her tent in the camp, Santos's goons had worked Jake over. Rather thoroughly, it appeared, judging by the number of dark spots splotching his skin.

Jake straightened and their gazes slammed together. The look in her eyes must have been easy to read because, without looking down at the bruises covering his torso, Jake said, "Yeah. And it hurts like a son of a bitch, too. I'd sell my soul for some painkillers right now."

Lauren tried to smile, but she was certain it came off as a more of a grimace. "Aren't you supposed to tell me that it looks worse than it is?"

"I'm not that good a liar," Jake said cheerfully. Then he leaned over the driver's side door, put the jeep's transmission into drive, and walked around to the back of the vehicle. Lauren followed him, digging her feet into the ground as she helped him push the jeep into the fast-moving river. It would have been a more poignant moment had they stood on the bank of the river and watched as their only means of transportation disappeared downriver, but they didn't. Instead, they found a hiding place in some leafy bushes behind a tree and hunkered down to avoid being spotted by the rebels who were following them.

Lauren held her breath as the sounds of shouting drew nearer and didn't realize that she had scooted closer to Jake on the floor of their makeshift camp until her shoulder bumped his arm. She was sitting on her beach bag, the canvas rough through the thin fabric of her swimsuit. Jake sat beside her on the ground, wearing nothing but his tan cargo shorts. He shifted positions, and his hair-roughened calf rubbed against her own freshly waxed one. His feet were bare and dirty, but he hadn't seemed to mind going barefoot. Lauren wondered how he'd managed to toughen up the soles of his feet. She must have missed that tip in her *Secret Agent's Handbook.*

They remained silent as the rebel troops searched for them, and Lauren hoped they'd soon spot the jeep at the bottom of the falls and call off their hunt. Rather than cooling off as midnight approached, the air in the jungle seemed to be getting warmer and more humid. Or perhaps it was simply her proximity to Jake that was heating the air around them.

Lauren started to shift away from him—all that smooth hard skin so close to hers was making it difficult to draw a deep breath—but Jake stopped her by sliding his arm over her shoulders and pulling her even closer. With one strong hand, he pushed her hair away from her face and leaned in to whisper in her ear. Lauren's heart was pounding so hard that she found it difficult to comprehend what he was saying over the blood rushing to her head.

It's just the adrenaline, she admonished herself, attempting to rein in her libido, which had suddenly appeared out of nowhere. She forced herself to listen to what Jake was saying.

"Close your eyes," he whispered.

Lauren did so, but turned her head an inch to the side and whispered back, "Why?"

"The whites of the eyes are easy to spot in the dark," Jake answered, his warm breath stirring the wisps of hair at her neck and making her shiver. He must have taken that to mean she was cold, because he pulled her closer and enveloped her in his own body heat, which just made Lauren's desire grow even stronger.

She kept her eyes firmly shut, lecturing herself the entire time Jake held her. She was *not* going to have reaction-to-danger sex with him. She wasn't. No, no, no. She was going to resist the temptation to lean into him, to let herself relax in the comforting embrace of his arms. And she sure as hell wasn't going to rub her bare thigh against the rough material of his shorts. Or splay her hand across his firm abdomen. Or turn and raise her lips to his in a kiss that was as heated as the jungle air surrounding them.

Okay. So she was lying. She was going to do all those things. And Jake was going to react by fisting his hand in her hair and kissing her back with such passion that Lauren felt as if she were being consumed by the heat.

He thrust his tongue into her mouth and Lauren sucked him in with equal fervor. She hadn't even realized that he'd lowered her to the ground until she felt the hard seam of her beach bag digging into her shoulder. She slid her arms around Jake's back, her fingers gently kneading his taut skin, mindful of the bruises Santos's men had inflicted upon him.

It dawned on her then that Jake found it easy to spin his tales of danger and excitement because those stories weren't really about him. When the threat was real, he accepted his duty stoically, without fanfare or heroics. He simply did what needed to be done to complete his mission. Afterward, he might glam it up—make it seem as if he always knew he'd make it out alive—but perhaps that was just his way of dealing with the fear that came with knowing that every op might be his last.

Jake grunted when she passed her hand over a particularly deep bruise, and Lauren felt a rush of tenderness that was quickly replaced with want as he untangled his fingers from her hair and ran his hands down the length of her sides, making her shudder. The evidence of Jake's desire pressed into her through the thin fabric of her bikini and Lauren opened her legs to him, rubbing against his erection until he groaned into her mouth.

"Lauren, we've got to stop," he whispered roughly, but his hips pulsing against hers belied his protest.

"Do you have protection?" she asked, her hands gripping his firm buttocks while she squirmed against him. She wished she could believe that her instantaneous response to Jake was a result of her being forced to run around nearly naked all day, but she knew it wasn't. Jake had shown himself to be a man she truly admired, his quiet strength and sense of humor giving her the confidence she needed to push her own limits. And never once had he treated her as if she were incapable of keeping up, as if she were nothing but a lame-brained liability. Instead, he'd listened to her opinions and treated her like an equal.

There was something awfully sexy about that.

"Condom. Right rear pocket," Jake said, his voice sounding strained, as though he were struggling to speak.

Lauren chuckled breathlessly and pushed Jake off of her as she dug into his pocket and pulled out the foil-wrapped packet she found there. They lay on their sides, facing each other, and she reached out, hearing Jake's sharp intake of breath when she moved her hands to his zipper, her fingers tickling the hard muscles of his abdomen.

Around them, the jungle quieted, the thick foliage of the bush they were hiding under cocooning them in their own private world. The humid air licked languorously at Lauren's skin, while Jake's tongue did the same to the sensitive spot just below her ear. Time seemed to slow, then stop altogether as Jake untied the knot at the nape of her neck.

Lauren arched her back as the ties holding her swimsuit top in place dropped, leaving her breasts exposed to Jake's searing gaze. He skimmed his hands slowly up her rib cage, the rough skin of his palms on her skin sending shivers down her spine.

"You're so beautiful," he whispered, and Lauren looked up to find that he wasn't looking at her breasts, but was, instead, watching the expressions flitting across her face.

Instead of dismissing the compliment as she usually would have, Lauren smiled. "Thank you," she whispered back. Then she gasped with pleasure as Jake slid his hands up to cup her breasts. He moved his fingers slightly, the pads of his thumbs brushing against her aching nipples.

Lauren closed her eyes, waves of pleasure washing over her as Jake lowered his mouth to tease her nipples with his tongue. She felt a throbbing between her legs and was overwhelmed by a primal need to do something to ease the pressure building inside her. With a purr-like sound, she put one leg over Jake's hips, opening herself to him and smiling with satisfaction when she heard him groan.

Her smile turned to a chuckle when Jake grabbed the condom from her and growled, "Give me this damn thing, you tease. How much longer do you think I can wait?"

Jake ripped the packet open with his teeth, trying not to get distracted when Lauren "helped" him by sliding the zipper of his shorts down over his engorged cock. God, it felt good when she touched him like that.

He closed his eyes, the condom forgotten as she sucked her index finger into her mouth and then slowly circled the tip of his penis. If she didn't stop, he was going to come right now—and to hell with the condom.

Jake reached down to pull Lauren's hands away from him. No, he definitely didn't want his first time with her to end like that. Not with her as ready for him as he was for her.

He sheathed himself in the condom and then turned his attention back to Lauren, surprised to find that she'd already shed her tiny, tantalizing bikini bottoms. She lay there in the darkness, her glorious hair spread around her, one bare foot sensuously gliding up his leg, the warm heat at the juncture of her thighs driving him wild with need, and Jake ignored the voice inside his head that kept asking,

"Why me? She could have any man—any *rich* man—she wants. Why would she settle for me?"

Fuck that.

He didn't care *why* she wanted to have sex with him. It was enough right now just to know that she did.

Then all thoughts fled from his mind when Lauren put a hand on his shoulder, gently pushed him to the ground, and then straddled him, burying his throbbing cock all the way inside her heat. Jake tried to hold back as wave after wave of hot pleasure washed over him, tried to slow Lauren's movements as she rode him, her head thrown back as she murmured his name over and over.

He felt the tension building inside himself and knew he couldn't last much longer, and he grabbed Lauren's hips to steady her, to keep her with him as he bucked against her, lifting, reaching for release. She pulsed against him then, her legs clenching his sides tightly as she spasmed around him. That was all Jake needed to let go, his own world going black with the force of his orgasm.

And then, it was over, their muscles giving out as Lauren rolled off him. Jake kept his eyes closed as, with Herculean effort, he threw one arm over Lauren's shoulders and pulled her to him, her spine against his stomach, her hips nestled against his crotch as they both breathed deeply to regain their strength.

When Jake finally let go of her and sat up to find his discarded clothes, Lauren blinked up at him dumbly for several seconds.

"Wow," she whispered once she had her breath back.

"I'll second that," Jake agreed. Then he held out her bikini bottoms, holding the thin scrap of metallic fabric awkwardly between his thumb and forefinger. Lauren grabbed her suit and quickly got dressed, frowning when it occurred to her that Jake was acting awkward, though she didn't know why.

"Uh, what's going on here?" Lauren asked, feeling more than a little awkward herself.

Jake turned to look at her, his green eyes full of a self-mockery Lauren didn't understand until he spoke. "The urge to have sex after a stressful situation is normal. It happens all the time. It's just the adrenaline, nothing more than that."

"So you think I would have done the same thing with anyone?" Lauren asked, incredulous that Jake was trying to convince her that what they'd just shared meant nothing.

Jake shrugged. "Sure."

Lauren's gaze was steady as she looked back at him. "You're wrong, Jake. This wasn't just about scratching some primal itch. I like you—"

"You don't know me," Jake interrupted. He rubbed one hand along his jaw and shook his head impatiently. "I'm not the hero you think I am. I was going to leave you with Santos while I checked out the camp, even knowing you might be in danger."

"Why?" Lauren asked, tilting her chin to look at him when he stood up. She was surprised that he had admitted this to her after spending the last several months pretending to be exactly what he was now protesting he was not. What she wanted to know was, why now? Why, when she had just made it obvious that she was interested in him, was he intent on discouraging her? She also didn't point out that, despite what he'd said, he had come back to rescue her after she'd screamed. He'd admitted that much to her during their long hike out of the jungle earlier. So why was he trying to convince her now that he didn't care what happened to her? Unless what he was really trying to do was to convince *himself* that he didn't care . . .

"If I had to, I would sacrifice you to complete this mission and save the people of Isla Suspiro further suffering," Jake said bluntly.

Slowly, Lauren unraveled herself from her sitting position on the ground and got to her feet. "You know, Jake, it seems to me," she began, bending down to pick up her beach bag, "that is exactly what a real hero *would* do."

CH@%!*R
7

"Where is the American? I have it arranged it so that a reporter will discover the man's body at Tomas's estate this morning."

Rafael Santos narrowed his eyes and briefly considered lying to his brother. He knew how Emilio would react to the news that the spy had gotten away. Unfortunately, he didn't have much of a choice. The CIA agent had disappeared . . . along with the woman Rafael had begun to think of as his good luck charm. He wasn't certain which one made him angrier.

"He escaped, but my men believe he is dead. He went over the falls at Nuevo Rios. No one could survive that," Rafael said into his cell phone. He refused to let himself worry about the temper tantrums his brother threw whenever things did not go his way. Although Rafael was a year younger than Emilio, he had learned a lesson his brother had not—life did not always go the way one planned.

When Rafael had been young, he had been certain that he and Tomas would rule Isla Suspiro together, as a team. He did not know exactly what had turned his oldest brother against him. All he knew was that by the time Rafael was old enough to hold a position in the government, Tomas had come to think of him as the enemy.

But he couldn't allow the people of Isla Suspiro to suffer for the dissention within the Santos family. Tomas didn't know it, but Emilio kept Rafael informed about the workings of the new government. It had been Emilio who told him that Tomas—like the dictator before him—had become corrupt, taking bribes from honest businessmen to ensure their places of business would not be destroyed by Tomas's army and skimming profits from his own companies rather than increasing his employees' wages.

It was up to Rafael to challenge his brother's position and bring prosperity to the island. This was his destiny.

And as Emilio cursed and accused him of incompetence for allowing the American to evade capture, Rafael's resolve strengthened. He was weary of Emilio's constant censure and the way his brother had of acting as if he were the one in charge. As Rafael disconnected the call, he made a decision. He had the funding he needed. His troops were trained and ready. Emilio wanted Rafael to wait until tomorrow to act. There was a festival today to celebrate the end of the rainy season, and Emilio reasoned that Tomas's army would be tired and hungover after the day's revelry. But Rafael figured that a large part of Tomas's troops would be out enjoying the festivities this afternoon and, thus, his mission would be easier to complete than if he waited until tomorrow.

Yes, he would attack today.

Perhaps that would finally prove to his brother who was leading this charge.

You are one stupid son of a bitch.

That thought kept running through Jake's mind as he and Lauren slowly made their way down the mountain to where she assured him a helicopter would arrive later that morning. She'd taken a helo tour of this area when she'd first arrived on the island and had apparently memorized the tour operator's schedule. Jake had been duly impressed.

As a matter of fact, everything about Lauren Devlin impressed him, which was why he couldn't believe he'd been stupid enough to push her away after she'd slept with him. What kind of idiot was he anyway?

The kind of idiot who couldn't believe that a supermodel like Lauren would have sex with the *real* Jake Haven—not the one who embellished the truth and pretended to be a superhero, but the man he really was inside. Still, that didn't mean he couldn't have let Lauren continue believing his lies . . . at least until after he'd gotten laid again.

Jake sighed and put a hand on Lauren's leg to help steady her as she dropped down onto the outcropping beside him. She was driving him nuts wearing nothing but that little bikini that left little to the imagination. When she looked up at him with her big blue eyes, Jake had to fight the urge to take her right there on the cliff and to hell with knowing that she thought he was something he wasn't. He hadn't realized that his BS job had worked so well. Before this op, Lauren had always treated him with a sort of cool detachment. He never knew that the stories he'd told her about his exploits in the field—some exaggerated and some not . . . well, okay, *most* exaggerated but a few not— had convinced her that he was some larger-than-life hero. If he'd been smart, he would have thanked God for that and just kept his mouth shut.

Since when had he grown a fucking conscience?

"Is something wrong?" Lauren asked, licking that luscious bottom lip of hers and blinking up at him innocently, as if she had no idea that just watching her suck her bottom lip into her mouth made him hard.

Jake stared intently at the rock face of the cliff. He had to stop thinking about Lauren's bikini, Lauren's lips, and anything to do with Lauren sucking anything. He had to stop thinking about Lauren, period.

Pretend she's Race, he ordered himself, then almost burst out laughing. Yeah, right. There was no man alive who had *that* good an imagination.

"No," he answered shortly. "I'm just thinking about what I need to do once we get back to the other side of the island." *Liar.*

"Oh. Well, obviously, we need to let Tomas Santos know about the delivery trucks," Lauren said, scooting backward in preparation for dropping down to the next ledge.

Jake scrambled down first and held out his arms to make sure she didn't fall, although she didn't really need his help. He'd worked with female agents before, of course, and wasn't some Neanderthal who expected them to whine and complain and not know how to do their jobs, but Lauren wasn't exactly the same as other agents. He didn't have the heart to tell her that there was no such thing as "intensive" field agent training. He wasn't sure why Martha McLaughlin had lied to her—most likely because she was a bitch and she wanted Lauren to continue providing intel without giving her a chance at a real promotion.

It was dirty and underhanded and just the sort of thing he would have expected from Lauren's handler.

After this op, Jake was going to recommend that Lauren be considered for a real field agent position. And if that meant he'd have to battle Martha McLaughlin over it, then that's what he'd do.

"We're almost there," Lauren said excitedly, interrupting his thoughts.

Jake glanced over his shoulder to see that they were nearing the clearing where Lauren had indicated the helicopter tour company made their landings. Intent on keeping the conversation light, he jumped down to the next outcropping and said, "That was a good idea about sending the jeep down the falls without us."

Lauren's cheeks flushed with pride at the compliment, and Jake realized that he'd never seen her blush when people praised her good looks. As a matter of fact, she was more likely to give her admirer a smile that didn't quite reach her eyes and respond with a cool but polite "Thank you" than take the compliment to heart.

"I can't take all the credit. I got the idea from my *Secret Agent's Handbook*," she admitted as she slid onto the rock next to him.

Jake blinked. "Your what?" he asked.

"My *Handbook*," Lauren said. "My handler told me all the agents have them."

Jake closed his eyes. Oh, God. He was going to kill the bitch.

When he opened his eyes again, Lauren was frowning at him. She reached into the bag she had slung over her shoulder and rummaged around for a moment before pulling out what looked to be an ordinary novel. "Yours may be different than mine. I mean, it would be suspicious if we all carried around the same book, right? But what's inside is probably pretty similar. You know, once you look at it through the special lens."

She was beginning to sound desperate, so Jake swallowed and nodded. "Yeah. Mine works the same way," he said.

Lauren slowly put the book back into her bag, watching him the entire time. Jake knew he could be a convincing liar when he had to be—he wasn't certain if the skill had come with the job or if he'd gotten the job because he already had the skill—but he knew he'd botched this one when Lauren glanced away. She swallowed several times, as if trying not to cry, and Jake felt as if someone were stabbing him in the heart with each passing second.

"I'm sor—" he began, but stopped when she rounded on him furiously and held up one hand to make him shut up.

"No. Don't you dare apologize. I'm the one who fell for it. The whole thing was a lie, wasn't it?" she asked, but didn't give him time to answer. "Of course it was. There's no such thing as intensive field agent training, and this book is nothing more than a sophomoric prank that Martha McLaughlin assumed I was too stupid to figure out. Well, it looks like she was right. She got me good. Ha, ha. Joke's on me." With that, Lauren reached back into her bag and pulled out the book. She thumbed through the pages for a moment, her expression so full of self-disgust that Jake couldn't stand to watch her, so instead he looked up at the lightening sky and wished he could rewind the last five minutes and do them over again.

"I'll bet you can get these stupid things at any bookstore, right?" Lauren asked, but Jake refused to answer.

Without another word, Lauren gave the book one last disgusted look, pulled back her arm, and threw the offending object into the jungle with all her might.

CH@%!*R

8

"The American is coming this afternoon," Tomas Santos announced as he pushed open the door to Emilio's office at the Isla Suspiro Rum Company headquarters.

Emilio slowly swiveled in his chair to face Tomas and then nodded. Yes, he had expected the CIA agent to show up here after Rafael had foolishly let the man escape from the rebel camp. He had not believed for one moment that the man was actually dead. Emilio prided himself on his ability to always stay four or five steps ahead of other people. Most of them were fools, so anticipating their every move wasn't difficult.

"It's a trap," Emilio said, leaning over to pull open one of his desk drawers. He didn't know if the American had discovered Rafael's plans, but he was not going to take any chances. The American agent had to die.

Emilio extracted a white envelope from the drawer and held it out to his brother, who had stepped inside Emilio's office and closed the door. "These are photos of the man, taken yesterday at Paradise Resort. I doubt you'll have any trouble recognizing our youngest brother's henchmen. You will also see that the man went willingly. None of Rafael's men have weapons." At least, it didn't appear so in any of *these* photos. Emilio had been careful to destroy the three that clearly showed the gun that had been pressed into the CIA agent's back when Rafael's men had come to take him away.

"Who's the woman?" Tomas asked, frowning.

"She's one of the models here for the photo shoot. I don't know what she was doing with the agent, but I'm certain she knows nothing of this matter." He assumed that Rafael's henchmen had left the woman at the hotel since Rafael had made no mention of her. Besides, she was a model. What danger could she possibly pose?

"And you believe the American was expecting Rafael's men?"

"Yes. I think the CIA wants to see you stripped of your power, and they are now making deals with our brother to take over in your stead. I believe the American was sent to assassinate you," Emilio stated bluntly.

Tomas rubbed his forehead as he studied the photos laid out on Emilio's desk. When he looked up and met his brother's gaze, his own eyes were dark and unreadable. "What do you propose I do about it?" he asked.

Emilio hid his surprise. He was not accustomed to Tomas asking for his opinion where politics were concerned. "Let me deal with it," he said smoothly. "That way, the man's disappearance cannot be traced back to you if I'm mistaken."

"How will you know if you're wrong?" Tomas asked, eyeing him curiously.

One side of Emilio's thin mouth drew up in a mockery of a smile. "I won't," he answered.

"And you have no qualms about killing an innocent man?" Tomas leaned forward and watched his brother, his elbows resting on his knees, his hands clasped loosely in the space between them.

Emilio had to force his teeth to unclench, to gaze back at his brother without a hint of guile in his eyes as he answered, "Not if it means removing a threat to my beloved brother's life, I don't."

Tomas's gaze remained fixed on him for a long moment before he finally nodded, unclasped his hands, and, with the slowness of one who is weary beyond his years, pushed himself up from the chair and quietly left Emilio's office.

Lauren winced as the makeup artist hired for the Isla Suspiro Rum shoot smoothed thick cover-up over the bruises she had acquired the day before. She wasn't certain which were more prominent—the bruises on her body or the dark circles under her eyes from lack of sleep. Good thing the makeup artist had experience covering both.

As Lauren had predicted, the helo tour arrived at the base of the waterfall at 9:30 that morning, and Jake had bribed the pilot to take them back to the resort immediately. Lauren had taken a shower and hurried to dress while Jake did the same. He had an appointment at one o'clock with Tomas Santos at Santos's home, which was part of the rum company's walled-in compound, where today's photo shoot was taking place.

They'd commandeered one of the resort's vans to transport everyone involved in the shoot from the hotel to the rum company. The compound itself was impressive—fifty acres of lush green land enclosed on three sides by a concrete wall topped by ten-foot-high wrought-iron bars. The fourth side was bounded by the Caribbean Sea, the beach patrolled round the clock by guards with machine guns.

Their driver had told them that there would be a parade this afternoon honoring the gods for putting an end to the rains and threat of hurricanes that plagued the island throughout the summer and early fall. On their ride to the compound, they'd passed vendors already setting up stalls to provide the townspeople with food and drink. Most workers had the day off, and Lauren could already hear the pop of fireworks and the shouts of children beyond the compound's gates.

"Looks like the people of this island take their festivals seriously," Jake said as he breezed into the makeup tent that had been set up for the photo shoot and handed Lauren a paper cup of coffee. "There are already hundreds of people lining the street outside, trying to get good seats for the parade."

He had told her that he planned to head back up to the rebel camp after his meeting with Santos, and Lauren could tell that he'd expected her to insist on coming along. But she hadn't. There was no use in either of them pretending that she was anything but what she was—a pretty face that could get them into presidential palaces and parties, and nothing more.

She sighed dispiritedly. She knew exactly why she had been so gullible. She'd wanted so badly to be part of something important. After a lifetime of being treated like cotton candy fluff that would melt at the slightest hint of rain, she had wanted someone to believe that she could be something more.

"Come on, drink up," Jake encouraged, crouching down in front of her and laying his warm hands on her bare knees.

For today's shoot, she was wearing a nearly sheer dress with a red bodice and multicolored scarf-like pieces of fabric that made up the filmy skirt. Her sandals were red, with four-inch-high heels that sank into the thick grass when she walked. Thanks to the makeup artist's magic, Lauren knew she looked great, but she had never felt worse about herself than she did right now.

Obediently, she took a sip of the rich dark coffee Jake had brought her. She needed the caffeine. Besides, she didn't have the spirit to argue.

When she lowered the cup, Jake leaned forward and surprised her by putting his forehead against hers. "Don't give up on yourself," he said. "You did great out there."

"Hey, don't do that. You'll mess up her makeup," Brad Klein scolded as he poked his head inside the tent.

Ignoring the photographer, Jake planted a light kiss on

Lauren's freshly lipsticked mouth before standing up and stretching as if he didn't have a care in the world. Lauren, however, noticed his grimace as the sore muscles around his ribs pulled. She'd seen him take some aspirin from the promotional pack on the side of one of the rum bottles in her room this morning, but it didn't seem to have killed the pain. She should be grateful—her bruises only hurt when she touched them.

Brad scowled at Jake before turning his attention to Lauren. "We could have gotten some shots in earlier if you'd been down to the lobby at 10:30 like you were supposed to be. The client wants us to do a plant tour at 11:30, so now we don't have time." He snorted and gave Jake a smarmy smile that made Lauren want to throw something at him. "These supermodels are such divas. They're all the same."

Lauren watched as Jake narrowed his eyes dangerously at the other man, his jaw tightening as he clenched his teeth. She almost wished that Jake would deck the obnoxious photographer. Instead, he drew in a long, calming breath and fixed his gaze on her before saying softly, "That's because you only see what she wants you to see."

She blinked up at him, stunned that this man that she barely even knew had summed her up so accurately. And as Jake held out a hand to help her up off her chair, Lauren began to wonder if the reason that he knew so much about her was because they were so much alike.

Give them what they expect. Wasn't that her motto? Maybe that was Jake's credo, too. Maybe that was why he cloaked himself in bravado, because when you gave people what they expected, they didn't look any deeper to try to find the real you. Because if no one ever got close to the real you, they didn't have the power to hurt you.

Lauren took Jake's hand and looked—really looked—into his eyes. She had seen the real Jake out there in the jungle, the one who cared about a lot more than just getting laid or playing some one-dimensional movie-star hero. He did a good job of hiding *that* Jake from the rest of world . . . but, then, Lauren knew all about creating illusions to sell something that wasn't real, didn't she?

"Come on, let's go," Jake said, squeezing her fingers.

Lauren squeezed back. "Lead on," she said, and then swayed after him in her four-inch heels as he pushed past the photographer and led her out into the sunshine.

The plant tour was more for show than anything else, Lauren figured as the photo crew followed the plant manager across the scrupulously clean linoleum floor. The plant was scheduled to shut down at noon so the employees could enjoy the festivities, and their little parade was most likely a way to help increase the workers' morale.

And, boy, did it seem like they needed it.

The Isla Suspiro Rum Company employees' expressions were about as drab as their brown uniforms.

"These people don't seem very happy," she whispered out of the side of her mouth to Jake. She tried to keep a smile plastered on her face, but it wasn't easy with the discontent that seemed to be pouring off the rum company's workforce in waves.

"No, they don't," Jake agreed.

The plant manager stopped near a pile of neatly stacked cardboard boxes with the company's name and logo stamped in black on the side. The sight reminded Lauren of the boxes she'd seen in Rafael Santos's tent, and she frowned, wondering for the first time why the rebel leader had purchased rum from the company that was partially owned by the brother he planned to overthrow.

She knew that Brad would complain about the creases on her forehead if he happened to look over and see her frowning, so she looked away as she continued to think. Maybe the rum had been in the delivery vans Rafael's men had stolen? If so, it probably had seemed silly to waste it.

"And here we come to the end of the line," the plant manager said as the photo crew gathered around him. "Once the bottles are filled, they're put into boxes and

taken by truck to the port to be shipped around the world."
He waved toward a half dozen metal doors that looked like
Lauren's garage door at home. She assumed that the rum
company's delivery trucks would be backed up into the
open bays to be loaded.

Nothing out of the ordinary there.

She turned her attention back to the boxes and noticed
that each box had a two-letter code stamped at the bottom
left-hand corner. The codes varied. One box was stamped
with the letters *VG*, another with *OX*, and another with *CI*.
Lauren was curious, so she nodded her chin toward the
boxes and asked, "What do those codes mean?"

The plant manager got a look on his face as though she
had just asked him what the cockroach content of their rum
was, but before he could answer, a strange sort of energy
rippled through the workforce surrounding them.

Lauren glanced up to see a man who looked remarkably
similar to Rafael Santos striding toward them. He was
about fifteen feet away when another, thinner man came
running down a narrow staircase that led to a second floor
of what appeared to be offices. Earlier, Lauren had noticed
the thin man watching their progress from the windows
above. His scrutiny had made her uneasy for some reason,
but she had dismissed the feeling. Now, as the man approached, she felt her uneasiness returning and turned to
Jake to voice her concern.

"Who's that?" she whispered.

"Emilio Santos. He runs the rum operation," Jake answered. "The other man coming toward us is his older
brother, Tomas, the president of the island."

Lauren nodded as the elder Santos brother stopped next
to the plant manager.

"Welcome to Isla Suspiro," Tomas Santos said, smiling
a broad smile that seemed to falter as his gaze landed on
Jake.

Her eyes narrowed. That was odd. The president had
never met Jake. Why, then, was there a spark of recogni-
tion in the older man's eyes?

"Tomas! What are you doing here?" Emilio Santos said with forced cheerfulness.

"I thought I would welcome our American guests," Tomas answered.

"And now you've done so. I would guess the leader of our little island has more important things to attend to," Emilio said, shooting a conspiratorial smile at the photo crew.

Lauren could never say what prompted her to do what she did next, but something—call it women's intuition or a hunch or just dumb luck—urged her to repeat her earlier question. "So tell me," she said, "what *do* those codes on the bottom of the rum boxes mean?"

CH@%!*R
9

Was the American model's question a ploy to get him to take his attention off the agent sent here to kill him?

Tomas felt a bead of sweat drip down the side of his face. It was warm in the plant—Emilio insisted that overhead fans were enough to cool the workers down on the production floor. The offices above, of course, were air-conditioned. But Tomas couldn't blame his perspiration only on the temperature. He was unarmed and had not expected to come face-to-face with the assassin.

Every person entering the compound was searched at the gate, but Tomas was not foolish enough to believe that his guards were infallible. A clever killer could smuggle a weapon in, especially one who was traveling with a seemingly innocuous group such as the model and her entourage. Before Emilio's offer to deal with the CIA agent himself, Tomas had been prepared to meet with the man in his office, with a gun in his hand and his own armed guards there to protect him.

It was possible that Emilio was wrong, that the American had not made a deal with Rafael and was not here to kill Tomas. However, the pictures Emilio had given him had convinced Tomas that this scenario seemed the most likely. Why else would the CIA agent go willingly with Rafael's men?

No, it was probable that Emilio was right. And perhaps the model was trying to distract his attention so that the assassin could complete his mission right here on the production floor.

Tomas had lived for so many years with a price on his head that he should have become accustomed to the constant fear. But he hadn't. It infuriated him that he cared so much for the people of his country and only wanted to do what was right for them, yet in return he lived every moment under the threat of being killed. It was bad enough that his own brother wanted him dead. The CIA's double-dealing, even though he had cooperated with them at every turn, was too much.

In typical Tomas fashion, he had decided to meet this threat head-on. He had been wrong to think that it would be best to allow Emilio to handle the problem. This was his domain, his life. He would be the one to take care of the CIA.

"The codes help us to separate the product for shipping," Emilio said smoothly from beside him.

Tomas frowned and allowed his gaze to slip to the stack of cardboard boxes for a split second. He knew nothing of these codes, but that didn't mean much. Emilio was more involved in the running of the rum business than he was.

Why, then, did he have the feeling that his brother had just lied?

"Oh," the model said, twirling a lock of her long dark hair around the index finger of her left hand. She seemed satisfied with Emilio's answer, but then her smooth forehead creased with the tiniest of lines. "I'm not certain I understand," she said in a breathy voice. "What does *OX* mean?"

Tomas kept his gaze focused on the assassin, only half-listening to his brother's response as he tried to figure out what to do next.

"I'm not certain. I must admit that I spend more time focused on the company's financial state than in memorizing our shipping codes," Emilio said with a forced laugh.

The model looked as though she might ask another question, but Emilio cut her off. "My brother and I must be going now. We hope you enjoy the rest of the tour. We're looking forward to seeing the final photos from your shoot."

With that, Emilio took a step backward. Tomas, however, was not about to turn his back on an assassin. Instead, he walked forward until he and the CIA agent were separated by only a few feet. If the man wanted to make an attempt on Tomas's life, he could give it his best shot.

Up close, Tomas noticed that the agent was more muscular than he appeared from a distance. If he was surprised that Tomas had approached him, he hid it well. There was nothing but mild interest in the man's dark green eyes.

"I believe we have an appointment at one o'clock," Tomas said. "If you're available now, I think we should take care of whatever it is you came to Isla Suspiro to do."

The agent nodded and stepped away from the group. The model took a step toward him, but stopped when the man gave an almost imperceptible shake of his head. Tomas glanced at his brother, hoping he had also seen what had just happened. It would be helpful if Emilio could keep an eye on the woman while Tomas and the American talked.

Just then, a whistle sounded, indicating that the company would be closing for the day. Emilio waited until the noise stopped and then waved toward the second floor. "Use my office," he said as the workers around them began to file silently out of the plant.

Tomas nodded. He knew his brother kept a loaded pistol in the top drawer of his desk. With the plant quickly emptying of employees, there would be no witnesses to the CIA agent's death. And if Tomas was not successful in killing the agent before he himself was killed . . . Well, he suspected his brother would take care of the situation if that were to happen. There was only one way out of the upper offices—the narrow staircase that Emilio had hurried down moments before. Should the American attempt to escape, setting a trap for him would be simple.

Emilio Santos watched his brother disappear into his office and tried to contain his glee. God had indeed blessed him this day. There was no way he could lose.

First, he would kill his brother and the American agent. He would set it up to appear that Tomas had killed the CIA man. Then he would move his brother's body to the beach, where he himself would "discover" it early tomorrow morning. He would rally Tomas's army and have them lie in wait for Rafael's troops. Since he knew exactly what Rafael's plans were, slaying his younger brother would be easy.

In less than twenty-four hours, Emilio would have everything he had ever wanted.

No one could stop him now.

Jake winced as he took a seat across from Tomas Santos. Damn, his ribs hurt. The painkillers he'd taken that morning must have worn off. He supposed he could have asked Santos for a couple of aspirin—there had to be some lying around the rum plant since their big promotion was to package hangover relief with their liquor—but he didn't like admitting weakness, especially not to a stranger.

Only let them see what you want them to see, right, Haven? One side of Jake's mouth drew up in a self-mocking smile. Yeah, maybe he and Lauren weren't so different.

"The CIA suspects that your brother and his troops are preparing for an attack," Jake announced bluntly, ignoring the persistent stab of pain in his side. "I was sent here to try to discover who might be funding the rebel army so that we might be able to cut off your brother's source of funds and end this conflict without bloodshed. I now believe that we're too late, that a coup attempt is imminent. Are you prepared to fend off such an attack?"

Across from him, Tomas Santos remained seated behind a large desk, his dark eyes unreadable. When they'd first entered the office, Tomas had surreptitiously opened one of the desk drawers, obviously searching for something that he did not find. Jake assumed he had been looking for a weapon. Since Jake himself was unarmed but for the slender knife hidden in his pocket, he was glad that Santos had not found what he was looking for.

Jake could understand the man's uneasiness—he hadn't been expecting the CIA to pay him a visit, after all—but Santos had nothing to fear from him. Jake wasn't here to harm the man, only to warn him of his brother's impending attack.

"You're not here to assassinate me, then?" Santos asked.

Jake's eyebrows drew together as he frowned. "Of course not. You know you have the United States' full support. Why would you think that my government had sent someone here to kill you?"

Santos pursed his lips and shook his head for a moment before releasing a relieved breath. "It seems that I owe you an apology. My life in politics has apparently made me paranoid."

"It's an endeavor that could drive any sane man crazy," Jake said with a short laugh. "I plan to go back to your brother's camp later this afternoon to see if I can discover when and where he plans to launch his attack. Unfortunately, my government can't provide you with any more assistance than that, but hopefully it will be enough for you to squash this rebellion and continue your efforts to stabilize the island's economy."

Tomas leaned back in his chair and clasped his hands across his lean stomach. In this relaxed pose, he looked ten years younger than he had just minutes before. Jake could only guess how difficult the man's life was, trying to bring this island out of poverty and despair and into prosperity and hope. Over the years, Jake had run into his share of despots and dictators, and he was impressed with Santos's seeming regard for the welfare of his people. Yes, he lived much better than the average inhabitant of the island in his walled estate surrounded by armed guards. Still, he truly seemed committed to improving the lot of the people here—something that could not be said of many of the world's leaders.

"I don't understand my brother," Tomas admitted. "He could have had a powerful position in my government, but instead he chooses to raise an army against me. We used to share the same dream for our country. I don't know when that changed. Or why."

"Some people believe that their way is the only way," Jake said. "Perhaps your brother couldn't accept that anyone but him could rule the island correctly." *Either that or he wanted everything for himself,* Jake thought, but didn't voice his opinion. Some men hated sharing wealth or power with anyone else. Frequently, it was this, rather than any lofty idealism, that caused men like Rafael Santos to rise up against their governments.

But since the enemy in this case was Santos's own brother, Jake kept his mouth shut. Some people were so loyal to their families that even when presented with hard evidence of their treachery, they refused to see it. Which, he supposed seconds later, was why it had been so easy for Emilio Santos to have plotted against his older brother without anyone suspecting that he was a traitor. It was only when Emilio flung open the door to his office, pointed a 9-mm at Tomas's head, and fired his first shot that Jake realized his error.

He should have focused his attention not on the obvious threat of Rafael Santos, but on the snake right here in Tomas's own garden.

As Tomas fell and Emilio swung around for his second shot, Jake dove for the floor, mentally cursing himself. He should have gone over a backup plan with Lauren this morning. She wouldn't know what to do if he disappeared. Most likely, she would come looking for him, and Emilio would kill her, too.

He was so stupid not to have planned for the possibility of his own death. And now Lauren's blood would be on his hands. She didn't have the training for this type of situation. God damn her handler for lying to her about that fucking handbook. As if some book could cover all the eventualities an agent in the field might face. For that, she'd need intelligence, a quick wit, and a hell of a lot of courage.

Too bad he wouldn't live long enough to tell Lauren he believed she already possessed all three.

CH@%!*R
10

Where the hell was he?

Emilio Santos wiped the sweat off his upper lip with the back of one hand as he scanned the darkened production floor below. He'd personally escorted the tour group out of the plant and checked the entire facility to ensure that he was alone with his brother and the spy before turning off all the lights except those to the second-floor offices and then entering the security code to lock down the building. Once the plant was secure and there was no way for either Tomas or the agent to escape, Emilio had made his move.

He'd removed his gun from his desk earlier, when he'd first seen Tomas come to greet the model and her crew. He had no idea what had possessed his brother to come to the plant this afternoon, but he was glad now that he had. It had made Tomas surprisingly easy to kill.

Emilio had expected his bigger, stronger, older brother to put up a fight. Apparently, however, might was no match for a bullet to the brain.

Had Emilio not been so angry, he might have laughed at his observation. As it was, the spy's escape had put a damper on Emilio's sense of humor. He couldn't believe the man had thrown himself against the second-floor window, crashing through the glass and falling to the floor below. Emilio had raced to the broken window and looked down, expecting to see the man lying in a pool of blood. Instead, he saw nothing but shards of shattered glass littering the linoleum floor.

Emilio clattered down the stairs as quickly as possible, leaving his brother lying gasping for his last breaths in Emilio's office. He would have paused to make certain Tomas was dead had he not been afraid that this would give the American time to get into position at the bottom of the stairs. With Emilio's only escape route blocked, he would be trapped and at the mercy of the spy.

He had no intention of being at anyone's mercy ever again.

With his gun trained on the darkness surrounding him, Emilio crouched down over the pile of shattered glass and looked for anything—a trail of blood, some torn clothing, anything that might help lead him to the American.

When he saw a suspicious spot on the floor, he reached down and trailed his fingers through the wetness. Looking up, Emilio Santos smiled.

The CIA agent was bleeding.

And like any predator, Emilio knew that all he had to do to catch his wounded prey was to follow the scent of blood.

Where the hell was he?

Lauren pulled on the locked door of the Isla Suspiro Rum Company's headquarters for the tenth time in as many seconds and considered the damage to her pedicure if she were to attempt to kick in the door with nothing but her high-heeled sandals for protection.

She knew that Jake planned to go back up to the rebel camp when he was finished meeting with Tomas Santos, but hadn't seen him leave the plant. The photo shoot had been set up within full view of the only road leading from the plant, and she'd been watching for Jake to reappear. It had been over an hour now and he had remained locked up inside with Tomas Santos the entire time.

They couldn't have had that much to discuss, and Lauren was getting worried. The photo shoot had ended, and the crew was waiting for her in their air-conditioned van. They wanted to leave now, before the streets got too packed for them to drive. The revelers outside the gates of the compound had gotten louder and more raucous and, according to their driver, it was only going to get worse as the afternoon wore on.

Lauren ignored the impatient beep of the van's horn as she pulled her cell phone from her purse. She was not leaving without Jake.

She scrolled to her log of incoming messages and found Jake's number. She hit dial, pressed the phone to her ear, and waited for it to ring.

"Lauren, come on. We're going to get stuck here all bloody night if we don't leave now," Brad shouted.

She scowled and put her hand over the mouthpiece. "Go without me," she yelled back. The trip back to the resort would take over two hours with the streets clogged as they were with people. If she were forced to endure the pretentious photographer's company for that long, one of them would have to die. And it wasn't going to be her.

The van took off without so much as a token protest from any of the crew.

Assholes, Lauren thought, turning her attention back to her call.

The phone rang once, then twice, and then, abruptly, the call was dropped. Lauren frowned and held the phone out to look at the display. She'd thought reception would be good here, but maybe she'd lost her signal. But no, there were five bars showing—the strongest signal she could get.

Then what—

Lauren heard the unmistakable sound of a gunshot from inside the plant and gasped.

Ohmigod. Knowing that he'd be searched before his meeting with the president, Jake hadn't brought his gun. That must mean that someone was shooting at him.

But what was she supposed to do? The doors were locked, the only windows on the outside of the building were two stories up, and she didn't have any brilliant ideas. Briefly, she wished she hadn't thrown away her *Secret Agent's Handbook*, but she immediately dismissed the idea and scoffed at herself. What good would it have done anyway? The stupid thing was just a joke.

Lauren pulled at the door again, feeling frustrated and helpless when it wouldn't budge. She slumped against the warm metal and closed her eyes. Jake was in danger, and there was nothing she could do.

She jerked upright and nearly dropped her cell phone when it rang.

"Jake, is that you?" she said.

Her heart seemed to stop when Jake's voice came on the line. Thank God, he was okay.

"I don't have time to explain anything right now. Can you call me back?"

"Sure," Lauren answered, but the phone had already gone dead. She redialed the incoming number and waited for Jake to answer, but it just rang six times and then rolled into his voice mail.

She didn't leave a message.

Suddenly, the window above her exploded and Lauren covered her head as shards of glass rained down on her. She peeked through her fingers and saw a chair land a few feet away in the thick grass. When the last of the glass finished tinkling merrily against the concrete walkway, she looked up to find Jake dangling from the windowsill. As she watched, he loosened his hold and dropped into the shrubs surrounding the building. She rushed to his side and heard him groan as he tried to move.

"Jake? What's going on?" she asked, reaching out to help him up.

"No time," he gasped.

That answer, of course, made absolutely no sense to Lauren. No time for what? Unfortunately, Jake couldn't clear up the mystery since he had rolled off the hedge, landed facedown in the grass, and promptly passed out.

Then it was her turn to gasp when there was another gunshot and the ground at her feet erupted. Bits of dirt and grass leaped up like popcorn from a hot pan and struck her bare legs. Lauren looked up at the broken window to find Emilio Santos aiming a gun at her. She didn't wait for an explanation. Instead, she grabbed Jake under the armpits and tugged, her heels burying themselves in the soft dirt as she grunted with the effort to drag two hundred pounds of dead weight out of harm's way.

She pulled with all her might, silently praising her personal trainer's efforts to whip her into shape as she managed to lurch around the corner of the building just as Emilio squeezed off another shot.

Still holding Jake under the armpits, Lauren wildly looked around for a means of escape. They were at the back of the plant, near the loading dock. Several delivery trucks painted dark brown with the Isla Suspiro Rum Company name and logo on them were parked on the pavement. Damn, she wished Jake had had a chance to show her how to hot-wire a car.

Lauren chewed on the inside of her cheek. Maybe she wouldn't need to hot-wire one of the delivery vehicles. Someone might have left the keys in the ignition, figuring the truck would be safe from thieves parked here in the gated compound.

"Jake, come on. Wake up," she urged, glancing from his prone body to the nearest delivery truck twenty feet away. When he didn't even twitch, Lauren knew what she had to do. She hated to leave him unprotected, but she had no choice. She couldn't drag him that far fast enough to outrun Emilio, who she expected was on his way outside right now. She had to take the chance that one of the vehicles would be accessible. If she didn't, she and Jake would both die right here on the pavement.

She rolled Jake over onto his back and then forced herself to leave him as she ran across the loading dock toward the line of vehicles. The trucks were more like oversized UPS vans than the semis used in the United States to transport goods. Lauren figured with Isla Suspiro's roads in such poor condition, many of them pockmarked with potholes large enough to hide several small children, semis couldn't be used until the roads were improved.

Lauren clambered onto the running board of the first vehicle she came to and jerked on the door handle, but it was locked. Cursing, she jumped down and ran to the next van, her high heels sinking slightly into the hot pavement.

When she tugged on the next door, it opened, and Lauren sent up a silent prayer that the keys would be in the ignition. She jumped into the driver's seat and felt around on the steering column for the keys, but the ignition was empty. Not willing to give up, she checked the top of the dashboard and then fumbled around in a pile of loose change, hoping the driver had left his keys there. Next, she slid her hand into a pocket on the side of the driver's door, gasping with relief when her fingers closed around a set of keys.

"Yes," she shouted through gritted teeth as she pulled the keys out and hurriedly tried to fit one after the other into the ignition.

The sound of a door opening behind her made her falter, and Lauren knew she only had seconds before Emilio spotted her. She pulled the last key from the ring and shoved it into the ignition. This one had to fit.

The key slid into place, and Lauren cranked it toward the dashboard. The van's engine coughed to life as Emilio Santos appeared in Lauren's side view mirror

He took aim.

She slammed the transmission into drive and floored the accelerator just as the passenger side door flew open.

Jeez. What now? Did Emilio have backup?

Lauren was just about to jerk the steering wheel to the right to try to dislodge the intruder when she realized that it was Jake who was trying to get inside the van. She kept her foot pressed to the gas pedal and ducked as Emilio's bullet shattered the window beside her and exited through the front windshield. -

"Drive," Jake shouted, throwing himself across the passenger seat.

"What do you think I'm doing?" Lauren muttered as she struggled to keep the swaying van on the narrow road. Up ahead, the road branched off into three different directions. The left route would take them to the main gate and through the center of town, but the roads would be clogged with revelers, making them easy to spot. Not to mention that they'd have to get through the phalanx of armed guards, who were almost certain to have been warned to stop them.

The middle road led down to the beach, but Lauren had no idea what they would do to escape once they got there. The rightmost road meandered through the compound and would put them out in a quieter part of town, but the road on that side of town wasn't much more than a rutted footpath through the dirt. With the heavy delivery van loaded down with boxes of rum, Lauren feared they might end up stuck up to their axles in mud.

As they approached the crossroads, she eased up on the gas.

"What do we do?" she asked frantically, turning to Jake.

Beside her, Jake was pale and sweating, and Lauren noticed blood dripping down his arm. "Have you been shot?" she asked, her eyes wide with shock.

"It's just a nick," Jake answered, sounding as though he were talking through clenched teeth. "Emilio was standing with his back to me and I was about to knock him out with a bottle of rum when my cell phone rang the first time you called. If I hadn't clipped him on the shoulder with the bottle when he turned around, I'd be dead now."

Lauren winced. So that's why he'd hung up on her. Why the hell hadn't she thought that calling him might give away his position? God, she was so stupid. No wonder her handler thought the idea that she could be a real field agent was a joke.

"I left my phone downstairs and had you call me back to make Emilio think I was still down there. That's how I managed to get upstairs and escape."

Well, at least she she hadn't been *totally* useless, Lauren thought with no small measure of self-disgust.

"Rafael Santos is staging his coup this afternoon," Jake said, interrupting Lauren's thoughts. "At least, that's what I gathered from a phone call I overheard between him and Emilio. Rafael called after Emilio shot Tomas and Emilio took the call while he was searching for me. Emilio didn't tell Rafael that there's no need for him to overthrow his brother. Tomas is already dead, and I think Emilio is setting a trap for his younger brother. I suspect he's the one who pitted his brothers against one another. He's wanted the power all along." Jake pressed his hand to the gunshot wound on his arm to stem the bleeding and bit back a shout of pain. Jesus, that hurt. He'd kill for a fucking aspirin right now.

"We have to stop Rafael," Lauren whispered. If they didn't the island would be thrown into another cycle of revolution and civil war.

Jake closed his eyes and tried to think, but he didn't see any way to stop events from unfolding exactly the way Emilio Santos had planned. They could try rallying Tomas's army, but why would they listen to a supermodel and a stranger from America over Emilio, who, as Tomas's right-hand man, was surely someone they trusted? By the time Rafael Santos launched his attack and Jake and Lauren were proven right, it would be too late.

He shook his head and held his breath as another wave of pain washed over him. "Do you have any ideas?" he asked.

Beside him, Lauren laughed bitterly. "Who, me? All I am is a pretty face. Haven't you realized that by now?"

Jake grimaced as he twisted in his seat to face the woman next to him. "That's bullshit, Lauren. You kicked ass out there in the jungle yesterday. You escaped from the rebel camp, took out one of Rafael's men who would have shot me if I'd been down in that pit, marched for hours without complaint, and came up with the idea that got us out of there and saved our asses. You're a damn fine field agent, and I'm proud to be on this op with you."

Lauren was already shaking her head. "That was all because of that stupid joke of a handbook. Martha McLaughlin's right. I thought she saw something more in me, but it was all just a lie to shut me up. The Agency doesn't believe in me."

Jake glanced behind them to make sure Emilio hadn't had time to follow them yet. Then, even though he nearly passed out with the effort to move, he slid across the seat and put a hand under Lauren's chin to tilt her face up to his. Her blue eyes were troubled, and Jake wished he had the time to kiss her worry away, but now wasn't exactly the right moment to stop and declare his feelings for the brave woman he'd fallen in lust with when they'd met and then fallen in love with the day before. She was so much more than she even knew.

"It doesn't matter what anyone else believes, Lauren. It's what *you* believe about yourself that makes a difference. When you believed you were capable of being a field agent, you *were* capable of it. The only difference between who you were yesterday and who you are today is what you think you can accomplish. Neither Martha McLaughlin's endorsement nor that handbook you thought contained all the answers were the source of your power. *This* is," he said, reaching up with his free hand to gently push her hair away from her temple and tap his fingers on the smooth skin of her forehead.

Lauren pulled her bottom lip into her mouth and slowly began to nod. Then, in a gesture he was beginning to find charmingly familiar, she straightened her shoulders, readying for battle.

Jake bit back a smile. He didn't want her to think he was laughing at her, because he wasn't. Instead, he was falling more in love with her with each passing second.

"I have an idea," she said. Then she reached up to squeeze his hand, pressed a kiss to his palm, and released him, saying, "Fasten your seat belt. It's gonna be a bumpy ride."

CH@%!*R
11

As Lauren laid on the horn and stood on the accelerator, her heart was full of hope. First, she hoped this crazy plan of hers didn't get them both killed. She also hoped her hunch about Rafael Santos was right. Finally, she hoped that the Jake Haven she'd come to know on Isla Suspiro was planning to stick around for a while, because he was a man she could easily imagine herself falling in love with.

He believed in her. And while she supposed it shouldn't matter, that she should feel confident enough in her own abilities to not need anyone else's opinion of her to fill her with courage, just knowing that he thought she was worthy made all the difference.

She took a deep breath and fixed her gaze on the gates up ahead. A half dozen of Tomas Santos's troops were standing in front of the heavy wrought-iron bars, waving at her to stop. In a few seconds, she knew they would stop waving and start pointing their machine guns at her, but she didn't falter.

"Get down," she yelled at Jake as the guards raised their guns.

"You, too," he yelled back.

They both crouched down to shield themselves as best they could. Lauren kept her hands on the steering wheel, the delivery van pointed like a missile, straight ahead. She hated to think that the guards might not move out of the way, but she had no choice. Emilio Santos would never let her and Jake out of here alive.

The first bullets broke the windshield and landed high in one of the cardboard boxes that were stacked against the thin bars separating the cargo area from the passenger area of the van. Lauren felt something wet and sticky dripping onto her head and assumed it was rum, but she didn't dare take her hand from the steering wheel to see if her guess was correct. As long as it wasn't blood . . .

"Aim for the center of the gates. That's where they'll be the weakest," Jake said.

Lauren raised her head so that she could see over the dash, but then ducked when another round of bullets peppered the van. The temperature gauge flew into the red zone. Damn, they must have punctured the radiator.

"Come on, this has to work," Lauren muttered to herself as she closed her eyes, her hands holding tightly to the steering wheel as they crashed into the gates. There was an awful, high-pitched screeching as metal ground against metal. Lauren smelled radiator fluid mixed with the sickly sweetness of rum.

She jerked the transmission into reverse, and the tires squealed on the pavement as she backed up to make another run at the gates. Startled, she screamed when one of the guards jumped onto the running board next to her, but didn't give him the chance to bash in the window that was already damaged from Emilio's earlier shot. Instead, she threw the van into drive and peeled out. The guard quickly jumped off, since remaining where he was when they rammed into the wrought-iron gates would have been tantamount to committing suicide.

The gates screamed in protest when she hit them again, but this time they moved far enough apart for the van to squeeze through. The revelers outside, alerted by her honking, had moved away from the compound's entrance and stood watching, clapping and hooting as if this were a part of the festivities.

Lauren drove ten feet from the compound and stopped the van. Hurriedly, she unbuckled her seat belt and swung around to roll open the divider between her seat and the cargo area.

"What are we doing?" Jake asked, after removing his seat belt and standing up.

"Giving out free rum," Lauren answered. "I don't think Rafael will harm the people of Isla Suspiro. If we can bring the party inside, to the manufacturing plant, maybe we can show Rafael what's happened to Tomas and end this thing without bloodshed."

Jake reached up to grab a case of rum from the top of one stack, his face turning a shade of green Lauren had never seen before. But he didn't complain. Instead, he tossed the box on the passenger seat and ripped it open. Then he pulled out one dark brown bottle and squinted at the plastic container that had been shrink-wrapped to the bottom. Unlike the single-dose packages of promotional aspirin that had been glued to the side of the smaller bottles of rum, the rum company must have decided to ship full-sized bottles of aspirin with their larger bottles of rum. Grabbing his knife from his pocket, Jake slit the plastic and separated the pills from the rum. Then he popped open the lid of the aspirin container, shook out two tablets, and washed them down with a mouthful of liquor.

"Hurry, we've got to get the crowd to help us before Santos's guards get here," Lauren urged, pulling her own case of rum off a stack and ripping it open.

"What makes you think Rafael won't harm them?" Jake asked.

Lauren met his gaze briefly and then shrugged. "It's just . . . he said something when I was with him, back at his camp. It made me think that maybe he and Tomas didn't have such different visions for the people of this island after all."

"I hope you're right," Jake said. Then he threw open the delivery van door and shouted, "Free rum! Get your free rum here!"

The crowd around them surged forward. Lauren saw the dark brown hats of Tomas Santos's guards as they attempted to force their way through the thickening crowd, but the revelers didn't pay them any notice. She crossed her fingers and started handing out bottles. Soon, the van was engulfed with people. When one of the guards finally reached them and grabbed Lauren's arm to pull her out of the van, she yelled, "Everyone, the president's army is here to protect you today. Please, show them your appreciation. Come on, hug a soldier."

A large woman in a brightly colored dress turned to the man who had a hold on Lauren and enfolded him in her arms. Around them, Lauren saw other soldiers being patted on the back, hugged, and even kissed by the grateful people of Isla Suspiro, who, many for the first time in their lives, had enjoyed a period of peace since Tomas Santos's election, in large part because of the efforts of Santos's army. The people's appreciation for this peace was enthusiastic, and Lauren couldn't help but grin when she saw the frustrated look the guard shot her from where he was being held captive by the large woman's embrace.

"You should *write* a secret agent's handbook," Jake said wryly from the other side of the van.

Lauren blushed and stammered out a "thank you" as she went back to handing out bottles of rum. Her first case was soon emptied, so she reached for another one and then another. With each box she emptied, she backed the van closer and closer to the rum plant, luring the revelers into the compound while the guards looked helplessly on.

As the empty boxes stacked up, she noticed that they were all stamped with the letters *VG* on the bottom left-hand corner. She hadn't bought Emilio's explanation for what the codes meant, something about the way his eyes had shifted when he answered told her that he was lying. But she didn't have time to worry about that now. When she looked up to hand out another bottle of rum, she found herself face-to-face with none other than Rafael Santos.

Lauren glanced over at the looming building of the Isla Suspiro Rum Company plant, shrouded in darkness. Party-goers had flooded the compound, but they seemed to avoid the manufacturing plant, perhaps because it reminded them of work on a day of play.

"Rafael, how good to see you again," Lauren said loudly to alert Jake that the man they sought was here.

"Ah, my good luck charm. I was very disappointed when you disappeared yesterday," Rafael said smoothly, reaching up to clasp Lauren's hand with his own.

Jake stepped forward and put his arm around Lauren's shoulders. "She's CIA. If anything happens to her, I will hunt you to the ends of the earth and kill you."

He voiced the threat so calmly, so rationally, that it took Lauren a moment to realize what he had just said. She looked up at him, wide-eyed, and had to blink several times to get her mouth to work.

"Jake," she protested with a half-laugh, but her stomach was fluttering madly.

Rafael Santos gazed coolly at Jake, taking his measure. If Lauren hadn't been so flummoxed by Jake's sudden pro-tectiveness, she might have suggested they get out a ruler. This was obviously one of those "whose dick is bigger" moments. She figured Jake won when Rafael let go of her hand and nodded. And when Jake leaned over her and she felt his erection pressing into the small of her back, she nearly gasped. Well, well, well. Guess she didn't need a ruler after all.

Jeez. Where had that come from? She'd thought he was in serious pain, but apparently not. And if he could get aroused just by standing near her . . . Sheesh. Was it hot in here, or was it just her?

Lauren fanned her suddenly warm face and tried to slow her racing heart. She was jerked back to the seriousness of their situation, however, when Jake announced to Rafael, "Your brother is dead. Emilio shot him."

Rafael Santos stepped back as if Jake had just slapped him. "Pardon me?" he said.

"Tomas is dead," Lauren repeated, jumping down out of the van with Jake behind her. "That's why we were doing this, to lure the people of Isla Suspiro here in the hopes that you wouldn't attack your brother's men."

"My brother is dead?" Rafael said. He put a hand to his forehead and rubbed, as if something were paining him.

"You should be happy. Wasn't that what you were planning to do here today? Kill your brother and take over the island?" Jake asked.

Rafael raised his gaze to them, his eyes full of sadness. "No. I was merely going to take back my family home and force my brother to acknowledge my rightful role in the government. He banished me two years ago, using his troops to keep me hiding in the jungle like some sort of leper. I owe it to the people of Isla Suspiro to aid in their economic recovery, to be a voice for their rights, to ensure that their leaders are not taking their money and using it to line their own pockets. I know Tomas let the power corrupt him, but the worst thing that could happen to the people would be if someone—even I—were to overthrow their duly elected leaders. That would only throw the island back into chaos. I would never do such a thing."

Lauren swallowed hard and looked over at Jake, who looked as ill as she felt. "Why do you think Tomas had been corrupted?" she asked.

Rafael shrugged his broad shoulders and gazed down at the grass beneath his feet. "Emilio told me about the money. About the bribes and about Tomas's illegal drug scheme and how he knew he couldn't be stopped because of his position as president."

"What illegal drug scheme?" Jake asked, frowning.

"The drugs that are hidden in the rum," Rafael said, with a wave toward the delivery van. "Tomas bought shipments of drugs from America—some that were past their expiration date and had to be pulled from the shelves, others that were not approved by your FDA, and still others that simply require a prescription that the purchaser does not wish to obtain. Then he sold these drugs via the Internet and shipped them back to the United States. To escape detection at Customs, he had the drugs packaged with our island's rum. If anyone were ever to inspect a shipment, it would appear that the rum comes with aspirin, as our advertisements state. Instead, my brother was shipping Viagra, Oxycontin, Vicodin, Percocet, Cialis, and other drugs to the United States."

Lauren jerked her gaze back to the van, which was nearly empty by now. Several revelers had taken over handing out the bottles, and the rum supply was almost gone. She squeezed her eyes shut and said, "That's what those codes were for. They told the person picking up the shipment which drugs were packaged inside."

Jake coughed and Lauren opened her eyes to look at him. "That explains it," he muttered, and Lauren choked. So much for him getting turned on just by touching her. All the boxes in their delivery van were marked with *VG*—Viagara, Lauren presumed.

"Where is Emilio?" Rafael asked, a hard look coming over his features.

"He was in the plant the last time we saw him," Jake answered. "Tomas is there, too. In Emilio's office."

"Wait a second," Lauren said as Rafael turned to leave them. "I don't think Tomas knew anything about this drug operation. When I asked about the codes, he seemed surprised and looked to Emilio for an answer. It was Emilio who lied. There's no way he couldn't have known what those codes meant. He had to be involved."

Rafael frowned. "Emilio did seem to have a lot of cash to donate to my cause," he murmured under his breath.

"They could have been in on it together," Jake suggested.

"It's possible. We may never know," Lauren said.

"Perhaps not," Rafael agreed and started toward the

manufacturing plant. When a gunshot rang out, he began running, with Jake and Lauren right behind him.

They reached the loading dock at the same time, just as Emilio Santos staggered out of the building, his chest covered in blood. His body lurched when he was shot again from behind. He swayed at the edge of a four-foot drop-off, his eyes locked on the trio who had frozen on the pavement a few feet away.

"I should have had it all," he whispered. Then, without another word, he fell, facedown, onto the concrete.

Lauren looked up to find a bloodied Tomas Santos standing in the open doorway, his hands clutched around a small black pistol.

"We keep this in the plant to kill the rats," Tomas said, his eyes glazed over with shock. And then he crumpled, going down like a balloon that had suddenly lost all its air.

Rafael leaped up onto the loading dock while Jake bent down to feel for Emilio's pulse. When he looked up and shook his head, Lauren knew that Emilio Santos would no longer pose a threat to his brothers. Lauren pulled herself up and into the manufacturing plant, taking the steps up to Emilio's office two at a time to find a phone so she could call for an ambulance since she had left her cell phone back in her purse in the delivery van.

When she got back downstairs, she found Jake awkwardly watching Rafael as he sat on the floor cradling his oldest brother's head in his lap.

"Emilio planned this all," Jake said quietly as he pulled Lauren outside to wait for the ambulance. "Unless Tomas is lying, which I doubt he has the presence of mind right now to do, he just told Rafael he knew nothing about the drugs. He said that Emilio warned him that Rafael was going to try to overthrow the government, that Rafael claimed he wouldn't be satisfied until he and he alone ruled Isla Suspiro."

Wearily, Lauren shook her head and sighed. All of this could have been avoided had Tomas and Rafael just talked to one another instead of believing the lies their brother had told them.

"So, how does it feel?" Jake asked, smiling down at her with a strange glint in his green eyes.

"How does *what* feel?" Lauren leaned into him, craving his strength. She felt as though she were about to collapse and didn't know how Jake managed to remain upright after all he had been through the past two days. He was a hell of a lot tougher than she was. She marveled at how different he was from the image he showed the world. He wasn't some one-dimensional movie hero, but a man committed to do whatever he had to do—even sacrifice his own life—to do what was right.

She wrapped her arms around his waist and buried her face in his chest, inhaling the scent of sweat and rum and Jake.

"How does it feel to have almost single-handedly saved this island from a civil war? These people"—Jake waved at the revelers behind them, the families with children, the young people squealing with delight while their elders looked on with serene smiles—"owe their futures to you."

Lauren breathed in deeply and felt the tears welling up in her eyes. *Stop that*, she ordered herself. According to her *Secret Agent's Handbook*, spies never cried. Instead, she tightened her hold on Jake and looked up at him with a wobbly smile.

"It feels like you were right," she said. "I am whoever it is I believe I can be."

Jake smiled back at her and leaned down to kiss her with a light touch that instantly turned hotter, leaving them both breathless. "Do you believe you're the sort of woman who might agree to go out with me once we get off this island?" he asked, sounding charmingly unsure of himself.

Lauren laughed and pressed herself to him, feeling his arousal poking into her stomach. "Yeah, I believe I'm that sort of woman."

"Good," Jake said as he leaned down to kiss her again.

After another few breathless moments, Lauren pressed

her lips to the sensitive spot just below Jake's right ear and rubbed her hips against his erection. "If that ambulance would hurry up, we could get back to the resort and take care of this little problem," she said with a throaty laugh.

Then Jake Haven, a man who two days ago Lauren had believed would do just about anything to get laid by a supermodel, shocked her speechless when he took a step back, clasped her hands in his, and solemnly said, "What I feel *here*"—he reached down and cupped one of her hands at his crotch, his arousal clearly evident to her touch—"is nothing. It will be gone in an hour. But *this*"—he pulled her hand away from his erection and put it against his heart—"will last forever."

And Lauren was so overwhelmed that all she could do was to smile up at Jake and think, *My hero*.

Epilogue

"We need to pass emergency legislation to increase funding for health care," Rafael Santos said, pacing the floor of his brother's office overlooking the Caribbean Sea.

Tomas Santos sighed and rested his head in his hands. "We've already flown in hundreds of obstetricians and midwives from America. The new hospital will be finished in a week. I don't know what more we can do."

The men looked up when there was a knock on the door. Tomas's pregnant assistant entered, waddling over to his desk with a sheaf of papers that needed to be signed. She was followed by the head housekeeper, also very pregnant, who wheeled in a cart with the lunch she had prepared for the men.

"This is all Emilio's fault," Rafael muttered, once both of the women had left.

"God rest his soul," Tomas added. He was the superstitious sort and didn't believe in speaking ill of the dead.

Fortunately, the American CIA agents had not confiscated the money from Emilio's illegal drug operation, with the caveat that Rafael and Tomas shut it down immediately. Those funds had been poured into building hospitals and improving the roads leading to those hospitals, as well as bringing in the medical staff the island needed for the enormous increase in births expected to begin within the next few weeks.

Tomas supposed he should be angry that his brother's folly had led them to this, but in a way, he saw the pregnancy epidemic as a sign of hope. Perhaps all of the new lives on the island would only make the people work harder for peace and prosperity. That was what he chose to believe, anyway.

And if there was one thing Tomas Santos had learned in his life, it was that you could accomplish anything . . . if only you believed.